To Pete,

Read with me . . .

All best,
Shawn

Stubblefield

STANLEY WILSON

Llumina Press

Requests for permission to make copies of any part of this work should be
mailed to Permissions Department, Llumina Press, PO Box 772246, Coral
Springs, FL 33077-2246

This is a work of fiction. All names, characters and events are the product of
the author's imagination. Although references are made to real persons and
places, their context is also a product of the author's imagination.

ISBN: 1-932560-91-2   1-932560-92-0
Printed in the United States of America by Llumina Press

Library of Congress Cataloging-in-Publication Data

Wilson, Stanley D., Ph.D.
  Stubblefield / by Stanley Wilson
      p. cm.
  ISBN 1-932560-91-2 (alk. paper) -- ISBN 1-932560-92-0 (pbk. : alk. paper)
  I. Title.
  PS3623.I5858S785 2004
  813'.6--dc22

                                                      2003027666

To Debrah and Noelle,
beloved wife and daughter

ACKNOWLEDGEMENTS

Heartfelt appreciation to my dear friends and fellow writers, Trip Quillman, Claudia Lewis and Mariana Sintay, for reading first drafts of every chapter. Your literary counsel and encouragement helped shape this novel.

I want to acknowledge an enormous debt to Brenda Peterson, a gifted writing coach and one hell of an author. Thank you for demystifying the writing process and for teaching me to take personal experience and craft it into a big story.

Thanks also to Marti Kanna and Joan Wolfe at New Leaf Editing in Seattle, Washington. I am especially grateful to Joan for editing a manuscript that made *War and Peace* look like a novella. I am also indebted to my talented sister, Dianne Nicholson, grammarian extraordinaire, for additional editorial assistance.

I am grateful to Ana Gonzalez for wandering into abandoned and desecrated Stubblefield Cemetery outside Walla Walla, Washington, and taking the photograph that appears on the cover. Thanks to my friend Cory Parris, of Cory Parris Photography, for an inspired cover design.

Eric Schiller, author of more than 80 books on chess, offered valuable advice that enlivened the scenes involving the great game. Dr. Michael Gladych, a beloved friend and enlightened elder, shared intimate details about his World War II battle experiences. Many thanks to Tom Dowd for granting me access to the Whitman College archives, yielding valuable information about the history of Stubblefield Cemetery, as well as the "Walla Walla Jesus." I would also like to thank Al Citron, retired Seattle Police Detective, for answering all my questions on investigative techniques and police interrogation. No one knows more about trauma than E.R. physician, Tom Robbie, M.D., and I am grateful for his medical advice. Much appreciation to Silver Wolf Walks Alone for a wonderful primer (Sacred Sage: How it Heals) on Native American rituals – for a copy write Wendy Whiteman, PO Box 2216, Ranchos de Taos, NM, 87557.

Residents of Walla Walla believe the town is as much a state of mind as a place on the map. Thanks to Bob France for helping me recapture the mood of our former haunt and to Whitman College for providing an exceptional education. Never let it be said that the brothers of Phi Delta Theta let our education get in the way of our learning.

I owe thanks to Deborah Greenspan and everyone at Llumina Press, a publishing company created by writers for writers. Your skill and enthusiasm have made the process of publication an unexpected delight.

Finally, I am immensely grateful to my family for their unflagging support. The care and feeding of a first-time novelist is no small task, yet no one has encouraged my writing more than my best friend and cherished wife, Debrah. Noelle, now a young woman but always the best daughter in the world, read key sections of the manuscript and gently reminded me of the complexities of the teenage psyche. My sister, Darlene McGlocklin, has rooted for this novel at every step along the way. Special thanks to Lorin Wilson and Yvonne Lovejoy, my father and mother, for the many sacrifices they made to attach me securely to an insecure world.

Grateful acknowledgement is made for use of the following:
"*Satisfaction,*" The Rolling Stones
"*Shout,*" The Isley Brothers
"*Louie, Louie,*" The Wailers
"*Respect,*" Aretha Franklin
"*Babe, I'm Gonna Leave You,*" Led Zeppelin
"*The Trouble Is,*" Back Pocket
"*I Put A Spell On You,*" Creedence Clearwater Revival
"*Stop In The Name Of Love,*" The Supremes
"*Unchained Melody,*" The Righteous Brothers
"*Hotel California,*" The Eagles
"*Aqualung,*" Jethro Tull
"*Mechanical World,*" Spirit
"*Round & Round (It Won't Be Long),*" Neil Young
"*I-Feel-Like-I'm-Fixin'-To-Die,*" Country Joe and the Fish
"*Little Wheel Spin and Spin,*" Buffy Sainte-Marie

"On the human chessboard, all moves are possible."

—MIRIAM SCHIFF

"Her image passed into his soul forever and no word had broken the holy silence of his ecstasy. Her eyes had called him and his soul had leaped at the call."

—JAMES JOYCE
A Portrait of the Artist as a Young Man

"Guard your soul carefully so that you do not forget the things your eyes have seen or let them slip from your heart for as long as you live, and make them known to your children and your children's children."

—DEUTERONOMY 4:9

CONTENTS

Chess had become a full-fledged obsession, a way of life that gave me an improbable high and a feeling of extraordinary competence. In chess I found the stability I'd lost following my mother's shocking death. Was it an illusion? Of course, but the rules and logic of the game held me together like emotional glue. When I sat down at the board and moved the pieces, I knew what to expect. I forgot about bad memories and shed my sense of fragility. Maneuvering my opponents into inferior positions and converting the advantage into a win gave me power and control. There was in chess a degree of logic and consistency that I found sorely lacking in the game of life. Chess was fair. Life was unfair. Chess made sense. Life made no sense at all. In its perfect order, chess became a refuge from what I'd witnessed on the Aurora Bridge and the chaos that resulted in my inner world. I had been given a gift more structured and logical than anything anyone could have ever dreamed up. I was not about to let it go.

Chapter 2
The Dare

I considered Harvard because of what my bookish and like-minded class-mates at the TAG Center referred to as "the prestige thing." To attend the oldest university in the country at age seventeen would have given me a second sense of power, after chess.

In the end, I chose Whitman College, Washington's oldest institution of higher learning. Considered by my father and his academic friends to be the finest liberal arts college on the West Coast, Whitman had historical character and an Ivy League feel and was less than five hours from my home in Seattle.

Whitman College. Founded in 1859 by the Reverend Cushing Eells in honor of Marcus and Narcissa Whitman, frontier missionaries massacred by a band of Cayuse Indians in 1847. Located in Walla Walla, Washington, population 20,000, ten miles north of Oregon, ninety miles west of Idaho, and two hundred-ninety miles east of the Pacific Ocean.

Whitman College. Student body, 950. Highly selective admission process with ninety percent of entering freshmen in the top three percent of their graduating secondary school classes. Equally co-educational. A liberal arts and sciences undergraduate college, independent of sectarian and po-litical control. *"Whitman offers an ideal setting for rigorous learning and scholarship and encourages creativity, character, and responsibility."*

With so much to recommend Whitman, it might have been my first choice anyway, but this small college had also won three consecutive U.S. Collegiate Chess Championships (1963, '65 and '67). This lock on the na-tional chess championships began with the arrival of Dr. Zdenek Zaleski, the Polish International Grandmaster. Conferred by the World Chess Or-ganization, International Grandmaster is, other than World Champion, the highest and most prestigious title a chess player can achieve. Once one of the top ten players in the world, the chess community considered Dr. Zale-ski an even better instructor. And one of his former students, Vladimir Primalov, a Russian, was widely considered to be the third best player in the world, behind only America's Bobby Fischer and Russia's Boris Spassky.

Dr. Zaleski first contacted me one year before I was eligible to attend college. He wrote a letter after I'd won two "A" tournaments in a row, sweeping older, more experienced opponents. I was stunned when his anno-tated commentary questioned the caliber of my play. He concluded: "You are a fine young player with <u>enormous potential</u>. However, like most prodi-gies, you do not understand the true purpose of the opening and attack,

Slider chuckled. "The popcorn man in that little triangle-shaped store a block from campus. Where Boyer runs into Main. The pharmacies here won't sell 'em to minors, and it's too embarrassing anyway."

Ethan started laughing.

"What's funny?" Slider asked.

"Oh, back home, there's this pharmacy where the high school kids go for rubbers. Not that I was going through a lot of 'em, but about a month ago I had a date with a girl I thought would put out so I went there with my buddy Alan and his girlfriend, Kathy. Alan and Kathy were high on pot, and we go in and I say, 'I'm gonna need some rubbers.' And the pharmacist says, very professionally, 'what kind would you like?' And Kathy, who's this boisterous type anyway, blurts out, 'Big ones!'"

I cracked up.

Slider chuckled again. "So did you get the rubbers?"

"Yeah."

"Did you score?" I asked, caught up in a new kind of conversation.

Ethan rolled his eyes. "I did, but I put the damn thing on inside-out and it came off."

"Smooth move," Slider quipped.

"Yeah, and three weeks later it led to a pregnancy scare," Ethan added.

"But she wasn't pregnant, I take it." Slider again.

"No, thank God!"

I've never even seen a rubber. I'm probably the only virgin in the freshman class.

We returned to Davis-Jacobs, admiring enormous, century-old maples and pink horse chestnut trees along the way. Slider mentioned he was attending Whitman on what amounted to a baseball scholarship. With Ethan and me sitting on the edge of his bed, he unpacked a small trunk and a canvas duffel bag. Out came an assortment of socks, underwear, T-shirts, toiletries, school supplies, sneakers, baseball trading cards, baseball gloves and baseballs. At the bottom of the box he had a *Sport* magazine with Bob Gibson on the cover, several copies of *Playboy* and a scrapbook that chronicled his own exploits on the diamond.

We soon learned Slider was as obsessed with baseball as Ethan and I were with chess. Since I'd followed the Triple-A Seattle Rainiers from age eight, I could cross over into Slider's world. And I did. I explained how my beloved Rainiers once had an eleven-run inning while I listened on the console radio in our basement, munching on a plate full of canned pineapple. Superstitious, I ate pineapple every night for a month during the September pennant drive. When the Rainiers won the Pacific Coast League championship, I knew the pineapple had made all the difference. Slider and Ethan had a good laugh and my first day at college seemed a resounding success.

———————

That weekend, at Slider's suggestion, the three of us drove to La Grande, Oregon, to watch the Whitman College football team (dubiously named the Fighting Missionaries) play an away game against Eastern Oregon College. It was a two-hour drive into the mountains. Since I was the only one with wheels, we took my Chevy and split the cost of gas. Slider called "shotgun" and sat in the front seat smacking his gum and wisecracking the whole way. Ethan sat in the middle of the back seat, leaning forward between us, while both of us laughed at Slider's vulgar stories of jock life ("golden waterfalls" in the shower, lighting farts, belching the "Ode to Joy") as a Wa-Hi Blue Devil.

As we crossed the state line, Slider launched into an explanation of the Greek system at Whitman. He told us five national fraternities maintained chapter houses near the campus and then proceeded to trash four of them. In his "unabashed and unbiased" opinion, they were either "potheads," or "colorless, odorless and tasteless." However, Phi Delta Theta, a.k.a. the *Phi Delts,* were "numero uno" to a man. Top dogs! According to Slider, the three of us absolutely must pledge Phi Delta Theta or else remain Independent, outside the fraternity system. Of course, that would mean missing out on a party life and best women.

"What makes the Phi Delts so good?" I asked.

"Not good, Bryan. *Great!* Listen carefully. I've lived in Walla Walla for the last three years. Trust me, this is common knowledge. All the jocks are Phi Delts, the coolest guys are Phi Delts, the campus leaders are Phi Delts. Everyone who's anyone wants to be a Phi Delt. *We* are going to be Phi Delts. All for one and one for all!"

At halftime we stepped down from the bleachers and went looking for a concession stand. We followed the enticing smell of burgers and popcorn and found one behind the end zone on the far side of the stadium. Standing in line was a jocular fellow with an enormous girth and a voice like a foghorn. Slider pulled us aside and told us his name was Oliver "Bigdog" Bowens. Even without the name, my first association would have been to Oliver Hardy, of Laurel and Hardy fame. Bigdog took up a lot of space and not just physically. He was, according to Slider, the Phi Delt Rush Chairman, not to mention the most popular student on the Whitman campus. "Be cool, but be yourself," Slider advised us as we approached the line.

"Let the big dog hunt!" Slider exclaimed, grabbing his fat friend from behind.

"Hey, *Slider* . . . my man! Long time no see."

"Not since the summer rush party." They embraced and slapped each other's backs, two large bodies in a ferocious bear hug.

Bigdog said, "How they hangin'?"

"Low," Slider answered, grinning as usual. "Hey, let me introduce you to my two best buddies. This is Bryan Matthews, and this is Ethan Maclean."

"Oliver Bowens," he said, first shaking my hand and then Ethan's, "but everyone calls me Bigdog."

"Good ball game, huh?" Ethan said. Whitman was up a touchdown at the half.

Bigdog enthusiastically grunted his agreement, wolfing down a jumbo hotdog he chased with beer from a large plastic cup. After swallowing, he licked his lips and replied, "Enjoy it, 'cause when the conference games start, we're gonna be in a world of pain."

"Whitman is not known for its stellar football teams," Slider added dryly.

"So I hear," I said, wanting to say more but afraid of saying something stupid.

As we approached the front of the line I wondered why Bigdog was in line when he already had food. When his turn came he ordered another hotdog and two bags of peanuts. Turning to us, he said, "I'd pick up the tab for you guys, but it'd be a violation of rush rules and some rat bastard from another fraternity would be just chickenshit enough to report me."

"Don't worry about it," Slider said. Ethan and I nodded in agreement.

Bigdog looked directly at me. "Hey. Could I catch a ride back with you guys?"

"Sure," I answered, wondering how he knew I was the one driving.

———————

The Fighting Missionaries won 52-42, which I think qualifies as a shootout. We sauntered to the parking lot and found Bigdog leaning heavily against the front bumper of my Chevy, still drinking from his plastic cup. He was drunk. Ethan called shotgun and everyone piled in. I backtracked through the mountains to Highway 125, heading north to Walla Walla.

We were on the road less than five minutes before I realized Bigdog was checking out Ethan and me to determine whether we were worthy of pledging Phi Delta Theta. The conversation was casual and laced with the kind of adolescent banter that included insulting one another in a no-holds-barred, but harmless sort of way. On learning we lived across the hall from one another, Bigdog asked, "Have you guys had a chance to check out Slider in the shower? The guy needs a flashlight to find his dick in the dark."

"Yeah," Slider countered, "and Bigdog needs a bookmark to find his dick in the folds of fat."

I laughed so hard I swerved slightly onto the shoulder, though no one seemed to notice.

Bigdog shot back, "Don't believe Slider, the guy's a major wanker."

"What's a 'wanker?'" I asked, risking the possibility that Bigdog would think me too green to become a brother.

Bigdog answered, "A wanker is a guy who spends too much time floggin' his dog."

Slider took issue. "For the record, gentlemen, I am not a wanker."

Bigdog replied, "There's only two kinds of liars in the world. Those that say they never have and those that say they've quit."

When the laughter died down I said, "So wankers like to spank the puppy?"

Bigdog chuckled. "Right. Beat the meat."

Having heard a million expressions for masturbating at the TAG Center, I said, "I get it. You're saying our pal Slider here has been known to stroke the dolphin."

Bigdog was laughing now. "Whip up a batch!" he roared.

"Peel the carrot. Pop the cork!" I added.

Ethan and Slider went into hysterics.

When they quieted down, Bigdog said, "Pound the pud."

"Choke the bishop."

"Choke the chicken."

I had one left. "Rough up the suspect."

Bigdog sputtered something about my being too much, caught his breath and said, "Shit, Bryan. You made beer go up my nose! I give up. You win."

Five minutes later, we passed the drive-in movie theater at Milton-Freewater, a little town just south of the Washington-Oregon border. Ethan called our attention to a Disney cartoon playing on the big outdoor screen. I slowed down and stole a glance. As usual, the irascible Donald Duck was upset with one of his nephews, who appeared to be trying to smooth Donald's ruffled feathers. Bigdog did a decent Donald Duck imitation, saying something clever about the reputation Whitman women had for being in love with their books. When the group laughter died down he mentioned he and his parents were taking their first trip to Disneyland over Thanksgiving break.

I took a chance. "I don't think that would be a very good idea."

The car went silent. "Why not?" Bigdog asked, surprised by the sudden seriousness in my tone.

"You'll be swarmed. The kids will think you're a new ride."

An excruciating moment of silence followed. Then Bigdog broke into great gales of laughter, high-pitched howls that infected the rest of us. He doubled over into Slider's lap in the back seat and actually began wheezing. For a split second I was afraid he wouldn't get his breath. Finally he gathered himself, sat up and said, "Oh God, Slider. You didn't tell me he was funny, too. You're all right, Bryan."

Only then did I realize what had appeared to be a chance meeting had been prearranged, but I was okay with it. I liked Bigdog and he appeared to like me, making any deception on Slider's part worthwhile. As we crossed the state line, Bigdog caught his breath and "worded" the three of us. "If you guys want to pledge Phi Delta Theta and join the best God damn fraternity in the U.S. of A., I can personally guarantee you're in."

Slider, Ethan and I pledged Phi Delt six days later, at the end of a hectic rush week. Even though Bigdog had guaranteed my acceptance, I was surprised when he knocked on the door of our room in Davis-Jacobs and congratulated Ethan and me for being part of the 1968 pledge class. I embarrassed myself by letting out an uncharacteristic whoop.

Our first chess class didn't meet until Wednesday, the second week of September, as Dr. Zaleski had been delayed in New York while serving as marshal for an international chess tournament. By then I'd heard all kinds of stories about him: that he had twice defeated sitting World Champions; that he was a Raja Yoga master and a close friend to Einstein; that he had helped hunt down Nazis after World War II; that he had been a pioneer in the field of mathematical modeling; that his unrealistic expectations had pressured a former Whitman chess student into a schizophrenic break. Not knowing what was and wasn't true intensified his powers of intimidation.

Ethan and I had no trouble finding the Zaleskis' home, an impressive, beautifully restored old mansion on Alvarado Terrace, a few blocks from the Phi Delt house. Alvarado Terrace, one of the few streets in Walla Walla not named after a tree, was lined with a canopy of them. The house, painted white with green trim, had two stories and a row of pillars across the front. Tasteful landscaping accentuated the overall good looks of the place. My heart pounded against my chest as I knocked at the front door.

Zdenek Zaleski opened the door. A powerfully built man in his midsixties, he looked more like a retired prizefighter than an International Grandmaster of chess. A bulked-up Kirk Douglas with the air of a swashbuckler and eyes the color of cold steel, I could see how he'd earned his nickname "the Polish Rifle." "This must be Bryan and Ethan," he said, after glancing at a grandfather clock in his entryway.

"Bryan Matthews," I said, offering a handshake. "Sorry if we're too early."

"I'm Ethan Maclean," Ethan said, also sticking out his hand. "Yeah, looks like we're twenty minutes early. I hope we're not intruding."

"Come in," Dr. Zaleski replied, but he made no attempt to put us at ease. We followed him into a huge study, an impressive room with floor-to-ceiling, built-in bookcases and a rolling library ladder with gleaming brass railings. A fringed Persian rug, an intricate design of cream, green and burgundy, covered the dark hardwood floor. The walls were wallpapered above walnut wainscoting, the perfect accent to the dark green leather furniture.

Dr. Zaleski's chessboard, sixty-four maple and cherry squares, had been inlaid into the polished top of a sturdy walnut table. Traditional, wood-carved pieces were set up for a new game. Something about the inlaid chessboard seemed familiar. I took a moment and let my mind drift, studying the miter-shaped bishops, the knights with their arched necks, and the powerful queen, ready to move in any direction in a straight line. Testing the heft of the various pieces jiggled loose the memory. It looked identical to the chessboard that appeared in my dream at age six, the night after I had discovered chess at the Matthews family picnic. The board with the white queen missing.

Just then, a small and sprightly woman entered the room and Dr. Zaleski introduced us to his wife, Reva. She spoke good-enough English, but with an accent stronger than his and different in a way I couldn't identify. She had a wise face, sparkly eyes and snow-white hair. Her manner was friendlier than her famous husband.

"This is a beautiful rug," Ethan told her, struggling to make polite conversation.

"Thank you," she responded in her deep accent. "Zdenek stole it from a Persian chess player in nineteen thirties, around the time Persia became Iran. We've held on to it ever since."

"I did not *steal* it, Reva. And he was born in India." He looked at Ethan and me. "I won it fair and square from Sultan Khan in Tehran. Have you heard of him?"

I nodded enthusiastically. "I've seen his name in my game collection books."

"A brilliant player who always wanted to get to the middlegame without having to study a lot of opening moves. It was his downfall as a player and it cost him an extraordinary rug."

Reva chuckled and excused herself.

Fifteen minutes later, three boys and a girl joined us. Dr. Zaleski formally introduced Ethan and me to his returning students, who checked us out like birds of prey. About Ethan, Dr. Zaleski said little, other than to mention he was a late bloomer and excellent tactician. "Look out when Bryan is playing White," he warned them with a gruff little laugh. "If you make the slightest mistake, he'll hand you your head. And, he scored a perfect sixteen hundred on his SAT's!" I blushed and wondered if I could back up his confidence in me.

Dr. Zaleski then gave brief biographies of the four returning members in the program. The one girl in class was Joan Levy, a quirky Jewish girl from Brooklyn who wore only black. A Julliard-trained concert violinist, she had coarse, dark hair and a horsy face drawn into a perpetual frown.

Slight of build, Miles Fletcher had thin, sandy brown hair and the odd look of a career mathematician (bow tie, soft plastic pocket protector, assortment of ballpoint pens). He and Joan Levy exchanged smiles that left me with the impression they were more than teammates.

Jeremy Kramer had been the number two player until Dr. Zaleski bumped him down to three, behind Javad Azizi and me. A cheerful sort, Jeremy wore gold, wire-rimmed glasses and had a Beatles mop of long brown hair, parted down the middle.

Javad Azizi, Whitman's number one player, reminded me of a cross between Omar Sharif and a Bedouin prince at home on his desert throne. Javad seldom spoke. When he did, his words came out clipped with an upper class British accent that broadcast arrogance, at least to me. A junior, Javad was considered the top collegiate chess player in the country, which gave me two years to wrest the mantle from him. I had no intention of inheriting the number one ranking via his graduation.

"You are here," Dr. Zaleski intoned, "for 'Chess Praxis: The Zaleski Method,' a Socratic approach where I *will* teach you the underlying logic of any board position so you can build and maintain a winning attack. In short, I will teach you to think like a Grandmaster." He then launched into a lecture on the power of having two bishops working together to control both colored diagonals. Watching him talk excitedly about the long-range power intrinsic to bishops took me back to those nights when as a six-year-old I would fall asleep with a chess piece in my hand, absorbing its magical power.

As he concluded the hour, Dr. Zaleski discussed the correct technique for correcting a bad bishop. To demonstrate his point he passed out photocopies of a middlegame board position, the light blue ink still emitting its chemical fragrance. "All right, hotshots," he said, "which position is strongest, White's advanced knights or Black's two bishops, one of which is bad? By the way, it is White's move. Speak up if you have the answer and be prepared to explain your thought process."

I looked briefly at the diagram, closed my eyes and waited for the pieces to begin moving into various positions, as they always did. By doing this, I could, more often than not, come up with the one move that would lead to an advantage. It sounds far-fetched, but it's simply watching the candidate moves and choosing the one that best maximizes my strength and exploits my opponent's weakness. This time the answer jumped out in a matter of seconds. I said, "White's position rules. The correct move is bishop to the queen rook one."

"Yes!" Dr. Zaleski exclaimed, nearly jumping out of his chair. "And that's precisely the move Jose Capablanca made in 1934 when this game was played. Then, a much younger Zdenek Zaleski, playing Black, moved rook to the king knight one. After that, what would Señor Capablanca do? Can anyone tell me without my re-diagramming the position?"

"Pawn to rook five," I answered without hesitation. Years of playing blindfold chess (learned serendipitously in response to my father's strict "lights out" rules) made it easy not only to see the board, but also to work out the next logical move.

"Yes. Yes!" Dr. Zaleski said, barely containing himself. "A brilliant move and *exactly* what Capablanca did. And I answered by moving my queen rook to the king bishop one. Now what should White do?"

"Pawn to bishop five," I answered.

"Yes, Bryan. A *brilliant* move! The support points for young Zaleski's knight outposts are totally undermined. Capablanca has created a superior position. The rout is on, and I had no choice but to resign ten moves later."

No one said a word. They were busy studying the photocopy, trying to manufacture in their heads the moves I'd suggested, which happened to be the identical moves the legendary Jose Capablanca had made more than thirty years before.

Jeremy Kramer broke the silence. "Jesus, Bryan. That's pretty impressive stuff. Makes me feel better about getting bumped down to number three."

Joan Levy squinted at me. "You can play blindfolded, huh?"

I nodded self-consciously, but secretly loved the adulation.

"I knew it," she said, shooting a hostile glance at Javad Azizi.

Ethan looked up from his diagram. "Nice goin', Rooms. Maybe you could take about half an hour tonight and explain what you just calculated in thirty seconds."

Javad scowled, attempting to look disinterested, but not quite pulling it off. I had served notice.

Three weeks into the semester, on a Friday during Homecoming Week, Slider invited Ethan and me to his parents' home on Pleasant Street. He promised us the best burgers we'd ever tasted, hard-to-get Coors and a nationally televised baseball game featuring the Dodgers, his favorite team. His folks were out of town for the weekend, salmon fishing on a chartered boat at Ocean Shores.

Ethan and I turned the corner onto Slider's street and did simultaneous double takes at the rig parked in his driveway. Slider leaned against a full-sized milk truck painted white with brown spots like a Guernsey cow. On the side, printed in large black lettering, *Country Charm Dairy* promised "Always Freshest!" along with a local phone number. Poised to greet us, Slider showed off his patented 'S.E.G.,' fraternity-speak for shit-eating grin.

"What's this?" I asked, climbing out of my car.

"I call it the Milker," he answered with obvious pride.

"Yes, but what is it?"

"I bought it for two hundred bucks when the dairy went out of business. It needs some work, but it's running. We can start taking it to parties."

"Cool." I poked my head inside and wondered if it was safe.

Ethan disappeared into the truck. "It smells like sour milk in here."

Slider looked at me and shook his head with an expression of mock disgust. "See, that's the thing about milk trucks, Ethan. They often smell of milk. Are you *sure* you graduated from Parachute High School?"

Ethan emerged from the truck to defend himself. "Isn't it possible to clean up spilt milk?"

Slider ignored him. "Enough of your token admiration and hostile envy, gentlemen. It's Coors time!" As always, he wore a T-shirt with a message. He seemed to have an endless supply, each one a conversation piece. This one read, *"We Don't Care. We Don't Have To. We're the Phone Company."*

We headed for the kitchen where Slider served a round of beers. I busied myself with a city map of Walla Walla spread out on the boomerang-patterned Formica tabletop. "Trying to learn your way around town?" I said.

"Oh, sorry," Slider apologized, "let me get that out of your way."

"No," I replied, stopping him, "this is interesting. I want to look at it." Walla Walla was shaped like a football with the nose pointing slightly up, spiraling in the direction of the Idaho panhandle.

"Why'd you have it out?" Ethan chimed in.

"Oh, the old man and I had a bet. He said Russell Creek and Reser Creek met up north of Reser Road. I bet him five bucks and won."

I pumped a fist like a victory salute.

Slider laughed. "You guys want cheese on your burgers?"

We both answered yes and watched him slice off big chunks of cheddar from a brick the size of a shoebox. Looking back at the map, my eye followed the red line for Reser Road until it ended, seemingly in the middle of nowhere. At the end of the line there was a little cross and the number nine in bold type. I looked down the Walla Walla Points of Interest list in the bottom right corner of the map. It read: *#9. Stubblefield Cemetery.* "Why is Stubblefield Cemetery a point of interest?"

Slider flipped our burgers with a metal spatula, catching them in midair and laying them down gently in the skillet. Then he tossed the cheese slices, Frisbee-style, on top of our burgers. His eye-hand coordination truly amazed me. "You got me," he answered. "No one ever goes out there, anyway. The place is abandoned, not to mention haunted."

"Oh come on, Slider," I said. "A haunted graveyard? Give me a break."

Slider took out a Walla Walla Sweet Onion for the burgers. His slices were enormous, nearly a half-inch thick. When he finished slicing he said, "A hundred years ago Stubblefield was the only graveyard in Walla Walla. According to the legend, they stopped using it because the gravediggers kept turning up dead on the job. Murdered. Three men in one year. So they abandoned the place and started burying people closer to town."

"Did they catch the killer?" I asked.

"That's the spooky part. The victims were buried in fresh gravesites, the ones that they'd just finished digging. No sign of struggle, just suffocated beneath a mound of fresh dirt."

"This has got to be bullshit!" Ethan said.

Slider stared at him. "I know it sounds that way, but a lot of people swear it's true. My dad, for one. He grew up in Walla Walla and Stubblefield hadn't been closed for that long when he was a kid. He heard all the stories."

"Like what?" I asked.

"You won't believe it anyway." He slid a lazy Susan onto the table, filled with more onion, lettuce, dill pickles and tomatoes.

I suppressed a smile. "Probably not, but I still want to hear the story."

"Okay," Slider said. "You remember Kooskooskie?"

"Yeah."

Slider looked at Ethan to see if he was following. Ethan said, "I remember Kooskooskie." Kooskooskie was a camping area in the foothills of the Blue Mountains, maybe fifteen minutes east of town on Mill Creek.

Bigdog had driven the three of us out there for a late night keg party during rush week, a blatant violation of the rules.

Slider continued, "Well, long before the Phi Delts used Kooskooskie for keggers, a Mormon sect lived out there. The Morrisites. In their heyday, which was around 1850, there were maybe seventy of them."

"So who was Morris?" I asked, in between sips of beer. Anything more than a sip and I'd embarrass myself with the hiccups. God knows what would've happened if I'd chug-a-lugged like most of the guys in the fraternity.

Slider used the spatula to flip cheeseburgers onto our plates, then handed us each an oven-warmed bun. "Joseph Morris. People called him 'Praying Joe' or 'The Dreamer.' He started out in Salt Lake City, but his belief in reincarnation got him in trouble with Brigham Young. After being asked to forfeit his life he left the church and high-tailed it along with some of the faithful."

"What happened then?" Ethan asked as he helped himself to condiments.

"He never made it out of Utah. A lawman killed him in cold blood, but his followers kept going and settled up on the bluff above Kooskooskie."

"Is this part of the legend or historical fact?" I interrupted, heading over to the sink to wash my hands.

"Historical fact," Slider answered. "I did a term paper on it my senior year. If you don't believe me, there're books on it in the archives of the Whitman library."

"I believe you. I just want to know where the history ends and the legend begins."

Slider speared some pickles for his burger. "Anyway, their new leader out at Kooskooskie was a Welsh preacher named William Davies. He told everyone the new colony was 'The Kingdom of Heaven.' And they believed him, and referred to Davies as either the 'Holy Ghost' or the 'Voice of God.'"

"God! Do you believe how gullible people are?" This was Ethan.

"It gets better," Slider told us. "When Davies' son was born, he proclaimed him to be a reincarnation of the Messiah, and the faithful believed that, too. There's a picture of the boy as a six-year-old in the archives, all decked out in his ceremonial robes."

Ethan followed up. "Did people in town have any idea what was going on out there?"

Slider nodded. "Yeah, and they thought Davies was a nut case, but they pretty much left 'em alone. At least at first. They called him Mormon *Davis,* not even getting his name right, and sarcastically referred to his son as the 'Walla Walla Jesus.'"

Ethan and I chuckled.

Slider paused to chew after taking a huge bite out of his cheeseburger. "Here's the best part. A second son was born and Davies dubbed him 'God the Father.' The word spread. Now they've got the Father, the Son, and the Holy Ghost out there."

Out and out laughter from Ethan and me.

Slider was on a roll. "Well, one day, a Morrisite named Grover Andrews came to town to pick up supplies. Andrews was a tough guy, with a reputation as a loudmouth and a bully. People in the colony called him the 'Destroying Angel.' A jack-of-all-trades named Tex Pearson starts ribbing him about the 'Walla Walla Jesus' and implies there's polygamy and incest in the colony."

"Which there probably was," Ethan interjected.

Slider nodded. "Andrews decks Pearson and the townsfolk gang up on him. In the melee, Pearson bites off Andrews' thumb, wraps it in his handkerchief and puts it in his pocket. He tells Andrews he's going to feed it to his pigs. Andrews mounts his horse to leave, but before he rides off he waves his bloody hand at Pearson and tells him he's as good as dead. That the Destroying Angel will get his retribution."

I cringed at the thought of Grover Andrews' maimed thumb.

"Did he get him?" Ethan asked, biting off a mouthful of cheeseburger.

"Okay, this is where the legend starts," Slider said, draining his beer. "Andrews dies that winter, don't ask me how, and they put his corpse in a casket to be buried out at Stubblefield. Guess who digs his grave?"

"Tex Pearson," Ethan and I said in unison.

"Right. One of his jobs is official town gravedigger. Only Tex doesn't make it home that night. When Davies and the Morrisites bring the casket out the next morning they find a fresh mound of dirt, but no hole to put it in. Since Grover Andrews was the only scheduled burial, someone gets a shovel and starts digging. Voilà, there's Tex, stiff as a board. The sheriff is summoned and he assumes one of the Morrisites got even for separating brother Andrews from his thumb, but there's no way to prove anything so the murder goes unsolved. Davies and the Morrisites insist it was the work of the Destroying Angel. That Tex had finally reaped what he'd sown. Anyway, Tex is put back in the grave he dug and Andrews is buried a respectable distance away."

"And the graveyard has been cursed ever since?" Ethan asked.

Slider nodded again. "Right. Because two more gravediggers met the same fate, face down in the grave they'd just finished digging. Both times, the coroner determined they were buried alive. People said it was the work of the Destroying Angel. That's when they started burying people in town. At Mountain View."

"It's a great story," I said, "but the part about the graveyard being haunted is a crock."

Slider frowned. "Maybe so, but my parents forbid me to go out there. They're not kidding either. If I go anywhere near Stubblefield, my dad says he'll kick my butt all the way to the state line."

"Have you been out there?" Ethan asked.

"No way!"

I was taken aback by the intensity of Slider's reaction; he was usually Mr. low-key.

"You guys don't get it," he said. "This is *not* a joke. No one in his right mind goes out there. It's just not done. The cemetery is abandoned, it's been desecrated, and it's a place where at least three people have been murdered."

"You really believe this story, don't you," Ethan noted, trying to get his mouth around his second four-inch high cheeseburger.

"I don't believe in ghosts, if that's what you mean, but I'll tell you this. I wouldn't go out there for a night in bed with Raquel Welch."

"I would," Ethan and I said, again in unison. The three of us broke into laughter.

Ethan picked up the map, pointed at the little cross and said, "Number nine . . . Stubblefield Cemetery. Doesn't the number nine have some sort of mystical significance?"

"It does in Greek mythology," I answered. "The Hydra, the monster that Hercules killed, had nine heads. And the Muses were known as 'The Nine.'"

Ethan finished chewing. "Who were the muses? I forget."

"The nine daughters of Zeus and Mnemosyne, the ones that presided over the arts and sciences. There were also nine rivers in hell, and in Milton's 'Paradise Lost,' the angels that were kicked out of heaven fell for nine days."

Slider looked at Ethan. "Now aren't you glad you asked?"

Ethan smiled. "Do you know anyone that's been out there?"

"Halloween. Two years ago. Some guys on the football team went out after practice, but it was before dark."

"What a bunch of chickenshits!" I said without thinking.

"Oh yeah?" Slider shot back. "I dare *you* to go."

"Let's do it," I said to Ethan, making a pretense of courage. "Worst comes to worst, we never come back and become part of the legend, the latest victims of the Destroying Angel."

Shortly after midnight, Ethan and I headed out of town. We'd gone a good four miles on Reser Road before coming to a stop sign at Foster. "We're lost," I offered.

"Slider said if we get to Foster we've gone a couple hundred yards too far, so double back and go slowly."

I did and we found an unmarked dirt road. I took it, turned on my brights and drove uphill for about a quarter-mile. "This can't be right," I claimed, "it's like we're driving into someone's wheat field."

"Just keep going," Ethan said. "It shouldn't be too far."

Thirty seconds later, we came to a pair of ruined stone pillars that marked the entrance to Stubblefield. Just beyond the pillars a stand of large trees lined both sides of the road. Dark, fingerlike branches brushed my windshield. In the headlights we could see a decrepit concrete archway, darkened and discolored by time. When we reached the archway, I stopped the car but didn't put it in park or set the emergency brake. Dried-out, dead ivy clung to the base of the arch on the right side, creating the illusion of black tears dripping toward the earth below. "Sure you want to do this?" I asked Ethan.

He hesitated and laughed nervously. "It does look pretty fuckin' spooky, but we've come this far. Let's at least drive in and check it out. We don't have to stay long."

Driving slowly closer, we could read "Stubblefield Cemetery" across the top of the archway and then, to the right and below, "1863." Directly under the arch itself we made out the rusted remnants of a wrought iron gate leaning heavily against the old wall. Although in a current state of ruin, the gate would have once been ominous. The top was adorned with a single row of black, spiky spear tips, pointing menacingly at the heavens. Some wise-ass had spray painted "Those who enter will not leave!" on the concrete.

"Did you see that?" I asked Ethan.

"Oh yeah! Kind of ups the ante, doesn't it?"

The dirt road that led us under the arch was rutted and in bad repair. "Lock your door," I said, swallowing dryly. My voice didn't sound right. I'd already locked the door on my side and was ready to wheel the car around and get the hell out at a moment's notice.

We drove cautiously another hundred feet to where the road seemed to end. Mercifully. My brights were still on but there wasn't much to see. No tombstones or monuments, nothing since the archway that would indicate this had once been a place for burying the dead. "Let's stop here," I said, my voice not carrying well. I pulled off the road and backed around, leaving the car at a ninety-degree angle so I could get out fast without having to turn the car around.

"Shut off the engine," Ethan said, his voice no more than a whisper.

I did. He rolled down his window and I followed suit. The wind sighed and, a moment later, dead leaves rustled. "I could use a beer," I said, my mouth as dry as dust. Slider had given us two bottles of Coors for the road. A "going away present," he called it.

Ethan patted his pockets. "Where'd I put the church key?"

"You hung it around your neck."

"Oh," Ethan laughed, only it came out as more of a shaky wheeze. I took some comfort in knowing he was as scared as I was. At least he seemed to be. He cracked the beers and we sat there, sipping and looking from side to side. "Should we get out?" suggested Ethan. "You know, sort of check the place out?"

I shook my head. "I don't think so. I don't want to step on people's graves. It's bad luck, not to mention creepy as hell."

"Did you know families used to picnic at the cemetery?"

"You're kidding, right?"

He picked at his beer label with a thumbnail. "No, I read it some-where."

We sat quietly for a minute. "What's the most scared you've ever been?" Ethan asked.

"What?"

"What's the most scared you've ever been?"

The first thing that came to mind was my mother stepping off the Aurora Bridge, but it wasn't something I shared with anyone, not even my roommate and new best friend. "I don't know," I answered. My eyes had adjusted to the dark. I could just make out the woods Slider had described when he told us about the search for the Stubblefield killer. *Alleged killer,* I reminded myself. I sat quietly, nursing my beer and contemplating calling it a night.

"What was that?!" Ethan whispered.

"What?"

"Did you hear that?" he asked, still whispering.

"I didn't hear anything."

"I thought I heard voices."

We went silent and strained to hear the night sounds. Nothing.

"It's because we're in a graveyard," I explained. "The night's playing tricks on us."

Ethan relaxed against the passenger door. "I don't hear anything now," he reported.

I downed my last swig. "I say we get the hell out of here." I'd never finished a beer so quickly.

"Yeah. Just let me get rid of this beer first."

Ethan got out of the car and began to relieve himself in the bushes. It was a ways back to town so I got out and joined him. "Buddy piss," I said, finding a spot a few feet away.

"Should we cross swords?" Ethan asked, chuckling.

I laughed and buttoned up my Levi's.

A spine-chilling scream split the night. Ethan and I looked at each other in horror. The sound came from farther inside the cemetery. I rushed back to the car and grabbed the flashlight from under my front seat. We followed the beam, carefully jogging through a field of dry, tangled weeds in the general direction of the voices. To our left, we saw sunken gravesites and an outcropping of very old gray and white gravestones. One had been dug up and leaned against a tree. Ahead of us, two girls wrestled awkwardly with a guy, but he shook them off.

When we got close enough, I yelled, *"What the hell's going on?"*

The tallest of the girls, the screamer, looked into the beam of my flashlight and let out another cry for help. "Stop him!" she pleaded.

The teenage boy could barely stand, but managed to push the screamer to her knees and shove the other girl back a few steps. Then, with the side of his foot, he shoveled dirt into what looked like an open grave. A fourth person, another guy, moaned from a prone position at the bottom of the hole. Judging from his inability to get up and climb out, I assumed he was the more intoxicated of the two.

"Knock it off!" I yelled at the top of my lungs, to no effect.

"Fuck off," the standing drunk told me.

"Hey," I yelled again, stepping closer. Without warning, he threw a right-handed haymaker at me. The blow was as telegraphed as it was unco-ordinated. I easily ducked it before slamming my forearm into his chest. He fell awkwardly and landed on the seat of his pants, gasping for air.

"Wow! Way to go!" the shorter girl exclaimed.

I'd dropped my flashlight, and now I picked it up. The light still worked. I considered using it as a weapon if the situation called for it. My father had taught me how to defend myself but I'd never actually been in a fight.

Ethan reached down into the open grave, doing his best to pull out the second drunk. The guy was dead weight so I helped, grabbing hold of his belt. Together, Ethan and I were able to drag him out. The screamer had settled down a little and we all just stood there a second trying to figure out what to do.

"How'd you get here?" I asked, not seeing a second car.

"We're parked over there. We came in the back way." This was the shorter girl. She pointed to the far side of the cemetery. "Can you *please* get me and my girlfriend out of here?"

"Sure. What're your names?"

"I'm Vicky Spotts," she said. "Thanks for helping. My friend screaming her fool head off is Leslie Vanzandt."

Ethan asked, "Are these guys your boyfriends?"

"No," Vicky answered. "Tweedledee and Tweedledum here are a couple of *fucking immature idiots* we should've never gone out with in the first place."

"I'm Bryan Matthews and this is my roommate, Ethan Maclean."

"Are you 'Whitties?'" Vicky asked.

"Yeah," Ethan said. "Freshmen. We can run you back to town. If you want."

"Great. I'm sure as hell not going anywhere with these jerk-offs!"

Vicky had a mouth on her. I aimed the flashlight in her general direction. She looked cute, but it was hard to tell without actually shining the light in her face. "What should we do with them?" I asked, referring to the two guys.

Leslie, tall with short blonde hair, said, "Bob lives on Browne. It's only a mile or so from here. Let 'em walk. Neither one's in any condition to drive, anyway." Before she had sounded frightened, now the anger had set in.

Bob, the one we fished out of the open grave, was virtually passed out at Vicky's feet. She pushed him hard onto his side, reached into his jeans pocket and yanked out a set of car keys. He scarcely noticed. Then she turned to me. "Where're you guys parked?" she asked. "I want to get out of here."

We headed back to my car.

The guy I'd knocked over called out, "Gimme the car keys. You can't leave us out here!"

Vicky yelled back, "Up yours!"

"Bitch!"

"Who's driving?" Vicky asked, ignoring the insult.

"I am," I told her, shining the beam of my flashlight on my car.

She climbed in the front seat with me. "You ride in back," she told Leslie. My heart thudded harder than when I decked her drunken friend.

"We appreciate this," Vicky told me, her voice softening.

"Yeah, thanks," Leslie added.

"No problem."

Pulling back onto Reser Road, I turned to Vicky. "I thought this was the only way in or out of the graveyard."

She swiveled to face me. "There's an old county road that heads kind of north and east. It doesn't have a name but we call it Farmer's Road, 'cause it goes through a wheat field."

"Where does it come out?"

"It goes about a half a mile and comes out on Foster," she answered, scooting closer.

"It's not on the map," I said, excited by her boldness. "I was looking at a city map earlier tonight."

"It wouldn't be. It's just a really bumpy Podunk dirt road that isn't maintained, but it still goes all the way through to Foster. That's how we got here tonight."

"Why would you use that road instead of the one we took?"

Leslie answered from the back seat. "There's a cop that sometimes watches the entrance you used. He busted a friend of ours for coming here."

Vicky added, "Caught her naked with her boyfriend in the back of a station wagon."

"What happened?" Ethan asked.

Vicky answered. "He made her get out of the car and wouldn't let her put her clothes on until he got his jollies. Montrose is his name. Now he watches the Reser entrance and hopes he'll get lucky again. At least that's my theory. So we use the Foster entrance."

"So you've been there before?" I asked, wondering how I could get a date with this girl.

"Once or twice, that's all," Vicky replied.

"I don't want to be rude," Leslie told her friend, "but it's nearly one o'clock and I need to get home. This night has been altogether too much."

Vicky directed me to Leslie's house and then walked her to her door. When she disappeared into the house, Ethan leaned forward over the back seat. "You could score tonight, Bryan. This Vicky's hot for your program."

"No way," I argued, entirely out of fear. Fear that came from suspecting he was right.

"Don't be a fool. Go for it!"

I paused before making a confession. "It'd be my first time."

"Don't worry about it. Just let nature take its course." We heard a door close and watched Vicky walk back to the car. "Jesus, check out the cans on her."

"Cool it, Ethan."

He punched my shoulder. "Just drop me off at Davis-Jacobs and go for it."

Vicky approached us, a little sashay in her gait.

Between my headlights and the street lamp I got my first really good look at her. She was kind of cute, like I'd thought, but in an unconventional way. A bottle-blond with dark roots, she wore too much eye makeup. The peroxide and mascara made her look cheap, an impression enhanced by her voluptuous body. She slid next to me in the front seat, a pink cashmere sweater tight across her breasts.

"What now . . .?" Vicky asked. It was clear from the pause she tacked onto the end that she wasn't ready for the night to be over.

"Bryan's going to run me back to our dorm," Ethan answered, before I had a chance to say anything and blow it. I glanced in the rearview mirror and saw him grinning like the Cheshire Cat.

"That sounds good," Vicky replied. She then told us what had happened before she and her friends ended up at Stubblefield. It had been a comedy of errors fueled by testosterone and a case of beer.

We dropped Ethan off. He hadn't even shut the car door before Vicky slid closer and whispered, "I'll show you a good place to park." The idea of being alone with her scared me, but what scared me most was that she said it without a trace of anxiety. Sort of like, "The phone book is on top of the counter." Had I not been speechless, I might have chickened out and made up an excuse to take her home.

I followed Vicky's directions to a secluded area not far from the Walla Walla Country Club. Having studied the map on Slider's kitchen table, I was somewhat oriented, which was good considering my anxiety. Crossing railroad tracks, we pulled onto an unpaved road that reminded me of the road leading into Stubblefield. Vicky then instructed me to make a sudden left, which led downhill into woods. "Kill your lights and pull in over there," she said, pointing to a spot under some big, leafy trees.

I turned off the engine. "Where are we?"

"Yellowhawk Creek, between two ponds. If we'd taken a left back there on Taumerson and gone about four miles east, we'd end up back at Stubblefield."

"I'll pass on that."

"There's only a few houses out here and none of them are close." She hesitated before adding, "We're totally alone."

"Is Vicky short for Victoria?" I stalled for time, too nervous to make the first move.

"Yeah. Victoria Anne Spotts."

"Nice name."

"Thanks."

"Uh, how long have you known Leslie?" *Kiss her, you idiot!*

"Since seventh grade. We were in band together."

"What instrument did you play?"

"Cello," she laughed.

"What's funny?"

"Leslie said I chose the cello so I could have something between my legs."

I laughed, a little too hard. It came out like a whinny. *You're scaring the crap out of me!*

She put her hand on top of mine, long nails touching the backs of my fingers. "I like you."

"I like you, too."

"You're cute, and you must be a brain if you got into Whitman." She pressed her breast against my arm.

I fidgeted with the collar of my T-shirt. There was no moon but the night was wild with stars. I rolled down my window to a chorus of crickets and looked at Vicky.

She kissed me, pushing her tongue deep in my mouth. Her mouth tasted bitter, like beer.

I acted like I knew what I was doing and put my arms around her. Ever so cautiously, almost like it was an accident, I placed my left hand gently on her breast. Pretty much the same move I'd used on Andrea Bennett at Lake Chelan a few months before. My only move.

Vicky shuddered and pushed me away. For an anxious moment I thought I'd gone too far, too fast, but then realized she was pulling off her pink sweater. Seeing Vicky in her brassiere caught my breath. If there is some unknown sexual point of no return, I'd passed it.

"Help me with my bra," she said. "It unhooks in the back."

Turning her back to me, she tossed her sweater on the dashboard. She had beautiful moon-white skin, the complexion of a girl who spent all her time indoors. I ran my fingertips down her sides, giving her goose bumps. I don't know why I did that, but it made her wriggle while I worked on the clasp, giving me an excuse for being slow.

Vicky faced me. Her breasts were larger than I could have ever imagined. Milky white and perfectly shaped, they shined translucently in the starlight coming through the windshield. Stupidly, my mouth dropped open and I might have even gasped. I gawked without the slightest attempt to look away. Vicky's chest would have been a glorious sight for any seventeen-year-old boy, but for one who'd never been closer to seeing bare breasts than the centerfold of a Playboy, it was an indescribable experience.

"Do you like 'em?" she asked, her voice soft and velvety. "They just exploded when I started taking birth control pills my sophomore year."

"They're . . . incredible!" I said lamely.

"Leslie calls me 'Jugs.'" She cupped a breast in each hand and brushed her fingertips over her nipples.

Vicky's seductiveness and language totally disarmed me. I'd never even imagined girls acted or talked like that, much less interacted with any. I'd wandered into very unfamiliar territory. "I can see why," I noted, aching to touch her again. "But I have to tell you something." The words tumbled out of my mouth. "I just turned seventeen."

Vicky laughed. "Oh God! I was afraid you were going to tell me you were a fag. I don't care about your age. Anyway, I won't be eighteen till October." She leaned over and kissed me.

"You smell good!" I told her, inhaling her scent. Her hair smelled smoky. I was doing okay at this point. We kissed again, harder this time. I took her breast in my left hand and squeezed it gently. She started breathing hard and I felt her fingernails on the back of my neck. Her excitement was contagious. I took her nipple and rolled it between my thumb and forefinger, first prizing its softness and then marveling at how taut it became.

"Don't you want to suck on them?"

When I did, she arched her back and moaned.

"Harder. Suck harder!"

I had a hard-on a cat couldn't scratch. Vicky made some comment I didn't quite hear about the bulge in my jeans. I was wondering what she'd said when she put her hand on my crotch and began rubbing. "It's not fair," she complained in a playful voice. "I'm half naked and you have all your clothes on."

"Okay." I unbuttoned my Levis, grateful for the way she took charge.

"Pull your pants down."

"Okay." Yanking my pants down, my penis sprung out and stood at attention. She took it in her hand and squeezed me with idiotic force, hard enough that I could feel myself pulsing in the palm of her hand.

"Ooh, I like it. Let's get naked and get in the back seat," she said impatiently.

We finished undressing and climbed over the seat, where Vicky lay on her back and spread her pale white legs without a trace of modesty. Her body was beautiful, enticing. I followed her over the front seat and gently positioned myself on top of her, bracing myself on my arms.

"This is your first time, isn't it?" she whispered softly into my ear.

"Yeah," I confessed. "Am I doing something wrong?"

"No. You're perfect. Put your finger in me."

I was completely unprepared for how wet she was. I put in a second finger and a tidal wave of lust washed over me, head to foot. She showed me the best place to touch her and moaned when I found it with my fingertip. I heard myself whisper, "You're wonderful!"

"Get off me a little," Vicky said after I'd played with her awhile, enjoying the slick wetness and earthy smell that came from between her thighs.

I pushed myself up on my elbows and knees. Vicky reached down and took my hard penis in her hand. Slowly, expertly, she guided me inside her.

I pushed myself all the way in and relished the warmth pulsing up from my groin. What can I say? Lying still deep inside of her was more physical and intoxicating than I could have possibly imagined. *This is infinitely better than chess*, I thought stupidly.

"Kiss me while you do it to me, okay?"

I kissed her deeply. We breathed into one another's mouths. She nibbled playfully at the tip of my tongue and gently bit at my lower lip. "Move in and out of me," Vicky said.

"Okay," I whispered, again doing what she asked. The sensation of my chest pressing against her breasts excited me all the more.

A moment later she laughed. "Not *all* the way out, you silly!"

Sliding back into her, I moved my hands over the curves of her breasts and ran my fingertips over her nipples.

"Pinch my nipples a little. It helps me come." Again, her language shocked me, but I can't say I didn't like it. When I pinched her, she thrust her hips, pulled away and thrust again.

Raw excitement took hold of my body and I came before I knew what had happened. "I'm sorry," I apologized, disappointed in myself. I wanted desperately to please her.

"Don't worry about it. Just stay inside me." Vicky rolled a bit to her side, slid her hand between our bodies and placed it between her legs. Rolling back on her back she began playing with herself.

She's masturbating, I thought, amazed at her complete lack of propriety. In a few seconds she arched her back off the seat and pushed hard against me. Her whole body tightened for a moment before giving way to an intense shudder. "Oh God! Oh God, I love you!" she cried out before collapsing back into the seat, sticky with sweat.

We lay there awhile, spent. I pretended not to have heard the 'I love you' and neither of us said anything for a minute.

"That was amazing!" I said, breaking the spell.

"I'm glad I was your first."

"Me, too."

She groaned with pleasure. "Is sex great, or what?"

"That was definitely great," I agreed.

She kissed me again, less passionately. "It's pretty late. You should take me home. If I get home too late, my mom will ask a bunch of questions."

"I think we should get dressed first."

"Good idea," she said, laughing. "You're funny. Are you . . . am I going to see you again?"

I nodded enthusiastically. "Tomorrow, if it's up to me."

She laughed some more, leaned over the seat to retrieve her clothes and began dressing. "What sign are you?"

"I'm a Virgo, but chess players don't believe in astrology."

"You're a chess player?"

"Yeah. Number two on the chess team at Whitman," I answered, reaching for my T-shirt. It was awkward and cramped with the two of us dressing at the same time, but I was turned on watching Vicky's breasts sway back and forth while she pulled on her jeans.

She noticed where I had my eyes and smiled in the dim light. "You don't strike me as a chess player. At least, you're not like the guys in chess club at Wa-Hi."

"Are they out of it?"

"Yeah. Bigtime!"

"So, is it okay that I'm a Virgo and a chess player?"

"Yeah. It's Scorpios I don't get along with, and as long as you don't wear one of those pocket protectors when you're with me, you can play all the chess you want."

My turn to laugh. Vicky was fun and had a good sense of humor. I imagined she'd made it with a lot of guys, but I didn't care. "What's wrong with being a Scorpio?" I asked, keeping the conversation going.

They're so intense, and they always have to be in control."

"So what sign are you?" I finished tying my shoes.

"Scorpio."

I remembered how she'd said she loved me at the moment of her orgasm. It was inappropriate and it bothered me, but I pushed the memory from my mind, instead replaying what else had happened.

On the way to her house Vicky told me, "You're cute, Bryan. The girls are gonna be all over you. Am I really gonna see you again, or did you just say that to be nice?"

"No, I was completely serious. I want to see you tomorrow."

"Good. This is my house coming up, right past the street light."

I pulled over. "What's your phone number?"

"Do you have a pen?"

I reached across her body, dug a pen out of my glove compartment and handed it to Vicky. She wrote her number on my arm. "This way you won't lose it."

"I would hope not," I joked.

I walked her to her door. She kissed me one last time and murmured, "Don't get a big head, but you're a good lover, too."

I smiled like never before, swollen with newfound adolescent pride. It dawned on me as I settled in behind the wheel: *Wow! I screwed a girl in the back seat of my car.* Being sexual broke open an entirely new way of experiencing myself. Suddenly, I was more than just a chess prodigy or young intellectual. Dwelling inside me was a little monkey with an appetite for sex. The realization made me feel instinctual, manlier. That a girl would let me touch her bare breasts, that she would allow me to put myself between her thighs and come inside of her produced a medley of feelings I am inadequate to express. Of course it was exciting, but for me it was so much more than mere physicality. Having sex with Vicky Spotts let me feel embodied

and whole for the first time in my life. I simply don't know how to put it
any better.

Chapter 3
The Kidnap Party

Whitman offered and required completion of a general studies program, imperiously referred to as Antiquity and Modernity. I filled odd mornings (Monday, Wednesday, Friday) with Principles of Psychology, my afternoons with French grammar and Chess Praxis: The Zaleski Method – analyzing chess, dissecting chess, extrapolating and breathing chess. Resurrecting famous games for opening, middle and endgame strategy, for brilliant combinations, and most of all, the keys to winning. Calculus and Astronomy padded the even days (Tuesday, Thursday), with after-class Raja Yoga meditations led by Dr. Z (a nickname Dr. Zaleski encouraged) in the darkened, emptied auditorium.

Fraternity life stacked male energy into a fixture of parties (The Friday Afternoon Club, regular keg parties out at Kooskooskie and at the Phi Delt cabin) and the three R's: the R.F., (which stood for "rat fuck" – Bigdog's expression for a prank of grand proportion), rivalries, and reputation building. After all, Phi Delts ruled!

Ethan, Slider and I made regular appearances at all the right places and hung out with Bigdog during the rest of our free time. Good times with good friends. My freshman year was everything college should be.

Vicky Spotts and I got naked every chance we had, either in the back of my Chevy at Yellowhawk Creek, or in her basement bedroom after her mother had passed out with a bottle of Akadama Red Dot Wine. Vicky's father had been out of the picture for five years, living somewhere in Alaska and working on the oil pipeline. She told me he was an even worse boozer than her mother and refused to send child support. That I had no mom and she had no dad (which Vicky called a "happenchance") bonded us in strange way, though we barely talked about it. We barely talked about anything of any real importance.

From day one, Vicky felt threatened by how much time I devoted to chess. To her, my passion for the game was a personal affront, a blow to her image as the sexiest girl in town. "He'd rather play chess with Ethan than get a blow job from me," she told Leslie one night while the three of us cruised The Gut, what everyone called the main drag through Walla Walla. I responded, "What I really want is a blow job *while* I'm playing chess." My language was becoming as vulgar as Vicky's.

Chess wasn't the only threat, as Vicky became increasingly possessive. When I went home to Seattle at Christmas break, she insisted on calling me every night, ostensibly to see how I was. The real reason, we both knew, was to check up on me. During one of these phone conversations I mentioned running into a girl I knew from my years at the TAG Center. We'd literally bumped into one another jockeying for position in front of the seafood display counter at the Pike Place Market. When I told Vicky about it, her first question was, "Did you fuck her?" "Yeah, Vick," I answered. "I nailed her in the second aisle, right between the honeydews and the cling peaches!" She said she was sorry, but I could tell she didn't mean it.

As the spring of 1969 approached, Vicky's suspicious nature turned into downright paranoia. To placate her, I gave her my Phi Delt pin. It calmed her down for about two weeks and after that it only intensified her sense of entitlement. If I was a few minutes late to pick her up or couldn't come to the phone, she'd accuse me of seeing someone else on the side. When we were together, she claimed I was checking out other girls' bodies, especially girls who were slimmer or prettier.

Things came to a head. After burgers at the Arctic Circle one night, I ran her home, shut off the engine. Vicky was about to get out of the car when she suggested, "C'mon by after my mom goes to bed. Park down the block and come in through the basement door. I'll leave it unlocked."

I gritted my teeth and braced myself for the fallout. "I can't, Vick. I wish I could, but I have to get up early for a Calculus test. I should be studying right now."

"C'mon, Bryan." She took my hand and tucked it up under her sweater. "I'll make it worth your while."

"I can't. You'll just have to do without me till Friday night." I joked, trying to keep the conversation light.

"Please."

"Can't." I pulled my hand away.

She shook her head in disbelief. "Are you sleeping with somebody else?"

I slumped down in the seat. "Right, Vicky. When would I have time?"

"Well, why else would you turn me down?"

"I told you. I have an important test in the morning and I'm going to be staying up half the night as it is."

"So you'd rather study?"

"No," I said, exasperated. "I'd rather be with you. But if I did, and then I bombed the Calculus test, I'd be really pissed at myself."

She rolled her eyes. "You've never bombed a test in your life."

I heaved a sigh and started the car. "I'm leaving."

"Okay, okay." She smiled sweetly, ran her hands through her hair. "Don't leave mad. Kiss me goodbye."

I leaned over and took her in my arms. Our lips met. She kissed me harder than usual and took my lower lip between her teeth. When I tried to pull away she bit me, at first hard enough to hold on and then hard enough to cut me. The salty, metallic taste of my own blood filled my mouth.

Shocked, I rolled down the window and spit blood. "Jesus God, Vicky! That really hurt."

"Then we're even." She slammed the door and stomped into her house.

———————

The next day Vicky apologized and asked me to forgive her. Like a fool, I did, then accepted her invitation to a Saturday afternoon picnic hosted by her mother for a co-worker who was leaving the cannery.

I had just helped Mrs. Spotts carry a large ice chest full of beer and soft drinks to the backyard. After setting it down on the lawn, I joined Vicky at a picnic table under the shade of an old elm. She was engaged in conversation about the merits of a four-year college with one of her mother's friends, a soft-spoken redhead she introduced as Sharon. The strangest smile flickered across Vicky's face. Her expression didn't fit what she was saying. I didn't know what to make of it until I noticed a mosquito sucking blood from the back of Sharon's pale and freckled hand. Without thinking, I swatted it away, telling Sharon what had happened. She thanked me and wiped away a spot of blood with a paper napkin.

"Didn't you see it?" I asked Vicky, puzzled.

"I saw it." She shrugged her shoulders and made a face, as if to say, *so what?*

"You saw it, but you didn't say anything?"

"That's right."

Sharon shook her head and gave Vicky the same puzzled, disgusted expression I had. Excusing herself, she walked briskly in the direction of the house.

"What's your trip?" I asked as soon as Sharon was out of earshot.

Vicky grinned. "I thought it was funny."

"You thought it was funny that someone was getting bitten by an insect? That's your definition of funny?"

"Yeah. And if you knew Sharon you'd think it was funny, too. She's a royal pain in the ass, always lecturing me on why I should get out of town and get a college education. The hell with her if she can't take a joke."

"I don't get you, Vicky."

"What's to get?" she said with a disarming smile. "It's no big deal."

"It's a big deal to me. It's like what happened at The Pancake House." A week before, Vicky and I went out for breakfast. A kid at the next table put a saltshaker up her nose and when I informed the waitress, Vicky asked me why I told.

"What's your point?"

"My point is you don't get common courtesy. How would you like to be the next person to use a saltshaker that had just been up a kid's nose? How would you like a mosquito to suck your blood and have someone gleefully watch but not say anything?"

"I wouldn't care about either one. Why's this such a big deal to you?"

I drew a deep breath and surveyed the scene, envied the people laughing and enjoying one another's company. "Because it reminds me how cold you can be."

She got up and disappeared into the house. I ducked into the driveway when no one was looking and left without saying goodbye. As I drove away I asked myself whether Vicky was worth it.

I phoned Vicky the following evening, determined to end it once and for all. Her mother told me she was at Leslie Vanzandt's studying and wouldn't return until late.

I killed a couple hours reviewing Bobby Fischer's brilliant win over William Lombardy in the '60/'61 United States Championship, then drove over and waited in Vicky's driveway. My stomach twisted itself into a hard knot, but sitting there alone gave me some time to organize my thoughts and rehearse what to say. I'd never broken up with a girl and had no idea how to say the words.

Vicky drove up a few minutes before midnight and flashed me a big smile when she pulled alongside my car. She must have thought I'd shown up for some late night sex. Walking over to my car, she grabbed her breast with one hand, a gesture I found crude. "Hop in," I told her, my voice croaky with anxiety.

"What's wrong?"

I cleared my throat. "Hop in. We need to talk."

She got in and set a heavy textbook in her lap. "You're ditching me, aren't you?"

"It's not working, Vick. I like you a lot, and I thought my feelings for you might turn into love, but it hasn't happened."

"Is this about that damn mosquito thing?"

"It's not about any one thing. It's—"

"Are you seeing another girl?"

"No. Swear to God. It has nothing—"

"Don't leave me," she pleaded. "I know you love me even if you don't see it yet. You're just messed up because of what your mother did."

A cannonball to the stomach would have been easier to take. "What my mother did? What my mother did happened when I was six years old. It has nothing to do with us," I stammered, realizing it had been a mistake to confide in her.

"Oh, it most certainly does. My counselor said—"

I abruptly leaned back. "You're seeing a counselor? Since when have you been seeing a counselor?"

"Since you went home for Christmas and left me here to sit on my thumb. It was my school counselor's idea but I wouldn't need to go if it wasn't for you."

I paused to collect my thoughts. "I'm to blame for your problems?"

"I blame you for being a user. I'm like a tube of toothpaste to you. You've used me up and now you're gonna toss me away!"

"Did your shrink tell you that, too?"

"Yeah, as a matter of fact he did. He also told me you're fucked up because your mother killed herself in front of you. He says you can't make a commitment."

"Wow! Quite a guy, this shrink of yours. He's never even met me, but he's got me all figured out. I'm surprised he doesn't send me a bill."

"Sure, make a joke of it, Bryan. You're good at that, but the truth hurts and you know it!"

The truth did hurt. My head spun with self-doubt. "Look . . . we can't talk about anything without fighting. This is a perfect example of why we should stop going together."

"I know I can be jealous sometimes and I'll try—"

"No, this is it. I want my fraternity pin back."

She began to cry. I felt bad for her, but if I caved in I'd kick myself all the way home. And then I'd have to do it all over again. "I'm sorry, Vicky. Really sorry, but it's time to move on. You need to move on, too. Maybe go away to college and get that teaching degree you said—"

I never saw it coming. Vicky lashed out with both hands, lunging across the front seat and scratching my cheek and neck with her fingernails. She'd gone from desperate to enraged in the blink of an eye. "You fucker!" she screamed in my ear.

I almost hit her, a reflex, but stopped myself. "Jesus!" I yelled, grabbing her arms and restraining her. "I can't believe you did that." A trickle of blood ran slowly down my face, tickling my cheek. Fury burned its way into my veins. "Get *out* of my car. Now!"

"You can't do this to me, you . . . immature little fuck!"

"Get out of my car, Vicky. We are *done*. I mean it!" I pushed her hard against the passenger door.

Wild-eyed, she grabbed up her book and bolted, slamming the door with all her might. "We are *not done!*" she shouted through the closed window. She stomped in front of my car, stopped abruptly and tore my Phi Delt pin from her sweater, tearing the material. Holding up the pin for me to see, she threw it down and ground it into the cement with the heel of her shoe. Locking eyes with me, she pounded her book on the hood of my car. Spit flew from her mouth as her face twisted into an expression of utter hatred. "You're gonna wish you never met me!"

––––––––––

With Vicky seemingly out of my life, I had more time to concentrate on chess and a third opportunity to play Javad Azizi (he'd won the first two). A win would award me with first chair on our chess team.

I played White and began with my usual Queen Pawn opening. Javad countered with the Meran Defense, a sharp line with good chances for Black.

I knew the Meran, but there are countless, wild variations, and my book knowledge failed me. After twenty moves the board position was bewilderingly complex and Javad gained a lead in development. I resigned on the forty-second move, down two pawns with no chances for counterplay.

I stared at the board long after my classmates had left the room.

Dr. Zaleski took a seat across from me. "I was there when Akiba Rubenstein unveiled the Meran Defense," he told me in a nostalgic tone. "It was his new conception. His *baby*. I remember how he caught us all by surprise."

"When was that?"

"1924. It happened at an international tournament."

"In Meran, Italy. Right?"

He nodded. "If my memory serves me, we were at the Hotel Zima."

I was in awe. "Did you play Rubenstein at Meran?"

"Sure. And we played on two other occasions. I'm afraid he got the best of me all three times. Apart from Bobby Fischer, no one could create a transition to a favorable endgame like Rubenstein." He paused, closed his eyes and sighed deeply. Abruptly, he pulled himself from the memory and asked, "What happened in your game with Javad?"

"I got lost. I know the Meran, and I knew he was using the Blumenfeld variation, but I couldn't remember what to do after thirteen moves. And I couldn't figure it out, either. Obviously."

"Would you like to go through the moves and see where you went wrong?"

"Definitely."

We quickly recreated the first thirteen moves. Dr. Z asked, "So, what did you do next?"

"Bishop takes pawn, putting him in check. It still looks like the right move."

"Yes, it looks that way, but the advantage disappears after you exchange queens two moves later."

"I learned that the hard way."

"You'd have done better to use Rellstab's idea and castle. Or, even better yet, move queen to bishop three and castle on the next move."

I looked the board over and nodded agreement.

"Or, you could try this." Smiling now, he moved my bishop to an aggressive diagonal that aimed squarely at his castled king.

"Why didn't I see that?"

"That was Stahlberg's idea," he said, ignoring my question.

As always, Dr. Zaleski's encyclopedic memory amazed me. In chess there are hundreds of openings and thousands of variations. He appeared to know them all. I said, "I got impatient and played too aggressively, right?"

He nodded. "I have an idea, Bryan."

"What's that?"

"Why don't you stay in Walla Walla over the summer? Reva and I would be delighted to have you. You could move into the guest bedroom in the basement."

I wasn't certain I understood what he was saying. "Move in with you and Reva?"

"Sure. The basement is quite comfortable. It has its own bathroom and you'd have plenty of privacy to come and go."

"Wow! It's an incredible offer, but—"

"But what? In return for room and board you could do yard work and odd jobs that I'm too old or too lazy to do. We could spend the day studying chess and sharpening your game."

I felt the air deflate from my lungs. "I'm honored. And I'd love nothing more than to stay here and study with you, but my father would never allow it. He wants me home for the summer."

"I understand," he said, disappointed.

No more disappointed than I was. But I rationalized by reminding myself how dull Walla Walla would be with the fraternity house closed until fall semester. Besides, I'd be facing stiff competition in the summer tournaments at the Seattle Chess Club and would return for my sophomore year a better player.

My last final was in Astronomy and fell on a Thursday afternoon. I planned to stay over Friday, pack up my sparse belongings and say good-byes to my fraternity brothers. Then, after sleeping in on Saturday morning I would gas up the Chevy and make the five-hour drive to Seattle.

———

Ten days before the end of the school year, Slider and I teamed up for a quiet game of bridge in the Phi Delt card room. I'd just dealt a new hand when Bigdog blurted out, "A kidnap party!"

"A what?" Slider asked him.

Bigdog laughed so hard he started to wheeze.

"Easy, big guy," I cautioned, rising from my chair and slapping him on the back. I'd recently learned Bigdog was asthmatic.

"Oh, man," he said, collecting himself and taking a couple hits off his epinephrine inhaler. "This is gonna to be the R.F. of all time!"

"Let's hear it." This was John "the Baptist" Knowles, a religion major and one of the better Bridge players. He earned his nickname after nearly drowning in the Snake River at a high school senior class picnic. I'd grown wary of the Baptist during the hazing rituals of hell week (sleeping on stairs, eating tomato soup with a light bulb, Sisyphean calisthenics). A founding member of the campus "God Squad," he and his ilk proselytized fundamentalist Christianity to the point of being obnoxious.

"Okay," said Bigdog, barely able to contain himself. He tossed down his cards. "Listen up. We're the only fraternity that doesn't have a major social function the Friday night after finals. And it pisses me off."

"How'd that happen, by the way?" Slider asked, sorting his cards.

Bigdog shrugged his beefy shoulders. "Supposedly, we don't have enough money after buying the color TV for the Super Bowl. Fair enough." He coughed into his hands and paused to catch his breath. "I say we hold a kegger up at the cabin and kidnap everyone else's dates."

"What?" Slider and I exclaimed in unison.

The Baptist ignored us, looked at Bigdog. "We still don't have any money."

"Oh, bullshit!" Bigdog pushed his chair away from the table. "We can do the whole thing for under two hundred bucks if we get that high school band from Dodge. 'Pothole,' or whatever the hell their name is."

"I don't think it could be done," the Baptist said.

"Call 'em and hire 'em," Bigdog answered impatiently.

With an air of disgust, the Baptist threw his cards face up on the table. "I *mean,* how are we going to kidnap everyone's dates?"

"It wouldn't be that hard," Bigdog explained. "We find out the name of every girl that has a date with a guy from another fraternity and we make a list. Friday afternoon we call them down from their dorm rooms, haul their butts up to the cabin and party."

"We snatch the snatch," Slider quipped, caught up in the moment.

The Baptist shot Slider an angry look. He disapproved of the swearing and crude talk that was the fraternity norm. He'd once proposed fining brothers for using the Lord's name in vain and putting the money in a glass milk bottle labeled "God's Jar."

"How would you find out who has dates?" I asked, intrigued by the idea of any kind of party on the last day of school.

Bigdog shrugged again. "Don't we have guys who are pinned to girls in every sorority? The girls could do it for us. We'd have to tell them what we're doing, swear them to secrecy and get 'em to find out who's going to what function."

"Okay," I said, my analytical mind shifting into overdrive. "So we have a master list with a lot of girls' names on it, probably close to a hundred, but we don't have a hundred guys with cars to drive them up to the cabin."

"That *is* a problem," the Baptist agreed, nodding and looking to Bigdog for an answer. Though pious, the Baptist was not above participating in a cruel, immature prank that involved abducting college girls under false pretenses and infuriating their bewildered dates.

"Okay, let me think about that." Bigdog turned pensive.

"How about this?" Slider said, bouncing a tennis ball off the wall (where the ball came from I have no idea). "I got a buddy in town whose dad has a big open-air cattle truck. You could get a hundred girls in it easy. We could park the truck out past Seven Mile Creek and transport the girls out there in our cars. Then load 'em in and then make a run back to town to get one or two more. When the truck's full, when we've got everyone on the list, we haul 'em up to the cabin."

"Is the road wide enough for a truck like that?" I asked. I had misgivings about herding girls into a cattle truck, but it seemed wiser to shoot holes in the plan than voice my opposition.

"Yeah," Slider assured us. "A car coming in the opposite direction might have to pull over, but there's plenty of room. It'd work." He looked at Bigdog for approval.

Bigdog nodded with a wry smile. "It *would* work," he told us. "Listen. We get our list and everyone picks out a girl or two they know. Friday afternoon you call them down from their rooms and ask them to go for a Coke or something. Tell them you have a problem you need to talk about . . . you just broke up with your girlfriend or you're about to flunk a class. Make up something good. They'll fall for it."

"They will?" the Baptist asked.

"Yeah. You know how girls love to listen to guys talk about their problems. Then we drive them out to Slider's cattle truck, drop 'em off and head back for another girl on the list. I love it!"

"Don't you think some of them will bolt from the cattle truck?" I questioned. "Whitman girls are considerably less compliant than your average beast of burden."

"Not if we park it out past Seven Mile," Slider answered with local knowledge. "That's a *long* walk. Too far from civilization."

"Besides," Bigdog added, "they're gonna be happy about ending up at a Phi Delt function."

On a warm and cloudless Friday, the day after finals ended, we lured ninety-three of the ninety-seven girls with dates into our cars (two couldn't be found, two others refused to come down from their rooms). I "kidnapped" a sophomore named Paula Tucker by telling her I needed to talk about breaking up with my townie girlfriend. Paula sat next to me in French class and we'd become casual friends. I felt guilty about the half-truth, but rationalized. *Pranks are a part of college life.*

As planned, we drove the kidnapped girls past Seven Mile Creek to the waiting cattle truck. Slider had parked it off the road, one mile across the Oregon border in the foothills of the Blue Mountains. Thankfully, he and his townie buddy had done a good job of cleaning out the rig. A few girls complained about what was happening, but far fewer than predicted. When the last girl was loaded in, Slider's townie buddy got behind the wheel and drove the bumpy road that wound its way up to our cabin.

A caravan of about twenty cars followed the truck. Slider and Ethan went in Slider's milk truck with their dates, Marilu and Kathy. Marilu, Slider's townie girlfriend, was the stereotypical redhead with a temper, but I really liked her. She had no compunctions about telling Slider when he was out of line and helped keep his wild side in check. Dateless and not wanting to feel odd man out, I drove up in the Chevy by myself.

The Phi Delt cabin, built from cedar logs, was in good condition, which I found remarkable in that its only use was for parties involving kegs of beer and immature fraternity boys. A wealthy alumnus and former brother had built and donated the cabin. A modest brass plaque mounted on the wall just inside the front door read: "Donated by John Dutton, class of '52. I don't sweat much for a little guy!" No one really knew what the oft-quoted saying meant, but all agreed it was funny.

A keg of Michelob occupied one corner of the main room. The rough ride into the mountains made for a foamy beer, but no one complained. Wearing a puffy white chef's hat, Bigdog barbecued burgers outside the front door with all the condiments available on a nearby picnic table. The Baptist, beaming with ministerial kindness and charity, filled huge bowls with enough potato chips and onion dip for a small army, which was good because the party included one hundred fifty people.

The band we hired set up in the front yard. Four mop-haired high school boys, they came from nearby Dodge and, in a creative burst of imagination, had named themselves, "Dodge." They brought along an adequate sound system that Chainsaw hooked to a generator behind the cabin. Dodge played a lot of early Beatles and sang decent harmonies. As the night wore on, they took the usual requests from drunken revelers (*Satisfaction, Shout*) and even consented to play *Louie, Louie* twice.

All the brothers went out of their way to be charming hosts to our kidnapped guests. The few girls who seemed most upset received apologies, but also special attention and door prizes: an expensive vanilla scented candle and a package of amber incense sticks supplied by Bill "Deuce" Twohey, a confirmed hippie whose sister ran a head shop in the Haight Ashbury district of San Francisco.

At midnight, the band started packing up their gear. I decided to leave and headed down to the grassy clearing where everyone parked. Hearing angry voices, I gravitated toward a contingent of "townies," who'd shown up late and uninvited. Maybe ten people stood in an informal circle, off to the side of a dark blue Chevy Malibu with its headlights on. A tall guy who appeared to be drunk taunted a chubby Mexican girl. She pleaded with him to give her something he was holding out of reach and over his head. "C'mon Jerry! Give me my keys."

"No! Lemme drive. I can drive," he responded.

"No, Jerry. You *can't* drive. It's my dad's car and he'd have a cow. Just give me the keys, will you?" The girl seemed on the verge of tears.

Jerry's buddies urged him to hold out. Feeding on their attention, he refused. "Guess you'll be here all night, Yolanda, 'cause I'm driving your daddy's car whether you like it or not."

"Give them to me, Jerry!"

"Naw, but you can sit next to me if you promise to put your hand on my leg." At this, Jerry's drunken audience guffawed, again egging him on.

As the laughter subsided, another girl stepped forward and crowded Jerry, her face no more than a foot from his. She appeared to be American Indian. Tall and willowy, she wore jeans and an all-white football jersey with striped sleeves – the kind many of my fraternity brothers wore. I watched to see what would happen. She placed her hands on her hips, cutting an imposing figure. Her voice was untroubled, almost bored. "Give *me* the keys, Jerry."

"Fuck you, Lydia."

She smiled. "Okay Jerry, we can do this however you want. Either you give me the keys right now, or I'm going to kick your ass. It's up to you."

A full-fledged crowd had gathered. At least twenty people, mostly guys, heard her deliver the ultimatum. It seemed no one breathed. Including me. I turned to a guy standing next to me, a sweaty, farm boy type in bib overalls with a bottle of Pabst Blue Ribbon in each hand. "Can she back that up?" I asked in a hushed voice.

"Oh yeah!" he said, sounding hick enough to be spitting watermelon seeds. "That's Lydia Redstone. She's got a black belt in karate. No one messes with Lydia."

"No kidding," I murmured.

Jerry looked confused by his predicament. Hanging on to the keys might get him hurt. Responding to an ultimatum by a girl would cause him to lose face. A no-win situation. His best move, in my estimation, was to hand over the car keys and tell her to lighten up, but then my brain wasn't affected by alcohol and Jerry's was. After a moment of impaired deliberation, and to the delight of his drinking buddies, he told her, "Butt out, bitch! This is between me and Yolanda."

Lydia's ability to stay calm impressed me. "Don't say I didn't warn you, Jerry. This is your last chance. I'm going to count to three. If you don't place the keys gently in my hand by the time I reach three, I'm going to have to take them from you. Then do you know what's going to happen?"

Jerry stared silently, his Adam's apple bobbing.

The farm boy next to me blurted, "What's gonna happen?"

She turned slightly, but kept her eyes on Jerry. There was enough light from the headlights of the Malibu to see that Lydia Redstone was beautiful. "Then I'm going to separate Jerry from Moss and you're going to the hospital in a bucket." She focused on her antagonist. "One . . ."

One of Jerry's friends chimed in, "Don't give 'em to her."

"Tell her to fuck off!" This from a skinny kid with multi-colored patches on his jeans.

Jerry's eyes darted anxiously.

"Two . . ." Lydia said, her voice becoming forceful. As she said it, she took a giant stride backward and assumed a karate stance. "Three."

Jerry tossed the keys hard at her feet. Right away I saw it as a trick to maneuver her into a vulnerable position. As Lydia bent over to pick up the keys, Jerry stepped forward and got halfway through a kicking motion. She anticipated the move. Quick as a cat, she grabbed the leg he'd planted and jerked him off his feet. Jerry fell hard on his back, the air rushing from his lung with a barking "Huh!" She pounced on top of him and clutched his neck with her left hand, fingernails digging into flesh. Her right fist was poised to throw punches, but she held the first one at shoulder level. Instead of hitting him she said, "Want me to mess up your face? Or are you going to hand the keys to me?"

Barely audible, Jerry croaked, "Okay. Okay."

Lydia got off him. Fire shot from her eyes. If the drunken Jerry was foolish enough to try anything more, she was ready. I hoped he wouldn't. Jerry, shaken by the suddenness of what had happened, got himself on all fours. Breathing heavily, he picked up the keys and stood up. After placing them into the palm of Lydia's hand he staggered off into the darkness behind the cars.

The crowd broke up. I watched Lydia get in the Malibu with Yolanda. They sat in the front seat, talking and laughing. Yolanda looked over her shoulder and turned off the car's lights. I walked over to my car, parked alongside Slider's milk truck. As I fished for my keys, Slider, Ethan and their dates ran past me, piled into the milk truck amid their own raucous laughter. Drunken laughter. Ethan sat in the front passenger seat and the girls climbed in the back, where I knew Slider kept an old, beat-to-hell leather couch he'd scored at a neighborhood yard sale.

Slider trumpeted, "Bryan, my man. Would you follow us back to town? The Milker hasn't been herself and I don't wanna get stranded out here." He'd obviously had too much to drink.

"What's wrong with it?"

"Fuck if I know. She loses power. Somethin' pluggin' the fuel line."

"Sure, I can follow. But are you okay to drive?"

Leaning back in the elevated seat, Slider shot me a maniacal grin as the Milker roared to life. "First rule of driving. If I can get the keys in the ignition, I'm okay to drive!" He slammed the Milker into gear, grinding for several seconds before pulling onto the gravel road.

"Drive carefully!" I yelled after him, but I don't think he heard me.

I jumped into my car and followed. The Milker kicked up a sizable dust cloud so I trailed behind by several hundred yards. I could see his taillights bounce in the ruts. He was driving too fast, making me nervous. By the time I reached the paved highway near Kooskooskie, the only road back to town, the Milker had gotten way ahead of me. Slider had sped up.

"Oh shit!" I muttered, and stepped on it. He was going at least sixty. Safe in the milk truck was fifty, maximum, and the road was curvy. I got my Chevy up to seventy, trying to get ahead and pass. It was all I could think of: pass him and then slow down, force him to decelerate. Before I caught up, the milk truck shimmied, its taillights dancing to the right before it tumbled like a well-lit Christmas tree down a flight of stairs. And then the taillights seemed to drop fifteen feet before stopping their bizarre dance altogether.

"Ohmygod!" I cried out. Slamming on the brakes, I skidded to a stop on the gravel shoulder, between the Milker and the highway. I bolted from my car. The milk truck lay on its back, its wheels spinning in the moonlight.

The roof and sides had collapsed like a tornado-stricken Missouri mobile home. Someone was crying. Smelling gasoline, I got on my knees, reached across Slider's contorted body and turned off the ignition. There was no sign of Ethan.

"It's Bryan," I said to Slider. "Is it okay to move you?"

"I think so," he groaned, reeking of alcohol.

I got my arms around Slider's chest and pulled him from what was left of the front door entrance. He was conscious, but dazed.

From somewhere inside the collapsed wreckage, Marilu said, "I'm okay . . . I think. You okay, Kathy?"

Kathy was the one crying. "My leg hurts, but not too bad," she answered weakly. Her voice had no carry in the still night.

"Crawl over here by the front door. I'll pull you guys out," I told them. "Hurry!" The smell of gas was getting stronger. I didn't want us all to die in an explosion.

It was dark and hard to see. Arms reached out to me. Marilu. I grabbed on to her forearms and gently pulled her from the wreckage. Moaning, she asked, "Where's Ethan?"

"He's got to be here," I answered. "Are you okay?"

"I think so." A note of hysteria crept into her voice. "I think Ethan got thrown out when the truck rolled."

"Okay. Look for him while I get Kathy out." Marilu must have been in shock because she started running in the wrong direction.

"Marilu. Stop! The other way! Back there. The other way." I watched her stumble to one knee before turning around and heading back. She started calling Ethan's name, but he didn't answer.

Kathy crawled to where I was and began backing out, feet first. Slider got to his feet then staggered over to help. He pulled on Kathy's leg.

"Ow!" she shrieked. I reached around him and grabbed Kathy by the waist. I got a good grip on her belt and together Slider and I pulled her onto the ground outside the remains of the Milker. "It hurts," she cried. "Below my knee."

Carefully, we helped her to a safe distance from the wreck.

"Holy fucking shit," Slider said, burying his head in his hands. He looked to be okay physically, but the reality of what he'd done had begun to set in.

"If you're okay, help us find Ethan," I told him.

"Go ahead, both of you," Kathy said. "I think it's just a bad bruise. We have to find Ethan!" She hopped to her feet and limped off, dragging her right leg in the sandy soil.

"Stay away from the milk truck," I ordered. "If a spark gets to the gasoline it's gonna blow!"

Slider and I angled back towards the highway. It made sense that Ethan would have been thrown out along that pathway. Slider was also limping, but it didn't look like anything serious. Up ahead, we heard Marilu say, "I can't find him. It's too dark."

"This isn't happening!" Slider said.

"It *is* happening and we've got to find Ethan." I said in an authoritative voice. "I'll be right back. I'm going to get the flashlight from my car."

I was almost to my car when I heard Kathy shriek, "He's dead! He's dead! Oh God, he's dead!"

I bolted down the hill in her direction, a good fifty feet from where the Milker had come to rest. Ethan's head lay lifelessly in her lap. Seeing us in the faint light, she reached out with her hand and wailed, "Ethan is dead!"

"What have I done?" Slider whimpered, collapsing to his knees.

I kneeled and put my fingers on the side of Ethan's neck, feeling for a pulse. It was slick with blood. A lot of blood, and no sign of life.

"Do something!" Kathy screamed in my ear.

I tried not to panic. Groping in the darkness, I found Ethan's wrist and again felt for a pulse. This time I could detect a weak, but rhythmical throbbing. "He's alive," I announced, "but he's unconscious. We've got to get him to the hospital, and fast! He's losing a lot of blood."

A car sped by on the highway, followed by the sound of screeching brakes. Gravel flew as the driver put the car in reverse and backed hurriedly, coming to a stop near my car. The light from my headlights illuminated a dark blue Malibu. The doors flew open and two girls ran down the embankment to the milk truck.

"Over here!" Kathy screamed. "We need help over here."

"Please help us!" Marilu shouted.

They ran to us in the darkness. Lydia Redstone got to us first. I recognized her tall outline in the dim light. "What can we do?" she asked, her voice urgent.

"We've got to get my friend to the hospital," I answered. "And fast! Help us carry him to my car." I grabbed Ethan by the shoulders while Slider and Lydia each took a leg. Ethan weighed about two hundred twenty, but we managed to half carry him, half drag him up to my car. Yolanda opened the door to my Chevy without being asked and pushed the front seat forward to make room in the back.

There was a moment of indecision about how to get Ethan in, but Lydia dropped his leg and scooted across the back seat. She said, "Get him in here and haul ass!"

We left the front seat forward and more or less stuffed Ethan into the back. Lydia held his head in her lap. With the interior light on, I could see he was bleeding all over her.

Kathy saw the blood and started screaming again. "He's bleeding to death. Ethan's gonna die!" she wailed.

I bit my lip and turned to Yolanda. "Can you drive my friends here to the hospital?"

Before she could answer, Lydia said, "Yolanda. Do it. I'll see you when you get there."

"See you guys at the hospital," I said, running around my car and jumping in the front seat. Fighting tears, I accelerated to eighty before slowing down for a gradual turn. That last look at Ethan convinced me I had no time to waste. He was bleeding profusely and showed no sign of regaining consciousness. Normal time back to Walla Walla would have been about fifteen minutes from where the Milker rolled. I figured I could do it in less than ten.

I focused hard on my driving. Lydia spoke softly to Ethan. Her words were undetectable, but her tone was reassuring.

"Is he awake?" I asked.

"No, but maybe he can hear me. What's his name?"

"Ethan. Ethan Maclean. He's my roommate. My friend." Saying his name and my relationship to him made me choke up.

As I took a big turn before a farmhouse I realized Lydia was praying. "Holy Father," I heard her say, "don't let this boy Ethan die. Keep him alive till we get him to the hospital so the doctors can save him." Her compassion touched my heart. I blinked away tears and concentrated on the road.

"Can you drive faster?" Lydia asked. "I can feel him fading."

I slammed down the accelerator on a straight stretch and glanced down as the speedometer moved past eighty. Looking up, I saw the police car parked in a driveway near a trailer house with an outdoor floodlight. I flew past it and never considered slowing down, even after we heard the siren and saw the flashing lights.

"Are you gonna stop?" Lydia asked.

"No way."

"I wouldn't either."

The cop car was about a quarter-mile behind us and closing ground when I reached the city limits. He had to be doing close to a hundred. After looking in both directions, I ran the red light at the Suds Up Car Wash and squealed the tires making the hard left onto the main drag. Laying on my horn, I passed two cars that were already in the right lane. They probably assumed I was trying to outrun the police car that was now only two blocks behind, siren blaring.

"The hospital's on Alder. Right?"

"Yeah," Lydia answered. Leaning forward, she added, "Take a right at the block that comes after Reed and Bell's."

Without thinking, I put on my turn signal before taking the turn at forty miles an hour. Had the moment not been so tense I'd have laughed at myself. The tires squealed loudly and I nearly sideswiped a parked car on the opposite side of the road.

Lydia shouted, "There's an emergency entrance in back . . . right there!"

I turned hard again to the right, fishtailed into a well-lit circular driveway, straightened it out and hit the brakes hard, skidding to a stop three feet from large glass doors that said "Emergency" in bold red lettering. I laid on the horn and ran around to the passenger door to get Ethan. As I threw it open, the police car came skidding to a stop a couple feet behind us. He came within inches of rear-ending my car.

A big, fit-looking young policeman bolted from his vehicle in a rage. "Hands on the car, asshole!" he yelled, his hand reaching for a holstered gun.

"My friend is dying!" I yelled back, ignoring his command. I grabbed the still unconscious Ethan by the legs and started pulling him out.

"Put your hands on the car right now!" the cop yelled again, this time louder. And I ignored him again, even though I was afraid he was about to draw his weapon and shoot me.

A nurse and a male orderly ran through the automatic doors. The orderly glanced at the cop and said, "Give us a hand, officer." The orderly then grabbed one of Ethan's legs and helped Lydia and me lift him onto a gurney, which appeared out of nowhere. The cop just stood there with his hands on his waist, fuming.

"Oh Sweet Jesus!" the nurse said on seeing all the blood. "Call Dr. Benjamin. Stat!" she shouted at an overweight, middle-aged woman who'd drifted out to see what was happening. The woman, presumably a receptionist, turned and ran back inside the hospital.

When the orderly and nurse finished strapping Ethan onto the gurney, the cop poked his finger in my chest. "You're goin' downtown, pal." He was robust and good-looking, with straight black hair, cut short. A one-inch horizontal scar high on his left cheek gave him a dangerous, tough-guy look. Some kind of weird energy radiated from his being, a mix of menace and conceit.

The nurse, wheeling Ethan through the doors, shouted, "We need that kid inside, officer. To tell us what happened."

I turned my back and followed them into the hospital, no doubt pissing off the cop even more. Lydia was walking next to me, saying something to the effect that Ethan would be okay. It was hard to understand her because the hospital speaker system was blaring, *Code Red, E.R., Code Red, E.R.* They rolled Ethan quickly into an emergency room just off a small waiting area. "You can't come in here," the nurse said. "It's sterile. Just tell me what happened. And make it quick."

"He was in a truck that rolled doing about seventy. Actually, he got thrown from the truck. He lost consciousness right away and hasn't regained it. That was about twenty minutes ago. Maybe twenty-five."

"Anyone else hurt?"

"Three more injured people will be here in a few minutes." The double doors opened and I managed to catch a last look at my best friend. Ethan looked spectral as they rolled him under the brilliant glow of operating lights.

Her eyes shined with fear. "Are the other three hurt anything like this one?"

"No. One girl might have a broken leg."

She turned to Lydia. "Are you injured?" Her white football jersey and blue jeans were soaked in Ethan's blood.

"I'm fine." She gestured in the direction of the operating room. "It's not my blood, it's his."

Someone inside the operating room yelled, "Intubate him!" The urgency in her voice frightened me. *Not a good sign,* I feared. Tears again welled up in my eyes.

The nurse turned back to me. "Your friend in there smells of alcohol. Has he been drinking a little or a lot? Don't lie to me. It's important for the doctors to know."

"Probably a lot. *Definitely* a lot."

She shouted over to the receptionist. "Betty, we've got three more injured coming in a few minutes. Possible leg fracture." She turned back to me. "You're Whitman students, right?"

"Yeah. I mean I am, and my friend in there."

"Betty," she hollered. "Get on the horn and call Bob Sanderson, the Dean of Men over at the college. He'll be in the phone book." Abruptly, she disappeared through the doors, allowing us a quick glance of what was going on. It looked like bedlam inside.

I turned around. Lurking less than five feet away, the angry cop glowered at me. Hands on his hips, he struck an aggressive posture. "You're in a boatload of trouble," he growled. "Speeding, failure to pull over, running a red light, reckless driving—"

"Give me a break," I interrupted. "I was trying to save my friend's life. Your saw the shape he was in."

"Doesn't matter. I pull you over, you pull over!"

"Oh, come on, officer. If I pull over, we lose precious minutes and maybe my friend bleeds to death."

"What? You some kinda doctor in training? You so smart it gives you the right to drive like a bat outta hell 'cause you think someone might be dying in the back seat?"

"I did what I had to. Jesus! He's fighting for his life—"

Betty, the receptionist, stepped in between us and interrupted. "Excuse me. We need some information on your friend."

The cop said, "Listen, nurse whatever-your-name-is. I'm Officer Jack Montrose and I'm arresting this punk for a whole series of moving violations. You—"

She cut him off. "I'm not a nurse. And I'm sorry, officer, but we need some vital information about what happened in this accident. There are three more kids coming in injured and we have to know how to get in touch with their parents. When I'm done with this boy you can arrest whoever you want."

"Why can't you ask *her*?" Officer Montrose snapped. He gestured with his head to Lydia. The three of us looked at her simultaneously.

"I . . . I don't know any of these people," Lydia responded. "I just stopped at the accident and tried to help."

"Okay," Officer Montrose conceded with a snarl. "But I get the Whitman kid as soon as you're done with your questions."

I followed Betty back to the reception area and sat down at a small wooden-topped table. Someone had scratched a cross into the surface. My body felt like it weighed a ton. Lydia walked a step behind me. I told her, "I can't thank you enough for your help."

"Don't worry about it. My name's Lydia."

"I know. Lydia Redstone. My name's Bryan . . . Bryan Matthews."

"I know."

We exchanged curious looks.

"If you two are done with introductions, I'd appreciate getting some information here," Betty said.

"Sorry," we replied in unison.

Betty asked me for Ethan's full name and didn't bat an eye when I gave his middle name as Breedlove. She wanted to know if I knew how to get in touch with his parents. During a momentary break in her questioning, I glanced over my shoulder to get a bead on Officer Jack Montrose, who was nowhere to be seen. I hoped he might have left the hospital after reconsidering the circumstances, a hope that lasted all of ten seconds. He walked into view outside the E.R. glass doors, sucking hard on a cigarette and pacing like a caged animal.

"Okay. That's all," Betty told me, interrupting my thoughts. "By the way," she added, "you did good getting your buddy here as fast as you did. It might have saved his life."

"Tell the cop," I grumbled.

Lydia had gone to the ladies' room to clean up some. She returned at the same time her friend Yolanda walked into the E.R, followed by Marilu and a limping Kathy. Marilu spotted me and rushed over. "How's Ethan?" she asked. "Is he going to be okay?"

"We don't know. They took him in there," I gestured, "a few minutes ago. He's still unconscious. Where's Slider?"

"He got out of the car at Reed and Bell's. Insisted he was okay." Lowering her voice she added, "He told us the hospital would test his alcohol for blood and he'd be in even worse trouble than he's already in."

"You mean test his blood for alcohol," I corrected her.

"No. He said 'test his alcohol for blood.' Anyway, he said for you to call him at home as soon as there was any word on Ethan."

"Not a bad idea for him to stay away from here. There's an asshole cop outside who's hot to arrest someone."

At that, Marilu went over and sat next to a weeping Kathy, who was waiting to have her leg attended to. Lydia introduced me to Yolanda who immediately told us she was heading home. I thanked her for stopping at the accident scene and for bringing in my friends. She offered Lydia a ride but Lydia politely declined, giving me an unexpected boost.

After Yolanda left, Officer Montrose came back inside and strode up to me. He said, "You're done talkin'. Put your hands behind you. I'm gonna cuff you for the ride."

My mouth dropped open. "Please, officer. You've *got* to understand this. I was trying to save my friend's life. It would've been foolish—"

"I'm not gonna argue, college boy." He grabbed me roughly by the shoulder, spun me around and handcuffed my wrists. It was at this moment I remembered Vicky Spotts telling me about the cop who busted kids parked out at Stubblefield, how he'd refused to let her naked friend put her clothes on. Officer Jack Montrose.

"Officer Montrose," Lydia pleaded. "Be reasonable. The orderly told me another few minutes and his friend might have arrived dead. Pulling over could've cost his friend his life!"

"Right," Montrose said sarcastically. He pushed me hard in the direction of the front door.

Just then, Dr. Bob Sanderson, the Dean of Men, charged into the emergency room. Right behind him was a gorilla of a man in his late fifties or early sixties. The gorilla had sharp, intelligent eyes, no neck, and what looked to be a permanent scowl on his pockmarked, unshaven face. At that moment the scowl was directed at Officer Montrose.

Montrose stopped and stood at attention. "Chief. What're you doing here?"

Before the Chief could answer, Dean Sanderson motioned to my handcuffs and asked, "Bryan, do you mind telling me what the hell's going on?"

I stared at Officer Montrose and decided to let him answer first. He rolled his eyes. Looking back and forth between Dr. Sanderson and the Chief he explained, "I tried to pull the kid over from Kooskooskie all the way to the hospital and he acted like I was invisible. He was going over a hundred, ran a red light, nearly caused a couple of accidents."

Dean Sanderson and the Police Chief looked at me for a response.

I shook my head. "Not true."

Montrose snapped, "That's just it. This kid has no respect—"

Dean Sanderson interrupted him. "Bryan, this is Chief of Police Bud Carter. Tell Chief Carter what happened."

"I'd shake your hand Chief Carter, but Officer Montrose handcuffed me for some reason."

"Why is this kid cuffed, Montrose?" Chief Carter asked with in an authoritative, slightly agitated tone."

"Standard procedure. He resisted arrest."

"I haven't done a single thing to resist arrest, and you can ask anyone here."

"Uncuff him for the time being."

"But Chief—"

"Now!" the Chief bellowed.

Montrose undid my cuffs as roughly as he put them on.

Chief Carter turned to me. "Let's hear your version of what happened."

"A friend of mine, Spencer Klatt, totaled his truck on the way back from the Phi Delt cabin, which is up in the Blue Mountains."

"I know Spencer," the Chief said. "Goes by 'Slider.' Pitched for Wa-Hi. He okay?"

"Yeah. But another friend, my roommate . . ." I paused, tightened my mouth, "a guy named Ethan Maclean is in the operating room right now. He's unconscious and bleeding heavily from his head." A wave of emotion overwhelmed me and I began to cry. Lydia, who was standing alongside me, took my arm and pressed close. I leaned into her body for support, experienced an almost blissful feeling of being held.

Dean Sanderson looked at the bloodstains on Lydia's clothes. Then he placed his hand on my shoulder and said, "Take your time, Bryan. You kids have obviously been through a lot."

I cleared my throat. "Ethan got thrown out of the truck—"

"Dear God in heaven," Dr. Sanderson said to no one in particular. "Was Slider driving that milk truck of his?"

"Yeah."

"Was he intoxicated?"

"I don't really know," I lied. "I was driving behind him when it happened."

"The officer says you were driving over a hundred. Is that true?"

"No. Out around Seven Mile I was pushing eighty on the straight stretches, but there were no cars. Ethan was unconscious in the back seat and he'd already lost a lot of blood. A ton of blood."

Lydia chimed in. "I was in the back seat with him. We thought he was going to bleed to death."

"Right or wrong," I added, "I thought I had to get him to the hospital as fast as I could. That's why I didn't pull over. And I didn't even come close to causing an accident. I passed precisely two cars on the way to the hospital. Out on Isaacs, and both safely."

Dr. Sanderson stared at Officer Montrose. "You're planning to ticket this young man for speeding to the hospital to save his best friend's life?"

"The law's the law," Montrose answered angrily. "We ticket men who speed their pregnant wives to the hospital to deliver a baby." He looked at Chief Carter for support, but it wasn't there. Shifting his gaze back to Dean Sanderson he added, "And who are you, anyway?"

"I'm Dr. Robert Sanderson, the Dean of Men at Whitman College. Frankly, Officer . . ." he paused to read the white-on-black plastic bar on his chest, "Montrose. I find it hard to believe that, once you heard the circumstances, you would write this young man a ticket. And I certainly don't understand why you would need to handcuff him."

"I'm doing my job," Montrose responded.

Dean Sanderson turned to Chief Carter. "Bryan is one of our best kids. It seems clear his intention was to get a badly injured friend to the hospital. For God's sake, he might have saved Ethan's life!"

Chief Carter motioned for Officer Montrose to follow him over by an elevator. I suppose he didn't want to publicly dress down one of his men, but his voice carried enough that we heard every word. "Technically," he said, "you could ticket the kid for speeding, but if we weigh in the circumstances it seems he was just doing what made the most sense. Saving a life justifies his disobeying the rules of the road."

Montrose was easier to hear. "How do we know the kid would have died?' he snarled. "How do we know the kid won't die anyway?"

"We don't. Now go out to your car and run Bryan Matthews for priors. Unless he has a history of moving violations I'm gonna cut the kid some slack. And wait for me outside."

Montrose looked back at me with hatred so pure it frightened me. He turned on his heel and stomped out of the hospital, boots clicking loudly on the hard-waxed linoleum floor.

Chief Carter walked back and asked me, "How's your driving record?"

"Perfect, sir."

He nodded. "That's what I figured."

"Officer Montrose is a dedicated cop and he gets a little gung ho at times, but it's nothing personal. He's just trying to do his job."

If it wasn't personal before, it is now! I thought to myself. "Thank you, Chief Carter. I'm positive I did the right thing."

"I'm inclined to agree with you, son," he said, his gorilla looks belying a gentle side to his personality. He turned to Dean Sanderson. "I'm going to want a thorough investigation of this accident. If there's alcohol involved, I want to know about it."

"Absolutely," Dr. Sanderson said. "We'll cooperate any way we can."

Chief Carter abruptly left. I watched him walk through the glass hospital doors to join Montrose, who stood alongside his car, drawing hard on another cigarette. They began talking. Chief Carter shook his head and made animated hand gestures. When the Chief was finished, Montrose threw his cigarette to the ground and stormed off.

I thanked Dr. Sanderson for coming to my defense. He nodded and said he'd gotten a call from the E.R. about Ethan being admitted with a head injury. He'd also been told another Whitman student was in big trouble with an overzealous cop. Despite the late hour, he decided to roust his golfing buddy Chief Carter, who lived on the same street. I thanked him again. He excused himself to get an update on Ethan's condition. Lydia and I, left standing by ourselves, looked at one another. I felt embarrassed about crying in front of her and didn't know what to say.

"I have to get home," she said apologetically, "or I'll have some real explaining to do. Actually, I'll have some real explaining to do anyway."

"I'll drive you."

She smiled enough to show the gleam of perfect teeth.

On the way out of the hospital, I offered Marilu a ride home, but she said her parents were already on the way. She also told me Kathy had arranged for a ride from a sorority sister before she'd been taken to an exam room.

Dean Sanderson rushed over. "Ethan is conscious," he said, heaving a sigh of relief and ruffling the sparse hair on top of his head. "He has a concussion and a deep gash on his scalp, but they think he'll be okay."

When my eyes filled with tears, Lydia took my arm in hers again. We said goodbye to Marilu and Dean Sanderson and walked outside to my car. It smelled of blood and alcohol so we rolled down the windows.

"Just start heading toward town," Lydia told me.

"Okay," I replied, suddenly exhausted.

Once underway Lydia said, "You said you knew my name. When we were standing by the receptionist."

"Yeah. A guy up at the cabin told me."

"Why?"

"The drunk that had Yolanda's keys. You were about to send him to the hospital in a bucket and I asked some guy what your name was."

"Oh. Jerry Moss," she laughed. "What a loser baby."

"You said you knew my name, too. How was that?"

"My friend Yolanda pointed you out at the cabin. She told me you're the Whittie that goes with Vicky Spotts."

"Past tense, *please*. I used to go with Vicky. I broke it off over a month ago. Where am I taking you?"

"You know where Washington Park is?"

"Not really."

"Know where the State Penitentiary is?"

I nodded. "Yeah."

"Head toward the pen."

I drove in the direction of the poor side of town and through an industrial area, ending up on Carrie Street, two blocks from the railroad tracks and not far from the penitentiary. From there, Lydia pointed out her house. I pulled to the curb and shut off the ignition. "I can't thank you enough," I told her.

"Don't worry about it. Anyone would have done what I did."

"No, they wouldn't. The way you stepped in to help, with someone you didn't even know. You helped save my friend's life."

"I just hope he's okay."

"Yeah. Ethan's a great guy. Are you going to be able to get the bloodstains out of your clothes?"

"I don't think it'll be a problem. I'll soak 'em in cold water before I go to bed."

"If they're ruined, I'll pay for them."

"Don't worry about it."

Knowing this might be my only chance, I forced myself to say what had been on my mind. "I'd really like to see you again. You seem really nice and . . . " My voice trailed off under the strain of adolescent nerves.

"Like a date?" she asked, sounding surprised.

I nodded again. "Yeah. Like a date."

She looked at the front of her house, then back at me. "You sure you and Vicky Spotts are really broken up? I mean, it sounds like it just happened."

"Believe me, I don't want anything to do with her. Cross my heart and hope to die." I crossed my heart with my index finger.

She sighed. "Look. I'm really tired. This has been a crazy night. Why don't you call me tomorrow?"

"What's your phone number?"

"Jackson 5-4455."

"How about I call in the morning?"

She laughed. "It is morning."

I jumped at the chance to laugh with her. "I mean, sometime before noon."

She nodded, leaned across the seat and kissed me on the cheek. I couldn't tell if it was an encouraging sign or a kiss goodbye. Either way, Lydia Redstone was an angel. But would she be my angel? I was all packed up and ready to leave for Seattle, but everything had changed. I wanted nothing more than to spend summer break in Walla Walla.

I drove back to hospital for more news on Ethan, avoiding the main drag and the possibility Officer Jack Montrose might still be on duty. Or worse, off duty. A visceral fear seized me. I kept a sharp eye for police cars and reached the hospital without incident. Once there, I decided I'd given in to paranoia, though time would prove me wrong.

Chapter 4
First Love

Lydia. I woke up with her name on my lips, the continuation of an ephemeral dream. I'd never met a Lydia and the sound entranced me: *Lid—ee—uh*. A beautiful, if not enticing name. *Had I not read of an ancient country named Lydia, somewhere near the Aegean Sea?* I listened inwardly to the sound of the two consonants and three vowels, frolicking in my mind like happy schoolchildren. Without thinking I whispered her name aloud, taking a slow, three-step trip of the tongue down the palate, the same way Professor Humbert did when he sounded out Lo—lee—ta in Nabokov's controversial novel. For the next few minutes, I lay in bed thinking. Humbert had been destroyed by his inappropriate and doomed passion for the nymphet Lolita. Was it an omen? Perhaps. I confess to believing in omens at age seventeen, but it would have taken a lot more than that to deter me from pursuing Lydia Redstone.

I got up and showered, went to the SUB and read the *Walla Walla Union-Bulletin* over a bowl of oatmeal with bananas, raisins and brown sugar. No article on the accident. Not yet, anyway. I took my time, read about a hunger strike at the state penitentiary and returned to Davis-Jacobs, packing the rest of my possessions into boxes. All I could think of was how much I wanted to accept Dr. Z's offer so I could stay in town and get to know Lydia. Then I took a deep breath, said "Here goes!" and phoned her. It was just before ten and I wondered if it was too early, but couldn't wait another minute. The phone was picked up on the fifth ring, just as my heart began to sink. "Lydia?" I asked.

"No. This is Yolanda. I'll bet this is Bryan, from last night."

"Yeah. Hi. Did Lydia spend the night at your house, or vice versa?" I wasn't trying to be nosy. I was confused.

Laughing, Yolanda said, "We spent the night at each other's house. We're sisters."

"Oh." Now I was even more confused. *Is one adopted? Parent in common? Lydia is clearly Indian. Yolanda, Mexican.*

"How's your friend?" Yolanda asked.

"They think he'll be okay. But he had a bad concussion."

"I'm glad. I mean . . . I'm glad he's going to be okay. I went to Mass this morning and lit a candle for him."

"Thanks, Yolanda. That means a lot to me," I said, moved by the thoughtfulness of these teenage girls who offer prayers for a stranger. Sisters.

"I'll get Lydia."

I heard a muffled conversation and a giggle. A few seconds later Lydia came on the phone and said, "Hi." She sounded less enthused than I'd hoped for.

"Hi."

"Have you heard how Ethan's doing?" she asked.

"Pretty good, all things considered. I went back to the hospital after dropping you off. They told me he'd been talking to the doctors and nurses. He had a bad headache and some of what he said didn't make sense, but they saw his waking up as a good sign."

"Did you get to see him?"

"They wouldn't let me. Want to go visit him with me?"

She paused. "I'm not sure."

"As in you're not sure you want to visit Ethan . . . or you're not sure you want to see me?"

"I'm not sure." She laughed self-consciously.

I felt my body tense up. "It's really important to meet someone when you help save their life. I read that somewhere. Besides, if you don't see me I'll be forced to starve myself until you change your mind. That makes two reasons for you to go." I don't know where that came from, probably the newspaper article on the hunger strike.

"Are you always this good at guilt?"

"When the need is there, I can be *very* good."

She paused again, this time longer. "What are visiting hours at the hospital?"

"I don't know, but the nurse said it was okay to come during the lunch hour."

"Okay. Pick me up at noon."

I gassed up the Chevy on the way to Lydia's, but arrived in her neighborhood way early. I took the extra time to check out the industrial area that paralleled the railroad tracks. A series of small business lined one side of the tracks. Arrow Caster and Wheel Company. Superior Demolition and Salvage. Blue Mountain Diesel Service. City-County Storage. None of them looked to be thriving. Across the street, in what appeared to be a refinery, fifty-foot storage tanks loomed inside a cyclone fence.

I stopped to have a look. A rail-thin man in his early twenties approached me from behind a parked car. I tensed up, but relaxed some when he smiled. I rolled down the window and he said something unintelligible.

"What?" I asked.

He fixed his small brown eyes on me but didn't repeat himself.

I motioned with my head and asked, "Is that an oil refinery over there?"

"It's where they clean the tanks," he answered.

"Oh."

"The gas door is open," he mumbled.

I realized he'd repeated the first thing he'd said and looked in the direction of the refinery to see if a gate had been left open.

He gently touched my arm and pointed to the open gas cap on the side of my car. "D'ya want me to shut it?" he asked.

"Sure. Thanks. I must have left it open when I gassed up a few minutes ago."

He flipped it shut and smiled again, revealing crooked teeth that needed brushing.

"What's your name?" I asked him.

"People call me Slim 'cause I'm skinny, but my real name is Horace Tackitt."

"My name's Bryan. Do you like to be called Slim or Horace?"

"Slim. 'Cause when I was in school the other kids used to call me 'Whore Ass.' I didn't much care for that."

I shook my head in agreement. "No, I wouldn't think so."

"Hey. I got my picture in the paper last winter."

"No kiddin'? How'd you manage that?"

"It was 'cause I found a bunch of kitten babies that someone threw in the trash up at the storage company. Right up the street where them weeds is growin' out of the sidewalk. I was walkin' by an I heard 'em meowin' an I showed two guys with long hair that was drivin' by in a big truck with a green elephant painted on the side. They took 'em to a school and put 'em by the heater and kept 'em alive."

I nodded approvingly. "Good job, Slim."

"The paper said I was a hero on account a the kittens would a froze to death 'cause it was freezin' cold that mornin'. The picture showed me pointin' to the trash bin where I found 'em. Gladys cut out the picture an put it in a picture frame."

"Well, you were definitely a hero, Slim. And you helped me today by noticing my gas cap was open. If you hadn't closed it for me I might have scraped it against something and broken it off. You probably saved me quite a bit of money. Here, take this. You earned it." I handed Slim two one-dollar bills.

"Thanks. If it's okay I'll give this to Gladys, 'cause I don't understand money real well."

"You don't?"

He shrugged his bony shoulders. "Don't work much 'cept for sometimes pickin' onions."

"Who's Gladys?"

"My Auntie."

"You live around here, Slim?"

"On Carrie Street." He pointed, held the position as if posing for an art class.

"Where are your parents?"

"Mom died when I was still in school. She turned yellow from smoking too many cigarettes. At least that's what Gladys said, an my Mom was her sister. That's why she's my Auntie."

"Where's your Dad?"

Slim frowned. "He's in the penitentiary 'cause he robbed the Baker-Boyer National Bank with a gun. He was wearin' a mask made of my Mom's nylon stockings, but people could see through it an one of them knew it was him 'cause she learned him in school."

"Bummer. Crime doesn't pay, does it?"

"No, sir. Don't smoke, an don't rob banks. That's what I learnt from my parents."

I couldn't help but laugh. "Those are good lessons. Say, I'm going to visit someone who lives on your street. Do you know a girl named Lydia?"

"Lydia Redstone. She lives right across the street. She's a Injun."

"Yes, she certainly is."

"An she's pretty."

"Very pretty." A car rolled by, stopped in front of Blue Mountain Diesel service. Two men got out, unlocked the front door and went inside.

"An she's nice, but Gladys doesn't like me to talk to Lydia."

"Why's that, Slim?"

"Cuz Lydia's momma was a Injun whore."

I recoiled in my seat. "You sure about that, Slim?"

"Sure as shootin'."

"Because that means Lydia's mother was a prostitute. A woman who took money for having sex with men. Did you know that?"

"Yep. That's what Gladys told me. That's why Lydia had to move in with Mr. and Mrs. Cruz, the Mexican family."

"Look, Slim. I better get going or I'll be late."

"Late for yer date."

"You got it, Slim. See you around."

Slim waved goodbye and stuffed the dollar bills in his front pocket. I took off in the direction of Carrie Street, shocked, but also wondering if I could trust a retarded man's version of Lydia's past.

――――――――

The grimy gray walls of the penitentiary formed a perfect background for a neighborhood nearly overrun by weeds. Junk cars were parked in front yards and lean-to shacks were built up against run-down homes. It looked like the kind of neighborhood where a prison record wouldn't make one a pariah – night and day from Hawthorne Hills where I'd grown up, which bothered me more than I'd care to admit. My guess was that Slim's wasn't the only family that had a loved one up on the hill.

I parked in front of Lydia's and looked across the street, still thinking about what Slim had told me. Lydia's house, or rather the Cruz', assuming he had the story right, looked out of place. It was modest but well kept with an almost-new coat of white paint and blue-green shutters. The lawn was mowed and the flowerbeds added a splash of early summer color. The house to the immediate left still had Christmas lights up and the mailbox would have fallen over were it not leaning against a rusted-out barbecue. The house to the right was littered with broken and unfinished pieces of pottery.

Someone must have spotted me from the window because the Cruz' front door opened and Yolanda stepped out onto the front porch. She wore baggy gray sweat pants and a maroon T-shirt that said *"Property of Cougar Football."* She waved to me with more enthusiasm than I would have expected and definitely more than Lydia had demonstrated on the phone. I liked Yolanda, intuitively. Lydia followed her out ten seconds later, long legs up to heaven. She bent slightly at the waist and said something to Yolanda under her breath. They giggled and exchanged a hug before Lydia headed down the steps and crossed the cracked sidewalk.

I jumped out to get the car door. Lydia wore a short sleeveless cotton sundress. It was cornflower blue with a floral print, the perfect complement to flawless nut-brown skin that seemed to give off a gentle glow. Her hair was jet black, straight and shiny, parted down the middle and tucked behind her ears. As she got close I realized I'd been too anxious the night before to really notice her eyes. Large and bright, they were the color of dark chocolate, accentuated by high cheekbones, long eyelashes and a thin line of blue eye shadow.

"Pretty dress," I said, holding the car door for her.

She smiled. "Yolanda made it for me. She designed it and everything."

"Wow. Yolanda has a real talent, then. And she's your sister?" We pulled away from the curb. A black Chihuahua ran in front of the Chevy and into a yard on the other side of the street. An elderly woman behind a screened porch yelled at the animal to come inside.

"Yeah. Her parents adopted me when I was seven. Yolanda and I are sisters, but not by blood." At that, she began laughing and offered up another beautiful smile. It was not just her mouth, but also her eyes that made it so lovely.

"What's funny?"

"Actually, we *are* blood sisters. When we were little girls we cut our hands with a razor blade and mingled our blood. What I should say is that we're not related. She's Mexican and I'm Indian."

"Full-blooded?"

Her body tensed. "Me or her?"

"You."

"Cayuse and Commanche. Can't get any more full-blooded than that. Unless you're all Cayuse or all Commanche."

I nodded, embarrassed by my own intrusiveness.

We arrived at the Walla Walla Memorial Hospital and found Ethan on the Intensive Care Unit. He complained of nausea and a splitting headache from the concussion so we promised to make it a short stay. I told him how

Lydia had held him and prayed for him while he bled all over her in the back seat of my car. He thanked her profusely and called her an angel, which was interesting because I'd thought exactly the same thing. She blushed and gave me a playful dirty look before looking away. Ethan said his parents and sister were set to arrive that evening and he wanted to know how he looked. "Frankly, a little scary with those stitches," I told him, "but otherwise dashing." On the way out, I slipped him the secret Phi Delt handshake. We all thought the esoteric Greek stuff was bogus and it felt good to get a little smile out of him.

We stopped at the nurse's station. A nurse with curly brown hair and thick glasses put down a chart she'd been writing in and said, "Your friend is damn lucky he didn't bleed to death. It was that close. We gave him three pints of blood."

"Is he going to be okay?"

She nodded. "He suffered a closed head injury so his brain is swollen right now. When I asked him this morning if he knew what happened, he told me someone had stabbed him in the ear with a number two pencil. He also told me his 'corporate silver tips' were hurting."

"Corporate silver tips?" asked Lydia.

"We think he meant his legs. But he's much, much clearer now."

"That's good," I said. "Can we expect a full recovery?"

She nodded again. "Your friend was unconscious a relatively short period of time, which means he has an excellent prognosis."

Back in the car, I drove Lydia to the fraternity house, four blocks away. The place looked dead except for a few brothers loading up their cars to go home for summer break. I pulled in alongside the Rutabaga, a purple '48 Studebaker Commander that served as the official Phi Delt car. Supposedly, it could only make left turns, requiring the driver to plan trips perfectly by intentionally overshooting the final destination, then make left turns in ever decreasing concentric circles until he hit the mark.

Bigdog spotted me from the "Second Old" sleeping porch and yelled down for me to wait. A minute later, he emerged from the back door, huffing and puffing as he waddled up to my side of the car. "The word is you saved Ethan's life. You did good, little brother."

"Thanks. But I couldn't have done it without Lydia's help." I introduced them.

Bigdog bent down and said, "Thank you, Lydia, and that's on behalf of all the brothers."

She smiled shyly. "You're welcome."

Raising his head above her sight line, Bigdog rolled his eyes and feigned swooning over her good looks. Then he shook his head. "The kidnap party could've been the all-time R.F. Damn shame someone got hurt. Ruins the memory."

"We just saw Ethan at the hospital," I told him. "The nurse said he was going to be okay."

Bigdog's shoulders relaxed a little. "That's good. That's good." He watched Tom Brewster struggle to carry an overstuffed box to his car. "Slider told me you were leaving today."

"Maybe," I said, glancing over at Lydia. "I don't know. I might stay in Walla Walla. What're you doing?"

"I might go to England with my parents. Depends on whether dad can get time off from the forest service during fire season."

"Send me a postcard if you do."

"What's your home address?"

"Just send it to Slider. He'll get it to me, wherever I am."

"Deal."

After exchanging well wishes for the summer, Bigdog and I shook hands. Then he leaned through the window, gave me an awkward hug and said, "You're a good man, Bryan. See you in a couple months." I watched him disappear back into the house. Then I let the Chevy coast through the alley before turning left on Valencia.

"He must be a good friend," Lydia commented.

"Yeah. He got me into the fraternity."

She turned sideways to face me. "Where's home for you?"

"Seattle."

"But you might stay in Walla Walla?"

I wasn't sure how I should answer. "I was planning on leaving today. I guess it depends."

"On what?"

Take a chance, Bryan. What have you got to lose? "It depends on you." I held my breath.

She looked surprised. "What do you mean?"

I swallowed hard and forced myself to speak. "If I thought we could get to know each other better, I'd spend the whole summer in Walla Walla." She stared at me but didn't say anything so I added, "One of my professors invited me to stay with him and his wife, so I already have a place and everything."

"You'd stay here for the summer to get to know me better?"

My heart fluttered. "Yes, ma'am. I would if you wanted me to."

She cleared her throat. "Are you putting me on?"

"No. I'm completely serious."

Lydia looked confused. Skip a few beats and she said, "Why don't we go over to Pioneer Park and walk around the lake?"

"Okay," I answered with more cheer than I felt. I stopped at a Mom and Pop grocery store on Alder and went in to buy Wonder Bread for the ducks, two Cokes and a bag of potato chips for us.

When I got back behind the wheel, Lydia asked, "You'd really consider staying for the summer because of me?"

I nodded sincerely.

"You don't even know me."

"I saw enough last night to know you're compassionate . . . and brave." After pausing I added, "Pretty easy on the blinkers, too."

Lydia smiled, but with wariness. She wasn't exactly shy, but seemed less self-confident than I'd have guessed from the night before.

I continued up the street to Pioneer Park. It was a spectacular day. Eighty degrees, a few fleecy, white clouds drifting aimlessly over the Blue Mountains. We got out of the car and headed toward the small lake on the south side of the park. The air was sweet with the scent of freshly cut grass.

Lydia took off her sandals. She had a graceful, easy way of walking that conjured up the image of a she-wolf moving silently through a meadow. "You need to know something," she said abruptly.

"Okay," I replied. My heart hammered against my chest. We had stopped walking.

"I'm not fast like Vicky Spotts."

Relief. I imagined she was about to nix the idea of getting to know one another. "I didn't think you would be."

"Well, I'm not."

I shrugged a shoulder to indicate it didn't matter. It didn't.

At the lake, we fed the bread to the ducks and geese, making sure every bird got a fair share. Lydia tore off the crust and made doughy little balls, then fired several long strikes to birds on the far side of the small lake. I'd never known a girl who didn't throw like a girl. Lydia had an incredible arm. "Nice arm," I complimented her.

"Story of my life. I should've been a boy."

"Yeah, well I have to admit to being glad you're a girl."

"You're funny." She smiled at me, in spite of herself.

When the last of the bread was gone, we headed for the welcoming shade of the park's century-old oaks. I plucked a leathery, dark green leaf and leaned against a trunk. The day felt hotter by the minute. Lydia sat on the grass a few feet away, legs akimbo. She appeared to be double-jointed. More people trickled into the park. A couple in maybe their late forties walked past us and stared. The man threw down his cigarette, snuffed it with the toe of his shoe and gave us a malevolent, disapproving look. White boys and Indian girls weren't supposed to date in Walla Walla.

Lydia looked at me and made the "naughty, naughty" gesture by brushing the top of one index finger with the fingertip of the other.

"That doesn't bother you?" I asked. "I felt like saying 'hurry up and die.'"

"I'm used to it. Besides," she laughed, "in that guy's mind, you're the one who's slumming."

"And that kind of thinking doesn't bother you?"

"Sometimes it gets to me, but not today. Today is a good day to ignore the jerks of the world. Can I have my Coke or do you get both of them?"

"Oh, sorry." I handed Lydia a can of Coke. Taking a sip from my own, I tore open the bag of chips, sat down and put it on the ground between us. "Is it okay if I ask you a personal question?"

"Sure. Fire away."

"What's it like being an Indian in Walla Walla? I mean, I've only been here a year, not even that long, but the town seems pretty backwards to me."

"Tell you what. I'll give you the short answer, because the long one would take all day and I'll end up mad."

"That's fine. I was just curious."

"The short answer is it's not easy. I'm proud of my Indian ancestry and all that, but there's a lot of prejudice to overcome. We're supposed to be stupid. We're supposed to be lazy. We're supposed to be drunks."

"It's like strike three before you even come to bat."

She nodded. "We got, pardon my language, *screwed* by the United States government. We're still getting screwed!" She paused and drew a deep breath. "Sorry you asked?"

"No. It's true. The government waged war against you. Then the white settlers killed all the buffalo, stole the land and destroyed your way of life."

She hesitated. "Are you saying that because you want to get in good with me?"

"I'm saying it because it's a historical fact."

"That's not what they teach at my school."

"I went to a special school at the University of Washington. My history teacher had us read a couple of good books."

"What did you read?"

"*Black Elk Speaks* and *I Will Fight No More Forever*."

Lydia gave me a sideways look and nodded her head wearily. "I've read them both, but let's talk about something else," she said.

"Okay. You pick the subject."

Lydia gave me that wary look again. "Okay. Let's talk about age. I've never dated anyone older than I am."

"What makes you think I'm older? I skipped a grade."

"How old are you?"

"I turn eighteen in two months. There're only about seventy shopping days left."

"I'll remember that. What's your birthday?"

"August 26."

She laughed. "I turn eighteen two weeks before you."

"I guess that makes you old enough to be an authority figure to me. Keeps your record intact, too. See, that makes it okay."

"What record?"

"Never dating someone older."

"Are you always funny?" she asked.

"Only when I'm nervous."

"Are you nervous?"

"Oh, yeah!"

"Me, too."

"Good," I said. "That makes me feel better."

A group of children in colorful swimsuits splashed out into the lake, making a ruckus and scattering a large group of ducks. Lydia watched them and said, "Did you grow up in Seattle?"

"Yeah. But I was born in Black Diamond, which is a little south, near Mt. Rainier. We moved to Seattle when I was a year old."

"We, meaning your parents, or do you have brothers and sisters too?"

"Just my parents. I'm an only child." This was the moment I always dreaded. The hardest part of having a shameful personal history is exposing it when you feel vulnerable.

"I am, too, except for Yolanda. She's *like* a sister. So, do your parents still live there?"

"My dad does. He teaches engineering at the U.W. My mother is dead. She committed suicide when I was six." *You didn't do anything wrong. Mother did.*

"I'm sorry. God, you were only six?"

I nodded, surprised by a wave of grief. Usually, I was more cut off from my feelings.

"My turn to ask a personal question. If it's okay."

"It's okay."

"Did they tell you she killed herself, or make up a story about an accident?"

"They didn't need to tell me. I was with her when she did it."

Her eyebrows arched. "You were with her?"

I nodded again. "She took me for a drive in the middle of the night and then jumped off the Aurora Bridge, the highest bridge in Seattle. I watched her do it." *Why am I being so open to this girl I barely know?*

"Ohmygosh!" Lydia covered her heart with her right hand. There was a simple mother of pearl ring on her ring finger. I wondered what she'd say next because it would determine whether I could feel safe in telling her more. She said, "I lost my mom about the same age you lost yours."

"What happened?"

She plucked a dandelion, rolled the stem between the palms of her hands. "She didn't die or anything, but she's more or less committing suicide on the installment plan. With booze and cigarettes."

I had a million questions. Settled on the most obvious. "What do you mean you lost her?"

Lydia's eyes went hard. She looked off in the direction of the Blue Mountains to the southeast. "I don't usually talk about my mom," she said.

"That's okay. I probably understand that better than anyone you'll ever meet."

Her eyes softened. "I was taken from her when I was seven. The authorities said she was an unfit mother, which was one of the all-time understatements."

"Because of her drinking?"

"No, because she was mean as a rattlesnake. Hardly a day went by I didn't end bruised and on my butt."

"Your mother'd actually hit you? I mean with a fist?"

"Oh yeah. She believed in using her fists. She'd say, 'That's the way Big Momma raised me and it didn't do me no harm!' Of course, her own childhood did Momma a whole lot of harm or else she wouldn't have been such a bad alcoholic and all."

"Where's she now?" Recalling my conversation with her neighbor Slim, I chose to leave the "and all" alone.

"In Vancouver, B.C. At least I think she is. She could be dead, for all I know. I haven't heard from her and her boyfriend Jimmy in several years. Not since two Christmases ago."

I paused a moment. "Do you ever feel like you never had a mother?"

"Yeah. I do."

"Me too." I was afraid to ask but did anyway. "Where's your real dad?"

"Never knew him. He died in a car wreck when my mom was pregnant with me. His car hit a patch of ice and slid out of control. Do you know where Deception Pass is?"

"Yeah. North of Seattle, off the north end of Whidbey Island."

"That's where the wreck happened. Mom said he was probably drunk."

"I'm sorry."

"Anyway, it was after they took me from Momma that I went to live with Yolanda and her parents. Hector and Amelia. The Cruz' took me in and then legally adopted me when I was ten."

"Are they cool?"

"Yeah. They've been terrific. As close to a real mom and dad as I'll ever get. I've been lucky in that way."

"It's sad."

"What?"

"That neither of your parents gets to see how well you've turned out?"

"I never looked at it that way. I always think I'm the one that lost out."

"You both did."

A tall, dark-haired woman in her late twenties walked past us carrying an infant in a backpack. Her baby, dressed in all blue, slept with his face against it. Lydia followed them with her eyes then turned back to me. "Your mother doesn't get to see you, either," she said. "I'll bet she'd be proud you're a Whitman student."

"Yeah. Maybe I'm just kidding myself, but I like to think she *can* see me. Especially when I'm doing something good."

She smiled. "What would you most like her to see you doing?"

What a great question to draw someone out. "Playing chess. That's what I'm best at. I learned to play right after she killed herself, so she never got to see me play."

"Yolanda told me about that at the cabin yesterday."

"Told you what?"

"That you're some kind of chess genius. Vicky Spotts bragged about you to Yolanda. They sat right across from each other in Study Hall."

We continued to talk for another hour, first sitting under the trees and then moving over to the open-sided gazebo in the center of the park. Lydia asked a lot of questions about the milk truck accident, how it happened and what kind of person Ethan was. To a casual observer it might have looked like a straightforward, normal conversation between a teenage boy and girl, but on another level only we could tap into, there was the unmistakable undertone of a powerful physical attraction. There was also an emotional connection I couldn't quite understand, but felt compelled to follow. "I like you a lot," I told her when we got ready to leave. It seemed a simple distillation of my raw and tender adolescent feelings.

"Enough to stay for the summer?" she asked.

"I already told you that," I answered with a nervous smile. "The question is, do you want me to stay?"

"I do."

"Cool! I'll stay." *Now I just have to talk my father into it.*

"Then let's go get some pizza and celebrate," Lydia said, jumping to her feet. "You like pizza, don't you?"

"I love pizza!" I took her hand on the way back to the car. I was afraid she'd pull it away, but she didn't. Touching her in any way felt electric.

As we drove out of the parking lot she said, "Let's try not to go too fast, okay?"

"Okay."

"Really? That's not going to be a problem?"

"Not for me."

"Good."

Pizza Pete's was vacant except for one table crammed with five high school students, all of whom knew Lydia. She greeted them, but then we sat as far away as possible. With *Respect* playing on the jukebox, Lydia told me that rumors we were together would be all over town by nightfall. We devoured a large pepperoni pizza with extra sauce (her idea) and extra cheese (my idea), then headed back to the Phi Delt house.

There was literally no one there. I wondered when the place would be locked up for the summer. Lydia and I went downstairs to the TV room and watched back-to-back episodes of *The Invaders*, starring Roy Thinnes. I got a good laugh by pretending to have an abnormal pinkie, like the aliens who were trying to take over planet Earth. We heard someone come in the back door halfway through the episode, but they didn't bother coming downstairs. We had the room to ourselves. I wanted to kiss Lydia more than I'd ever wanted to kiss anyone in the world, but held myself back. By the time we left, I felt like I'd passed a test.

At nine-thirty, I drove her home. I walked her to her front door, rehearsing the perfect thing to say.

Lydia preempted me. "I don't think I've ever talked so much in my life," she said. "It's like I've been saving up for the right person to come along."

"That's good. I like hearing that."

"I can't believe all the things I told you." Her voice sounded almost musical. "Can I tell Yolanda I'm going to see you tomorrow?"

I beamed. "Wild horses couldn't stop me from seeing you tomorrow."

She laughed. "You're still being funny."

"No. Now I'm being totally serious."

"Do you want to kiss me?"

We embraced and closed our eyes, my fingers finding their way into Lydia's silky black hair. Our bodies pressed gently together and I lost a little of myself as the tips of our tongues touched for the first time. A boundary vanished, just for a fleeting moment, an experience I never knew existed. The kiss itself wasn't bold and sexual like when Vicky Spotts would stick her tongue halfway down my throat, but tender and sensual.

"Wow!" I exclaimed, looking into her eyes to see if she'd had the same reaction. "That was a great first kiss."

"That was a great *any* kiss!"

I stopped by the Zaleski's, confirmed their offer was still good, and slept one last night at Davis-Jacobs. Early in the morning, on the verge of hyperventilating, I called my father from the pay phone in the hallway. To my surprise, a woman picked up on the second ring. "Hello," she answered.

"Who's this?" I asked, first wondering if I'd dialed a wrong number and then if my father had hired a live-in housekeeper.

"This is Cat. Who's this?"

"Bryan. Richard's son."

"Oh, Bryan. I've heard so much about you. Let me get your dad. He's outside trying to remove that ridiculous stump."

I waited, realizing I must be the last student left in the dorm. The eerie quietness made me all the more eager to get my belongings moved over to Dr. Z's. *Please, Dad. Please!* I was wondering what the basement room looked like when my father picked up the line. "Hello, son," he said, clearing his throat. He was out of breath. "I was planting a rhododendron."

"Oh. I heard you were taking the axe to that cedar stump?"

"I was, but now I'm planting a 'Hurricane.' Big pink clusters, looks a lot like the Cotton Candy on the south side of the house. I'm putting this one just off the patio."

"Cool, Dad. Don't forget to make the hole twice as big as the root ball."

"Glad you remember what I taught you. You about to hit the road?"

"That's why I called, Dad." I gritted my teeth and shut my eyes. "Dr. Zaleski and his wife, Reva, have invited me to live with them over the summer. It's the chance of a lifetime to improve my chess. I *really* want to stay."

"You'd be living with your chess coach?"

"And his wife. They can put me up in a basement bedroom. Dr. Zaleski wants to work intensively with me on the weaknesses in my chess game."

"I didn't know you had any weaknesses."

"Huh! You'd be surprised. The number one guy owns me."

"I don't know, Bryan. You've been gone nine months—"

"Please, Dad. This is just too good an opportunity to pass up."

"I thought you were tired of Walla Walla."

"I am, but I'd have an International Grandmaster all to myself." *And I've got it bad for this Indian girl I just met.*

He paused a long moment. "Well, I guess it's okay. I don't want to be selfish and get in the way of your chess. You sure you wouldn't be imposing on the Zaleskis?"

"It was their idea."

"Okay. As long as you at least come home for a visit. Pop and I miss you."

I hopped up and down, spun a 360 and got tangled the phone cord. "I will. I miss you guys, too."

"Have you made arrangements to pay room and board?"

"It's covered. When I'm not studying chess with Dr. Zaleski, I'll be doing all kinds of chores around the yard. I might need a little spending money, though. In case I go on a date or something."

"Okay. If I send a check to your campus P.O. Box, will you get it?"

"Yeah. The mailroom of the SUB stays open for the summer. Thanks."

"Make it last."

I leaned against the wall. "Okay. Thanks. Who's Cat?"

"Cat is Catherine. My lady friend." The words hung in the air somewhere between Seattle and Walla Walla.

"Cool. How long have you been together?"

He laughed. "I guess we've been an item for about a month now. You'll meet her when you come visit. She's terrific. You'll like her."

"That's great, Dad."

We signed off. I couldn't help but think how easy he made it for me to stay. Not even a mention of getting a part-time summer job to earn spending money. That could only mean he and Cat were in love.

Early that afternoon, I moved in with the Zaleskis. Dr. Z helped me carry boxes to my new room, insisting on taking the heaviest one, which was mostly filled with chess books. When I finished unpacking, Reva gave me a grand tour of the house, as I'd previously only been on the main floor for chess class. My basement bedroom was the coolest room in the house. A blessing, since Walla Walla temperatures regularly reach the high nineties in July and August.

After unpacking, I went to the study and browsed Dr. Z's chess library until supper was ready. Reva had prepared a spicy chicken dish and doubled the recipe for garlic and onions. The house smelled wonderful. She seemed excited at the prospect of cooking for a hungry teenager and her hospitality made me feel at home. In between bites of dessert, rhubarb pie a la mode, Dr. Z told me we'd start our chess studies first thing in the morning. "After Bryan has breakfast," Reva reminded him. He nodded and said he would introduce me to an opening that would "change my life." I thought he was kidding.

A lineman for the phone company, Hector Cruz looked too young to have a daughter Yolanda's age. He had wavy black hair combed straight back and a thin, neatly trimmed moustache that gave him the dashing look of a swashbuckler. A fit man of medium height and build, he spoke with a very slight Mexican accent.

Amelia looked even younger than her husband, and every bit as attractive. She was darker skinned than Hector and nearly as tall. With her high cheekbones and large eyes, she might have passed for Lydia's biological mother. Amelia worked as the main cook at Viva Mexico, a little hole-in-the-wall restaurant next to the County Courthouse on Main Street.

I was nervous about making a good first impression, but Hector and Amelia put me at ease by asking questions about my freshman year at Whitman. What was my major, was it hard to get good grades, how competitive were the other students? Hector had attended a college in Mexico City and studied business administration. When he smiled, I noticed the braces on his teeth. From their interest, I concluded the Cruz' valued higher education. I hoped they were pleased Lydia was dating a college boy.

Yolanda, who'd been listening in, retreated to a back bedroom in response to a plea for help from Lydia. Amelia asked me where I was from and then what kind of car I was driving. I told her it was a '53 Chevy and she leaned forward in her chair to look out the front window. Fortunately, my car wasn't the kind that made parents nervous, unless they thought the mustard color was in unusually bad taste.

There was a lull in the conversation and Amelia abruptly excused herself, disappearing into the kitchen. The move appeared choreographed. Hector slid his chair closer to my end of the couch. I felt myself tighten up. He focused intense, dark eyes on me. "I don't know you, Bryan. You're probably a fine young man, but I'd like to speak to you frankly."

"Sure," I said, swallowing dryly.

He folded his arms. "Please don't take offense, but people who come from larger cities don't realize how small Walla Walla is. Trust me when I tell you that everyone here has their nose in everyone else's business. I'm saying this because Amelia and I want you to be careful, in case you and Lydia end up dating for a while. We don't want anything to happen that would damage Lydia's reputation. Do you understand?"

"Yes, sir. I understand perfectly." I wondered if we were having this conversation because Yolanda or Lydia told him I'd gone steady with a fast girl like Vicky Spotts.

"That means if you go to the drive-in, like you are tonight, you must assume someone is watching the two of you. And they will say things about you as soon as they get back to town. Do you understand me?"

"Yes, sir."

Just then, Lydia, Yolanda and Amelia all appeared through a swinging kitchen door. Lydia was wearing another sundress, this one bright red with a white fleur-de-lis pattern, with small irises at the top of the dress, and larger ones at the bottom. This dress was shorter than the blue one she'd worn the day before and did an even better job of showing off her long legs. *Hector should be lecturing his daughter, not me.*

"Pretty dress," I commented. "Is this another creation by Yolanda?"

Yolanda blushed and stared at the pink thongs on her brown feet.

"She's my own private designer," Lydia answered.

Halfway to the car I told Lydia, "You should be declared illegal in red."

She did a double take. "Meaning what?"

"Meaning you look too good for your own good."

"Don't forget I have a black belt in karate," she joked.

The Milton-Freewater Drive-In was showing two Clint Eastwood spaghetti westerns, *Fistful of Dollars* and *For a Few Dollars More*. I loved the "man with no name" but thought "man with no conscience" would be a more apt description of his character. When the first movie ended, Lydia and I got out of my car and walked to the snack bar to get some popcorn and Cokes.

I excused myself to go to the men's room and handed Lydia a five to pay for our snacks. When I came out a couple minutes later, I had to push through a knot of people and found her standing nose to nose with an irate Vicky Spotts. A large box of popcorn and two Cokes littered the ground at Lydia's feet.

Vicky hissed, "You can have him, bitch!" She wore a low-cut blouse that exposed a lot.

"Get out of my face, Vicky," Lydia warned. "Or you'll wish you did."

"What? You gonna pull a knife and scalp me?" Vicky mocked. A few people in the growing crowd snickered.

"I might just do that." Lydia's dark eyes flashed rage.

Elbowing someone aside, I stepped in between them and gave a push intended for Vicky's shoulder. I accidentally hit her breast instead.

"Keep your fucking hands off the merchandise!"

"Just leave us alone," I said to Vicky, taking Lydia by the arm and escorting her past several onlookers. They moved quickly aside, no one uttering a sound. Lydia went willingly the first few steps, but then bolted from my grasp, turned and dropkicked a half-full cup of Coca-Cola at Vicky. It hit her in the crotch, splattering her jeans and blouse with its sticky contents.

Venom spewed from Vicky's lips. "Fucking Indian bitch!" She looked under the influence of something.

This time I grabbed Lydia's arm and marched her back to the car. "God, that was ugly!" I apologized. "I am so sorry."

"You don't need to say you're sorry. You didn't do anything."

"I know, but she used to be my girlfriend."

"She's flipped out."

"Totally!"

She glanced over her shoulder, shook free from my hand. "I really wanted to smack her around."

"I know, but it's good you didn't."

"I suppose."

"What happened, anyway?"

"I was waiting for you to come out of the men's room and someone just *slammed* into me from behind, making me spill everything. I turned around and saw Vicky with a big smile on her face. She obviously did it on purpose."

"That's about her speed."

"Then she says, really sarcastically, 'Oh, I apologize. How clumsy of me.' She thought it was really funny."

"Did you say anything to Vicky after she bumped into you?"

"Not bumped. Slammed! I told her she owed me two dollars seventy-five cents."

"And Vicky said . . .?"

"Fuck off and die, you skinny Indian bitch!"

For some reason, this struck both of us as funny and we started laughing. "You nailed her good with the Coke. That had to be worth at least twice what we spent."

Lydia clenched her fists. "What a *bitch* she is!"

"World class. I should know."

She gave me a puzzled look, paused a moment. "Why did you go with her so long?"

"Don't ask."

"I'm asking. I want to know."

I drew a deep breath and blew it out slowly. "At first, she was nice to me. She was the first girlfriend I ever had and I liked the attention. When she started getting crazy on me . . . I guess I thought that's just the way girls are."

She folded her arms. "Were you, you know, having sex with her a lot?"

"Not really," I lied.

"Did you sleep with her?"

I slumped in my car seat, feeling caught. "Yeah. But she's the only girl I've ever slept with."

Lydia thought awhile. "I wish you hadn't done it with her. *Especially* her."

I could have said it was all a mistake and that I wished I hadn't slept with her either, but that would have been too big a lie. Instead I quoted Grandpa Matthews, "You can't un-ring the bell."

"How true." She twisted to look out the back window, maybe to see if the crowd had dispersed. "Will you take me home?"

"Oh, come on. I can't help it if I slept with someone before we even met."

"It isn't that. It's what just happened. Why can't I just go on a simple date like everyone else?"

"I don't know. Because it's Walla Walla. Because we were unlucky enough to go to the drive-in the same night Vicky did."

"Please. I really want to go home."

"Don't let her wreck our night," I pleaded, wanting to stay and see the second movie together. "That's exactly what she wants."

"I know. I'm sorry, just get me out of here."

I felt sick. I rolled down the window and fumbled to replace the awkward metal speaker on its stand. Tires crunching the loose gravel, I drove out of the drive-in, well aware we were being watched. Just like Hector predicted.

Lydia was distant on the ten-minute drive back to town. She stared out the passenger window and said nothing. When I crossed the state line I asked, "Are you okay?"

She nodded but didn't say anything so I let her have her silence.

I pulled to a stop in front of her house. Cars lined the street. They looked asleep, heavy and glum in the warm haze of the night. "Are you mad at me?"

"Yes," she answered softly.

"What did I do?"

She paused. "Nothing. You didn't do anything."

"Then why are you mad at me?"

Lydia looked at me intently and ran her hand across her forehead. She started to say something and stopped herself. Finally she said, "I'm mad at you because I like you. Because, if I let myself, I could like you a whole lot."

"I don't get it. You're mad because you *like* me?"

"I don't want to get hurt, Bryan."

"I have no intention of hurting you."

"I always get hurt."

"What do you mean?"

She gazed out the windshield. The haze made her neighborhood look remote and lonely. "That's a hard question to answer," she answered in an undertone.

"Try."

"Okay, my father hurt me worst of all and I never even met him. And then Jimmy, my mom's boyfriend, he was kind of like a father to me . . . he dropped me like I never existed when the authorities came down on my mom."

"Have you been hurt by boyfriends?"

"No, because I've never had one. I've dated, but I never end up going with anyone."

"How come?"

She met my eyes. "I never go out for more than three dates. It's easier that way."

"Is that because you're afraid to get close?"

"I guess."

Neither of us said anything for a while. The neighborhood was still and no lights were on in the Cruz' house. Lydia broke the silence. "For all I know you'll go back to Vicky Spotts."

"When hell freezes over. No, let me change that. I wouldn't go back to Vicky even *if* hell freezes over."

"That's what you say now, but if you want sex—"

"It's not *what I say,* it's a promise. I'm done with her. You saw what she's like. Believe me, I don't want anything to do with her."

She fiddled with the armrest, picked at a loose seam. "I want to believe you, but look at this from my perspective. You're a white boy going to Whitman. In three short years you'll be a college graduate with your whole life in front of you. I'm an Indian girl, born and raised in Walla Walla by a drunk. Indian girls are supposed to marry Indians, make babies and work our lives away in the canneries. We're stuck here. Face it, you and I come from different sides of the tracks. Figuratively *and* literally."

"We're more alike than not."

"No, we're not. And if you were Indian you wouldn't say that. You could read *Black Elk Speaks* and every history book ever written and you still won't understand what it's like. You have to be Indian."

"Okay, but I still see us as having a lot in common."

"Like what?"

"We both lost our mothers. My mother was an alcoholic, too. She killed herself right in front of me. And that was exactly one minute after she invited me to hold her hand and jump with her. You're not the only one in the car with a fucked-up mother."

She reared back as the shock registered. "Are you telling me your mother actually asked you to jump off the bridge with her?"

"Touching, huh? And I'll tell you something else. Something I've never told anyone in my life. *I was tempted.*" I swallowed back tears, scarcely believing I'd given away my most closely guarded secret.

She reached over and gently placed her hand on top of mine. "That's awful."

"I shouldn't have told you that."

"I'm glad you did," she whispered. "I feel honored."

I cleared my throat. "We're probably both messed up because of our mothers. But don't quit on me just because you're scared, because I'm scared, too. Give us a chance and see if we're supposed to be with each other."

A car came down Carrie Street from the opposite direction. We both shielded our eyes from the intrusive glare. Lydia said, "I should go in."

"Not yet. Please. I want to know why race has to matter?"

She looked away, in the direction of her house. "If you only knew what I'm going up against."

"Then tell me."

The front porch light began flashing on and off. "That's Hector," she said. "He doesn't like me and Yolanda to sit out front with dates because of what the neighbors might think." She shrugged her shoulders.

"Bummer. Why does the night have to end like this?"

"I don't know. Look, if I don't go in right away, Hector'll come out and embarrass me. I start my summer job at Bird's Eye tomorrow. Eight to five shift. Call me around five-thirty?"

"Okay." My heart felt like a stack of lead weights inside my chest.

Lydia got out and walked to the front door without looking back. I sat for a minute trying to figure out what had gone wrong. My head was spinning. The world suddenly seemed upside down, inside out, a jumble of confusing thoughts. There was only one thing I was sure of. I was falling madly, hopelessly in love with Lydia Redstone.

The fiasco at the drive-in made for a long night. I tossed and turned until two a.m., replaying what Lydia had said about our differences. She was right. Being Indian was something I was incapable of understanding. Reading about decades of broken promises and genocide was different from living out the oppressive consequences.

Reva had fixed a bacon-and-eggs breakfast with whole-wheat toast and raspberry jam on the side. The aroma wafted into the basement, luring me upstairs to join her in the kitchen. I dressed quickly and headed up.

"Dis is your place," she said with her usual smile. As I took my seat, she clanked silverware on the glass-topped, wrought iron kitchen table.

"Thanks, Reva." I felt uncomfortable in the unfamiliar surroundings of the kitchen, but pleased to have my own place at their table.

"De jam's homemade," she said with obvious pride.

"It looks delicious." I looked out the window, still thinking about Lydia. A hyperactive squirrel perched midway up one of the Zaleski's apple trees. He twitched his bushy tail and helped himself to some unripe fruit.

"Good morning," Dr. Z greeted us. "Can I talk you into a cup of coffee, Bryan? It's a mail order blend Reva smuggles in from Denmark. Not the weak American stuff."

"Sure. I'll try anything once."

He laughed. "Well, don't try that demon weed that's so popular with your classmates." After retrieving a small bag from the refrigerator, he poured a handful of whole, roasted beans into an old-fashioned coffee mill. He turned the crank, then poured the finely ground beans into a coffee-maker. I'd never believed the taste of coffee could live up to the aroma, but with a spoonful of fireweed honey and fresh cream from a local dairy, the Zaleski's brew was divine.

"This is sensational stuff," I told them.

"And legal," Reva quipped, causing us all to laugh. The summer was off to a good start. At least as far as the Zaleskis were concerned.

Dr. Z and I retreated to the study we used for chess class. Seeing it in the summer made me feel special. Having an International Grandmaster all to myself was too much.

"Here's the plan," Dr. Z said, his blue eyes even more intense than usual. "I want to spend at least a month studying one particular opening." He paused for effect. "The Stonewall Attack."

"An entire month on the Stonewall?"

"At least a month. And I expect you to be studying eight hours a day, five days a week. Any problem with that?" he asked in a stern voice.

"No." That did it for my summer vacation, but as long as I had evenings and weekends free for Lydia, I was okay with the arrangements.

"The Stonewall was absolutely made for you, Bryan. The great attackers have all used it at one time or another. My old friend Edgar Colle adopted it back in the twenties. So did Harry Pillsbury, who might have been the boldest planner I ever played. Even the positional masters like Jose Capablanca and Geza Maroczy used the Stonewall."

"I thought the Stonewall was out of favor."

"It is very much out of favor. Has been since the turn of the century."

"There must be a reason."

He glanced at his floor-to-ceiling chess library. "Because seventy years ago the Russian champion, Mikhail Tchigorin, discovered a relatively easy equalizing system for Black. Tchigorin bragged he could equalize as early as the third move. Ridiculous!"

I searched my memory. "I remember a more modern defense with the fianchetto of Black's king bishop?"

"Yes, very good, Bryan. That came later, and I have to admit, it gives White some problems. It also cost the Stonewall its reputation as a valid opening."

"Okay. So why are we going to spend a month on it?"

"At *least* a month," he corrected again. "I've been analyzing the Stonewall off and on for the last two years. I've discovered responses to Tchigorin's equalizing system *and* the fianchetto defense, responses that return the advantage to White."

"Cool! So the old equalizers don't equalize when your new ideas are put into play. That is beyond cool!" I was more than a little buzzed from a second cup of strong Danish coffee.

"Yes, it is . . . *beyond cool*," he said, poking fun at my adolescent vernacular.

"The Zaleski variation on the Stonewall Attack."

"That has a nice ring to it," he said.

"I'm going to adopt a new variation. I've never done that." As with music, a chess variation was an altered version on a known theme.

"You're going to do a lot more than adopt a new variation, Bryan. You're going to help me develop it."

His statement startled me. "I am?"

He nodded. "I'm stuck in a few places and need your imagination and analytic ability to find the correct moves. You and I are going to take the summer and resurrect the Stonewall Attack!"

On our fourth date, I surprised Lydia with a gift of a simple but lovely turquoise ring. The gemstone was light blue and mounted in a thin silver setting. I'd spotted it through the grimy window of a pawnshop on lower Main, Walla Walla's version of Skid Road. Slider and I had just left Lutcher's pool hall after playing snooker with a kid from Alabama who'd insisted on singing *Jimmy Crack Corn* throughout the game. I was commenting on how annoying the guy had been when I glanced in the pawnshop window and saw the ring. The ring's price tag said thirty-five dollars, but I got the man behind the counter, ugly and pockmarked in a greasy gray shirt, to give it to me for twenty, the sum total of all the spending money I had for the rest of the month.

I gave the ring to Lydia just outside the gazebo at Pioneer Park, but first I set her up. "This is where we came on our first date." I smiled like a fool despite my best effort to not give away the surprise.

"I know that."

"So, this must be our what . . . third or fourth date?"

"Fourth."

"*Fourth?* That can't be right! You never go out with a boy more than three times. Remember? You told me that the first time we came here."

She smiled. "I guess that makes you the exception that proves the rule, Mr. Smarty Pants."

I laughed and produced a small, slightly squished box from my back pocket. I'd wrapped it in the funny papers from the Sunday *Union-Bulletin*. "It's not a great wrapping job, unless you like Dick Tracy," I joked, handing it to her.

"What's this?"

"It's a present. Open it."

Lydia tore away the paper like a kid at Christmas, but then went into slow motion and gently removed the lid as if to elongate the moment. She found the ring between layers of cotton and held it up. "Oh, Bryan. It's beautiful!"

"Try it on."

She slipped it over the ring finger on her left hand and held her hand away from her body to better admire it.

"Does it fit?"

"Perfectly."

"Do you like it?"

"I *love* it! But what's it for?"

"I told you. To commemorate our fourth date. It's a world record."

"You're a nut!"

"No, I'm the lucky guy that got past date number three."

"I'm the lucky one." She removed the ring and examined it closely in the sunlight. "No one ever gave me jewelry before."

"It's Bisbee turquoise and Taxco silver. The man who sold it said it was good quality."

She put her arms around my neck and kissed me hard on the mouth, something I hadn't expected. When she took a step away, the afternoon sun provided a perfect backlight for her shining black hair.

"Remind me to give you jewelry more often."

She beamed. "Do you know what wearing turquoise means to an Indian woman?"

I shook my head. "I have no idea."

"Most people say it casts away the dark clouds and makes for blue skies, but according to Big Momma, my grandmother, it makes a woman beautiful to all men." She laughed. "Big Momma wore lots of turquoise."

"Nothing could make you more beautiful than you already are."

"That's sweet, Bryan. If I wear the ring every day, does it mean I'm your girlfriend?"

"It does. I want you to be my girlfriend."

"Then I will," she said, laughing again. She slid the ring back on her wedding finger and hugged me close to her body. I couldn't believe my good fortune. To have Lydia as my new girlfriend felt too good to be true.

Lydia had a ten o'clock curfew on weeknights, midnight on weekends. We stayed out until the last possible minute and then a few extra. I learned that she would become hysterical if you tickled her bare feet. That she preferred RC Cola to Coke or Pepsi. That she held four school records for the Wa-Hi track and cross-country teams. That she was afraid to go on a certain ride at the carnival because of a bad experience at the Pendleton Roundup. That at age six she put a foot through a television screen after her mother slapped her for changing the channel to The Mickey Mouse Club. That she had a pear-shaped birthmark on the inside of her left thigh. There was little holding back; it was like the two of us had saved up a lifetime of things to say and had a limited amount of time to get it all out.

One night after supper with the Cruz', Yolanda and I were goofing around on the back porch. It was hot and the aroma of barbecued chicken floated through the neighborhood air. Yolanda was teaching me how to thumb wrestle and the two of us were laughing hard because she couldn't seem to get through a single match without cheating. Yolanda had an easy laugh and we were well on our way to becoming good friends.

Lydia sat cross-legged on the grass about ten feet away, watching and smiling at our antics, but also distant, as if she were not quite a part of things. The phone rang and Amelia stuck her head out the door to tell Yolanda she had a call. Lydia motioned for me to come and sit next to her in the grass. "How come you've never asked me about my martial arts training?" she asked.

I shrugged. "I don't know. It seems kind of weird, having a girlfriend who could kick my ass."

She smiled. "Is that why you're so nice to me?"

"No. But tell me how you got into karate."

"Jimmy taught me. My mom's boyfriend. When I was six."

"That seems kind of unusual. To teach a little girl to fight."

"Not if you're an Indian girl. It's the way things are settled. You have to be tough or you get picked on."

"So Jimmy taught you to defend yourself."

"Yeah. When I was in first grade he watched me lose a fight. We were playing kick-the-can . . . the kids in my neighborhood and an older boy who was visiting a neighbor. We were arguing about the rules and the older boy tripped me and got on top. He weighed too much for me to get him off and when I started struggling he hit me in the face. I got a bloody nose and said 'Uncle.'"

"And Jimmy didn't like that."

"No, he didn't. He was furious with me. Called me a chicken in front of the other kids. I don't know what hurt worse, my nose or my feelings. I ran into the house crying."

"What happened then?"

"Actually, he came in and apologized. I couldn't believe it. Never once had my mom ever said she was sorry for anything. Jimmy said he should've done something, that it wasn't a fair fight because the boy was so much bigger."

"Yeah, he could've stopped it."

"I said something like that, but he said he wouldn't always be there. That I had to learn to fight my own battles. Then he took me in the back yard and started giving me lessons on how to take care of myself. My nose was still bleeding."

"He expected you to be tough."

"Yeah. Jimmy knew street fighting from growing up in the barrio in L.A. and I guess he thought it would be cool to pass it on. My mom never paid any attention to me so I ate it up. I tried really hard to please him, which in this case meant kickin' ass in the neighborhood. I fought with boys and girls. It didn't make any difference to me."

"Ever hurt someone bad?"

"Yeah, when I was nine I messed up two sixth grade boys. They were like twice my size."

"Did you get in trouble?"

"Not much because they picked the fight, and it was two boys against one girl. The Principal lectured me, but I didn't get suspended or anything. One boy's parents were mad because he was on crutches for a month, but there wasn't anything they could do."

A squeal followed by laughter came from inside the house. It was Yolanda, presumably still on the phone. I asked, "Did you stop fighting when you moved in with the Cruz'?"

"Not right away. Hector enrolled me in a summer martial arts class because they teach you not to fight unless you absolutely have to."

"What kind of martial arts?"

"Tae Kwan Do."

"Cool. And it worked? You stopped fighting?"

"It did work. I've never figured out why. Maybe because I learned to control my temper, or because no one wanted to mess with me any more." Lydia laughed and plucked a bright yellow dandelion from the patch of lawn between us. She smelled it, tossed it away and rubbed her nose.

"And you kept studying Tae Kwan Do?"

"Yeah. I joined Master Kim's dojo at the Jefferson Park Fieldhouse. I could walk there after school. I just loved it, and I ended up going three times a week for six years. We'd compete in tournaments in the Tri-Cities."

"Tae Kwan Do is Korean karate, right?"

"Yeah. There's a big emphasis on kicking, which is my strength because I have long legs and good balance."

Yolanda reappeared on the back porch. She must have heard the last part of the conversation because she said, "Being completely double-jointed helps, too."

"You're double-jointed?" I asked Lydia.

She nodded like it was no big deal.

"How does that help?"

"To deliver blows with maximum force you have to get your feet and joints in proper position, or else you'll hurt yourself striking your opponent."

Yolanda seated herself on the top step of the porch and said, "She's being modest. Master Kim says Lydia's the only student he's ever had who gets perfect leverage and it's because she's double-jointed. He says Lydia kicks like a mule!"

"Do you still study with Master Kim?"

"No, he moved his dojo to Boise two years ago. Broke my heart. Now I just practice on my own or with a few of his students who are still around."

"What was Master Kim like?"

"Tougher than a boiled owl, but with a great sense of humor. I think he's in his sixties, probably late sixties, but it's hard to tell 'cause he's so physically fit. When I think of Master Kim, I always see him smiling." She smiled.

"Is he from Korea?"

"Yeah. His parents dumped him on the streets of Seoul when he was a boy. He had to learn to fight to survive. When he was sixteen, he joined the South Korean Army and ended up teaching hand-to-hand combat to the other soldiers."

"Best way to learn. Teaching someone else."

She nodded. "I think Master Kim felt sorry for me. He knew I'd been taken from my mother and Jimmy. Hector probably told him." She looked at Yolanda. "Did he?"

Yolanda shrugged a shoulder. "Knowing dad, he probably did," she answered.

"Anyway, Master Kim knew what it was like to lose your parents and sort of took me under his wing. I became his pet project. By the time I was thirteen I'd earned my black belt."

"Will you show me some moves?"

"Sure."

Yolanda laughed. "You're in trouble now, Bryan Matthews!"

Lydia hopped to her feet, brushed grass from her bottom and stretched. "Stand there," she told me, "and whatever you do, *don't* move!"

"Got it." I stood where she told me to and froze like a statue.

Lydia moved about six feet away from me and assumed a karate stance. In the blink of an eye, she executed a powerful leaping kick to my head followed immediately by a spinning kick to the front of my neck. More amazing than her speed was the visible power she generated. She pulled both blows just inches short of my body. Had either landed, I'd have been on the ground and in need of first aid.

"Wow!" I exclaimed, my heart racing. "If there's a fight, I want you on my side."

Lydia and I made Fourth of July plans to go to the hydroplane races with Slider and Marilu. The race was to be held on the Columbia River near Richland, an hour's drive from Walla Walla. The Cruz' issued stern warnings about alcohol and pot consumption, the importance of making the right choices. Hector had heard of hippies spiking wine with LSD and told us that under no circumstances were we to take even a single swig from a passing wine jug.

The four of us left mid-morning, Marilu driving her VW van. We arrived a few minutes before noon, parking in a lot with several thousand other cars. The heat was already oppressive on the beach and scores of onlookers waded into the shallows of the wide river to cool off. The crowd was mostly young people, our age or slightly older, many openly guzzling cans of beer and premixed wine coolers. Somewhere in time, the hydroplane races had become an excuse for a beach party. A thousand blaring stereos competed with the sounds of raised voices and alcohol-induced laughter.

Slider found a bare patch of sand and grass and spread an oversized cotton blanket, a thoughtful donation by Marilu's mother. The air reeked of suntan lotion, sweat, and gasoline fumes from the pit area, a hundred yards or so away from our vantage point. Lydia put tanning lotion on my back and shoulders and handed the plastic bottle to me. "I don't really need it," she said, with a shy smile, "but you can put some on me anyway." She peeled off her cutoff jeans and an oversized T-shirt, revealing a yellow bikini that Yolanda had made especially for the occasion. It looked fabulous against her brown skin. I took my time spreading suntan oil on her shoulders and back and gave her a little kiss on the shoulder when I'd finished.

Slider and Marilu had brought along a big Styrofoam cooler containing two six-packs of Rainier beer packed in ice. According to Slider, it had been "claimed in the name of the people's army" from the stash Slider's dad kept in their cellar. I contributed a bag of oranges, some grapes and a good-sized watermelon. Marilu asked me if I was a fruitarian and I told her I resented the implication. We all laughed and then laughed even harder when Marilu, who was tiny, put the melon under her T-shirt to look pregnant. She then passed out cans of beer with her upper eyelids folded over, giving her the look of a deranged psycho in a trance. "Show me your I.D.'s," she said in a disembodied voice.

"Make her stop," Lydia told Slider, accepting an icy can. I'd never seen Lydia drink.

"What's she doing?" he responded, as he watched a gigantic crane lower one of the hydroplanes into the water.

"She's doing some weird trick with her eyes," I said. "It's making my eyes hurt to just to look at her."

Slider turned around and snorted when he saw Marilu. "That's not a trick," he told us with a maniacal grin. "*This* is a trick." He set down his can of beer and pulled five oranges from the grocery bag I'd set on the blanket. With an air of nonchalance, Slider began to juggle. As with all things involving manual dexterity, he was amazing, tossing and catching first three, then four, then all five oranges without a single drop.

A group of hippies next to us broke into spontaneous applause. I noticed them passing a fat joint and nervously scanning the beach. "Far fucking out!" one of them said, loud enough to turn every head within a thirty-foot radius. Lying sprawled out in the sand, he wore a torn, purple and white tie-dyed T-shirt. His eyes were bloodshot and half-closed even though the day was just beginning. Neither Lydia nor I had ever tried marijuana and, looking at this guy, I had no desire to. At the conclusion of Slider's juggling act, the longhair sat up and shouted over, "Hey. The rumor is there're some plainclothes narks in the crowd. So keep your eyes open. Okay?"

"Wide open, brother. Power to the people!" Slider answered with mock seriousness.

The rest of us nodded. Lydia wondered aloud whether we should move away from the dope smokers. I didn't exactly hear her because two of the hydroplanes were leaving the pit area and the roar of their Rolls Royce airplane engines drowned out her voice. Slider waited for the hydros to pull onto the course and explained there would be drugs on the beach no matter where we moved and not to worry.

Looking satisfied with Slider's advice, Lydia said, "Okay, we stay here. Do you want to see my trick?"

We all looked at her.

"Toss me an orange," she said to Slider.

"Orange to Lydia." He underhanded it.

She deftly caught it and held it in between the palms of both hands, behind her back. "Okay, here's the deal," she said, with a mischievous look. "Notice how my hands are clasped around the orange." She turned around to show us.

"She's showing off her cute bottom," Marilu said, her eyelids back to normal.

Lydia playfully gave her a dirty look. "Now, in a matter of seconds I'm going to be holding this same orange in front of me, only I'm going to get it there without unclasping my hands."

"Can't be done," Slider said.

"Oh yes it can," Lydia replied.

"It's impossible," Slider argued.

"Bet?" Lydia said.

"A buck," he answered, without hesitating.

"Get your dollar ready," Lydia said. She bent slightly at the waist and slowly raised up her arms behind her back. To our amazement, she lifted her arms over her head, keeping her fingers interlocked around the orange. Her shoulders made a popping noise.

"Oh, my God!" I said. I remembered Lydia acknowledged being double-jointed the day she showed me her karate kicks, but my mouth still dropped open.

"How'd you do that?" Slider asked, befuddled.

"It's easy if you're double-jointed," Lydia answered, looking amused.

"Do it again," Slider and I said in unison.

"Where's my dollar?"

"Okay, okay." Slider fished a dollar from his wallet and handed it to her.

She tossed it on the blanket, stepped on it so it wouldn't blow away and said, "This time I'll go front to back."

We made her do her trick five times, the last time in slow motion. She was a good sport and never complained. Then we tried it. It seemed physically impossible.

"Does it hurt?" Marilu asked.

"Nope."

"Can you do any other double-jointed tricks?" I asked.

"I can fold both legs behind my neck."

"Let's see it," I said, suppressing a smile.

She blushed. "Not with Slider watching."

Slider slipped me the look of a fellow conspirator and pretended to mop his brow, as if the day had suddenly gotten even hotter than it already was. He said, "C'mon Lydia. Double or nothing!"

"Forget it!"

I shot Slider a sideways glance. It was hard not to fantasize about Lydia with her legs wrapped behind her head.

Marilu said, "Okay, Bryan, your turn."

"What?"

"Your turn to show us a trick."

"I don't know any," I apologized, gritting my teeth with embarrassment.

"Sure you do," Slider said. "Everyone can do *something*."

Not me. I couldn't wiggle my ears, touch my tongue to the tip of my nose, snap my fingers really fast like Curly on The Three Stooges, or do anything that resembled a trick. I froze. Everyone was staring at me and I felt myself going away in my head. If I'd had a chessboard with me, I could've demonstrated the brilliant pawn stalemate Znosko-Borovsky gained on his forty-seventh move against Salwe at Ostende in 1907. With chalk and a blackboard, I could have shown them there is a remainder of two when you divide 12 by the 17th power, plus 8, by 6. My eyes fixed on an enormous billboard in the pit area. It advertised *Mercury* outboard boat motors, giving the name and phone number of several local dealers in the Tri-Cities. I considered telling my friends that the atomic number for the element mercury was eighty, that its valences were one and two, that Mercury was the smallest and innermost planet, that in Roman mythology Mercury was the son of Jupiter and messenger to the gods. But the game was to perform a physical trick. I shrugged my shoulders.

Lydia put her arm around me and said, "I don't care if he can't do a trick. He's a *great* kisser!"

Slider laughed and Marilu said, "Okay, show us your stuff, Bryan."

Lydia put her arms around me and kissed me passionately in front of God and everyone on the beach. One of the longhairs shouted over, "All right, brother! Go for it!"

Lydia had rescued me from somewhere deep inside myself. While the others were busy discussing teachers they'd had in common at Wa-Hi, I began thinking about my tendency to think too much. My head ached in the glare of the burning sun. Then I heard Lydia say, " . . . isn't that right, Bryan?"

"What? Sorry, I spaced out."

"Slider was thanking me again for helping get Ethan to the hospital the night the milk truck rolled. And I told him he didn't need to keep thanking me because I got to meet you." The dollar bill stuck out of the top piece of her swimsuit.

"Oh, right," I said, biting my lip. I felt out of it, like I'd just parachuted onto the beach and landed in the middle of the present scene.

Marilu said, "I should thank you, too, Lydia. The accident would've turned out a whole lot worse if you hadn't stopped to help."

"You're welcome," Lydia said. "You're both welcome. The worst part was dealing with that cop that tried to pull us over."

Slider looked at me with a puzzled expression. "You didn't tell me about that."

"I guess I forgot," I said, somewhat defensively.

"So, what happened?" Slider asked.

"This cop tried to pull us over on the way to the hospital. I was speeding and I refused to pull over because Ethan was in such bad shape. Anyway, the cop flipped out and tried to arrest me after we got to the Emergency Room."

"How'd you get out of it?"

"Dean Sanderson showed up with the Chief of Police. They stuck up for me."

"Sanderson showed up with Bud Carter?"

"Yeah. They're neighbors."

Marilu said, "I know I got there after you did, but I didn't see any of this."

"You were in the treatment room with Kathy," I explained. "This cop, Montrose is his name, put the handcuffs on me right after you left the waiting area. And then Dr. Sanderson and Chief Carter got there after that."

"Officer *Jack* Montrose?" Marilu asked.

"Yeah," I answered. "You know him?"

"I don't know him, but my older brother Ron does. He says Montrose is some sort of a legend. Only in a bad way."

"What do you mean?" I asked.

"Where do I start?! Ron played football with him in high school. Montrose had a reputation for hurting people . . . trying to tear up guys' knees, elbowing at the bottom of the pile, stuff like that. Oh, and he was a cat bopper."

"What's that?" Lydia asked.

"He'd drive around looking for cats he could run over."

"That's sick!" Lydia said, her face showing disgust. The Cruz' had a much-beloved tomcat named Taco.

"What an asshole!" I said, shaking my head.

"There's more," Marilu told us. "Montrose was always mean, but then he went to Vietnam and came back crazy *and* mean. My brother ran into him at the Sportsman Tavern a couple months ago. Montrose was bragging about coming back from Nam with a necklace of 'gook' ears. He said he actually enjoyed killing people, especially in hand-to-hand combat, because he liked to watch them die."

"Sick. How long was Montrose in Vietnam?" I asked.

"I don't know. Ron said something about him getting out early because he was willing to go into law enforcement. There was some kind of federal program for recruiting cops in rural areas."

"Oh, this is *great* news," I said. "The guy's a total psychopath and now he hates my guts because I defied his authority."

"Seriously. Watch your back," Marilu concluded. "My brother told me that if I *ever* get pulled over by Montrose, no matter how outrageous it is, to be polite and ultra-respectful."

"Too late for me," I said.

Slider nodded and then grinned. "Isn't it comforting to know they let guys like that carry guns?"

Lydia suddenly jumped to her feet and extended me her hand. "This is a depressing conversation," she said. "Let's go back to the van. I forgot my radio."

I felt relieved to be off the subject of Montrose and excited to think about being alone with Lydia in the parking lot. Seeing her in her bikini made me long to touch her, feel her skin next to mine.

"Careful, kids," Marilu warned with a knowing smile. She tossed a ring of keys to me.

"Yeah, right!" I said, feigning innocence.

The van was parked in the shade of a stand of cottonwood trees, but it was hot inside. I opened the sliding side door, giving it a minute to air out. "They say it's dry heat in Eastern Washington," Lydia quipped. We laughed to break the tension.

Then we got in, locked the doors and sat facing one another on the bare mattress in the back. The back windows were open for ventilation, but Marilu had installed ruffled blue curtains that gave the illusion of complete privacy. I leaned over and kissed Lydia on the mouth. The way she returned my kiss was different. More passionate. I looked into her eyes for some kind of permission and saw hunger. I screwed up my courage. "Do you want to . . .?" The rest of the sentence stuck in the back of my throat.

Lydia lay down on the mattress without speaking.

Heart racing, I lay down alongside her. Inhaling her scent, I whispered, "I love you." It was the first time I told her, or told any girl. The words came out naturally, spontaneously.

Lydia murmured, "I know. I love you, too."

We kissed a second time. My ears buzzed, not so much a sound as a sensation caused by raw excitement.

Lydia said, "Sometimes I wonder how I can love you this much when we've only been together a month. But I do. I love you so much!" Her voice filled the space around us.

My heart swelled. We kissed again, oblivious to the temperature in the van. "I'm really turned on," I told her.

She sat up with a shy smile. Reaching behind her back, she untied the top of her bikini and tossed it over the car seat. Her breasts were small but beautifully formed, with dark, prominent nipples. Her skin was paler where her top had been, which inexplicably added to my excitement. When she saw me looking at her she said, "They're not big, but they're good." She eased herself back down on the mattress.

"They're beautiful. *You're* beautiful," I said, kissing her one more time. I placed my hand over her naked breast. My breath quickened. Taking a nipple in my fingertips, I pinched it delicately, felt it grow hard under my touch. Then I took her breast in my mouth, tweaked the nipple with the tip of my tongue and began sucking, gently at first and then harder. Her skin was damp and tasted salty. A rivulet of sweat trickled down her chest and off her side, onto the mattress. I ran my hand between her breasts and slowly over her stomach. My hard penis pressed against her leg.

She moaned and we kissed deeply. "Make love to me," she whispered.

I moved away far enough to get a look at her. Her cheeks were flushed and her eyes half-closed. "Really? What about . . .? We don't want you to get pregnant."

"Don't worry. I've been taking birth control pills. The doctor gave them to me to regulate my periods." She removed the bottom of her two-piece, tossed it aside.

"You never told me—"

She shushed me and we kissed again, our lips and tongues touching playfully. When I couldn't wait any longer, I slid my right hand slowly across the smoothness of her belly and through a soft cluster of pubic hair. My fingers found a pool of wetness between her long legs.

"I can't believe how juicy I am," she whispered self-consciously.

"You're wonderful!" I said softly. Her body relaxed and I got naked. I slid my tongue down her neck and all over her breasts. I took my time touching her between the legs, drawing circles with the tip of my middle finger before gliding my finger inside her. She made a little moaning sound in the back of her throat and began rhythmically moving her pelvis to heighten her excitement. And mine. After moving on top of her body, I pressed against her crotch.

"Please. I want you to," she told me, her voice mingling with the drone of the hydroplanes on the river.

I put myself inside her, halfway at first and then all the way in, filling her completely. She held me tightly in her arms and moaned low in her throat. Being inside Lydia produced a kind of sensual pleasure I can find no words for, a pleasure so intense it temporarily erased all my thoughts. I fell into a natural trance that went unbroken for some time and only ended when she spoke unexpectedly. "There's something I want to try." Her voice sounded tentative against the side of my neck.

"What? I'll do *anything* for you."

"Pull yourself out of me."

I withdrew myself slowly. Lydia reached down, grabbed my slick penis and began rubbing it against the most sensitive part of her. I did a half pushup on my elbows, trying not to come.

"Bryan," she said, breathing fast. "I think I can finish." She spread her legs wider while continuing to stimulate herself with the tip of my penis. The temperature in the van climbed. Lydia's breathing quickened until her muscles went rigid and she gave herself over to her orgasm.

I took my penis from her hand and pushed myself back inside her while her body was still contracting. Placing her hand over her mouth, she muffled a scream of pure pleasure. I grabbed her high up on her arms and held on as my excitement mounted, tension running through my body like an electric current. Finally, my body began to tighten and I gave in to the pleasure of orgasm. My eyes rolled back in my head and I let myself go, all my energy flowing into Lydia.

We lay together spent and panting. A minute passed and Lydia made a joke. I can't remember exactly what she said, but it was something like, "Why did you make me wait so long to do this?"

We laughed and rolled onto our sides with our bodies still coupled. I whispered, "It's better when you wait."

She closed her eyes and sighed. "It couldn't have been better."

"You were wonderful!"

"I was afraid it would hurt the first time."

"It didn't?"

She shook her head. "Not at all."

"That's because we're a good fit."

"You would know. You're the one with all the experience," she teased.

"Okay. Be nice."

We lay there awhile, not saying anything more. Lydia pulled away from me. Sitting up, she asked, "How come it's still hard? Didn't I satisfy you?"

I rolled onto my back. "I couldn't be more satisfied. Anyway, it's only three-quarters hard. Sometimes it doesn't go down all the away."

"Knowing you, it probably has a mind of its own."

"Lydia, if you were a guy and you were naked with a girl who looked like you do, you wouldn't be able to get it down, either."

She threw her head back and laughed. "Compliments will get you everywhere."

"I'm counting on it."

"Three quarters hard, huh?"

I nodded. "Yup. Three quarters. That's about right."

"Will it get *four quarters hard* if I do this?" She stroked and squeezed my penis with her fingertips.

I closed my eyes and moaned. "It's up to seven eighths," I lied, my erection absolute.

"Liar!" she said, giving me an extra hard squeeze with her hand. "Maybe this'll do it," she said, straddling my body and guiding me back inside her.

I took Lydia by the shoulders, pulled her towards me and kissed her. She straightened up, undid her ponytail and shook out her mane of hair. When she leaned over to kiss me again it swept against my neck and shoulders, tickling me. Reaching up, I ran my hands over her breasts and gently squeezed her chocolate brown nipples. Lydia was moving slowly, first swaying her hips and then rocking back and forth in a way that made the pleasure almost unbearable. I opened and closed my eyes, dimly aware of the musky smell of our overheated bodies. For a second time, I drifted into a dreamy state where there was little left of me save heightened senses. *Now I am in heaven,* I thought.

Lydia's second orgasm came out of the blue, like an unexpected but welcome guest arriving late to a party. She shuddered uncontrollably. I grabbed her bottom and pulled her all the way into me, thrusting until I lifted her body completely off the ground with a climax of my own. She flopped on top of me and we lay motionless for some time, breathing heavily, our eyes closed.

A strange and unnerving question wound its way deliberately through my consciousness: *Am I Lydia Redstone or is she Bryan Matthews . . . or are we one in the same person?* I had to open my eyes to stop the buildup of anxiety. Looking at her body and then mine helped me reconstitute a boundary, as if I needed reassurance we could return to the beach as two separate beings.

I rolled off and we lay side by side for a minute or two. There were voices from somewhere close to the van, maybe a few cars away. I was worried we'd been overheard until I heard an angry woman say, "Well, next time let's not go for a last swim." I had to laugh.

"How do you not go for a last swim?" Lydia whispered, giggling.

"You got me."

Lydia wiped sweat from her stomach and thighs. "If only Yolanda could see me now."

"Are you going to tell her?"

"Sure. We're sisters. We tell each other everything. Do you mind?"

"No."

"Are you going to tell Slider and Ethan?"

"No. I don't think so."

She smiled. "Good. I don't want you to."

On the drive back to Walla Walla, Slider introduced us to Led Zeppelin. After punching in the 8-track tape of their debut album, we listened to a soulful Robert Plant singing *"Babe, I'm Gonna Leave You."* When the song ended, Lydia looked at me and whispered, "Are you going to leave me, now that you've had your way?" She was joking around, but there was a hint of anxiety in her question. The kind of anxiety a girl can't shake when her own mother has abandoned her. One I could relate to.

"I will never leave you," I promised. "Not in a million years. Not for anything!"

"Cross your heart and hope to die?"

"Cross my heart and hope to die."

She kissed my cheek and cuddled up next to me, her body radiating heat. "You're even smarter than I thought."

I memorized the sensation of her touch. That way I could take her with me wherever I went. Within minutes, she fell asleep in my arms, worn out from the sun and the beer and the excitement of first sex. I breathed in her earthy smell, a combination of vanilla and sweat, and wanted to lick every inch of her body.

The drive home was hot, the air dense with the threat of a thunderstorm. Marilu and Slider left the front windows wide open and the warm air scattered Lydia's long hair across my face and lips. It felt like black satin caressing my cheeks, whisking away any residue of doubt over the vulnerability that came with loving her so completely. I wished the moment would never end. Closing my eyes, I held on to the feeling until it gave way to a most distressing thought: *Can anything that feels this good really last?*

————————

The thunderstorm broke just after midnight and awakened me near the end of a dream. I'm alone in the fraternity house. It's dark and quiet, a few hours before dawn. I'm roaming from room to room searching for someone to talk to. I call out, hear my voice disappear down a hallway. I wander into the front yard. There are no clouds and no stars. Everything is black, white, or shades of gray. I want to be with Lydia so I head off in the direction of her house. I'm walking down the middle of Alvarado Street. There are no cars, no signs of life. Suddenly, the entire scene is brilliantly lit, as if someone had turned on long banks of powerful lights at a baseball stadium. On both sides of me yellow daffodils sprout from the blackness of the earth, sped up, like in time-lapsed photography. Each daffodil forms a trumpet-shaped central crown and grows to a disproportionate height. Their stalks are strong and vibrant, greener than life. A row of red and white tulips pops up in front of the daffodils. I watch this madness of growth. The flowers reach ten feet tall, then twenty, and don't stop until they tower over me, a good fifty feet in the air. The street has become a continuous corridor of dazzling spring colors. At the end of the corridor there is a woman. She is wearing a gauzy, white dress and sits in a white leather chair. It's my mother. I walk closer. Her eyes, greener than mine, penetrate to the core of my being. "What do the flowers mean?" I ask. "They mean you're in love," she answers. "Anything else?" I ask. "There is nothing else!" she replies. Without so much as a goodbye she gets to her feet and walks away. Her bare feet barely touch the ground as she disappears into a fine mist. I climb into the white chair and nestle into the spot she has vacated, but the chair has gone as cold as frost on a windowpane.

Chapter 5
"Radar Doesn't Lie!"

My summer lessons produced dramatic results. I put in fifty hours a week of intense study and played scintillating chess with Dr. Z. In every game, he found a way to bring some deep strategic concept to life. Capture toward the center to avoid pawn islands. Destroy a flank attack by counterattacking in the center. Place a knight on the square in front of an isolated pawn. Keep rim pawns close to home. Use pieces, not pawns, to occupy holes in the enemy position. Start the attack on the side where you have the most space. Coordinated rooks are best used on adjacent files because they control more relevant squares.

Dr. Z was right. The Stonewall Attack was a simple and elegant attacking machine that fit well with my aggressive style. The theme for our lessons was always the attack: how to begin the attack, develop the attack and complete the attack. Attack, attack, attack! Following a rule he attributed to the great Jose Capablanca, Dr. Z urged me to break the habit of using single pieces to strike and destroy enemy targets. "Smash your opponent with an attacking complement of three or four pieces," he commanded me with a level stare late one afternoon, when I'd erred by coming after his king with only a knight. "Don't be a sniper. Overwhelm your opponent! Attack with more force than he can use in defense!"

By August I had improved enough to play even up with Dr. Z. I couldn't have been happier with my progress, but when I offered him a draw in the last of four consecutive draws he snapped, "Bryan. Why are you not defeating me?"

His question caught me completely off guard. "I'm sorry. I don't understand."

"What's not to understand? It's a simple question. Why are you not defeating me? Why have you *never* defeated me?" Dr. Z was practically shouting.

Dr. Z could be a taskmaster, but I'd never seen him so upset. A Raja Yoga master, he lived and breathed the Eastern concept of detachment. "But you're . . ." I intended to say he was the better player. Something told me that would only make the situation worse.

Arms folded, Dr. Z stared right through me, but said nothing more.

My body felt like it had shrunk in half. Had I not heard every agonizing tick of the grandfather clock in the entryway, I would have thought time stopped. I cleared my throat, but still no words followed.

Finally Dr. Z said, "You are my student. I am *asking* you a question. Why did this game end in a draw?"

I took a deep breath and tried to calm myself. "It ended in a draw because I traded dark-squared bishops on move eighteen. And it turned out to be a mistake."

"Then why on earth did you make the trade?"

"It was a mistake."

He erupted like one of the five active volcanoes in the state of Washington. "No. That's *not* why! And my patience is wearing thin."

I shook my head. "I'm sorry, then. I honestly don't know why I made the mistake. I had a bad bishop and I thought—"

"No, Bryan," he bellowed, slamming his fist on the chessboard. The pieces migrated from their final positions. I flashed on an enraged Nikita Khrushchev pounding his shoe on the podium at the United Nations, threatening to bury the United States. Dr. Z was talking again. "Enough of your excuses. I will tell you why you are making silly mistakes and getting draws instead of wins. It is because you are afraid to defeat the grandmaster."

"What?"

"Bryan," he intoned. "Every day you gain the advantage on me. You accumulate a series of small advantages, something you do as well or better than anyone I've ever coached. And I mean *anyone*. Look back at games we've played this week. Monday you had a healthier pawn structure. Tuesday you had a material advantage and control of the center. Wednesday you caught me with an isolated pawn and a buried piece that was so hemmed in it was worthless. Today you got ahead in the space count and had superior mobility. But it doesn't matter what your advantage is because you keep finding ways to make a mistake so I can eke out a draw. Stop making mistakes and beat me!"

I swallowed hard. "Okay, just for the sake of argument, let's assume I'm finding ways not to win. How am I supposed to get past it? How am I supposed to put you away?"

"The same way we all do the first time we break through and defeat the master. It's simple." He took a little of the edge off his voice. "Forget you are playing Zdenek Zaleski, International Grandmaster, and concentrate on the game in front of you. Play the *game*, not your opponent. *Win* the game!"

The next afternoon I did just that. I opened with the Stonewall Attack and built up tremendous kingside pressure. His play was sharp and he mounted an impressive counterattack, but lost control of several critical squares. Remembering his advice, I focused on the board position and not who was sitting across the board. On the thirty-fifth move, I advanced my king bishop pawn, tightened the noose and checkmated him six moves later. Dr. Z could have resigned, but he played it out, probably wanting me to have the satisfaction of actually checkmating the Grandmaster.

"Congratulations, Bryan," he said, beaming with satisfaction. He reached across the board and shook my hand. "Are you aware of how well you played?"

I nodded. "I think it might have been my best game ever."

"Yes, I think so. But why? What made it your best game?"

"No mistakes."

"No mistakes, Bryan. Get this tattooed somewhere on your body so you never forget it. Chess games are seldom won. They are almost always lost!"

"I think I've got it. Can I skip the tattoo?"

Dr. Z smiled. "Your game lends itself to forcing errors," he explained. "Attack, let the tension build and seize the initiative! Keep the pressure on until your opponent makes a mistake, however small it is. Given enough pressure, even Grandmasters make mistakes."

———————

That night, Dr. Z and Reva met Lydia and me in the elegant oak and marble dining room of the Marcus Whitman Hotel. The "Marc," as the brothers called it, was reputed to be the nicest place to dine in Walla Walla and the Zaleskis wanted to celebrate my victory in style. As we finished our desserts, Dr. Z announced that I would defeat Javad Azizi when school resumed for fall semester. He had no doubt about the outcome.

"I hope you're right."

"I am right," he said. "And, there will be more than the number one ranking at stake."

"Why's that?" I asked.

Dr. Z's eyes lit up. "Next February, Vladimir Primalov is coming to the U.S. to do a tour. He's playing in several select tournaments and one of them is the Candidates' Tournament in San Francisco. As you know, Vladimir was my student. And he's flying up to Walla Walla for a visit."

"Wow!"

"Who's Primalov?" Lydia asked, looking first at Dr. Z and then me.

"He's a World Championship contender. The third best player in the world, after Bobby Fischer and Boris Spassky." I looked imploringly at Dr. Z. "I'll get to meet him, won't I?"

He laughed. "You'll do more than meet him. He offered to play an exhibition against me and I told him I had a better idea. Get this." Dr. Z bristled with excitement. "Primalov has agreed to an exhibition game against Whitman's number one player. It's going to be in the Harper Joy Theater, open to the public."

My jaw dropped. "You have *got* to be kidding!"

Lydia said, "So if Bryan beats Javad, he gets to play the third best player in the world?"

Dr. Z smiled confidently. "*When* he beats Javad."

———————

The next morning I could barely contain myself. Without knowing why, I felt a sudden urge to go by and say hello to Mom Waters, my freshman year housemother at Davis-Jacobs. Mom had endeared herself to me by noticing

I was out of sorts after the breakup with Vicky Spotts and providing some much-needed support ("Bryan. Let me explain teenage girls to you . . ."). On a separate occasion, she loaned me twenty dollars when I ran out of spending money. After Davis-Jacobs was razed for the new science center, Mom moved into a place down the street called College Apartments. Before driving over, I picked a spectacular bouquet of purple and white dahlias from Reva's flower garden.

Mom's door was ajar and Mozart played on her modest stereo system. I peeked in and saw her sitting on a blue corduroy couch with lace doilies on the arms. Her eyes were closed. A noisy air conditioner in the window failed in its attempt to keep up with the heat. She looked like she might have fallen asleep. After debating whether I should interrupt her I said softly, "The Magic Flute?"

"Bryan Matthews!" she exclaimed, coming instantly to life. "Come in and sit yourself down. Yes, I believe it is 'The Magic Flute.' Good for you." Mom had pale, papery skin and liver-spotted hands. Her room assaulted my senses with the thick, mothballed odor of an elderly woman's space. Everything smelled old, an effect magnified by the room temperature, which, like Mom Waters, was pushing eighty.

"Are you sure it's a good time?"

"Of course it is. What a pleasant surprise! I always like to see my boys and now that they've torn down Davis-Jacobs, well, I guess I'm not going to have much to do."

"I heard you were going to help out over at Anderson Hall."

"Yes, I am," she replied, smiling. "But those are girls over there, Bryan, unless you failed to notice. And I'm partial to my boys."

"Oh, here. These are for you." I handed her the dahlias, which I'd placed in a jumbo Arctic Circle Coke container.

"They're lovely! Thank you. I'm going to cut the stems and put them in fresh water so they'll last longer." She walked stiffly into the kitchen. Alongside the couch stood a flimsy-looking end table, home to a gaudy antique lamp, a music box and a lovely crystal objet d'art with the engraving, *Chance cannot change my love nor time impair.* A twinge of sadness momentarily gripped me as I imagined a younger Mom Waters in love.

A little bookcase with maybe ten books graced the corner of the room. I glanced at the books one by one: a well-used copy of *The Joy of Cooking,* *Gone With the Wind,* a timeworn family *Bible, Little Women,* and a paperback *Common Birds of the Northwest.* A split-leaf philodendron had been trained over the top of a display case featuring at least twenty ceramic salt and pepper sets.

Mom returned with the flowers neatly arranged in a green vase. She placed them carefully on the glass-topped coffee table and smiled. "You're back for school early."

"Actually I never left," I told her. "I've spent the whole summer with the Zaleskis."

"You didn't go home?" She seemed surprised.

"No. I had a chance to study chess all summer with Dr. Z . . . uh, Dr. Zaleski, and I couldn't pass it up." I left out the part about the new girlfriend. Mom had suggested I stay away from girls for a while after the debacle with Vicky.

She mopped her brow with a white handkerchief. "Oh, where are my manners? The hottest day of the year and I haven't asked you if you want something to drink. Would you like a glass of iced tea?"

"Sure. That sounds great." This time I followed her into the kitchen. She opened the refrigerator and removed a full pitcher of iced tea.

"Would you mind pouring it, Bryan? I'm afraid my arthritis has flared up. It doesn't usually happen till the weather turns cold in the fall, but I guess I won't be so lucky this year."

"Sure. No problem." I pried loose an ice tray from the freezer section of the fridge, which was virtually a solid accumulation of frost. Mom Waters put out two glasses and I filled them with ice and tea.

"Here's to your sophomore year," she said cheerfully. We clinked our glasses, producing a light, sharp ringing sound.

"And to your health," I added.

She smiled appreciatively. "Thank you, Bryan."

"It looks like College Apartments forgot to clean and defrost your fridge before you moved in," I said as tactfully as possible.

"It hasn't been cleaned for a long time, that's for sure. I'd do it myself, but it's a bit much for me. If I get down on my knees I might not get back up."

"Can I do it for you?"

"Oh, Bryan. That's not necessary."

"I know it's not necessary, but I'd like to do it. It'd give me something to do."

"Are you sure? It's so doggone hot."

"That'll make it defrost easier. Really, I want to."

"My goodness. That would be wonderful. There's not much in it right now because I spent the last week with my good friend Ella in Dayton. I haven't been to the grocery store since I got back yesterday afternoon."

Mom was right. The main section of the fridge contained only a halfempty carton of milk, an unmarked margarine container with really old leftover broccoli, an expired bottle of Benadryl, an open can of Hershey's chocolate syrup and bottles of mustard, mayonnaise and ketchup. The vegetable drawer had some rubbery celery and a bunch of carrots with suspicious black spots, which I promptly threw out. The freezer compartment was empty except for a carton of vanilla ice cream. I put the ice cream and condiments in a large stainless steel pot and packed them in what was left of the ice after making us each a second glass of iced tea.

Mom took an unopened box of baking soda in her cupboard, mixed about a fourth of it in a saucepan with warm water and gave it to me. "Use this," she explained, "it makes a good scrubber, but it's not so gritty that it'll scratch the surfaces."

For the next hour I defrosted and cleaned the fridge while Mom sat at the kitchen table and told me a good portion of her life story. I mostly listened, asking a few innocuous questions here and there. Her husband had been a marginally successful logger who died in the woods when Mom was in her early forties. He was killed tying chokers on a logging truck when a thick chain snapped and hit him between the eyes. They had no children and Mom never remarried. At this point in her story she retreated momentarily to her living room and returned with the crystal I'd admired a few minutes before. "I want to show you something," she told me, setting the heavy piece on the kitchen table.

I nodded appreciatively. "I noticed it when I first came in. It's beautiful!"

"Thank you. Daniel gave it to me for our twentieth wedding anniversary. It says, 'Chance cannot change my love nor time impair.' Isn't that lovely?"

"It's perfect," I answered.

"He bought it at a fancy store in San Francisco, but it comes from Ireland. When you get to be my age you don't put much stock in *things,* but this is my most prized possession."

"I can see why. I'd like to give something that beautiful to my wife someday. Assuming anyone will have me."

Mom laughed. "Oh, Bryan, I can't imagine you having any trouble with the girls. Not with those green eyes of yours. You just have to pick more carefully."

I blushed a little and got back to work. When the refrigerator looked squeaky clean I plugged it back in and joined Mom at the kitchen table. I had sweat stains all the way through my T-shirt. Mom said, "Thank you so much, Bryan. It looks like a brand new fridge!"

"You're welcome." I downed the watery remainder of my iced tea and asked, "What's this?"

On the kitchen table was a small figurine, a black horse rearing up on its hind legs. Made from clay, it bore an uncanny resemblance to one I'd seen as a boy. The tail had been broken off and lay on top of Mom's old Silvertone radio. I picked up the body of the horse and was examining it when she said, "I've had that little horse almost my whole life."

"What happened to his tail?"

"The morning I went to Ella's I knocked it over reaching for the salt-shaker. Clumsy me. I seem to be all thumbs these days."

"It's really well done. Where did you get it?"

"My mother gave it to me when I was ten. I was absolutely crazy about horses in those days. Like most young girls, I wanted a real horse, but we couldn't afford one so my mother, bless her heart, bought me this little figurine."

"You could fix it with a dab of glue."

"My hands aren't steady enough. I'd just make a mess."

"I can do it. I've got the skilled hands of a surgeon." In succession, I quickly tapped each fingertip to my thumb and gave Mom my most winning smile.

Mom laughed and went to a drawer between her now gleaming refrigerator and not so gleaming sink. After rummaging around for a few seconds she handed me a tube of Elmer's glue, the clear kind that dries fast. "Here it is, Dr. Matthews. Let's see if you can save my horse."

I squeezed a little dab onto the tip of the built-in applicator, applied it to the body of the horse and fastened the tail at the point of the break. The glue had a sharp, chemical odor that stung my nostrils. "It's a clean fracture," I said to Mom, wiping off the excess with tip of my forefinger. "Your horse is going to be just fine."

"Thank you, Bryan. Again."

"When I was just a kid my mother used to make things from clay," I told her. "She was really good. An artist. She had a little studio in our basement with a kiln and everything. One day I walked in just as she finished sculpting a little horse that looked almost identical to this one. Same size, same confirmation. The only difference was it wasn't rearing up like yours. I remember my mother holding it delicately in her wet hands and asking me if I liked it. I told her I loved it, or something to that effect. Know what she did?"

"No, what?" she asked with a wan smile.

"She closed her hands around the little horse and pressed it back into a shapeless ball of clay." I demonstrated for Mom Waters. "Then she handed me the round ball of clay and said, 'The little horse is still in there, Bryan. See if *you* can find him!'"

Mom Waters stared at me, absorbing the meaning of the story. "Oh, Bryan. That's a wonderful story! I've never said a single thing that memorable. Your mother must have been quite a woman."

My body tightened instantly. *Why'd she refer to my mother in past tense?* I'd certainly never shared anything about my childhood with her. "You knew my mother was deceased?"

"I'm sorry, Bryan. I didn't mean to make you uncomfortable, but yes, Dean Sanderson told me what happened to your mother. Before you moved into Davis-Jacobs."

"He told you about my mother? I mean, he told you what happened to her?"

She nodded. "Yes. He did."

"What did he say?"

"That she committed suicide when you were a youngster."

"I didn't even know he knew."

She looked almost wounded. "Was he wrong to tell me?"

"I don't know. It's just seems so private. It's embarrassing."

She nodded sympathetically. "I imagine it would be. My grandmother took her life. She put her head in an oven and turned on the gas. The same way that poet did a few years ago. What's her name? The one that wrote *The Bell Jar.*"

"Sylvia Plath."

"That's the one. I can't remember names any more."

I shook my head in disgust. "What a waste. To throw away a life."

Mom Waters sighed wearily. "We can never really know why someone would take their life. It's too complicated. But I think it's safe to say they wouldn't have done it unless they were suffering terribly."

"I think it's pretty selfish to kill yourself when you have a child to raise. That's what makes it so hard to forgive her."

"But if you were *her,* with her circumstances and her frailties, you would have done the exact same thing."

I took a moment to think it through. "I never looked at it quite like that."

She shrugged. "Well, that's the way I see it. Maybe you should try looking at it my way. It helps us find the compassion we need to forgive those who left us behind."

"I'll try."

She picked up her little horse figurine and gently tested its tail. The fast-drying glue held firm. Mom Waters smiled, looked at me and said, "Sometimes things that have been broken and put back together turn out to be stronger than if they'd never been broken at all."

I phoned Lydia to find out about the first day of her senior year. Yolanda answered and we chatted for a few minutes, mostly her filling me in on all the cute boys in her classes. Yolanda was desperate for a boyfriend and, according to Lydia, horny as a goat since hearing of our recent sexual escapades. When Lydia came on I asked, "How'd it go?"

"Okay. I pretty much got the classes I wanted except for English."

"What's the problem with English?"

"I got Mr. Howlett. He's really hard. A taskmaster. We're going to have to do a literary analysis of *The Great Gatsby.*"

"Ah, the great American novel."

"You've read it?"

"Yeah."

"Good," she said, her voice brightening. "You can help me."

"What's in it for me?"

"The pleasure of my company."

"Deal. How about the pleasure of your company tonight?"

She sighed. "Can't. Mr. Howlett gave us homework that's due tomorrow. A two-page typewritten essay on the most memorable thing about my summer."

"Tell him about losing your virginity."

"Very funny, Bryan!"

We talked for ten minutes and signed off, signaling the first time we'd gone a whole day without seeing one another since meeting in June. Classes for me didn't start for another week so I drove up Isaacs to the Suds Up

Car Wash. After spray washing my car, I headed out Highway 12 toward Dixie, a long, arrow-straight stretch of road where I could put the pedal to the metal and blow off any residual water. At eighty miles an hour I flashed on Officer Jack Montrose, got a queasy feeling in my stomach, backed off the accelerator and turned around.

Before returning to the fraternity house I stopped at Reed and Bell's for a root beer float. Just as the carhop handed over my order, someone—Vicky Spotts—opened the passenger door and sat down in my front seat. She appeared ill, with dark circles beneath her eyes. Her complexion had broken-out and she'd gained a considerable amount of weight. "Can we talk for a minute?" she asked.

"Do I have a choice?"

She narrowed her eyes. "Don't be a butt. I need to talk to you."

"The last time we talked you took a chunk out of my face. Or have you forgotten?"

"Sorry about that. I lost my temper."

"Right. And then a few weeks later you lost your temper at the drive-in and made a scene in front of Lydia. Are you sorry about that, too?"

"That, I'm not sorry about. She's a bitch and she stole my boyfriend."

"Look, Vicky. I'm not trying to be rude, but I've got to get back to the fraternity house, so say what you have to say and get it over with."

She took a deep breath, pursed her lips and exhaled. "I just want to know if there's a chance for us to get back together."

I started shaking my head before the words came out of my mouth. "No. It's not going to happen."

"Because you're with . . . her?"

"No. I am with Lydia, but that's not why I'm not with you. I'm not with you because we didn't work out. We've been over this before. I don't want to talk about it again."

"So is it true love? Is she the one?"

"C'mon, Vicky. There's no point in talking about this."

"Would Lydia do this for you?" She rotated her right arm and showed me a series of nasty cuts extending from her wrist to her elbow.

"Jesus!" Without thinking I grabbed her arm and pulled it closer for a better look. The cuts looked fairly recent and deep enough to have caused a substantial loss of blood. A few appeared infected.

"Want to see the cuts on my stomach and legs? They're deeper." Fat tears began rolling down her cheeks.

"No, I don't. Does your mother know you're doing this?"

"She knows." She let out a high-pitched half-laugh half-shriek that startled me. "Half of Walla Walla knows!" I looked at the cars around us to see if anyone was paying attention. They weren't. She wiped the tears with the back of her hand, opened my glove compartment without asking and took a napkin to dab at her eyes. It was a reasonable thing to do and yet I felt violated.

"Are you still seeing that shrink?"

She nodded. "He says I'm cutting on myself to show everyone how hurt I am. But it's not that complicated."

"So what is it?"

Her eyes glazed over. "I like it. It gives me a feeling of relief."

"From what?" Wrong question. I regretted it as soon as the words left my mouth.

She jerked her head angrily. "From what you've done to me."

"I'm sorry you're hurting, Vicky. I *really* am. And I hope to God you stop doing that to yourself. But it doesn't change anything. We're done."

"Because you're fucking Pocahontas."

I turned in my seat, livid. "That's it. Get out of my car."

"Gonna make me?" she asked, with a weird smile. She unbuttoned the top two buttons on her blouse and carefully extracted a long silver chain. A razor blade dangled from the end, not the safety kind, but a thin piece of steel with two sharp edges. She took the blade between her right thumb and forefinger and turned it in her hand, making it gleam in the fluorescent lights from above my car. She glazed over. "You'd think this thing would be slicing up my big boobs, but it doesn't. It only cuts when I want it to. I have complete control."

"Vicky. Please get out of my car before you do something we both regret."

"Regret? Did you say *regret?* Good choice of words, mister."

Two images raced through my mind. The first had me feeling the shock of cold steel carving my face to the cheekbone. The second one had her cutting open her own left wrist, blood spurting. I swallowed hard. "Just get out of my car!" I said it loud enough for the person in the car to our right to look over and frown.

At that, Vicky inflicted an elbow to wrist cut on her left arm, slowly and deliberately, like a skilled surgeon taking pride in practicing her craft. I watched transfixed as a horrible thin line appeared on her pale skin, watched as it turned red and oozed a considerable quantity of dark blood. "Bye for now," she said, her eyes flickering with a weird silvery light. Then she got out, but not without first wiping a bloody forearm on my car seat.

The match with Javad took place the second Friday in November. Butterflies crowded my stomach as I walked from the fraternity to the Zaleski's house. The autumn air was unusually crisp and two days of rain had turned a million fallen leaves into a red-orange paste. I arrived early, thinking about our previous games. We'd played three times and I'd lost three times, but I felt a newfound confidence after my one-on-one summer tutorial with Dr. Z.

The match began on time, but only after Dr. Z announced the winner would earn the right to play Vladimir Primalov come February. I drew White and opened pawn to queen four, intending to play the Stonewall

Attack, my weapon of choice. Javad knew of my recent success in playing the Stonewall and countered my intentions by playing pawn to queen bishop four – the Benoni Defense. The Benoni, considered suspect when it was first introduced in the early 1800's, was now considered a respectable, even forceful defense. A favorite of Alekhine and Tal, two former World Champions, it gave rise to active positions and aggressive play. I was surprised he'd chosen it. Aggressive play and rapid-fire tactics were my forte, not Javad's.

I refused the temptation to capture his pawn—which is what he wanted—and we ended up with a closed center in a variation of the Benoni called the Blockade System. We exchanged pawns on move thirteen and I got my queen into play two moves later, aiming her squarely at his castled king. I made a series of middlegame interference moves that blocked Javad's line of attack while allowing me to swing my king rook to the opposite wing. The board became impossibly complicated. Knowing Javad's game, I felt confident he would want to simplify. When I set him up with the chance, he initiated a wholesale exchange of knights and bishops, leaving me with the better heavy pieces for the endgame.

Javad resigned on the forty-second move. He congratulated me with a faint smile and a bewildered shake of his head. Dr. Z gave me an affectionate squeeze on the shoulder. The others looked up from their respective games to acknowledge what had happened. Joan Levy, who disliked Javad for being sexist and anti-Semitic, grinned from ear to ear. Ethan gave me the thumbs-up sign. Miles and Jeremy smiled and nodded their congratulations. To the best of my knowledge, it was the first time Javad Azizi had ever lost to another college player. The mantle had been passed.

Had there been any doubt about the improvement in my game, it vanished. A light had gone on and I suddenly *knew* what was most important in any given situation. I could now answer Dr. Z's most frequent questions. "Which side has the better position?" "Where are your weak squares and how can you improve the placement of your pieces?" "Should you build up or resolve the tension in the center?" "What is the most efficient way to pierce my defenses now that you've completed your development?"

I excused myself, acknowledged the congratulations of my teammates and left through the front door. Lydia and Yolanda were at the curb, leaning against the Cruz' Malibu. The rain had stopped but their hair was wet, as if they'd been there awhile. "Who won?" Lydia called out. I smiled broadly and pumped my fist in the air. She let out a little shriek then dashed up the steps and into my arms. "You get to play the Russian!" she shouted. She gave me another hug and planted a hard kiss on my mouth. There were tears in her eyes, which caught me off-guard and touched me in a way I am still unable to describe.

"You guys are supposed to be in school," I said with a smile.

"We thought this would be worth cutting for," Lydia replied.

"Glad I won." I hugged her again.

"And we're going to celebrate tonight," she said, taking my hand and leading me down the steps to the cherub-faced Yolanda, who gave a kiss on the cheek and more hugs.

"What're we doing?"

"I can tell you this much," Lydia replied. "It involves the back seat of your car and the woods out by Kooskooskie."

Yolanda plugged her ears. "I didn't hear that."

Lydia and I parked a couple miles past the bridge at Kooskooskie, well hidden behind a tangle of blackberry vines that had overgrown an ancient collapsed wooden shack. On the way back to her house, I passed a police car in the parking lot between the VFW and All Seasons Rentals. It looked like Officer Montrose, causing my stomach to twist with fear. I glanced at the speedometer, felt relief on seeing I was under the speed limit. The police car pulled onto the main drag and began following us, maybe a hundred yards behind. "Shit!" I said.

"What's wrong?" Lydia asked.

"There's a cop behind us. I think it might be that Jack Montrose."

"What makes you say that?"

"I saw him."

"Bummer." She turned around and looked. The police car had closed to within fifty feet.

It wasn't late, a few minutes before ten, but the streets were virtually empty. "I'm going to do something," I told her. Normally I turned off on Second to get to Lydia's house on Carrie, but this time I took a right turn on Park to see if I was right about being followed.

"Is he following us?" Lydia asked, without looking back.

The police car continued straight on Isaacs. I heaved a sigh of relief.

"Are you sure it was that Montrose guy?"

"Pretty sure. He pulls the late shift and I know for a fact he'd like nothing better than to bust my balls."

"Perish the thought!" Lydia smiled and slid her hand high on my leg.

"That was wonderful," I told her when we got to the front door.

She hugged me tight to her body. "I love you," she whispered.

I melted into her warmth. "I love you, too."

"Sleep tight."

"You, too."

I headed home on Ninth the way I always did. The police car was parked at the intersection at Moore. Too late to whip a quick left on Rees. I reassured myself I hadn't done anything wrong and checked my speedometer. Twenty-one in a twenty-five.

As I passed the police car I glanced over and saw the unfriendly face of Officer Jack Montrose. He held something in his right hand and it looked enough like a gun to scare the bejesus out of me. Beyond any doubt I knew he would pull me over. Montrose wasted no time; he pulled out on my tail and put on his flasher lights. I eased the Chevy to the curb and turned off my ignition. *Act like a limp dick*, I told myself, a strategy that seemed intuitively right. Montrose strolled to my car. My stomach tightened. "Did I do something wrong?" I asked politely.

"As a matter of fact, you did. Let's see your license and registration." His voice was authoritative, but reasonable.

I retrieved both and handed them to him. He pulled a small leather book from under his arm and began writing out a ticket. I looked up at him with a blank expression. "Excuse me. What did I do?"

"Out a little late, aren't you?"

"What? It's ten o'clock."

He grinned. "That's right. You're a college boy. I almost forgot."

"Why are you . . . what did I do wrong?"

"You were speeding."

"Oh God, no way was I speeding! I saw your car as soon as I turned the corner and kept my speed under twenty-five."

"I got you with the radar gun at thirty-seven."

"No way, Officer Montrose. Swear to God I checked my speedometer! I was going twenty-one."

"Not according to the radar."

"Then the radar has to be off."

"Sorry, just had it calibrated this afternoon. You were going exactly thirty-seven. If anything's off, it's your speedometer."

I fell temporarily speechless. The lights went off in a small house on the other side of the street and it occurred to me how utterly alone I was. Finding my voice I said, "You were waiting for me, weren't you?"

A half-smile crossed his face. "I get a lot of people for speeding in residential areas. Tonight's your night, college boy."

"But you knew I was going to turn down Ninth. You know how I go home from my girlfriend's, and you waited for me."

"I've got better things to do than to set a trap to catch you speeding," he sneered.

"Then why aren't you doing them, instead of being parked on a side street in the middle of the night where there's no traffic whatsoever."

"But that's not exactly true, is it. If there was no traffic whatsoever, I wouldn't have caught you breaking the speed limit."

"Officer Montrose, this isn't fair. I was not speeding and you know it." So much for the limp dick approach.

"I'm not going to argue with you. And, guess what? This time you don't have the Dean of Men to bail you out. Sign the ticket and go home." He pushed the ticket pad and a pen in through the window, jarring my left shoulder.

"This is bull . . ." Jaw clenched tight, I fought the urge to throw it back at him. "What happens if I refuse to sign it?"

"You go straight to jail, which is just fine by me. Or, you can sign it and go to traffic court and tell the judge how *unfair* you think it is to get caught speeding." He snorted derisively.

"You're enjoying yourself, aren't you, *Officer* Montrose?"

"Let me tell you something, college boy. I'd enjoy this a whole lot more if you were man enough to step out from the safety of your car." His voice carried some real menace.

"You'd like that," I replied. "You've got a gun and a club on your belt and—"

"Just sign the ticket and shut the fuck up!"

I scribbled a signature and thrust it back to him.

He ripped off a carbon copy, shoved it in my face and snarled, "Let me tell you one more thing, college boy. You so much as roll a stop sign, you forget to use your turn signals, you cross the street outside the fuckin' crosswalk, and I'm gonna be on you . . . like stink on shit! Do you understand?"

I nodded, terrified.

Montrose walked back to his car and got in, slamming his own door.

My body shook with fury. "Fucking asshole!" I muttered under my breath and waited for Montrose to pull out and drive off. Only he didn't. He sat there, arms folded across his chest, waiting for me to go first. After a good minute I pulled away from the curb and drove back to the Phi Delt house. Cautiously. Montrose followed me all the way home, not breaking contact until I pulled into the alleyway behind the fraternity. After turning off the engine I closed my eyes and fantasized about kicking Montrose in the nuts, watching him writhe in pain. If only I knew karate, like Lydia. I wanted to tear the bastard from asshole to elbow, but an enormous ball of fear came rolling in right behind the rage.

Bigdog approached me the next day with the blueprint for still another prank. His idea was to sabotage the dedication of the new Whitman College flagpole, an event scheduled for the first week of December. He planned to stack old tires over the top, however many it took to obscure the fifty-foot pole. The "R.F." would take place in the dark of night. If caught in the act, Bigdog had ready a letter of explanation he'd typed out on stolen Whitman College letterhead. The letter carried Dean Sanderson's forged signature and authorized an "Inter-Fraternity Tire Cutting Contest" to be held in the morning just before the dedication. I declined without giving it any thought. Running afoul of the law might mean having to deal with Officer Montrose.

The prank went off without a hitch. After dropping off a truckload of tires, Bigdog and his cohorts rigged a pulley system to hoist a tire to the top of the flagpole, then began dropping them over, one at a time. This was no small accomplishment, even for Badger, a fraternity brother whose résumé of incredible feats included the ability to screw a light bulb in its socket using his ass and throwing an ordinary playing card over our three-story fraternity house. The flagpole feat required that he climb a long ladder they'd rented from a local tree cutting service, place a tire over the ball on top of the pole and proceed to push the ladder far enough from the pole to allow the tire to drop down to the bottom.

Come Sunday morning, Martin Scribner, Ph.D., the very proper President of the Whitman College, showed up for the dedication along with his very proper wife, Eileen. Joining them were ten of the schools most prestigious alumni, as well as various local dignitaries who'd made sizeable contributions toward erecting the flagpole. A reporter and photographer from the Walla Walla Union-Bulletin were also there the cover the event. Of course, the story became the prank rather than the dedication and President Scribner was furious.

———

The Phi Delt house bustled with activity over the final days of the term. The telephone outside my room was constantly in use as brothers spoke to family and made last-minute Christmas vacation travel arrangements. Bigdog and Chainsaw were flying to England from Seattle. The obese Bigdog promised to "roll" London Bridge, which meant lying on the pavement and rolling the length of the bridge while counting the number of revolutions to get from one end to the other. I offered to take care of Bulldozer, the softball-sized Russian tortoise who roamed his off-campus apartment. That way Lydia and I would have a place to be alone.

My father sounded only slightly disappointed when I told him I wanted to stay in Walla Walla to prepare for my upcoming chess match with Vladimir Primalov (and thus avoid separation from Lydia). He readily consented, which I attributed to his amorous relationship with Cat. We agreed to mail our gifts ahead of time and talk long distance on Christmas day. He couldn't say for certain if he and Cat would attend the Primalov exhibition in February.

I did my Christmas shopping in downtown Walla Walla and took a box of wrapped presents to the post office. I waited in line twenty minutes, directly behind a woman holding a fussy infant son with a ripe diaper. The postal worker who was helping me, a friendly hippie named John, assured me my box would get to Seattle before Christmas Day. Out of bills, I paid him four dollars thirty-seven cents in change and left the building.

Officer Jack Montrose was waiting for me at the curb. Alone in his squad car, he motioned for me to get in the front seat. The car reeked of cigarettes and, if I was not mistaken, the sharp scent of fear.

"What is it?" I asked, my heart working up to a gallop. Sitting next to Montrose felt like reaching into a den of venomous snakes.

"You hear about the vandals that got to the new Whitman College flagpole couple weeks ago?"

I nodded. "Of course. Everybody in town heard about it."

"Right answer. Just wanted to see if you were stupid enough to deny it. Know how much it cost the college to remove the old tires and repair the pole?"

"I have no idea."

"Neither do I, but it's a damn shame if they have to pay a penny. Whoever did it should pay. What do you know about it?"

I tried to keep my voice even. "Nothing."

He traced the outline of his facial scar. "Give me a name and I'll forget where it came from. No one has to know you told on one of your fraternity brothers."

"There's no one to tell on. If someone in our fraternity did it, I'd know about it. That was much too big a deal to keep quiet."

He snorted. "You're lying, Matthews. Tell me who did it and I'll forget the bad vibes. We could start over. Be buddies."

"I can't tell you who did it because I don't know."

"Know what, Matthews? I wouldn't be surprised if you were in on it."

"I wasn't. Can I please go now?"

His expression turned malevolent. "No, you may not!"

"Okay, but I can't answer your question."

He leaned in close to my face. "I heard your fat friend did it. What's his name? 'Hotdog.' Nod your head if I'm right and you can go."

"Bigdog? You mean Bigdog?" I felt claustrophobic, like there wasn't enough space or air for the two of us.

"Yeah, that's it. Bigdog."

I shook my head. "He wasn't in on it. If he was, I'd have heard all about it, and I haven't heard squat."

Montrose sneered. "I don't much like you, Matthews. Know why?"

Because you're a neo-Nazi pinhead who envies anyone with more than a teaspoon of gray matter? "You think I was disrespectful when I didn't pull over on the way to the hospital."

"That's only part of it. I got notice you're goin' to court on that speeding ticket."

"You said I could take it to court." I looked up and saw Amelia Cruz walking toward us carrying two medium-sized boxes, one under each arm. She appeared to be headed toward the post office and hadn't yet seen me. But people always look into police cars to see if anything interesting is happening and I figured it was a matter of time before she spotted me.

He gave me a vicious look. "You'd be better off payin' the ticket and stayin' outta my way."

Amelia made eye contact with me. She shifted the boxes under her left arm and strode purposefully toward Montrose's car. When she reached it she bent over and knocked on the passenger side window. I lowered it without asking permission. "Is there something wrong, officer?" Amelia asked, her face creased with concern.

"Police business, ma'am. I take it you know this boy?"

"Yes, I know Bryan very well. Is he in some kind of trouble?" She reached in and placed her hand on my shoulder.

Montrose shifted in his seat. "No, not exactly."

"Can I go then?" I said, putting my hand on top of hers.

Montrose affected a friendly tone. "Sure. Why not? You give me a call if you hear anything about that vandalism over at the college."

My hands trembled as I got out. I watched Montrose pull into the sparse downtown traffic.

"Is that the cop that gave you the phony ticket?" Amelia asked me.

"Yeah. That's him."

She looked into my eyes. "You look like you could use a hug."

"I could."

She set her boxes on the sidewalk and held me close to her. My tears surprised both of us.

Christmas Eve, the Zaleskis and I drove over to Candy Cane Lane, a well-to-do neighborhood that competed for holiday prizes for best outdoor lighting. Afterwards, we went home and opened presents from under a tree Lydia and I had cut in the Umatilla National Forest. Reva and I had decorated it with multi-colored bubble lights, glass ornaments and tinsel. I'd gotten Dr. Z a sturdy looking briar pipe that I thought fit his personality. For Reva, I bought a pair of down slippers because she was always complaining the wood floors were colder than the ones she got used to growing up in Russia. Their gift to me was a leather jacket from Italy, reddish brown like mahogany and soft as baby skin. It could have been a tad larger in the shoulders but I didn't care.

Christmas day I spent with Lydia at the Cruz'. She'd told me to expect a few presents under the tree and I arrived with several of my own. I bought Hector a Swiss Army knife that included a little pair of scissors for trimming his moustache. For Yolanda I bought a good pair of pinking shears, since she was forever cutting out patterns and sewing clothes. "I'm big on scissors this year," I joked as I handed Amelia her gift, a cookbook I'd special ordered through the University Bookstore in Seattle. It was called *Authentic Recipes from Old Mexico* and I secretly hoped she try out a few on me. I gave Lydia a pair of cowboy boots she'd tried on at the Frontier Western Apparel store next to the Fairgrounds. Thrilled, she kissed me a little too passionately in front of Hector, who told her to mind her "P's and Q's." To my surprise, to *everyone's* surprise, she told him to mind his own business.

My court date got scheduled for January 8, which was good; I wanted it over and done with before my February 18 match with Vladimir Primalov. I hoped Montrose would have better things to do than to show up in traffic court, but pretty much knew that would be too good to be true. I arrived at the Whitman County Courthouse fifteen minutes early, took a nervous pee in the men's room and located my name on a roster of cases to be heard in Courtroom B. I found it without asking for directions.

I surveyed the room. Five rows of wooden benches, a long bookshelf with an impressive set of law books, American and Washington State flags at the front and a door in between that read: "To Judges Chambers and Court Reporter." Taking a seat in the middle of the room, I looked over the other ticketed drivers. A middle-aged woman in a wheelchair with her purse slung over the back scrutinized some papers. An overweight man in a gray pinstriped business suit tugged at his collar and read the meager *Union-Bulletin* Sports section. His shirt and suit had been purchased at a time when he'd worn a much smaller size. Seated near him, a nervous young man in shabby clothing fingered a well-worn baseball cap. He worked his teeth with a toothpick, which I hoped for his sake he'd lose before the judge appeared. In the front row, an elderly woman carried a black cane and appeared to have difficulty breathing. A young woman with big hair and a rhinestone-studded jacket accompanied her.

Montrose strolled in just moments before a hefty woman bailiff asked the courtroom to "all rise." His presence seemed to drop the room temperature by ten degrees. The Honorable Judge Bertram Meyer walked in from a door to the left of his elevated podium, struck his gavel down decisively and asked us to be seated. I looked over at Montrose, who had taken a seat in the front row. I thought he might not have noticed me, but then he turned and very deliberately eyed me. He was trying to look intimidating, which wasn't hard given his imposing size and irritable disposition. I returned his stare, feeling simultaneously annoyed and frightened.

The bailiff called the first case a few minutes after nine a.m. She named Sarah Wilkins, the elderly woman with the cane. The big-haired blonde helped Mrs. Wilkins to her feet and announced to Judge Meyer that her mother had a serious case of emphysema. The defendant had parked in a "loading only" zone to avoid a long walk and produced a note from her doctor stating she should refrain from walking more than thirty feet. She explained to the judge that she had only gone into the Save More Pharmacy to pick up a prescription and that her car was in the loading zone less than five minutes. He dismissed the case. I privately wondered how this woman could possibly be competent to pilot a two-ton automobile. *Yet I'm in trouble for no reason other than the fact that some yahoo cop has a grudge against me.*

Next up was a man in his early twenties named Seth Jones. He'd disposed of his toothpick, but walked up front wearing the weathered cap I'd noticed when I first sat down. It read "John Deere" on the front. Seth was chewing gum furiously and scratching behind his ear when the judge ordered him to kindly remove his cap. When the judge asked him to raise his right hand and swear to tell the truth, the whole truth and nothing but the truth, Seth raised his left hand. The judge snapped, "Your other *right* hand!"

Montrose let out a ragged and inappropriate burst of laughter and exchanged "Do you believe it?" expressions with the bailiff. Seth had also been ticketed for speeding, only he was caught doing forty-two in a thirty-five. *Allegedly caught,* I corrected myself, thinking his ticket could be as bogus as mine. Seth explained that he'd just gotten oversized tires for his truck and hadn't had his speedometer recalibrated. Handing the judge a receipt that showed he'd now done so, he asked the court to excuse him for going only a few miles an hour over the limit. Judge Meyer lectured the entire courtroom. "Intent to speed, or lack of intent, is irrelevant under the law. You're either speeding or you're obeying the law. It matters not whether you intend to speed." He proceeded to uphold the twenty-five-dollar fine and sent Seth on his way, taking any hope I had for leniency with him.

I was called next. I walked up front and was sworn in, unintentionally glancing at Montrose as I swore to tell the truth. Judge Meyer read my ticket aloud and noted that Officer Jack Montrose, who wrote the ticket, was in attendance. Turning to me the judge said, "With radar involved, this looks pretty straightforward, Mr. Matthews. What do you have to say?"

"There's just no way I was speeding, your Honor. I had just dropped off my girlfriend and turned onto Ninth Avenue when I saw Officer Montrose's car parked a block ahead, just past the railroad tracks by Rees. The last thing on earth I would do is speed past a policeman so I went slowly and watched my speedometer. I was going twenty-one, and my speedometer's accurate."

"And how do you know that?"

"I recently checked it against the mileage posts just outside town on the way to Dixie. It was right on for five miles."

The judge looked over at Montrose. "Officer Montrose, could your radar have been off that night?"

Montrose rose and replied in a clear voice. "No, your Honor. It had just been recalibrated the day of the infraction. I've attached a copy of the certification to the back of Mr. Matthews' ticket."

"Yes, I see that. Thank you, Officer." Looking back at me Judge Meyer said, "Alas, Mr. Matthews. If I'm forced to choose between the Police Department's finely honed electronic equipment and the mileage posts on the way to Dixie, I'm afraid I'll have to take the former."

"I have no doubt that Officer Montrose's radar was functioning properly, your Honor." I was perfectly aware of jumping into scalding hot water, but couldn't stop myself. I didn't want to stop myself.

Judge Meyer looked bewildered. "I don't understand," he said, looking over at Montrose and then back at me. "If you accept that the radar was working properly, then what are you doing in my courtroom contesting this ticket? Radar doesn't lie!"

"The radar didn't write the ticket, your Honor."

A stir of voices washed over the courtroom. Someone behind me and to my right said, "Oh shit!" loud enough for the bailiff to say, "Order in the courtroom!" It reminded me of a Perry Mason episode, when Perry pointed out the real killer and pandemonium broke loose. I turned enough to see Montrose snarling at me, his body rigid with anger.

Judge Meyer merely looked incredulous. When the room quieted he cleared his throat. "Let me make certain I'm understanding you, Mr. Matthews. Are you suggesting that Officer Montrose's radar gun was working properly, that it would have gotten you going . . . uh, what did you say . . . uh, twenty-one miles per hour, and that, in spite of that, Officer Montrose wrote you a ticket for going thirty-seven?"

"I'm saying that as God is my witness I was not going thirty-seven miles an hour. I'm saying that I was going exactly twenty-one. As I told the court, I saw Officer Montrose as soon as I turned the corner onto Ninth. I'd have to be the stupidest person in the world to accelerate and speed right past a police car. I'm saying that I was *really* careful to stay under the speed limit."

Judge Meyer waved the ticket for everyone in the courtroom to see. "Yes, Mr. Matthews, but I said 'radar doesn't lie,' and you said, 'the *radar* didn't write the ticket.' Like . . . the radar didn't write the ticket, Officer Montrose did. To me that would imply that you believe Officer Montrose acted dishonestly. That he deliberately wrote you a ticket based on a lie."

"I'm saying I know for one-hundred percent certain I wasn't speeding."

"May I address the court, your Honor?" Montrose said in a belligerent voice, his jaw jutting out absurdly.

"Yes, please do," the judge answered, before reaching for a glass of water. I wished I had one.

"There's a history here, your Honor. Mr. Matthews thinks I gave him a bogus ticket because of a little run in we had several months ago. He was speeding then, too, but he got out of it on a technicality. Now, he'd rather question my integrity than accept the fact that I caught him speeding a *second* time, and on an occasion where he can't avoid responsibility for his actions."

Judge Meyer looked to me for a response.

"That's partly true, your Honor, the part about there being a history. But the technicality Officer Montrose is referring to was not a technicality in any sense of the word. Police Chief Carter himself told Officer Montrose not to write that first ticket because I was speeding on the way to the hospital to save my friend's life. And Officer Montrose is right when he says I think this ticket is bogus, because it's the very definition of bogus. That's why I chose to fight it. I was written up for going thirty-seven in a twenty-five at a time I knew I was being observed by a police car. That alone should tell you something is off here. Officer Montrose doesn't like me and—"

"Whoa!" Judge Meyer said, interrupting me and slamming down his gavel. "Let's stick to the facts around here and keep personalities out of it.

This is a court of law. I don't know how you got the idea that Officer Montrose dislikes you, but—"

"I got the idea he doesn't like me because he told me he doesn't like me!" Quid pro quo. The judge interrupted me. I interrupted the judge.

Judge Meyer looked over at Montrose who was giving me his best "You better keep your mouth shut" look! Montrose turned to the judge and said, "I never said any such thing, your Honor. I'm a professional law officer. Even if I did dislike a particular citizen I would keep it to myself and treat him fairly under the law."

"You told me you didn't like me in your squad car a few days before Christmas. Just outside the post office. And I'm quoting you. That's *exactly* what you said."

"Wait a minute, Mr. Matthews," Judge Meyer blustered. "Stop right there! I've had about enough of this. Officer Montrose is not a man who would write a bogus ticket or try to intimidate a citizen. Did you know he volunteers his free time to coach Little League football? Did you know he has served his country and is a decorated Vietnam veteran?"

Did you know he brags about his necklace of 'gook' ears? I wanted to say. Instead I folded my arms. "I put my hand on the Bible a few minutes ago and swore to tell the truth. I swear to God Officer Montrose told he didn't like me. I swear to God I was not speeding the night he wrote me this ticket. I'm under oath and I'm telling you the truth."

Judge Meyer said, "Mr. Matthews, I'm going to advise you to stop disparaging this fine police officer or you'll find yourself in contempt of court. And I'm ruling against you on this ticket. If the radar says you were speeding, then you were speeding. It's that simple no matter how complicated you'd like to make it. Pay the cashier the twenty-five dollar fine on your way out and consider yourself lucky."

I kept my mouth shut, though I gave strong consideration to asking Judge Meyer the procedure for appealing his ruling. For that matter, I also considered spitting on the floor of his courtroom. I turned and walked out, conscious of the disbelieving stares of the remaining defendants. By keeping my eyes on the exit door I avoided looking back at Montrose. I marched to the cashier's window, paid the court its filthy lucre and stomped out of the courthouse.

I'd parked a block away in a parking lot for courthouse visitors. As I reached my car a familiar voice behind me barked, "Matthews!" Startled, I jerked around to see Montrose no more than three feet behind me. How he got that close without my knowing spooked me.

"What?" I blurted out. The image of Montrose sneaking through tropical vegetation in a Vietnam jungle came to mind.

"The next time you fuck with me is the last time!" Spittle flew from his mouth.

I stood dumbstruck at the door of my car, a spider of fear crawling down the length of my spine. No words came from my mouth.

"Do . . . you . . . understand, college boy?" Montrose demanded, his eyes blazing murderously.

"I do understand. I get it. I won't mess with you any more." My voice shook so hard it seemed unrecognizable. For a moment I wondered if he even heard me.

"You, by God, better not!" The cords in his neck bulged hideously.

Scrambling to get behind the wheel, I fumbled the car key trying to get it into the ignition. My arms felt like rubber. I retrieved the key from the floor mat and stole a quick glance at Montrose a few feet away. Despite my words of submission, he looked close to snapping. Staring straight ahead now, a realization plowed into me as I finally jammed the key into the ignition. Officer Jack Montrose wanted to kill me.

Chapter 6
Vlad the Impaler

With the Montrose altercation weighing on my mind, I threw myself into preparation for the match with Vladimir Primalov. I felt grateful for the distraction, though several times I'd find myself looking at a chessboard and notice my hand trembling. On one such occasion, Dr. Z detected an expression of fear and mistakenly assumed it had to do with facing the Russian Grandmaster. "Let it in, Bryan," he instructed me. "Take the fear tenderly in your arms and make friends with it."

I wanted to tell him it was a psycho cop who scared me, not Primalov, but kept the truth to myself. Still, Dr. Z's strategy of embracing the fear was helpful at those times my mind returned to the peril posed by Montrose.

My chess teammates worked as a group to annotate several of Primalov's recent games with Mikhail Tal and Boris Spassky. The idea had been Dr. Z's suggestion, an extra credit class assignment. Their efforts helped to familiarize me with Primalov's strengths, which included positional sacrifices and attacking from cramped positions. Weaknesses were harder to find.

Dr. Zaleski instructed me to read Vukovic's newest book, *The Art of Attack in Chess*. And he carved enough time from his busy schedule to play me two games a day, one with the White pieces and one with Black. In one of our more spirited games, Dr. Z uncharacteristically captured away from the center to open lines and then attack a castled king using the king bishop file. I looked across the board. "Is that a Vladimir Primalov move?"

Dr. Z smiled and nodded yes. "As best I can, I'm trying to adopt Vladimir's style of play. It's more modern than mine."

Reva, overhearing our conversation from the kitchen, shouted, "Just don't adopt Vladimir's personality!"

"There's no danger of that," Dr. Z responded, loud enough for his wife to hear.

"Is he really that bad?" I asked.

His smile disappeared. "It's one of Vladimir's most potent weapons. And he knows it. Be prepared for his antics or he'll stomp you into the ground."

"Even though I'm a lowly eighteen-year-old college student?"

"*Especially* because you're a college student! Think about it, Bryan. It is a no-win situation for Primalov. If he wins, it's expected, so it's no big deal. Were you to get a draw or, God forbid, a win over the number three player in the world, it would be a shocking upset. The proud Russian would be utterly humiliated. So it won't be enough for him to win, he will try to embarrass you. Trust me."

"If it's a no-win situation, why does he even consent to do the exhibition?"

"Ego, pure and simple. Vladimir Primalov would never even consider the possibility of being beaten by a college student. Believe me, I know him well. He is *supremely* confident, an egomaniac! Even the Russian public has grown tired of his boorish behavior. And they *adore* their Grandmasters. They're held up as national heroes."

"Back to charm school, Comrade Primalov."

"Do you know what we called him on the European chess circuit?"

"*Time* magazine called him 'The Russian Prima Donna.'"

"Yes, and he is a prima donna, as temperamental and conceited as they come. That's for sure. But those who knew him best referred to him as 'Vlad the Impaler.'"

"After Dracula?"

"Indeed, because Vladimir's goal is to suck the very life out of his opponents. He wants to win just like you and I do, but first he wants to intimidate you, grind you into the board. Toward that end he can be rude, brash, loudmouthed, insulting, even menacing."

I leaned back in my chair. "Menacing? How can a chess player be menacing?"

"Did you ever see the heavyweight champion 'Sonny' Liston just before a fight was to begin? When the referee was giving the boxers final instructions? Liston was a convicted felon who learned prizefighting in prison. He liked to stare down his opponent, give him a murderous glare from inches away right before a fight was to begin. Most of his fights were over before the first punch was thrown. That's what Vladimir Primalov tries to do. He glowers at his opponent and gets him thinking about things other than chess."

I smiled. "And what happened to Sonny Liston?"

"What?" he asked, with a puzzled expression.

"What happened to Sonny Liston?"

"What do you mean?"

"1964, Dr Z. What happened to the big, bad Charles 'Sonny' Liston when he got in the ring with the young upstart Cassius Marcellus Clay?"

"He lost."

"Yeah, he lost! I watched the fight with my father. Sonny Liston was a seven-to-one favorite and got his butt kicked all over the ring on national television. And I'm not going to be intimidated by Vladimir Primalov."

With so much happening, I forgot to tell Bigdog that Jack Montrose had mentioned his name in connection with the flagpole prank. When I did remember, I found him in his third-floor room at the Phi Delt house and closed the door. Big Brother and the Holding Company blared in the next room, which was good. I didn't want to be overheard and the walls of the house were paper-thin.

"What's the deal, Bryan? You seem sort of spaced lately."

"What do you mean?"

"You never even asked me about Christmas in London."

"Sorry. How was London?"

"Cool. I saved Chainsaw's life. First day we were over there. He forgot the traffic goes the wrong way and stepped off a curb without looking. I jerked him back or this limey asshole would've pancaked him. Death by mini-Cooper!"

I laughed. "Good work, Bigdog. Now we've both saved a brother."

He grinned from ear to ear. "All in a day's work."

"Did you roll London Bridge?" I was referring to Bigdog's pastime of being rolled along the ground to measure distances.

"I rolled it on a Saturday night. We were wasted. It was one hundred sixty-eight revolutions, if I remember correctly. Chainsaw counted along with Simon, our British friend. Remind me to tell you some Simon stories."

"Go for it."

"Okay. We're driving around London and Simon's hanging his head out of our rental car, yelling, 'Rotten hat, lady! Rotten hat!' It sounds funnier when he does it 'cause of his Cockney accent. He screams it at every woman that's wearing a hat and he's *really* into it! He *hates* women's hats. Says they make him crazy!" Bigdog laughed at the memory, triggering an asthmatic wheeze in his throat. "But you came up here for a reason. What's up?"

"Okay. I go to the Post Office before Christmas to mail some presents and this cop, Montrose, the one who hates me—"

"The prick that wrote you the phony speeding ticket?"

I nodded. "Anyway Montrose corners me when I come out of the Post Office and asks me who rat fucked the flagpole."

"And you tell him you don't know squat."

"My exact words."

"So what's the problem?"

"Well, Montrose says someone already told him who did it. And he names you. Only he refers to you as 'Hotdog.'"

Bigdog let out raspy laugh. "Hotdog. That's good."

"I told him it couldn't possibly be you because I'd have heard about it. But I think he knew I was lying."

"I still don't see the problem."

"The problem is the cops are hot to nail someone for this and it sounds like someone ratted you out."

Bigdog laughed. "Bryan. I like you. I liked you from the day we met at the football game in La Grande. You're a good brother, but you are *so* green."

"What do you mean?"

He hand-combed his dark hair. "It doesn't matter if someone ratted me out. I don't give two shits who told this Montrose guy I was in on it because it wouldn't be anyone who's really in the know."

"Explain that to me."

"Connect the dots. Only four people *really* know who did it. That would be me, Chainsaw, Slider and Badger, because it was our gig. Other people may *think* they know we did it, but they weren't there so they can't prove it. Ergo, I have nothing to worry about because brothers don't rat out brothers. It's the code of silence."

"So you have no worry?"

"Zero, ought, naught, goose egg, zip, zilch! Nada!"

This time I laughed. Bigdog cracked me up. "And the code is foolproof?"

"Absolutely! Look, I got called into Sanderson's office the day after we did it. I'm always the number one suspect when something like this goes down." He smiled smugly. "The code of silence is foolproof. It has to be. I told Sanderson I knew nothing about it. What can he do? Chainsaw isn't going to confess. Slider isn't going to confess. Badger isn't going to confess. We keep quiet and it doesn't matter who thinks we did it. Silence really is golden, Bryan. You just have to trust the code!"

"Bryan. It's time I told you about my friend Arthur Dake." Dr. Z and I braved the cold and took a brisk walk after stuffing ourselves on Reva's cabbage rolls and rye bread. Eight days were left before my exhibition game with Vladimir Primalov and Dr. Z was pulling out all the stops to build my confidence.

"I've heard of him. The Grandmaster who lives in Oregon, right?"

"Yes," Dr. Z answered. "Only Arthur's an *International* Grandmaster."

"Oh." The puff of steam from my mouth reminded me the temperature was in the teens. The walk had been my idea. Now I had second thoughts.

"Arthur is someone who never picked up a chess piece until he was seventeen. Seventeen! Think of it! He had dropped out of high school to become a merchant seaman and was bumming a bed at the YMCA in downtown Portland. While he was there, a couple down-on-their-luck Russian immigrants taught him the moves. This is where it gets interesting. Five years later, Arthur Dake defeated the great Alexander Alekhine and became the first American to beat a sitting world champion." He paused and looked at me, presumably to see if his message was sinking in.

"Wow!" I exclaimed. "That's unbelievable."

"It is, but believe me, it happened exactly like I told you." Dr. Z paused to wipe his runny nose. "Certainly you understand why I'm telling you this story."

"If Arthur Dake can beat Alekhine after five years of study, Bryan Matthews can beat Primalov after more than ten. Or something like that."

"Yes, but I want to give you more than hope, Bryan. I want to give you *faith*. I want you to go into that game with a *conviction* that you can defeat Vladimir Primalov. Because you can!"

"You really believe that? I mean . . . I do, but sometimes I think you expect Primalov to manhandle me."

"Let me tell you something, Bryan. There isn't a chess player alive who could manhandle you. Lose? Yes. Manhandle? No."

"What about Bobby Fischer?"

"He could beat you, but he wouldn't destroy you in the process. Not since last summer, anyway. You have a great gift! I watch you play. I play against you every day, and yet you never cease to amaze me. The combinations and sacrifices you come up with, the way you exploit positional advantages and pounce on your opponent's mistakes. Sometimes I just stare at the board and marvel at the moves you dream up."

"Thank you. Do you think I'm lacking confidence?"

"You're a hard one to read, Bryan Matthews. Reva assures me you have all the confidence in the world, but I don't always see it. I'm not sure you know how good you are."

I stopped walking under a streetlight a block from the Zaleski's house. I will never forget this moment. Shrouded in frozen fog, the neighborhood stood as still as a painting. The cold had turned Dr. Z's nose red and made his movements appear tense. I looked him in the eye. "I want to explain something. And I hope you don't think I'm just full of myself because I'm only eighteen. Reva is right. I *am* confident. I don't care if Primalov is the third best player in the world. I don't care if he's better than I am. I'm at the top of my game right now and I know his tendencies backwards and forwards. He's goin' down!"

––––––––––––

Vladimir Primalov's chartered plane, a twin-engine Beech 18 Super H, landed at the Walla Walla City-County Airport on a wintry, sunless Saturday afternoon. His flight had originated in San Francisco, where he'd spent five days trouncing an impressive field at the California Open, a tune-up for the United States Open to be held the first week of March in Harrisburg, Pennsylvania.

Dr. Z and Reva picked up Primalov at the airport and drove him to The Pony Soldier Inn, chosen because it was walking distance to the venue. Primalov was traveling without his wife, Iroda Primalova, who'd been forced to stay behind in Moscow because of visa problems. This was a disappointment for Reva, who told me she and Iroda had become close friends during the years Dr. Z coached in Leningrad. Reva explained how the KGB was loath to allow married couples to leave Mother Russia together, as they were more likely to defect.

A photo of a scowling Primalov was given front-page treatment on the Sunday *Walla Walla Union-Bulletin*. The big Russian looked the part. A

tall, robust man in his mid-forties, he exuded both power and supreme confidence as he descended the steps of his chartered plane. According to the
companion article, a bevy of reporters and photographers had been on hand
to greet him.

We were set to square off at the Harper Joy Theatre the following evening. Posters appeared in the windows of downtown business and were
tacked to telephone poles all over town. They read: *The Whitman Chess
Program – "A Celebration of Brilliance!"* Professionally done by The
Printer's Inkwell on Main, they featured black and white headshots of the
two of us. Primalov's photo showed him glowering at the camera, his neck-
tie loosened and dark hair looking wild and unkempt. Below it read:
*Vladimir Primalov, Russian International Grandmaster and World Cham-
pionship Contender.* My photo, one I'd never before seen, caught me gazing
downward at a chessboard, my chin resting on my right fist like Rodin's
Thinker. I had no idea when it was taken, but my best guess was that Joan
Levy was the photographer, as she would occasionally snap pictures of fellow chess team members. Below my photo were the words: *Bryan
Matthews, Whitman Chess Champion and American National Master.*
Given the political tension and military rivalry between our respective
countries, the college played up the America versus Russia theme. At the
bottom of the poster were the particulars. Harper Joy Theatre, Sunday,
February 18, 8:00 p.m. Live game commentary by Dr. Zdenek Zaleski, International Grandmaster and Whitman chess coach. Arrive early! No one
will be admitted after the game begins. Admission: one dollar with Whitman College Student Body Card, five dollars to members of the community.
Proceeds benefit the Whitman College Chess Program.

Mercifully, Sunday morning arrived and I woke shivering in my bunk on
Second Old, my electric blanket cranked to the max. I'd managed a good
night's sleep despite a bizarre dream (I drive to Jack Montrose's house, tie
a chain around a small leafless tree in his front yard and drive off, pulling
the tree out by its roots).

Lydia stopped by at lunchtime, but only for a few minutes. Reva invited
her to stay for tuna salad sandwiches and canned pickles but she declined,
thinking she would be a distraction. I walked her out to her car and accepted a good luck kiss. She drove off after telling me she would say a
prayer for me to play my very best. Watching her turn the corner and disappear made me inexplicably sad.

I trudged back indoors where Dr. Z asked me to join him in the den for
some last minute advice. "Any questions, Bryan?"

"Actually, I do. I've been wondering . . . when Grandmasters, or World
Championship contenders like Primalov lose to less-skilled players, is it because they take them too lightly, or is it something else?"

"I wish I knew. I've been upset many times over the years, and I've taken out more than my share of Grandmasters who had higher Elo ratings. But your theory is as sound as any I've heard. Sometimes the better player overplays by attacking prematurely, assuming the defensive skill of his opponent is inadequate."

"There must be other reasons."

"Sure there are. It can be as simple as a bad night's sleep, or even showing up drunk."

"A Grandmaster would allow that to happen?"

"It happens more than it should. There was a Russian Grandmaster in the thirties by the name of Vissa Ivanowich. We called him the Czar. A gifted player with the perfect balance of attack and defense, like Botvinnik and Spassky. Unfortunately, the Czar loved his Vodka more than he loved the game of chess and it cost him from time to time. But don't expect something like that to happen with Vladimir Primalov. He likes his Vodka as much as any Russian, but he's much too disciplined to do anything foolish."

"I know that. I guess I'm looking for some kind of an advantage. Something I can take to the board with me."

Dr. Z smiled reassuringly. "You have an advantage if you draw White and get to play the Stonewall Attack. Vladimir won't be expecting it because it's out of favor."

"Okay, let's assume I'm lucky enough to draw White and let's assume I catch Primalov by surprise. I still don't see why that would be an advantage against a World Championship contender."

"The advantage is there because of all the hours you've studied the Stonewall. Your preparation for the opening sequence is superb. It couldn't be better! You've mastered the matter of move order and you're flexible enough to adapt to whatever Vladimir does. You know every possible theme that occurs in Stonewall pawn formations. You know how to maximize the effect of your good Bishop and minimize the effect of your bad Bishop. You know exactly how to build a fortress of dark-squared pawns and deliver mate using different pieces. I tell you, if you draw White tonight, you'll give Vladimir a run for his money."

"You're not just saying that?"

"No. I'm serious. Think of it this way, Bryan. When it comes to playing the Stonewall, you *are* a Grandmaster!"

I smiled. "Ooh, I like that!"

"Good."

"And if I draw Black?"

"You'll still make a fine showing. As I've told you before, so much of the work is done before we come to the board. This was not always true in years past. Your opening preparation is sound whether you play White or Black. That's why I have so much confidence in you."

"Thanks."

He shook his head and looked up at the ceiling.

"What is it?"

"I was just thinking how I'd love to be inside that mind of yours to-night, to borrow your creativity, your tactical skill for one game against Vladimir Primalov. To be back in my prime and put my former student in his place."

"I'll try and do it for you. If I play my best chess—"

"It's not the chess that worries me most. It's Vladimir's penchant for intimidating his opponents. Don't give him the chance to upset you. Don't even look at him during the game."

"Am I supposed to look away every time he looks at me?"

"Yes!"

"I'm not going to be intimidated by looking at him. Maybe if he makes killer moves, but not because of the way he looks at me."

"You look nervous now and you haven't even started."

"I am nervous, but I'll be fine once I start moving the pieces. I always am."

Dr. Z smiled and shook his head.

"What is it?" I asked.

"I hope you're right. I hope you can contain your nerves, but I'm telling you, Vladimir's psychological tactics are legendary. When he defeated Bobby Fischer at the Varna Olympics in 1962, he did it by being rude and obnoxious. Oh, he made some great moves, too, but he won because he got inside Bobby's head."

"How does he do it?"

"He does it by *hating* them. He hates his opponent and he hates to lose and you can actually feel his hatred across the board. It's like you're swimming in it, and it affects the level of your play. Let me tell you something. If something should happen tonight and you come away with an advantage, Vladimir will direct his menace at you and you *will* feel it."

"Okay, I'll be nervous, but I'm not going to be afraid of the guy."

"How nervous are you now?"

"I've got enough butterflies to blot out the sun."

He raised his eyebrows. "You all right?"

I nodded. "Like I said, I'll be focused as soon as I sit down at the board. I'm sure of it."

"That's good. There's a fine line between nervousness and excitement." Eyes wide, he took a deep breath and released it slowly through his pursed lips.

"Do *you* have butterflies, Dr. Z?"

"I'm too old to get butterflies. Nowadays I get moths, but there is much more room now in my stomach."

The temperature hovered in the mid-twenties as I walked from the frater-nity house to the Harper Joy Theatre. Winter squeezed the barren trees in its vice grip. It was only a couple blocks, but the crisp air cleared my head like a tonic. And Dr. Z's warnings had had the paradoxical effect of settling me down. *He's doing his raja yoga thing,* I thought to myself. *Now, if I can just do my part.*

A group of at least fifty people waited in line for the front door to open, hugging themselves in bulky parkas and stomping feet on the pavement to ward off the cold. Someone recognized me as I cut behind the building to the backstage door. Dressed like Nanook of the North, he called out, "Go get 'em, Bryan!" That precipitated several shouts of encouragement from the others. I turned and waved, recognizing a fellow who sat across from me in French class, a Beta named Steve Fadden, in danger of failing because of his talent for confusing verb tenses. *My God! Even the Betas are pulling for me.*

I knocked on the backstage door, thankful for my gloves. The door magically opened a few seconds later and a grim-faced Javad Azizi appeared. "How're you doing?" he asked, his British accent as crisp as the night air.

"Pretty good, considering."

"Primalov's already here. He got here about a half-hour ago with Dr. and Mrs. Z."

"What's he like? Dr. Z won't allow me to meet him until right before we start."

Javad closed the door as quickly as possible. "Rude, just like everyone says."

"Did you meet him?"

"I guess so. We were introduced. He's not exactly friendly."

"So I hear."

"He just finished checking out the stage a few minutes ago . . . the seating, the board, the pieces, the time clocks, the monitors, the chairs, the lighting, backstage, you name it. A bona fide control freak."

Dr. Z spotted me as he came through the door that went onto the stage. "Bryan," he exclaimed, "I was beginning to wonder when you were going to show up. How're you doing?"

"I'm fine. Ready to rock'n'roll." I unzipped my leather jacket and pulled off my gloves as he walked over to greet me. Just seeing him had the effect of steadying my nerves.

"Excellent!" He shook my hand. "Let me show you the setup before the place fills up. I believe they're only minutes from letting people in. It's damn cold out there and they don't want the early arrivals to freeze to death."

I followed Dr. Z up some carpeted steps and onto the stage. The wood floor was creaky, reminding me of the ancient Whitman gymnasium where we played pickup games of basketball. Looking out at the vacant seats made my stomach flip-flop. I quickly focused on the board, recognizing it as Dr. Z's favorite, one we had played on a hundred times. "You approve of the board?" he asked with a knowing grin.

"Oh, yes. I definitely approve." I knew the grain of the maple on every square of that board, the exact heft of every piece. A master craftsman made it after World War II, a friend of Dr. Z's in his native Poland. *Home field advantage,* I thought, suppressing a smile.

"Quiet, please!" signs were posted all over the room. No one knew if our Walla Walla audience would know the first thing about chess etiquette, but Dr. Z told me privately that anyone creating a distraction would be asked to leave. Barry Palmer, the manager of the Harper Joy Theatre and a former bouncer at the infamous Rathskeller Tavern in Coeur d'Alene, would do the honors.

Joan Levy waved from the back of the theater. As usual, she was dressed in all black and, from a distance, appeared to be wearing black lipstick. She and Jeremy Spencer would act as ushers and monitors to keep the room quiet. Ethan was twenty feet off to my right, situating the blackboard Dr. Z would be writing on to provide his live game commentary. Only it wasn't an ordinary blackboard, it was a smooth, hard white-colored panel. Reluctantly, Vladimir Primalov had given his consent to allow an ongoing written commentary, thus informing attendees how the match was going. No one asked for my permission, but I thought it was a terrific idea. As explained to me, Dr. Z would gear his comments for beginning to average chess players, writing down key points as the game progressed. Examples: "White wants to attack the Black rook but needs more firepower," or, "Prevents Black from trading his knight for the bishop . . . advantage White!"

Ethan spotted me and ran onstage, shaking my hand with more enthusiasm than he'd exhibited at any time since his head injury. "Did you get a program?" he asked, his face flushed with excitement.

"Not yet."

"Here." Ethan took a folded program from his back pocket and handed it to me. "Joan and Jeremy and I are passing them out as people take their seats. When play starts, I'm in charge of duplicating all the moves on the big chessboard." He motioned over to the mock chessboard. Made from felt and mounted on a backing of plywood, it measured six- by six-foot. Someone in Theater Arts had done a good job, constructing it especially for the occasion. At Dr. Z's direction, Ethan had placed the big board directly in front of the stage and just to left for the benefit of the audience. As soon as Primalov or I completed a move and pressed the time clock, Ethan would move the same piece to the same square on the mock chessboard. It was large enough that anyone in the theater would easily be able to follow our moves and situated so as not to block the view of the stage.

I said, "If I blunder, maybe you could forget to show everyone."

Ethan let loose an uneasy laugh. "No way you're going to blunder. You're going to make me proud, Rooms."

"I'll do my best."

Dr. Z said, "You will do your best ever, Bryan. You've proven to me you play your best under pressure."

"Then I ought to be sensational."

Joan stuck her head in a doorway and called out, "They're opening the doors. Here they come!"

"Let's go backstage," I said quickly to Dr. Z. Not wanting to be in the position of greeting people and becoming distracted, I wanted to be out of sight.

Dr. Z and I ducked behind the curtains and through the door that took us backstage. We walked down a few steps and into a hallway lined with stage props and storage containers. From there he showed me to my dressing room, smaller than I had imagined but large enough for a couch with a horrid floral print. The room smelled of mildew and stale cigarettes. The carpet was ruddy brown and in bad shape, worn from years of makeup stains and cigarette burns. The wall opposite the couch had a large mirror surrounded by lights and next to that there was a closet with a row of empty hangars. On the wall was a sign that read: *Note to actors – Before exiting to receive the adoration and praise of your fans, please double check your appearance or face the wrath of the costume needle ninjas.* Dr. Z patiently watched me take it all in and said, "I'll be back in about a half-hour to introduce you to Vladimir. You want a Coke or anything?"

"A nice cup of tea would be great, if they have it."

"I'll have Miles bring you one. Meanwhile, just relax. You're very well prepared for this, Bryan. Enjoy your moment in the limelight. You're going to play *fantastic* chess."

"Thanks," I said as he left the room. I sat on the couch and took out the program Ethan had handed me. *"A Celebration of Brilliance!"* was written across the top and then, in bold capital letters, PLEASE REMAIN QUIET DURING PLAY! Below that was my opponent's biography. *Vladimir Primalov was born April 12, 1924, in Moscow, Russia. He fell in love with the royal game after being given a chess set for his fourth birthday. In 1946, he became a student of Grandmaster Zdenek Zaleski and within a year won the USSR championship for young masters. He earned the Grandmaster title that same year and went on to win the 1958 National and World Open events. Vladimir's best results include wins in tournament play over World Champion Bobby Fischer and former World Champion Mikhail Tal, the "Riga Magician." In 1966, in Berdichev, Ukraine, Vladimir tied for first with Boris Spassky in a tournament that featured no less than 39 Grandmasters! A fierce competitor with a reputation for striking fear in his opponents, he is known on the European chess circuit as "Vlad the Impaler," after the real life barbarian who inspired Bram Stoker's Dracula. In 1967, Vladimir became an instructor at Moscow's famous Botvinnik Chess School. His Elo Rating of 2788 is the third highest in the world!*

Someone knocked and I heard Miles Fletcher say, "It's me, Bryan. I've got some hot tea for you."

I opened the door and accepted a cup and saucer without inviting him in. Miles had a nervous habit of flipping his hair from his eyes and I didn't want his random energy around me. I thanked him and abruptly shut the door after receiving his good luck wishes.

My bio read: *Bryan Matthews was born August 26, 1951, in Black Diamond, Washington. He learned the moves at age six, watching his grandfather and uncle play at a family picnic. It wasn't too long before he won both the National Elementary School title and Scholastic K-12 Grade Championships. Then, at the tender age of ten, he "played up" and won the National Chess Championship in the sixteen and under division. Time Magazine has called Bryan " . . . the most promising American prodigy to come along since Bobby Fischer." By age eleven, as a student at the University of Washington's "Talented and Gifted Center," he was teaching chess to college-level students. Bryan says he enjoys chess because of the logic and complexity of the game and because it teaches some of life's most important lessons – like thinking carefully and avoiding acting on impulse. Off the board, he enjoys mathematics, listening to Dylan and spending time with his girlfriend.*

The reference to Lydia was unexpected, but I liked it and figured she would too. It had to be Dr. Z's doing, possibly in collaboration with Reva, who had recently taken a real liking to Lydia. I wondered if Lydia was already in the building and tried to feel her presence, but couldn't get past the butterflies. As arranged by Dr. Z, she, along with Hector, Amelia and Yolanda, would be seated in the first row. After that, it was first come, first seated. Bigdog had informed me there would be a large contingent of fraternity brothers, at least thirty and all on their best behavior. Deuce Twohey, Phi Delta Theta's unofficial source of pot and other hallucinogens, had promised to arrive early, sit close and "beam" me "a radiance of positive vibes." Conspicuous by his absence would be my father. I'd invited him, but he begged off at the last minute, citing heavy snowfalls in the mountain passes. Thinking about who would and wouldn't be there turned up the volume on my pre-game jitters and sent me in search of the backstage men's room.

I left my dressing room and reentered the hallway, filled with framed posters of plays and musicals from all over the world. Richard Burton as *Hamlet. Today, I am a Fountain Pen,* by Israel Horovitz. Passing a washing machine and dryer, I entered into a large open area, its ceiling lined with plumbing pipes and a sophisticated sprinkler system. Hanging from the largest pipe a sign read: Costume Construction and Wardrobe Storage. Indeed, there were costume racks that went the length of the building.

I knocked on the bathroom door and let myself in when no one responded. The floor was concrete with a drain in the middle, the walls a collage of newspaper art, magazine articles having to do with theater, Screen Actor Guild cards, front covers from Playbill, Life, and Newsweek. There was at least one mirror on each wall and a fire extinguisher in the corner. One framed poster showed a variety of ways to do women's hair and another how to tie different kinds of ties. I regretted not having the time to learn the proper way to tie a bow tie.

Sitting on the toilet I glanced at my watch. It was seven-thirty. The game was scheduled to begin punctually at eight. *God, how I'd love to win this game for Dr. Zaleski!* With that thought my butterflies intensified and I wished the time would move more quickly.

I returned to my little dressing room and began a breathing meditation to calm myself. "Pranayama," Dr. Z called it. After five minutes of watching my breath, he let himself in without knocking. "It's time to introduce the combatants," he said, his voice booming off the walls of the small room.

I got off the couch and followed him down the hallway to Primalov's dressing room. Once there, Dr. Z smiled at me and knocked gently. The door opened and the big Russian appeared with a Sports Illustrated in his hand. The cover showed "Pistol Pete" Maravich looking to the right while passing the basketball to his left, number 23 in his L.S.U. uniform and baggy socks. Primalov noticed me looking and made the magazine disappear behind his back. Dr. Z introduced us in a jovial manner, keeping things light.

"Pleased to meet you," I said, shaking Primalov's beefy hand. He wasn't exactly giving me the Sonny Liston stare down, but there was not a flicker of warmth in his steel gray eyes. His eyebrows looked like tangled brown wire thickets behind a pair of black-framed glasses, the kind worn by Senator Barry Goldwater. I wondered if the Vlad the Impaler nickname was a cruel reference to his mouthful of crooked teeth.

"Zdenek tells me you beat top college player from Iran for right to play me," Primalov said. Then he busied himself by brushing a bit of dandruff from the shoulder of his smart-looking navy suit.

"Yes. Javad Azizi. He'll be on stage, monitoring."

"Zdenek tells me you are promising student."

"Thank you. Dr. Zaleski is a wonderful coach, as I'm sure you know."

"He is best." He turned to face Dr. Z. "Not that it matters to outcome of game, but when do we draw sides for White or Black?"

Despite Dr. Z's repeated efforts to prepare me, I was taken aback by the absolute arrogance of this comment. I looked wide-eyed at Dr. Z, my jaws tightening into hard knots of tension.

Dr. Z casually answered, "If it's all right with you, Vladimir, I thought we'd draw sides on the stage. The audience will get a kick out of it."

"A kick?" Primalov asked.

"The audience will *enjoy* it," Dr. Z explained. "It will add to the drama."

"Fine," Primalov said. "We will need drama."

"Okay. We'll see you on stage in fifteen minutes," Dr. Z told him.

Primalov grunted and turned his gaze on me. "Play well." It came across as a command, not an exhortation.

"Thank you," I said, but he had already closed the door in our faces.

Dr. Z put his arm around me and walked me down the narrow hallway. "His arrogance is a good thing, Bryan. He's showing you that he's overconfident. That can only help." He gave my shoulder a reassuring squeeze and left me alone in my dressing room where I spent the longest fifteen minutes of my life.

I can't even remember what I was thinking when someone knocked on my door and said, "Showtime." It was Barry Palmer, the theater manager. The time was exactly two minutes before eight o'clock.

I jumped to my feet and checked myself one last time in the mirror. I'd chosen to wear a comfortable pair of brown dress slacks and a white sweater. Barry Palmer escorted me to the entrance to the stage where Dr. Z was waiting.

"Courage!" Dr. Z whispered, an earnest expression on his weathered face. Turning to Mr. Palmer he asked, "How's the crowd?"

"Seating capacity's 312, so I guess it's about that."

"It's full?" I asked, surprised.

Barry Palmer nodded enthusiastically. "Best crowd since 'The Importance of Being Earnest.'"

"Great!" Dr. Z exclaimed, rubbing his hands together as if he were still out in the cold.

Vladimir Primalov stopped a few steps behind me. "Who will make introductions to audience?" he asked.

"I will," Dr. Z answered. "Follow me."

We walked on stage to polite applause. I scanned over and saw Lydia, smiling nervously. She wore black slacks and a silk beige blouse that shined in the bright theater lighting.

When the applause died down, Dr. Z stepped to the front of the stage and announced, "Welcome to *A Celebration of Brilliance!* We are all honored to have in Walla Walla, my old student, Vladimir Primalov, a contender for the World Championship of chess." More polite applause. "Mr. Primalov has agreed to play this exhibition game with Whitman's number one chess player, Bryan Matthews." More applause, this time louder.

When the audience quieted, Dr. Z said, "Gentlemen," and motioned for us come forward. Walking to center stage I swallowed hard and again looked at Lydia, who gave me a smile as our eyes connected. Next to her, seated left to right, were Yolanda, Hector and Amelia. Three rows behind them Bigdog sat with Slider and a large contingency of fraternity brothers. Deuce Twohey was pressing his fingertips to his temples and nodding slightly with his eyes closed. I forced myself to stop looking at the audience and directed my attention to Dr. Z.

Dr. Z projected his voice. "We will use a two-stage process to determine who plays White and who plays Black. On top of the chessboard you see two ordinary Whitman College coffee mugs, donated by our own irrepressible Mrs. Beatrice Wallace at the Student Union Building." Scattered laughter around the room. "Taped to the bottom of each mug is a single number, either 1 or 2. In a moment, our guest, Grandmaster Primalov, will choose one of the two mugs. If he chooses the one with the number 1 hidden on the bottom, he will have the right of picking one of the two envelopes in the Evans Cup, fittingly being held by Javad Azizi, who helped us win it at the Collegiate Chess Championship." On cue, Javad lowered the Evans Cup, showing the audience it held two manila envelopes.

"If Grandmaster Primalov picks the mug with number 2 taped to the bottom, Bryan Matthews will have the right to select one of the envelopes. Inside each of the envelopes is a miniature flag, one Russian and one American. If Grandmaster Primalov or National Master Matthews chooses the envelope with the flag of his own country, he will have the right to choose either White or Black. If he chooses an envelope with the flag of his opponent's country, his opponent will choose White or Black. Okay, Grandmaster Primalov, if you would be so kind as to pick one of the mugs."

Primalov, his face expressionless, looked down at the board and reached for the mug on the left. He turned it over and showed the number 2 to Dr. Z and me.

Dr. Z said, "Grandmaster Primalov has selected the mug with the number 2 on the bottom." He paused to show it to the audience. "That means Mr. Matthews will have the right to pick one of the two sealed envelopes from the Evans Trophy."

Javad walked over and held out the ornate silver trophy, the size of a large flower vase. After glancing at Lydia, I closed my eyes and reached in, pulled one of the envelopes and handed it to Dr. Z.

Dr. Z. accepted the envelope and took a deep breath. He, too, would be silently hoping and praying to find an American flag inside. Then, without hesitation, Dr. Z tore open the envelope and pulled out the miniature Stars and Stripes. The crowd applauded, eliciting a frown from Grandmaster Primalov. I assumed he was reacting to the audience showing partisanship, not to the fact that I'd have first choice of the white or black pieces. "What will it be, Mr. Matthews?"

Keeping my best poker face I nervously shrugged a shoulder. "I'll play White," I said, giving me the opening move and the opportunity to use the Stonewall Attack. I wanted to jump up and down, give Dr. Z a hug.

Dr. Z then opened the other envelope, removed the miniature Russian flag and placed it in a small holder on the side of the board with the black pieces. After placing the American flag on the White side he gestured for us to take our respective seats. "Mr. Matthews will play White and move first," he said to the audience. "I would ask that you be *absolutely* quiet so as not to break the concentration of either player. Thank you for your consideration."

Sitting down, I was aware of facing in the direction of Lydia, but restrained myself from looking at her. It was time to concentrate. I got in a comfortable position and promptly moved pawn to queen four, pressing the time clock that started Primalov's clock running. In accord with chess etiquette, I pressed the button on the time clock with my right hand, the same hand I used to make my move. I had chills. Racing through my mind and body was a thought, not unlike a shooting star Lydia and I had witnessed on a freezing night in November – *God, how I love this game!*

Primalov answered pawn to queen four, no hesitation. After pressing the time clock, he straightened in his chair and glowered at me from two feet away. Sonny Liston in a suit.

I ignored him and focused on the board. My next moves were used to steer play into the Stonewall pawn pattern. On move four I played knight to queen two to prevent Primalov from countering with the so-called Double Stonewall, a favorite defense of the great Jose Capablanca.

Primalov made predictably good moves as he exerted control on the center and prepared to castle on the kingside.

On my fifth move, I went pawn to king bishop four, completing the Stonewall pawn pattern. Now I could anchor my king knight at the powerful king five outpost and exert a commanding influence on Primalov's territory.

Two moves later, Primalov moved his queen bishop pawn onto my side of the board. It was a good move theoretically, an approach used successfully by Rotlewi in a 1911 game I'd studied, but it gave me no problems. Having anticipated the move, I promptly created a retreat for my threatened bishop.

Primalov castled and mumbled something, loud enough to understand if I spoke Russian. I glanced over at Dr. Z, but he was busy commentating with his chalk. Reva, however, sitting immediately in front of Dr. Z's blackboard, had raised her eyebrows, apparently in response to Primalov's comment.

I looked across the board at my opponent, who had folded his arms and affected an impatient expression. I would've liked to have asked him what he'd said, but it is against the rules to speak to your opponent unless you are resigning, offering or accepting a draw, or adjusting a piece that isn't properly centered on its square. I moved out my king knight, getting ready to position him at the formidable king five outpost. I had gained no advantage, but the game was unfolding nicely for me, according to plan.

After stationing my knight at the powerful outpost, I castled. Next I moved queen to bishop three, the kind of aggressive move that had been my style since learning to play the game. Leaning back in my chair, I became vaguely aware of Dr. Z writing his live commentary on the blackboard followed by the murmurs of a few spectators in response. I imagined he'd written something like, "Bryan signals his intention to mount an attack on Vlad's kingside."

My last move had earned Grandmaster Primalov's full attention. He took a sip of water, set down his glass quietly and refolded his arms. The ice clinking in his glass was the only sound in the room. Deep in concentration, his eyes bored into the chessboard as he analyzed his position. Eight minutes later he moved his dark-squared bishop to a more defensive square.

I had a number of good moves available on my twelfth move, but a voice inside kept repeating Anderssen's maxim, "Attack! Always attack!" The conditions seemed ripe enough so I moved my king pawn forward in attack, simultaneously converting my "bad" bishop to a "good" one.

After studying the board for another five minutes, Primalov defensively pushed his king rook pawn, parrying my latest bishop threat and creating an escape square for his king.

I noticed my fingers were ice cold and began rubbing my hands together. Primalov looked up from the board, annoyed. I stopped, but it registered that the Grandmaster's concentration was less than ironclad. *Keep the pressure on,* I told myself and proceeded to capture his bishop, offering my outposted knight in exchange.

Primalov captured back with his queen. A tic seemed to have developed in his left eye, or maybe it had been there all along and I hadn't noticed.

Without hesitation, I again advanced my king pawn forward in attack. I now had earned a clear positional advantage with a stronger pawn structure and control of critical squares in the center. Primalov stared at the board, loosened his tie and took another drink of water.

I motioned to Javad to bring me hot water for my tea and noticed Dr. Z was writing something on his live commentary blackboard. When he finished, an excited murmur raced through the audience. Someone made a shushing noise.

Primalov retreated his knight to the eighth row. I had him back on his heels.

At this point, I had made only fourteen moves and used less than seven minutes off my time clock. Standard time control allowed each of us forty moves in two hours followed by another hour each for all the remaining moves. Now I deliberately took some time off the clock, not only because I wanted to hold onto my advantage, but also because I wanted Primalov to sweat. Ten minutes later I moved pawn to queen knight three, reminding my opponent I could easily mount a threat on the queenside, as well.

Primalov again said something in Russian. He mopped his brow, stared at the board and then up at the ceiling as precious minutes ticked off the clock. Desperate for counterplay, he moved pawn to bishop three.

I turned up the heat, moving my queen onto his side of the board where it closed in on his king.

Primalov then precipitated an even exchange of pawns and put me in check with his rook. After pressing his time clock he caught me by surprise by crossing his index fingers to form the letter "X." At the same time, he said, "Nichya?"

I didn't need to speak Russian to understand. He was saying, *"Would you like a draw?"* My immediate reaction was anger. It was improper for him to offer a draw while my time clock was running. By pressing his clock, he'd automatically started mine. Moreover, offering a draw when I had a forced reply to his check put me in the position of wasting time considering the offer while he thought about his next move. I looked up from the board and saw Primalov smiling, showing me a mouthful of crooked teeth. He looked charming, gracious. *He expects me to accept the draw. I would be able to tell my grandchildren I earned a draw at age eighteen with a World Championship Contender.*

I found myself looking in the direction of Dr. Z, but he was frantically writing something on the blackboard, no doubt informing the audience that Grandmaster Primalov had offered me a draw. I looked back at the Russian. He was still smiling, waiting for me to take the draw. But, on the verge of perforating his kingside, I didn't want a draw. There was no guaranteed win but, unless I blundered, I could see several ways to make him miserable. For one thing, his king would have no secure refuge and he would constantly be on the defensive. Smiling nervously I looked at Vlad the Impaler and said, "No, thank you." At that, I removed his check by taking his rook with my knight and pressed my time clock. Another murmur made its way through the audience.

Primalov's face went scarlet. He glared daggers at me. My heart was hammering but I met his eyes and glared back. He then looked over to his former coach, Zdenek Zaleski, as if he could do something to intervene. Dr. Z refused to make eye contact. I knew Primalov wouldn't offer a draw a second time and that he was more dangerous than ever. Scowling, he redirected his attention to the board and, after an exchange of pawns, mounted a weak threat against my queen bishop pawn.

I ignored the threat and began a bold demolition sacrifice on his kingside, swooping down to capture his king rook pawn with my dark-squared bishop. He could have had my bishop for a mere pawn, but didn't dare take it knowing I'd have had his king on the run and an eventual win.

Primalov studied the board with fierce concentration and took my queen pawn with his knight, thus pinning my bishop pawn.

I answered by removing the pin and intensifying the attack on his kingside, while forcing him to defend his knight. I now had both bishops and my queen within three squares of his beleaguered king.

Primalov defended with skill that demonstrated why he was a World Championship contender. Using his king bishop, he put my castled king in check, a move I saw coming. Still, the slightest slip on my part and my wealth of threats would disappear in a puff of smoke.

On his twenty-sixth move, Primalov moved queen to king bishop seven, infiltrating my defenses and threatening mate at my king knight one square. The crowd gasped when Ethan duplicated the move on the large mock chessboard, but I'd anticipated it and made an effective reply, moving knight to king knight three. This not only eliminated the threat of checkmate, but also freed up my rook to drive out the enemy queen while attacking his knight on the back rank.

Beads of perspiration appeared on Primalov's brow. He loosened his tie and then made his move, cleverly threatening my queen and managing to get a pawn in exchange for his remaining knight.

Using the standard point count system I was the equivalent of two pawns up after only twenty-eight moves. Primalov hadn't given up by any means, but with his position wide open he must've been in a state of shock. I used the next move to increase the pressure, trying to take away any glimmer of hope the Russian might still have. He responded by moving his queen into a defensive position.

That made it my move. I studied the board with an intensity I'd never before achieved. I was playing the pieces and not my opponent, the way Dr. Z had taught me. My concentration was single-pointed, absolute, as I searched for a way to enmesh Primalov's black king in an inescapable mating net. The pieces began to move in my imagination.

And then I saw it! A queen move so brilliant I knew at once I would shock the chess world. Chills raced up my spine and down my arms. Because it looked too good to be true I played out every possible way the Grandmaster could slip the noose. Satisfied there were none, I looked at Primalov himself. He had taken off his wristwatch and set it alongside the board, but was studying the board maniacally and wouldn't look up. With plenty of time on my clock, I repeated my analysis and the moves that led to checkmate to make sure I wasn't missing something. Primalov had no way out.

Unable to stop myself, I looked up from the board and smiled at Lydia in the first row of seats. Oh God, she was beautiful. Drinking her in with my eyes, I could feel my soul. I wanted to cry and almost did. *Does she know why I'm smiling? Does she know I am on the verge of defeating Vladimir Primalov, the third best chess player in the world? Does she know this is the sweetest moment of my life?* She met my eyes and sent me a dazzling smile in a timeless moment of connection that demonstrated the intensity of our love.

Returning my attention to the game, I moved queen to king knight five, then pressed my time clock for the last time. Primalov recoiled from the board, as if someone had thrown a venomous snake in his lap. It was a sacrifice that, one month later, the editor of *Chess World* would call, " . . . one of the deadliest 'quiet moves' in the annals of chess!"

It is difficult enough for a man like Vladimir Primalov to resign, but even more difficult when the opponent is an eighteen year-old college student. Complicating matters for the Russian, Dr. Zaleski, his former mentor, was providing live commentary to an audience expecting me to be thrashed in public. His massive ego notwithstanding, Primalov nonchalantly tipped over his king with his right index finger and said, "I resign." He knew his position was hopeless and had seen enough of me to know I wouldn't blunder on my way to checkmate.

The audience was momentarily stunned into silence until Joan Levy blurted out, "It's over! Primalov resigned." Realizing I'd won, everyone in the room jumped to their feet and applauded wildly. I got out of my chair. Primalov stood and graciously shook my hand as flashbulbs popped and several photographers rushed the stage. Primalov said something to me that I couldn't hear and when I shrugged my shoulders he leaned forward and shouted into my ear, "I *said* . . . are you all the time this good?"

"I don't know," I answered, tears filling my eyes.

Looking bewildered, Primalov shook his head in disbelief.

Dr. Zaleski appeared on stage and shook my hand first. "What a move," he said. "What a move!" He turned and shook the hand of his former student.

Primalov looked at Dr. Z and half-shouted, "You should have warned me about this boy, Zdenek." Dr. Z gestured with his palms up, as if to say, *"How could I have known he'd play the game of his life?"*

We watched as Primalov pivoted and walked off the stage in the direction of his dressing room. When he was out of sight, Dr. Z grabbed me by the wrist and raised my right hand in victory. The audience cheered again and a few of my fraternity brothers, led by the boisterous Bigdog, started pumping their fists and chanting, "USA! USA! USA!"

Lydia jumped onto the stage and kissed me on the mouth. She tasted of lipstick. Hector and Amelia were bashful about coming onto the stage so I leaned over and shook hands with each of them until my chess teammates began mobbing me. Ethan said, "I knew you'd win, Rooms! I just knew it!"

Javad Azizi shook his head. "That might be the greatest move I've ever seen."

Bigdog and Slider had made their way down to the stage. Bigdog yelled, "Phi Delts rule!" Slider didn't say anything, but his big gummy grin spoke volumes. He, too, had tears in his eyes.

Reva was hugging Dr. Z about ten feet to my right. I broke free to get in on a three-way hug.

"You vant to know vat Vladimir said in Russian?" Reva asked over the noise of the crowd.

"What?" I asked, unable to hear her.

"Vladimir said someting in Russian . . . at start of game. Do you vant to know vat he said?"

"Yes!"

"He said, 'Stonewall is a *child's* opening!'"

"Oh." The Russian, in fact, *had* underestimated me.

I accepted still another congratulatory embrace from Dr. Z, who hugged me so hard I thought my ribs might crack.

Lydia reappeared and wrapped her arms around my neck. "Way to go, Bryan," she shouted. "Way to go!"

I felt delirious with joy. Her opinion was worth more than all the others combined.

Chapter 7
Stubblefield

Bothered by a recent bout of insomnia, I chose to spend the night at the Zaleski's. My basement room, weakly lit from a nearby streetlamp, cycled through shades of late-night gray. Nearly dark one moment, it brightened as the lamp turned on, briefly illuminating the corkboard neatly tacked with an article about my win against Primalov. A grainy photo showed the mayor of Walla Walla presenting me with the key to the city. Reva had saved the miniature flags from the tournament, one Russian and one American. They stuck out of the corkboard, the American one higher than the Russian, like banners casting faint shadows.

Late spring rains hissed against my one window. The drops cast light-patterns on my nightstand stacked with *Modern Chess Strategy, The Art of Checkmate,* and *The Chess Mind.* This week's review. A place to bury my thoughts. Could I smother my unease in grand strategies and tactical thrusts?

Montrose lurked at the back of my thoughts. I'd spotted him once or twice in his patrol car, but he was either parked and smoking a cigarette or headed in the opposite direction. On one occasion, I headed into Kentucky Fried Chicken late at night and saw him through the glass door drinking coffee with another cop. An abrupt, unexpected meeting of eyes followed. His eyes had narrowed and hardened, a warning to keep my guard up despite a reprieve of several months. I pivoted and hurried back to my car as if I'd forgotten something, then drove off in a near panic. I guessed my chess win had gained me more than public admiration.

Bothered by the memory, I thrashed in bed, knocking the phone handset from its cradle where I'd left it an hour or so earlier, shoved to one side on the blankets. The handset struck the floor. No dial tone. Instead, a drone, "If you'd like to make a call . . ." I leaned over with a groan, retrieved the phone and laid it carefully in place.

Lydia. I visualized her beautiful face, in profile, looking away. Our last conversation (Mill Creek hiking trail, Memorial Day, unambiguous sunshine) and dozens of others, photographed that picture. If I pulled back the camera, she would still be holding my hand, a smile would still touch her lips, but I now sensed in her a holding back, a turning away from the closeness I so craved. Not all the time, but enough to cause me to doubt her commitment. When I'd called her earlier in the evening she seemed distant, irritable. "Are you mad at me?" I asked, my insecurities in full bloom.

"No."

Uncomfortable silence. "Well, you didn't seem too happy to be with me today."

"Sorry."

A sour geyser ejected its contents into my stomach. "What's wrong?"

Audible sigh. "Nothing's wrong."

"You still love me?"

"Yes, Bryan. Of course I do. I just don't feel like doing cartwheels every time we're together."

"Okay. I love you too."

I got off the phone feeling defective and needy. Losing Lydia seemed incomprehensible, yet possible, and I wondered if she would someday pull away altogether. When your own mother has left you, it's not easy to feel confident about a teenage girlfriend.

———————

The second week of June in Walla Walla meant Pioneer Days, an arts and crafts festival traditionally held at Pioneer Park. Lydia and I pushed upstream against the crowd. I held her hand and wove through the current of people. Townsfolk of all ages crowded into dozens of makeshift booths where artisans sold pottery, macramé, bonsai trees, wildlife photography, knick-knacks, tie-died T-shirts, hand-tooled leather wallets and purses, pizza by the slice, hot dogs and ice cold sodas.

A country rock trio from LA named *Back Pocket* (unabashed Scientologists, high-end harmonies, feel good lyrics) performed an acoustic set, bowing to a city ordinance declaring no noise levels over ninety decibels. We sat in the grass near the big hill and listened to twenty minutes of music *("The trouble is . . . is that there's nothing to be troubled about.")*. Lydia said they sounded like Buffalo Springfield on a sugar high.

Next we browsed the booths. I found things I wanted to buy but, low on cash, my only purchase was a gift for Lydia, a coffee mug that read: *Have you taken your pill today?* We knew Hector would disapprove of the humor, but Lydia gleefully accepted it as one more way of asserting her independence.

We drifted over to the carnival area, scaled-down but in full swing. Young children and teenagers swarmed around a Carousel, Bullet, Tilt-O-Whirl, Paratrooper, and Octopus. "Do you want to go on one?" I asked.

She made a face. "Not really. I'm not into rides."

"Oh yeah. You had a bad experience."

"That'd be an understatement."

"I knew something happened but you never told me what it was."

"It's a long story."

"Tell me. I want to hear it."

She led me over to a wooden bench, using the moment to decide. "Okay, I was five and Momma took me to the Pendleton Roundup. It's a rodeo, but also like a state fair with fun stuff for kids."

"Like rides."

"Rides, game booths, pig races, 4H contests, dog and cat shows, all kinds of exotic chickens and bunnies that came from all over creation. I loved all the loud sounds and colors, the smell of the popcorn and that greasy food they sell. But going on the rides was my very favorite part. Anyway, mom bought me an all day pass and told me she'd find me when it was time to go home."

"You were five years old and she left you unsupervised all day?"

"That was my mom. All she did was give me some change for food and tell me not to go off with any strangers because there were a lot of weirdoes at carnivals."

"Were you scared?"

"I was when it got dark, because Momma had a history of forgetting about me and leaving me places. And, sure enough, she did. I spent a long time looking for her and finally saw her standing by a little trailer next to one of the rides. She was flirting with a big Mexican guy who turned out to be Jimmy, my sort-of stepfather. He was operating the Gravitron, which happened to be my favorite ride. Is it Gravitron or Graviton?"

"I'm pretty sure it's Gravitron. "

"Then what's a graviton?"

"In quantum physics it's a hypothetical particle."

She smiled slightly and watched a sad-faced juggling clown walk by. "So, she was talking to Jimmy and acting silly, laughing at nothing and making really obvious sexual overtures. I just watched her and Jimmy for a minute, not wanting to butt in, but I was so relieved to find her I finally ran up to her and grabbed her by the leg. I wanted to tell her about all the rides, about the candied apple I'd eaten, about seeing the view from the top of the Double Ferris Wheel, but she gave me a dirty look, like I was about to ruin something she had going with Jimmy."

"You were cramping her style."

"Yeah. One of her favorite sayings was, ' . . . men see kids as excess baggage.'"

"So what did she do when you ran up to her?"

She frowned. "She introduced me as her *only* child, like she wanted him to know there was only *one* piece of baggage to contend with. Jimmy looked at me in no particular way and asked if I wanted to ride the Gravitron. All by myself. I think my mouth dropped open and I looked at my mom to see if it was okay. I knew it would be, but I liked to pretend that what I did mattered to her. Momma said she didn't care. So I marched bravely into the Gravitron all by myself and chose a good place to stand, leaning against the wall. Jimmy slammed the entrance door shut and in a few seconds the mechanical gears engaged and the music came on. Then the ride started, slowly at first and then gradually building up speed like it's supposed to. Ever ridden on a Gravitron?"

"I don't think so. They didn't have one at Playland, the amusement park in Seattle."

"Well, you're inside this big cylinder that spins faster and faster until it pins your body up against the wall."

"Centrifugal force."

"Yeah. So, there I was, this skinny little five-year-old girl, flying around at a million miles an hour, thinking how lucky I was to have it all to myself. I'd been going on rides all day and had a pretty good idea how long they were supposed to last, but this one was a *long* ride. Extra long! I'm thinking I'm special because Momma has a friend who's giving me extra time. Finally, it dawned on me that something was wrong because the Gravitron wasn't slowing down and stopping. It just kept going and going, at top speed."

"God, Lydia. How long did it go?"

"I wasn't old enough to be a good judge of time, but I would guess it went at least ten minutes. Maybe more. All I knew was I wanted it to end . . . and was afraid it would never end."

"Do you remember what you were thinking?"

"Mostly I was just wondering where my mom was. I was terrified, which was unusual because I didn't scare easily, even at that age. I started getting weak and dizzy. Sick to my stomach. Then I started to cry and couldn't stop, which is a weird experience when you're spinning around. I just felt so helpless. You can't move in the Gravitron but you can scream, so that's what I did. I was screaming loud enough to get someone's attention, but the organ music was blaring and I figured no one could hear me."

"I would have flipped out."

"I *did* flip out! It was like the Gravitron took on a personality."

I closed my eyes and imagined. "Like you were in the jaws of a monster that preyed on little children."

"Exactly. Then I felt warm water running down my leg and realized I'd wet my pants. On top of everything else, this meant I was in big trouble with Momma, assuming I ever got out alive."

"What happened next?"

"More time passed. I just kept spinning around, spinning around, one revolution every couple seconds, pinned to the wall."

"That's awful." I got an image of little Lydia pinned against the wall like one of those pretty, dead butterflies you see in a museum.

"I started screaming louder and louder. Ear-piercing shrieks I hoped someone close by would hear. I'd given up on Momma. Nothing happened right away, but then the music shut off and the Gravitron began to slow down. For some reason that made me cry even harder and when the centrifugal force weakened I collapsed to the floor. Then Momma and Jimmy came rushing in."

"What'd she say?"

"When she saw I was hysterical she said, 'Oh, for *God's sake* Lydia, it wasn't that long!'"

I shook my head. "Unbelievable!"

"Yeah. She pulled me to my feet before I was ready, but I had no legs under me and no balance so I fell right back down. Then she jerked me to my feet a second time and started bitching at me for peeing my pants. Called me a little actress. To make things worse, I threw up on her shoe and she stormed away, swearing and stomping her foot on the floor of the Gravitron. Jimmy picked me up and carried me outside."

"And then what happened?"

"I tried to apologize to Momma for throwing up on her but she wouldn't hear it. She was furious. Meanwhile, Jimmy took out his handkerchief and started cleaning me up. I noticed he wasn't wearing his snakeskin boots and that the little trailer door was wide open. And then I noticed Momma's blouse wasn't buttoned properly."

I shook my head. "Why do people like your mother even have children?"

Her expression turned pensive. "Because they can't keep their blouses buttoned."

We looked at each other and cracked up. Nothing like a little comic relief to ease the pain that comes with a difficult childhood. I remembered my psychology professor saying humor was the highest defense. "So did Jimmy go home with you and your mom?" I asked.

"Yeah. He followed us in his truck. I wanted to ride with him. Can you believe it? I didn't even know him, but I'd have rather ridden home with this scary looking stranger than my mother."

"Who wouldn't?"

"He moved in with us that night, and don't ask me why he stayed when all the other men didn't, because I don't have a clue. It wasn't like he and my mom got along."

I gave it some thought, watched a smiling middle-aged man help an excited toddler step off the Carousel. "Maybe it was because of you."

"What do you mean?"

"It sounds like Jimmy liked you. You were a cute kid and he was more nurturing than your mom. Maybe it worked for both of them."

"I never thought of that."

The temperature had soared into the nineties. I fanned my face with my hand. "I say we skip the rides and get a snow cone?"

She nodded and we headed back to the concession stands. Once there, Lydia stretched over the high counter. "What flavors do you have?" she asked, expectantly.

The hair on my neck stood up. *"What?"* I wheeled around and scanned the crowd, expecting to see Vicky Spotts, who according to the Walla Walla rumor mill, had been stalking Lydia and me. But this time it was Officer Jack Montrose, easily recognizable even in civilian clothes and a tattered baseball cap. He leaned against a tree no more than twenty feet away, drawing on a cigarette and leering at Lydia's cheeky bottom, partly exposed in her frayed cutoff jeans. I stepped between Montrose and Lydia, blocked his view and shot him my best scowl. At that, Montrose threw back his head and let out a guttural laugh. Strolling away from the tree, he flicked his lit cigarette into a tangle of dry grass, not bothering to snuff it out. "Asshole!" I said too loudly.

Lydia whirled around and stared at me in shock.

"Sorry. That cop, Montrose, was checking out your bottom. I busted him."

"Oh, that's disgusting! Where is he?" she asked, craning her neck and simultaneously tugging at her cutoffs.

"He slithered off that way." I pointed in the general direction of the gazebo.

"Let's leave. I mean, I don't care if Montrose is here, I'd just rather be someplace less crowded."

"Fine with me. We can go out to Kooskooskie. Put our feet in the creek and cool off."

We finished our snow cones and bought Amelia a tortoise shell barrette, then headed back to my car, parked a few blocks away on Juniper. At the edge of Pioneer Park, Jack Montrose stepped into our path from behind the trunk of a sprawling oak tree. "If it isn't college boy and townie girl," he sneered. "I guess it's my lucky day."

"But apparently not ours," Lydia replied.

Montrose flashed a sardonic grin. "I figure you two have been together about a year now."

"So what?" I said.

He shrugged a shoulder. "Just wondering if you're gonna make Injun' babies any time soon?"

"Why don't you just leave us alone!" Lydia snapped.

"Come on," I told her, "let's get out of here." I put my arm around Lydia's waist and steered her toward the car, giving Montrose a wide berth.

We'd gone about fifteen feet when Montrose fired his parting salvo. "Hey, college boy. Your old lady's ass looks better when she's bending over. But then you probably know that."

Lydia spun around, grabbed the just-purchased coffee mug from a bag and fired a fastball at Montrose's head. He ducked, barely in time to avoid a serious injury, bits of ceramic exploding off the oak tree behind him. The slack-jawed look of shock on his face was easily worth the price of the mug. Even so, my stomach knotted. "C'mon!" I pulled her toward the car.

She struggled, shook free. "Where do you get off?" she yelled. "Prick!"

"Lydia, let's go!" I unlocked the car and got in.

She balanced, poised where she stood on the sidewalk, as if to gather in her anger and lob it at Montrose.

Montrose started forward, wary, gauging her movements. His eyes quivered with rage and he muttered something inaudible.

I slammed the heel of my hand into the horn, held it for a long blare. Strangers arriving at the festival stopped and gawked. Montrose spit in our direction and strode off. Lydia glared at me, but this time, got into the car. Because I'd kept the scene outside the courthouse a secret, she had no way of knowing how dangerous Montrose really was.

On July 20, 1969, Lydia and I drove over to Bigdog's apartment to join him and Slider and behold the media event of the century. We gathered in front of Bigdog's rabbit-eared TV and watched, like a billion other people around the planet, the Apollo spacecraft in lunar orbit. "Move over," said Slider, elbowing in with a bowl of buttered popcorn. Bigdog grabbed a handful and saluted the spacecraft on TV.

CBS, ABC and NBC were all on live. We held our collective breath and watched Commander Mike Collins pilot the lunar module to the surface of the moon. I'll never forget how we cheered when the fuzzy image of Commander Neil A. Armstrong appeared on Bigdog's screen. "Houston, Tranquility Base here," he announced. "The Eagle has landed!" When Armstrong said, "That's one small step for man, one giant leap for mankind," we went wild, whooping it up and proud to be Americans.

All except Slider. "This has got to be one of the all-time scams," he declared. "They're mocking this up on some back lot in Hollywood."

"Right, Slider," Bigdog replied in a sarcastic tone. "That's why Walter Cronkite is speechless for the first time in his life."

"Maybe he's a good actor," Slider offered, wiping his fingers on his Three Stooges T-shirt.

"Are you serious? Do you really think this is a fake?" I asked Slider.

"Let's just say I don't trust our government. Look at all the misinformation they've been feeding us on Vietnam," he answered.

"Didn't you see the Columbia blasting off from Cape Canaveral?" Lydia asked him.

"That was real enough, but who's to say the damn thing ended up in a perfect orbit around the moon, a couple hundred thousand miles away?"

Bigdog cautioned us, "Slider's on his second six-pack and he's in one of his feisty moods. Don't pay any attention to him."

The matter was dropped by the time the four of us sat down to a late dinner. Bigdog spooned his "killer" Texas chili into large bowls and served them with cornbread he made from scratch. We talked about how fast summer vacation was going and washed down our meals with beer.

When we finished eating, Lydia volunteered to clean up the kitchen and I offered to help. Bigdog's sink and counters were heaped with a week's worth of dirty dishes and it took us twenty minutes to get through them. Lydia handed me the last pan to dry. "Let's go out far enough that there're no city lights and look at the moon."

"Where do you want to go?" I asked. "The cabin?"

"That's too far."

Bigdog overheard us. "Stay and watch *Abbott and Costello Meet the Mummy*. It's a knee slapper." He let out a moan as he collapsed on the couch. The big guy had stuffed himself, as usual, spurring Slider to needle him about eating anything that didn't bite back.

"I've seen it," I commented. "It's not as good as *Abbott and Costello Meet Frankenstein*."

"Have Bryan take you out to Stubblefield." This was Slider, fiddling with the TV antenna and trying to stir things up.

Lydia looked at me with imploring eyes. "Would you?"

"I'm not sure I could find it," I said defensively.

"You found it the first time," Slider said. "You go out Reser and if you get to Foster Road you've gone about a hundred yards too far."

"Have you ever been there?" I asked Lydia.

She shook her head, causing her long braids to swing. "No, but I've heard about it since I was a kid."

"I was out there once with Ethan. It was spooky as all hell."

"I know," she smiled. "That's where you met the lovely Miss Vicky."

Slider said, "Bryan. Tell us the truth about your relationship with Vicky Spotts. Give us the straight poop. Once and for all."

Bigdog laughed hard enough to aggravate his asthma. "The naked truth!" he wheezed.

"You guys are wasted," I said, feigning disgust. Turning to Lydia I asked, "Why would you want to go to an abandoned cemetery that's supposed to be haunted?"

"Because I've heard of it a hundred times and never been there. Besides, it'd be a great place to check out the moon."

"I've got a bad memory of that place," I told her.

"You can have my last six-pack of Oly if you take her," Slider said. He seemed to take a perverse pleasure in coaxing people into going to Stubblefield.

"C'mon, Bryan. Just this one time," Lydia pleaded with a knowing smile. "It'll be fun."

"Okay," I agreed reluctantly. I rarely said no to anything that Lydia wanted and she'd been distant of late.

Bigdog broke into song. *"Whatever Lydia wants, Lydia gets . . ."*

Slider laughed and razzed me for being "whipped."

Lydia and I hung around until it got dark, thanked Bigdog for dinner and left about nine forty-five. I drove out past Prospect Point School and turned left, heading due east on Reser Road. It seemed a long way before we turned off the road and made out the pair of ruined stone pillars that marked the entrance to Stubblefield. They looked a bit less ominous than the first time, but I stopped the car. "Are you sure you really want to do this? We could just drive up into the mountains instead."

"No, I want to go in. This is kind of exciting."

"Okay." I gave her a nervous smile and turned onto the dirt road that led into the cemetery. On our left, a couple hundred yards away, was a house, supposedly the residence of the wheat rancher who owned the fields surrounding Stubblefield. Tree branches brushed my windshield, looking in the dark like charred arthritic fingers. We drove on through the discolored cement archway and past the rusted remnants of the wrought iron gate Ethan and I had noticed on my first visit. I parked where the road ended, thirty feet from where the few remaining tombstones and monuments began.

Lydia smiled, relaxed into her seat. "This isn't so scary." Though indistinct in the moonlight, the Blue Mountains were strangely beautiful.

I parked at an angle so we could see the full moon through the front windshield. A perfect pearl, it flooded the clear night with light. An unnatural quiet had settled over the cemetery, the loudest sound an occasional cricket. The air felt blood-warm, saturated with heat. Not a murmur of wind. A static charge seemed to gather around my car. I reached into the back seat and grabbed Slider's six-pack of Oly. I opened one for myself and offered another to Lydia.

"Just think," she said after taking a first gulp and eyeballing the moon, "there's someone walking around up there."

"I know. It's amazing! I can't remember. Are they actually on our side of the moon, or the dark side?"

"The dark side, I think. Which means they can't see us," she teased, sliding close and nuzzling my neck with her nose.

"Yeah, but the man in the moon can, so behave yourself."

I peeled the damp label off my bottle of Olympia. Printed on the backside of an Oly label you'd find one, two, three or four dots – supposedly vat numbers at the brewery. In the Pacific Northwest, one dot meant you got to first base with your date, two dots meant second base, and so on. My label showed four dots. Without speaking, I wiggled my eyebrows and showed it to Lydia.

She held the label under the windshield where there was enough light to read it. "Lucky you," she said with a big smile. "Do you want me to sign it for later or do you want to cash in right here and now?"

My pulse quickened. "Is that a sincere offer?"

"It doesn't get any more sincere."

"Now sounds good to me."

We kissed, Lydia hooking her right arm around my neck. Her lips seemed impossibly soft and moist. She licked my lower lip and slid her tongue into my mouth. "I want you," she said, lip-locked. Her hand slid down my chest and stomach and began fumbling at the buttons on my cut-off Levi's.

"What're you doing?"

Without speaking, she took me in her mouth. This was new territory. I swooned and threw my head back, weak with pleasure. I watched the moon disappear from view and everything else with it. Moments before I was ready to come I said, "I want to be inside you."

"You are," Lydia giggled.

"You know what I mean. Let's get in the back seat."

We tore off our clothes and climbed in the back. Lydia lay on her back and pulled her long legs up, holding the backs of her knees with her hands. "Hurry!" she said, slightly out of breath. Her voice betrayed a hunger, leaving me dizzy with expectation, but also frightening me in a way I'll never understand.

I kissed her and rested the palm of my hand on her belly. Lydia's skin was smooth and hot. When I pushed myself inside her, she let out a little yelp. Crazy with desire, I started thrusting, making no effort to be tender or skillful the way I usually did.

"Oh yeah!" she cried out.

Little light penetrated the back seat and I could only see her outline. In some way it made her less Lydia, less the sweet and beautiful girl I admired, more a naked body that needed to be released. A surge of aggression seized me and I pinched her nipples a bit too hard, out of my mind with pure sensation. She groaned and dug her fingernails into my shoulders. I pumped hard and fast until Lydia screamed, as if something was about to detonate in her belly. Never before had either of us been so utterly physical.

Then the backseat seemed to close around us until space disappeared completely and nothing was left but our naked bodies locked together. The instant I sensed an orgasm forming in my groin, Lydia grabbed my buttocks and squeezed hard. A weakness developed at the backs of my legs then all the muscles in my body seemed to collapse at once and I came for what seemed an eternity, an experience so intense and powerful that it became perhaps my strongest memory of being with Lydia sexually. Not only because it was so pleasurable, but also because it was an expression of our love and passion. Her orgasm came seconds later and afterwards we lay motionless, catching our breath and collecting ourselves. "Are you okay?" I finally asked her, a little embarrassed by our performance.

"I'm great!" she answered, panting and running her hands down my sweaty back. "How'd I do on the . . . you know?"

"I loved it!"

She giggled. A film of perspiration had formed on her upper lip.

"What?" I asked.

"It's a secret."

"C'mon. Tell me."

"Okay, but you have to promise not to tease me about it."

"I promise."

"Yolanda and I practiced on Amelia's homemade dill pickles."

I chuckled. "I don't think Amelia would approve."

"She most definitely wouldn't approve. And you should be careful. Your pickle's bigger than Amelia's. You could hurt someone with that thing!"

We laughed so hard I popped out of her, which only made us laugh harder. "I've been expelled from Paradise!" I told her, sitting up and running my hand along the inside of her thigh.

"Are there any more beers?" Lydia asked, pulling herself to a sitting position.

"Yeah, but a beer won't do it for me. I need an IV." I leaned over the front seat and strained to reach the remainder of the six-pack, which was lying on the passenger side of the floor. Lydia playfully grabbed my balls and I shrieked loud enough to frighten any animal life within a mile. "Oh, you're going to pay for that!" I threatened playfully. This was the best we'd been together since my victory over Primalov.

"Promises, promises."

I grabbed two bottles of beer and the church key and had just popped the top off her beer when we simultaneously heard a sound from somewhere in the night. "What was that?" I asked.

"I don't know. I heard it, too."

In the next moment we both heard the unmistakable sound of crunching gravel. Seconds later a car skidded to a stop twenty feet adjacent to us and just off the road. Its lights had been turned off. I looked over and felt my stomach clench into a tight knot. It was a police car. A spotlight trained into the back seat, striking the two of us like a knockout punch. We were temporarily blinded.

"Oh shit!" I said.

Lydia reached over the seat and grabbed the T-shirt she'd been wearing.

"Get out of the car. Now!" I knew his voice, sharp and cold, like a new razor blade. Officer Jack Montrose.

"Okay. Okay," I said. "We're cooperating." I pushed forward the seat and exited through the driver's side door, retrieving my cutoffs as I climbed out. Montrose's right hand rested on his gun. I knew we were in for it.

"Speed it up! And leave the beer where it is!" Montrose barked.

"Let me get my pants," Lydia said, her voice quavering with fear.

"No. Get out now!" Montrose demanded.

"Let her put her pants on," I said, as I finished buttoning my own.

"Shut up, college boy!" With remarkable speed and skill, Montrose slapped a handcuff on my right wrist, clicked it shut and cuffed me to the handle of my open car door with the other one.

"Can I please just get my pants?" Lydia begged him.

"No, you may not!" He grabbed one of her braids, yanked her through the open door and pushed it shut.

"Jesus!" she cried out.

"Not so rough, Officer!" I pleaded. "That's not necessary."

Ignoring my plea, he spun Lydia up against the car and forced her hands behind her. Demonstrating the same dexterity he did with me, Montrose produced a second pair of handcuffs and cuffed her hands together behind her back.

"This is really embarrassing," Lydia said, her voice tinged with anger. "Why can't I put my pants on?" She'd managed to get her T-shirt on before being pulled from the backseat, but that was all.

"In a minute!" Montrose insisted.

The spotlight from the police car hit Lydia low in the back, illuminating her bare bottom, and when she turned, the black vee of pubic hair. She crossed her legs and, still exposed, twisted sideways to hide herself.

"Look, Officer Montrose," I said. "I promised I'd never mess with you again. And I haven't. There's no need to use handcuffs for this. Teenagers park and drink beer. It's not that big a deal."

Montrose had gone around to the passenger side of the Chevy and was shining a flashlight inside the car. "Beer's one thing," he replied. "Fornicating in public is another."

"Oh, come on." I tugged helplessly at my handcuffs. "First of all, we're hardly in public and second, we weren't fornicating."

"Yeah, right!" he sneered, walking back to where he'd secured me to the car door. "Then why's your girlfriend's butt all sweaty?"

"Can't you please just let us go? We won't do it again." This was Lydia, appealing to a side of Montrose that I knew didn't exist.

"Shut up! Both of you. You're under arrest for underage drinking and lewd conduct."

"Okay, we're under arrest. Would you at least have the decency to let my girlfriend put her pants on?"

Montrose tilted his head, smiled at me like I was an amusing child, and slapped me hard across the side of the head. I felt my jaw pop. It wasn't broken, but my ear rang like a church bell. Eyes watering, I watched Montrose grab Lydia by the elbow and march her over to his squad car, pushing and shoving her along the way.

"You said I could get my pants," Lydia protested.

"I *said* . . . in a minute!" After muscling Lydia to the rear door on the far side of his car, he opened it and pushed her facedown in the back seat. Then he reached into the front seat and switched off the spotlight.

"What do you think you're doing?" Lydia demanded in a loud voice.

"Searching you for drugs." Excitement had crept into his voice.

The realization hit me like a baseball bat. Montrose couldn't search Lydia for drugs because all she wore was a flimsy T-shirt. He intended to violate her and there was not a thing I could do to stop him. A shiver seized my body as I flashed on the way he'd eyeballed her body during Pioneer Days. Everything was going wrong. I went weak in the legs, momentarily too frightened to speak.

The back door of Montrose's car was open and the interior light was on. I could see most of what was happening. I watched the bastard move his hands over Lydia's bare bottom, then under her T-shirt. "Nice titties!" he gushed, after rolling down the window so I was sure to hear him. He must have pinched her nipples, because she yelled, "God dammit! That hurt!"

I had to say something to stop the assault. Slack with fear, I willed myself to speak. "Please stop! We were wrong to come out here. But don't do anything to her. We can drive back to town and forget about this."

"Shut up!" Montrose bellowed, his eyes blazing.

"Swear to God we won't say a thing!" I added.

"Damn right you won't!" he laughed. "Neither will your Injun' split-tail."

Split-tail. An expression I'd never heard, fueling my loathing of the man. I concocted a lie. "I've got almost a thousand dollars in cash back at my room. You can have it all. Just let us go and we can all pretend this didn't happen."

"I already know you're a liar," Montrose said. "So I'll pass on the big bucks. I am gonna drink your beer, though." He laughed as if he'd said something drop-dead funny.

"You're not going to get away with this, Montrose!"

"Oh, but I will. Our dispatcher thinks I'm looking for some senile old fart that wandered away from Veteran's Medical Center. That's what, ten miles from here."

"It's *okay*, Bryan. I'll do a trick," Lydia said, her voice deliberate.

"No!" I yelled back at her. "It's not okay!" Too frightened to think clearly, I assumed Lydia meant a "trick," slang for an act of prostitution. Like she'd space out and do whatever Montrose wanted, whatever she had to do to get us out of this.

"Bryan!" Lydia shouted. "Listen carefully! I can do a trick!"

"No!" I screamed. "Don't let him!" Lydia wasn't putting up any resistance. It wasn't right for her to lie there passively, to let Montrose have his way. It made no sense. Lydia was a warrior. She should've been fighting for her life.

"On your knees, bitch!" Montrose demanded with a carnal relish. When Lydia didn't move, he grabbed her hips and jerked her into the position he wanted. She immediately plopped back down on her stomach. "You want it rough?" he asked. He slapped her hard on the bottom and pulled her back up to her knees. This time she stayed up and I was forced to watch Montrose touch her from behind. Smirking, he wiped his brow with his forearm and looked over at me.

"You're hurting me!" Lydia shouted.

Montrose backed out of his car and casually unbuckled his belt and lowered his pants. It took some effort because the belt had a big gun and other police gear on it. Addressing me over the roof of his vehicle, he said, "No drugs on her, but I did determine she just had sex." He snickered. "I call that good police work."

"Fuck you, Montrose!" I shouted.

"No, I think I'd rather *fuck her!* Never had any Injun' pussy." Montrose laughed, enjoying being in control. "You know, college boy, I have a decision to make and I think you can help me. I could settle for sloppy seconds here, or I could give it to her in the ass. What would you do?"

I went berserk, out of my mind with helpless rage. I screamed so loudly I almost missed the fact that Lydia was shouting something at me. I stopped long enough to hear her say, *"Just give me long enough to do my trick!"*

This time it registered. Lydia was pleading with me to do something that would buy her time to do her double-jointed trick. I had to think fast. A tornado of thoughts made my head swim. Insulting his mother was all I could think of. "Hey, Montrose. I hear your mother blows goats!"

Montrose looked up and bared his teeth. I had his attention.

"Your mother's a whore, Montrose. I hear she fucks donkeys in Tijuana!"

Montrose nodded his head and smiled the smile of a man who'd come to an easy and pleasurable decision. He pulled his pants back up and methodically rebuckled his belt. Grinning maniacally, he strode around his police car to where I was handcuffed, a distance of some twenty-five feet. He seemed in no particular hurry. Maybe he wanted to take his time, savor the moment.

Unattended, Lydia wriggled out of the car on her stomach, feet first, and stood on the spot just vacated by Montrose. Tiptoeing behind him, she effortlessly did her "trick," working her arms in front of her in preparation for combat.

Montrose glowered. "What did you say about my mother?" Even in the moonlight I could see his face had swollen with rage. With his malice now focused entirely on me, he was oblivious that Lydia stood six feet behind him.

I forced myself to look into his wild eyes and not at Lydia. "Did she diddle you too, Jack?"

"You're dead meat!" he growled. Veins bulging from his neck, he stepped forward and threw a vicious right hand at my head.

Bracing myself against the side of the car, I ducked and avoided the full force of the punch. Then I reared up, kicking Montrose with both feet and catching enough of his chest and shoulder to spin him around.

Now he faced Lydia. In a heartbeat, she whirled three hundred sixty degrees and karate-kicked Montrose in the throat, her bare foot making a loud slapping sound against his skin. He went down hard at my feet, smacking the ground like a wooden puppet with severed strings. Clutching his Adam's apple, he let out an awful choking noise. I hoped he would lose consciousness, but he collected himself and pulled his gun, a big ugly black hunk of metal. Stricken by fear, I kicked it barefoot from his hand, but not before it discharged into the heavens, making a loud popping sound. The gun flew over and hit his squad car, producing a cracking sound. Blind with pain, I shouted at Lydia, "Don't let him get his gun!"

Montrose raised himself to one knee and looked up at me. He snarled and drew back his lips, like a cornered animal. "You're dead, you little fuck!" he said, spittle flying from the corners of his mouth. He shook the pain from his hand and struggled to his feet, but Lydia was ready and waiting with another ferocious kick, this one connecting solidly with his groin. A horrible moaning sound escaped his body and he doubled over before falling to his knees. Gagging, he took another powerful kick that again caught him squarely in the face. I watched his head jerk back as he flipped over and landed with a thud. The force of Lydia's blows seemed superhuman. Montrose, eyes bulging, lay motionless in a cloud of dust, equidistant between his patrol car and my Chevy. Bleeding heavily from his nose, his face twisted into a grimace of rage and terror.

My heart pounded like a locomotive. I wanted to grab Lydia and run, but I was still handcuffed to the car and, besides, it felt like I had no legs under me. "Get his keys," I said, gasping for air. I desperately wanted free, wanted to be able to do something.

"Pig!" Lydia yelled at Montrose, who'd rolled over onto his stomach. I wasn't sure she'd heard me. She knelt down and unleashed a ferocious two-handed blow to the small of his back, her martial arts training again evident in her power. Her handcuffs were still in place, only her hands were in front of her now.

"Get his keys!"

Still kneeling, Lydia leaned over Montrose's inert body and fiddled with the keys fastened to his thick leather belt.

I watched Lydia contort her wrists and fingers as she tried key after key. With each failed attempt she dished out another blow to the area just below Montrose's kidneys. The sound of impact was impossibly loud, like when a soccer player makes solid contact with the ball. Each time she hit him she let out a guttural sound – half grunt, half scream, like a wounded animal fighting for its life.

Keys jangled against the steady hammering backbeat of my heart as I warned her, "Be careful. He might be playing possum!"

Montrose summoned whatever energy he had left and tried to crawl away from the blows, a sidewinder awkwardly rolling over onto his back. He choked out a word that might have been, *"Enough,"* but it was impossible to say for sure.

Lydia raised her manacled hands to the night sky, paused as if to absorb a mysterious force from the heavens, and delivered a final blow to his throat. I watched in that weird slow motion that happens when you're mind is in shock and can't give orders to the body. Montrose actually bounced off the ground, powdery dirt rising up and mingling with the sweat on Lydia's half-naked body. A desperate groan escaped from his swollen mouth, the eerie sound of a dying animal. Then his body wilted entirely, like his uniform had emptied out.

I watched Lydia with fascinated horror, too stunned to speak. Staring at her catatonically, my eyes refused to blink. She was no more than ten feet away, breathing rapidly in short gasps, body glistening in the oppressive night heat. Wanting free from the bondage of the handcuffs, she tried more keys. Finally, she found the right one and undid herself. She appeared to be in control of herself, purposeful. I tried to make sense of what had just happened, but couldn't. My mind went completely blank and there was only shaking in my body.

Lydia glanced my way, meeting my eyes. She was strangely beautiful in her savagery, a wild angel of vengeance. Given the way Montrose had violated her, there seemed a moral rightness to the murderous expression I saw on her face. She looked down at his body, lying prone in front of her. I followed her eyes with mine and wondered if his leg was twitching. *Is that merely an involuntary reflex, like the dead frogs in Biology lab, or is Montrose clinging to life?*

Reading my mind, Lydia looked up. "He's dead. I crushed his windpipe." She was out of breath, but detached. Getting to her feet, she wiped her forehead with the back of her hand, walked over to me and undid my handcuffs.

I stammered, "Are you okay?"

She nodded, walked back to Montrose and seethed out the words, "And you can rot in hell!" Like he could hear her from the other side.

Rubbing my sore wrists, I took five steps over to Montrose and, without thinking, kicked him hard in the ribs. I heard a popping sound, like snapping a dry twig in a silent room. I was so pumped up I'd forgotten my foot was sore from kicking the gun from his hand.

Lowering myself to my knees, I got close to his face to see if he'd actually stopped breathing. His eyes were glassy and open. Blood and sputum leaked from his mouth, running black down his chin and neck and puddling at the collar of his uniform. Shaky from an overdose of adrenaline, my bowels wanted to move. I heard someone say, "Oh shit, Lydia. Oh shit!" I recognized the voice as my own, though it sounded vaguely different, like when you hear a tape recording of your voice and wonder if it's really the way you sound.

"He asked for it." Light from the interior of Montrose's car illuminated pinpoints of fire in Lydia's dark eyes.

Thinking was impossible and yet, on some level, I knew I had to think. Two thoughts came – *I can't believe this is happening* and *my life will never be the same!* The two thoughts looped, formed a closed circuit and, to my dismay, started over again. I shook my head to stop the thoughts from repeating, but they kept looping. I shook my head again, the way I shook my Etch-A-Sketch as a child when I wanted to erase an image. The thoughts remained. Finally, I broke the circuit by asking a question, a question I would immediately regret. "Did you have to kill him?"

Lydia was pulling on her cutoff jeans, just retrieved from the back seat of my car. "I can't believe you'd say that!" she said indignantly. "You saw what he did, you know what he was going to do!"

"But, killing him—"

"Bryan, he was going to *kill* us! Don't you get it?"

I didn't get it. I didn't get anything. The enormity of what had happened decommissioned my brain. I became only sensation and feeling, no thinking other than the looping thoughts, which reemerged in the foreground of my awareness. I smelled the acrid odor of urine. Montrose had lost control of his bladder. His pants were soaked in a dark circular pattern at the groin. It made me think of a Rorschach inkblot, Dracula's cape in the urine stain.

"Bryan, come here." Lydia sounded far away, as if she was on the other side of the cemetery or wandering out in the woods.

I walked slowly over to Lydia and stopped two feet front of her. I was numb, an automaton. She slapped me hard on the face.

"What was that for?" I asked in a bewildered voice. My jaw stung, but time had restarted.

"You're in shock, Bryan. Wake up! I need you to think. We just killed a cop! He's dead! What are we going to do?"

I rubbed the sting from my cheek and wondered why she'd said *"we"* instead of *"I."* Gazing over at the fallen Montrose, another thought crept in. A thought as unexpected as the scene that had just played out in front of my disbelieving eyes. A thought that flew in the face of everything I believed about myself, everything I held true about Bryan Matthews the person. I could only allow this thought to penetrate my awareness for an instant. An instant. I delighted in the fact Jack Montrose was dead and that he'd pissed his pants on the way out. I reveled in his ugly death, his final humiliation. The thought appeared and disappeared in an imperceptible space of time. I concentrated on Lydia because she was outside my head, separate from this new awareness of who I really was. I said, "No one will believe us if we tell the truth."

"What?! Why wouldn't they?"

Her question registered somewhere behind my eyes and routed itself to a working area of my brain. I was thinking again, not enough to process what had happened but enough to answer Lydia. "I couldn't get the court to believe Montrose wrote me a bogus speeding ticket. How are we going to get them to believe what he did to you?"

"But there's two of us," she argued. "We *know* what he did!"

I reached down and rubbed my sore foot. "There's two of us, but Montrose is dead. He can't defend himself. They'll say we were judge, jury and executioner."

"We *had* to be. He was going to kill us. You heard what he said about looking for the old man out by Veteran's Medical Center. He had a ready-made alibi."

"You think so?"

She looked at Montrose's fallen body. "Think about it, Bryan. He was about to rape me. I mean, he did rape me, but he was about to put his *dick* in me. There'd be two of us accusing him. Not my word against his. Our word! He couldn't do that to me and let us testify against him. He'd be finished as a cop! He'd go to prison!"

"I suppose."

She put her hands on her hips. "He pulled his gun, for God's sake! He fired a shot! He was going to kill us. You don't rape a girl in front of a witness and leave them be."

I struggled to calm myself and think. "You're saying he was going to murder us and leave our bodies to rot."

She nodded vehemently, eyes wide in disbelief. "Yes! God, how can you be so smart and so dense? No one comes out here. They might not have found us for days. Weeks, if he hid our bodies in the underbrush. And no one would know he was in the vicinity."

"Bigdog and Slider knew we were here. This is the first place they'd have looked if we were missing. Besides, they'd find my car."

"It doesn't matter! Montrose would be long gone. He'd get away with it. Don't you see? That's why I had to kill him and now we're screwed. Or at least I am."

"What do you mean by that?"

"I was the one that killed him. You were just watching."

I glanced down at Montrose's fallen body. "I kicked him first. I spun him around so you could get him in the throat. At the least, that makes me an accomplice."

She shook her head. "It's not the same."

I felt sick to my stomach and close to vomiting. I looked up at the moon, partly obscured by a wispy cloud. *If we hadn't put a man on the moon we wouldn't have driven out here to get a good look. If Slider hadn't suggested we go out to Stubblefield . . .*

" . . . maybe I should tell the truth and take my chances."

Lydia was talking to me. I'd started to go away in my head. "The truth?" I asked her.

"If I say what he did to me I might get off and for sure you'd be okay."

"Forget it. It won't work."

"Why?" She folded her arms to stop herself from shaking. Her previous detachment had worn off.

"Because Montrose is a cop. You don't kill a cop and get away with it. Ever! They'd send you to prison for a long time. A long, long time."

"Why would I go to prison? The pig stuck his fingers up me." She spit in Montrose's direction. "And he was about to do more than that!"

"I know what he did. But we can't prove it. A prosecutor is going to say it's plausible that he was just patting you down for drugs. Or that we're making the whole thing up. And even if they believed he was about to, you know, rape you, they'll say it doesn't justify killing him."

"It doesn't?" she asked, incredulous.

"Not in a court of law."

"The hell with a court of law. I was defending myself. He violated me and he was going to kill us."

"Lydia, listen to me. In a million years they wouldn't believe a police officer raped you and planned to murder the two of us to cover it up."

She put her palms up. "But that's exactly what was going to happen. We were not going to leave here alive."

I paused to collect my thoughts. "Maybe you're right, but we can't prove it. You weren't in court with me six months ago. The judge acted like Montrose was Mr. Pillar of the Community. Cop killers are made to pay their debt, no matter what the circumstances."

She paused a long moment, stared at the corpse. "Then we really are fucked."

I'd never heard Lydia use the word "fuck." And a minute before I'd seen her spit for the first time. "Yeah, we are."

She grabbed her sandals from my car. "I say we get out of here."

I shook my head. "I don't think so. At least two people know we're out here. If they find his body in the cemetery, we'd be the prime suspects. My run-ins with Montrose are common knowledge. And people know you're a black belt."

"Slider and Bigdog wouldn't say anything."

"We can't count on that. They could slip up. If they've left Bigdog's apartment and run into friends, they might've already told someone we were going to Stubblefield. It's too high a risk."

She rubbed at her wrists. "Okay, so what do we do?"

"I don't know. I wonder if anyone heard the gunshot, or the yelling."

"The people in the house over there?"

I scaled my Chevy and stood on the roof, looking through the sparse trees at the ranch house. I felt dizzy, but somewhat relieved there were no lights on and no signs of life. A dog barked a long ways off, too far to be the rancher's animal. Moving carefully, I climbed back down, trying mightily to collect myself. *Think. Think of a way out. Turn it into a chess problem. You're facing checkmate and you must escape to keep playing. The game is never over as long as you have moves to make. Be a man. Control your own destiny. You outplayed the third best chess player in the world!* "Wait a minute, I have an idea," I announced.

"What?"

"Okay. We can't leave Montrose here because it'll be obvious he was murdered."

She flinched and narrowed her eyes. "We didn't . . . I *didn't* murder him, Bryan. I killed him in self-defense."

I nodded. "Okay, I'm just saying he looks like he was murdered."

"That'll be obvious no matter where they find him."

"Not if we stage a car accident." I walked over to Montrose's car, a white Plymouth Fury, and quietly shut the back door. I wanted the interior light off in the event someone drove by on Reser Road and looked up the hill into the cemetery. Or, more likely, if someone in the ranch house happened to look out a window and see light.

She cocked her head, slightly. "What're you saying?"

Establish a safe place in enemy territory. "We drive him out Mill Creek Road and wreck his car. Out by Kooskooskie. That's remote. Make it look like he was chasing someone and lost control. Or something like that."

"And then put his body behind the wheel?"

I nodded. "Yeah. If we do it right and get his car far enough off the road, it could be days before they even find him."

"How do we wreck his car to make it look bad enough to cause a fatality?"

I saw it in my mind, like when the chess pieces move for me. "I can slam it into the bridge at Kooskooskie. Then we can push it over the embankment. That'd do some serious damage. If we need to, we can smash it with boulders, make it look even more convincing."

She looked over at Montrose's patrol car. "So they find him in a wrecked car with fatal injuries."

"Why not? It makes sense. Cops are always getting in accidents because they're going too fast."

"They are? I've never heard of one."

I nodded, reassuringly. "It happened in Seattle last Thanksgiving. A cop was chasing a drunk driver on Highway 99 and he lost control and plowed into a parked car."

"What happened?"

"The cop died. And they charged the drunk driver with homicide even though he was six blocks away when the wreck happened. That's what I mean about making cop killers pay."

"Okay," Lydia said. "So we put Montrose in his car and one of us drives it and the other follows? Or what?"

Generate ideas and make careful calculations before you move. "Let me think about this. I'll drive his car. We can put his body in the trunk, but first I put on his uniform and drive through the east edge of town."

"Someone could recognize you," she said, tracing little circles in the dirt with the foot that helped club a man to death.

"Huh uh. I'm going to be going really fast. Like I'm chasing someone. Even if they don't see the uniform, they'll automatically assume it's a cop."

Her voice picked up momentum. "That's good. Then when they find the wreck, they'll also assume Montrose was the one that was after a speeder."

"Right. I've got to make sure someone sees me to establish Montrose was alive before the accident. There's bound to be someone going or coming at the Green Lantern, or using the Chevron Station."

She brushed something from the sole of her bare foot. "So what do I do?"

I paused to think. *Play to your strength. Accumulate advantages to find a way to win.* "Okay, I've got it. Whoever sees the cop car speeding will assume he's after a speeder, or that there's some emergency he has to get to. But it'd be much more convincing if they could actually see the car he's chasing."

"I lost you there," she said. "I can't be speeding in your car. Someone would tell them what your car looks like and they'd come after you for causing the car wreck. Like the drunk driver in Seattle."

"We're not going to use my car. We're going to use someone else's. If I only knew how to hotwire a car . . ."

"I know a car we can use," Lydia said excitedly. "Tammy Balfour keeps one of those hide-a-key things hidden on her Barracuda."

"Do you know where she hides it?"

"Right under the front bumper. She locked herself out of her car one day at school and I was with her when she got it. I know where she lives, too."

"What if she's not home?"

"It doesn't matter. The Barracuda'll be there. She can't drive it because she just got her third speeding ticket."

"Where does she live?"

"On Chestnut. We practically passed it on the way out here."

Plan ten moves ahead, but make sure the next move is the correct move. "Okay. Let's think this through. There's a lot of ways we could do it, but only two that make any sense. Plan one. We leave together in Montrose's car, steal the Barracuda and head out of town with me posing as Montrose chasing you in the stolen car. Then we stage the accident and drive back in the Barracuda. Dump it, get in my car and go home. If we move fast, we'd have the Barracuda less than an hour. Even if it gets reported stolen, we should be okay."

"Why do you say that?"

"Because it's Sunday night and Montrose is probably the only cop patrolling."

"And he can't hurt us any more," Lydia added in a low voice.

I glanced at his slack body and nodded. "Plan two, we could ditch the Barracuda out at Kooskooskie and walk back, but that would be too risky. It'd take a couple hours to get back on foot and someone might see us."

"I agree. Let's do plan one."

"Okay, give me a hand getting his uniform off."

I had my flashlight in the Chevy, but didn't need it with the bright moonlight. We first undid the buttons in front, then the cuffs on his sleeves. When I pushed Montrose onto his side to work his arm out of the uniform, the sudden movement released a rank odor – the coppery smell of human blood combined with leaking intestinal gas. "That's sickening!" Lydia exclaimed.

The stench overwhelmed me. I got up and ran to the edge of the woods, vomiting at the base of a scraggy tree. Most of my dinner came up, followed by foul, chemical tasting bile. I spit several times in succession, wiped my eyes and mouth on the sleeve of my T-shirt and walked slowly back.

Lydia waited for me by the back door of the squad car. The worst of the odor was gone. By rolling Montrose to one side, then the other, it was possible to remove his shirt. The idea of putting it on gave me the creeps and I was still feeling queasy, so I threw it in the front seat of his car. Next, we each grabbed an arm and dragged him to the trunk of his car, the heels of his boots making barely perceptible parallel trails in the dirt. My mind strayed, imagining soft footprints being left on lunar soil and longing for the uncomplicated life I'd enjoyed fifteen minutes before.

Needing the key to Montrose's trunk, I checked the ignition. No keys. "Shit! Did you see car keys on his key ring?"

"He wouldn't have car keys on his key ring."

"Shit! We have to find his car keys. Check his pockets."

"You check his pockets. I'm not reaching in the bastard's pockets."

"Okay, then get his gun. Pick it up by the barrel and wipe off your fingerprints before we put it back in his holster."

I knelt down and fished in each of his front pockets, but found no keys. *Think! Where would he put his keys? He pulled in alongside my Chevy, put the spotlight on us and walked around. If he didn't put them in his pockets, where would he put them?* I went back to his car and pulled out the ashtray, overflowing with stale smelling cigarette butts. No luck there. Reaching up, I flipped down the visor above the windshield. Keys jangled as they fell, hitting the steering column and landing at my feet. "We've got keys," I told Lydia.

I got out, walked behind the car and opened the trunk. Lydia had found the gun, replaced it in its holster and snapped it shut. "Did you wipe off the part you touched?" I asked.

"Yeah. It was still warm. We'd be dead if you hadn't kicked it away from him."

I nodded, halfheartedly, and bent to lift Montrose's body. But then I stopped. "We can't put his body in the trunk because he might leave blood behind. Or some other kind of evidence."

Lydia nodded in the moonlight. "So, what do we do?"

"Stuff him in the back seat."

"He'll bleed in the back seat, too."

"There's probably been blood in the back seat before so it wouldn't raise a red flag like blood in the trunk."

"Good point."

I opened both back doors of the squad car and together we strained to hoist the dead body part way into the seat. It reminded me of the time we'd pulled Ethan into the back seat of my Chevy after Slider had rolled The Milker and I wondered if Lydia made the same connection.

Getting Montrose to fit into the back seat proved a difficult task. He was a couple inches over six feet and must've weighed two-twenty, so lifting him was a problem in and of itself. In the end, we had to bend his knees and jam his torso into a tightly cramped space. After a lot of pushing, we managed to force shut both doors. We were both out of breath. Something felt wrong. I sighed heavily and rubbed my forehead.

"What is it?" Lydia asked.

"I don't know. Something's not quite right, like I'm missing something."

"Something important?"

I shrugged. "I don't know."

"Maybe it'll come to you. For now, I say we get out of here."

"Okay." I put on Montrose's navy blue shirt over my sweaty T-shirt. Cool and slimy at the collar, I realized his blood was touching my bare skin. I cringed and another wave of nausea swept over me, but there was nothing left to throw up.

"You okay to drive?" Lydia asked, having observed my discomfort.

"Yeah, just shaky." I climbed behind the wheel and waited for Lydia to get in the passenger seat. When she shut the door, I put the key in the ignition and fired the big Plymouth to life. Lights off, we turned around and headed slowly out the cemetery for Reser Road. Still no lights coming from the ranch house. With no cars in sight, I turned on the headlights and drove back in the direction of town.

We hadn't gone far when Lydia said, "I'm so pissed at you, Bryan!"

"What'd I do?"

"You blamed me."

"I didn't." My voice sounded unconvincing.

"The hell you didn't! You blamed me for killing him."

"How did I blame you?"

"You said, 'Did you have to kill him?' Those were your exact words."

My foot ached from kicking the gun from Montrose's hand. I wriggled my ankle. "That was a question, not an indictment."

"The implication was pretty clear."

"Okay, let's just say I wish you hadn't killed him."

"Great! Some *pig* is in the process of raping me and you accuse me of murder for defending myself."

"I'm not accusing you of murder, Lydia. I was questioning whether it was necessary to kill the man. There's a difference."

"I was fighting for my life! What was I supposed to do? Demand he remove our handcuffs? Go to town and file a complaint?"

"He was unconscious. It seems like—"

"Bryan, you're making me crazy! You yourself said they wouldn't believe us, that they'd take his word over ours just because he's a police officer."

"I know what I said."

"Look at it this way. Montrose is . . . Montrose was totally crazy. If he didn't get us tonight it would have been next week, or next month! Especially after the way we messed him up. Why do you not get that?"

I remembered the murderous look he'd given me outside the courthouse in January. "Maybe you're right, but let's not have this conversation now," I pleaded. "We have a lot of work to do."

"Fine, but I'm pissed."

"I've got that. Right now we have to think of every possible way this plan can go wrong. We have to anticipate the unexpected and be ready for it."

She took a moment to gather herself. "Like?"

"Like what if someone saw Montrose take the road into Stubblefield. What if someone saw *us* go in?"

She twisted in her seat. "What difference does it make if he dies in a car wreck fifteen miles away?"

"When Montrose shows up dead the first thing they'll do is try to reconstruct what he did tonight. Minute by minute. If they put us in the same place with him we're going to have to answer some questions."

"Won't they just assume he was chasing a speeder?"

"That's what we're hoping for, but we have to be prepared for every possibility. Just in case. If for any reason it comes up, that we were in the cemetery and Montrose came in, let's say he hassled us for being parked and we left with a warning. Don't say anything about having beer with us and say we left out Farmer's Road."

"Where's Farmer's Road?"

I checked the rearview mirror. "The back way out of the cemetery. On the other side of where we were parked. It runs into Foster, which runs into Five-Mile Road."

"Why don't we just say we left the usual way?"

"Because we just left in Montrose's car and that would mean my car was either right in front or right behind him. And it wasn't. So our story is that we skirted the wheat field and left the back way."

She nodded. "Okay, but I seriously doubt if anyone saw either of our cars going in or out."

"You're probably right, but it's possible the people that live in that farmhouse saw something."

She rubbed her wrists again. "Barely."

"What if they heard the gunshot? What if they reported it?"

"First of all, I doubt if they heard it. This is farming country, Bryan. People shoot at coyotes all the time."

"I hope you're right. Tell me where your friend Tammy lives."

"Turn right on Howard and go about ten blocks. To Chestnut."

In an exchange, disregard the pieces you're trading and consider how the board will look after the trading is completed. I followed Lydia's directions and let her guide me the rest of the way to her friend's house. A gold Barracuda was parked on the street, directly under a street lamp. I drove past it, scanning both sides of the street to see which houses had lights on. There were several and they all had good views of the street. The neighborhood was quiet, no one coming or going, nothing happening.

I turned on Center with the intention of circling the block. "Get down!" I shouted at Lydia. Halfway down the block a woman in a white sweat suit was walking an Irish Setter on a leash. They were on the sidewalk, heading toward us at a brisk pace. I pulled Montrose's cap down over my eyes and cursed under my breath. Lydia flopped over in the front seat, resting her head on my right leg, barely below the woman's line of sight. As I pulled even with the woman she smiled and gave a little wave with her free hand, presumably grateful for a police presence in her neighborhood. I nodded and gave her a little salute with my left hand, avoiding any chance of her getting a good look at my face. I drove on toward the end of the block, not speeding up, not looking back and wondering what she was doing out at such a late hour. When I got around to Chestnut the second time, I switched off the headlamps and parked a half block from the Barracuda. "Let's go over the plan," I said, removing Montrose's cap and wiping my forehead with the sleeve of his uniform.

Devote the time to anticipate small problems and prevent large ones. We took a few minutes to review the plan, paying extra attention to the orchestrated car chase at the east end of town. Lydia was about to get out of the car when I looked at her and said, "Wait a sec! Can you do anything with your hair to look less like you?"

She thought for a moment and touched her hair, which was double-braided. "How's this?" she asked. Taking a long braid in each hand, she pulled them in front of her face and tied them in a loose knot that covered the entirety of her forehead.

"That's good," I told her, nodding my head. At ten feet in bad light she would be virtually unrecognizable to anyone who didn't know her well.

She got out of the car, quietly closing the door and walking up the sidewalk. If Lydia was successful in stealing the Barracuda, it was agreed I would follow her at fifteen miles an hour through residential streets until we approached Isaacs. On reaching The Green Lantern she would gun the accelerator and I, the Johnny-on-the-spot police officer, would take off in hot pursuit. If for whatever reason she was unable to get into her friend's car, she was to continue walking up to the next block and I'd pick her up a few minutes later. If someone saw her, she would casually walk behind the closest house, cut through back yards and meet me on Maple Street, a block over.

I watched Lydia walk deliberately toward the Barracuda, hugging the far side of the sidewalk, where she could stay in the shadows. Despite all she'd been through, she was thinking. I felt awful for her. A man had violated her and she'd killed him, which was horrible enough, but her burden was made worse because I questioned her actions. Maybe Montrose did intend to kill us. Maybe Lydia was right. If the authorities bought into the staged accident and we got out of this mess, our relationship would need as much repair as Montrose's car. *How can things be so good one minute and so completely fucked up the next?*

Concentrating with Montrose in the back seat proved difficult. The idea of a corpse being right behind me was chilling. It sounds irrational, but I half-expected his dead body to spring to life, get me in a chokehold and squeeze the life out of me. I turned to give him a look. Face up and lifeless, his eyes stared blankly at the ceiling of his car, as if searching for a clue as to what had happened that he would find himself dead. His body reeked of sweat and, if I was not mistaken, alcohol. I hadn't before smelled the alcohol and I wondered if booze had fueled his total loss of inhibition. It was funny. Not funny, funny, but interesting, because out at the cemetery I'd considered pouring enough of our beer on Montrose to make it look like alcohol played a role in his fatal car wreck. The way it turned out, I didn't have to.

Stay focused. Don't let emotion get in the way of clear thinking. Checking the dashboard I found a toggle switch labeled "Siren," next to the police radio. My plan included hitting the siren as soon as I started chasing the Barracuda. A witness reporting a police car, siren roaring and speeding after another car, would make the idea of a fatal accident more plausible. My eyes scanned over the dash and fixated on the radio send button. It was on the left side of a microphone, attached to the main unit by curly cord. That gave me still another idea.

I looked up in time to see Lydia duck in front of the Barracuda, temporarily disappearing from view. My breathing quickened and I whispered *". . . please find the hide-a-key."* Thirty seconds later the lights went on inside Tammy Balfour's car. I glanced in the rearview mirror, then up and down both sides of the street, seeing nothing to suggest anyone had observed Lydia. A few moments later she pulled away from the curb, slowly but not too slowly, quietly and with lights off, as agreed. I breathed a sigh of relief, put Montrose's cap back in place and crawled out after her. My bladder was about to burst, but that was the least of my worries.

One block later Lydia turned on the headlamps. I followed suit. No one was on the streets. No sign of the woman walking her dog. It appeared the theft of the Barracuda had gone unnoticed. I turned a little too sharply onto Division Street and Montrose's dead body shifted in the back seat. Another whiff of alcohol mixed with the sickening scent of blood. A quick glance behind me indicated he'd fallen further off the back seat, further from view should anyone have a look in. No harm there. "Fuck you, Montrose. You lose!" I said out loud. "A girl killed you, tough guy. A girl with handcuffs on!" I laughed, but it came out wrong, sounding more like a little dog whose foot had been stepped on.

Ahead, the Barracuda made a series of herky-jerky movements and might have even stalled. Lydia, unaccustomed to driving a four-speed with a lot of power, appeared to be having difficulty with the clutch. *Just don't kill it when it's time for the chase,* I implored her, as if telepathically attuned. She got going again and pulled even with The Green Lantern, slowing for a red light. There were no cars in the parking lot and no sign of anyone coming or going. *Sunday night.* Washington had so-called "blue laws" and taverns were closed on Sunday. "Shit!" I yelled. *What else will go wrong?*

Sticking to the plan, Lydia turned onto The Gut and gunned the accelerator with a vengeance. The Barracuda jumped like a big cat, tires squealing. Rubber burned onto the pavement as Lydia fishtailed up the street, guaranteeing enough noise that everyone in the tavern would have instinctively looked out the window. I swore a second time. We had lost a strategic advantage.

Conducting a winning attack takes nerve! I flicked the Siren switch to the on position and heard it respond, a banshee in the quiet night. Pulling down Montrose's cap, I took off after the Barracuda, skidding onto The

Gut, a police car engaged in hot pursuit of a speeding citizen. Witnesses would assume I was after a wild teenager in a fast car, a menace to law-abiding society.

A block ahead, someone in a Ford Bronco heard the siren and pulled abruptly to the side of the road. My spirits lifted with the realization we'd been seen. A moment later, an attendant gassing up a Mustang in the Chevron station craned his neck to see what was happening. Behind him, two women getting out of a station wagon also looked our way. We had witnesses galore, all of whom would look in the fast-moving police car and see a man in a police uniform. Nothing out of the ordinary.

A series of thoughts raced through my mind. An investigation would begin when Officer Jack Montrose failed to report in from his late shift. Eventually he would be found dead in his vehicle. The Walla Walla Police Department would ask for witnesses to come forward to help them unravel the unfortunate death of a good cop, killed in the line of duty. The towns-folk would report a police car chasing a gold Barracuda, which by then would have been reported stolen by someone in the Balfour family. The police would know Montrose to be the officer speeding north on Isaacs at seventy miles an hour. And they'd assume he lost control minutes later, resulting in his untimely death.

Two blocks ahead of me, past the Suds Up Car Wash and across from the Blue Mountain Tavern, Lydia swerved right off Isaacs and took the sharp left turn onto Mill Creek Road. I switched off the siren, thinking there was no point in attracting any further attention. Lydia was hauling ass, going seventy-five on the straight stretches and making me nervous for her safety. Beads of perspiration broke out on my forehead. Not to mention injuring herself, an accident in the Barracuda would derail a plan that had no built-in margin for error.

I sped past a trailer house with a large dog tethered to the front porch. A floodlight illuminated a junk Edsel on cinder blocks, but no occupants were in sight. Distracted, I took a right turn too fast and brushed the branches of an overhanging cottonwood. Backing off the accelerator, I hoped Lydia would lose me in her rearview mirror and reduce her speed before reaching the fork in the road at Blue Creek Road. After a straight-away with a big dip, I took the fork and headed downhill, an old barn on my right. Thirty seconds later I spotted her taillights, a half-mile ahead and even with the historic site of the first sawmill built between the Cascades and the Rockies. Flooded with relief, I took a deep breath and tried to clear my mind.

It had taken us only ten minutes to reach Kooskooskie, which was really no more than a few summer cabins. With no grocery store and no gas station, there was little chance of being seen as the hour approached midnight. I continued on to the agreed-upon destination, just our side of the Oregon state line. I watched Lydia's rear brake lights glow bright red as she prepared to turn around on the far side of the bridge.

Slowing down, I tightened the lap seat belt and got the bridge in my sights, bracing myself for the impending collision. Then I depressed the send switch on Montrose's police radio, left it open and set it on the seat beside me. I accelerated one last time and smashed Montrose's car into the cement pillar at the near end of the bridge. Caught up in the moment, I forgot to check my speed, which had been my intention when the scheme first hatched in my mind. I wanted to be going about twenty miles an hour, but I think it was more like forty. The Plymouth cruiser had to weigh two tons and the impact with the cement pillar tore a big chunk of the right front fender completely off the car. Anyone listening to the police radio back at the stationhouse would've heard the earsplitting sound of metal twisting and glass breaking. The decibel level far exceeded my expectations.

My heart raced as I heard a hubcap bouncing off cement and hitting rocks as it rolled over and down the embankment. An instant later the radiator blew like Old Faithful. Steam poured out from under the hood, which had buckled in the middle, partly obstructing my view. My body ached and I felt momentarily stunned, like I'd taken really bad fall on unforgiving ice. I thought I was okay, but sat still to collect myself.

A woman's voice, crackling with static, came bursting through the radio speaker and into the car. "Car 17, come in, please."

I froze. Held my breath and said nothing. My ears were ringing.

"Car 17, do you read? Come in, please!" Clearer reception somehow translated into more fear.

Lydia was driving the Barracuda across the bridge toward me and at a pretty good clip. She was fifteen feet away, rolling down her window and looking concerned because I hadn't moved since the impact. Time to act fast.

"Car 17! Jack Montrose! Jack, are you all right?" The woman's voice was fast approaching hysteria.

I held my index finger to my lips to signal Lydia for quiet, took the microphone in my other hand and imitated the last sound Montrose made back at the cemetery, the sound of a frightened animal in the throes of death. Carefully switching off the send button, I wiped the parts I'd touched using Montrose's shirttail and let the mike drop to the floor of the car.

I got out to survey the damage. The entire front end was crunched and the fan belt had been pushed into the radiator. The car was perched precariously at the edge of the embankment. I realized how close I'd come to going over.

Lydia bolted out of the Barracuda. "Did you mean to hit the bridge that hard?"

I shrugged, noticed a wounded look in her eyes. She'd been crying. I looked at Montrose's car. The intact left headlight of the police car illuminated the numbers 1958 indented in the smashed cement pillar. "Let's get Montrose behind the wheel and push the car over the embankment."

"What were you doing on the radio?"

"I'll tell you later," I said, dismissing her with the wave of a hand.

"What if someone comes by?"

I rubbed the back of my neck. "I've been out here for three keg parties and no one's come by yet."

"But what if they did?"

"Say we stopped to help this poor cop who wrecked his car. Don't let them get a good look at your face and tell them to get to a phone and report it. Say we saw some speeders in a late model, dark car. Generic GM, not too specific."

She nodded approval. "Okay. What do we do now?"

"Let's put his uniform back on him. Hurry. We don't have any time to waste."

We opened the left rear door and dragged Montrose out, his head clunking hard on the pavement, like a coconut falling from a tipped grocery bag. I did a quick check for bloodstains in the back seat, but didn't see any. His face appeared to have taken on a bluish color. Touching a dead man was creepy and brought on another bout of nausea.

After considerable tugging and positioning, we managed to get Montrose's shirt on him and tucked it in with a reasonable degree of neatness. It took another couple of minutes to hoist him into the driver's seat and place his feet in the proper position. The effort exhausted us. I wiped down the steering wheel, then pressed his palms and fingers against it to put his fingerprints back in the places they belonged. If the authorities were to dust the steering wheel and find it wiped clean of prints, their suspicions would have been immediately aroused. This way, they'd find what was expected. I put the car in neutral and said, "Okay, let's push it over the embankment, but remember where you place your hands. Just in case they suspect something, we can't leave any fingerprints."

We got behind Montrose's car and, on the count of three, pushed as hard as we could. Our feet slipped on the gravel shoulder and the car refused to budge. I opened the driver's door and cranked the wheel as far to the right as it would go. We pushed a second time, but again the car wouldn't move. "Shit!" I swore. "We don't have time for this."

"Just leave it, it looks like a bad accident."

I shook my head. "Not bad enough to kill someone. I'm okay, aren't I?"

"I guess."

Never rush your reply. Take enough time to calculate in an unfamiliar position. I closed my eyes and considered several candidate moves. The best one seemed obvious. "Stand on the bridge," I ordered, "and get way out of the way." I dashed over and dove in behind the wheel of the Barracuda, which she'd left running. I jammed it into first, drove a hundred feet past the wreckage and turned the car around. There, I floored it, angling off the road and slamming its right side into the driver's side of Montrose's car, which shuddered against the bridge before shooting forward and hurtling

over the embankment, picking up speed as it went. When it reached the
bottom it hit a boulder half as large as the car itself. The windshield exploded in a spray of glass.

I got out and ran down the embankment to survey the damage, my injured foot killing me.

"How's it look?" Lydia asked, right behind me.

"Convincing," I said. Montrose's police car had flipped halfway onto its
side. Steam hissed from the radiator. A gold smear of paint from the Barracuda extended the length of the left front fender. The impact had distorted
the driver's door, but I managed to get it open, careful again to wipe off any
fingerprints. I reached in and also wiped my prints off the car keys, horsed
the gear lever back in drive and wiped it down. Montrose lay awkwardly
against the dashboard. His cap had fallen on the floor. His eyes were open
and bulging out of their sockets. The way they rolled up made it look like he
was trying to get a final look at the moon, desperately taking in a piece of
American history.

Learn to convert temporary advantages into permanent ones. Carefully, I
grabbed the microphone by its curly cord and placed it gently in Montrose's
cupped right hand. His last act had been to call in to the precinct. I tried to
look at the accident objectively. It appeared he'd hit the windshield with his
head. He wasn't wearing his seat belt and I wished I'd strapped him in before pushing the car over the edge. *Too late now,* I reasoned. I walked
behind the car and wiped off the areas in back where we'd pushed. Part of
the right taillight had been busted out.

Lydia asked, "Shall we get some boulders and smash it up some more?"

*Avoid moves that look good but yield no material advantage. Don't help
your opponent.* "No. It looks convincing the way it is."

"Okay, let's get out of here."

"Go ahead. Turn the Barracuda around and get in the passenger seat.
I'll be right there." I hurried down to the creek and washed off the blood on
my neck, the blood left behind by Montrose's collar. I couldn't stand the
creepy sensation a minute longer. I took off for the road above me, slipping
on a smooth rock and bruising my shin. Limping up the embankment, I
piled into the vacated driver's seat and headed the Barracuda back to town.

"What were you doing with the police radio?" Lydia asked right away.

"I radioed in the sound of the wreck. I made it look like Montrose tried
to call in, that the distraction had something to do with the wreck."

"But I saw you saying something into the mike."

"I was just groaning. Like Montrose did when he died."

She squeezed her eyes shut. "Oh. What do we do now?"

"I'm going to cut over to the Scenic Loop. Five-Mile Road connects with
Foster and that'll take us back to Stubblefield."

"We're going to leave Tammy's car in the cemetery?"

I shook my head. "No, we'll ditch it close to Farmer's Road and walk
into Stubblefield the back way."

"I've lived here my whole life and I've never heard of this Farmer's Road."

"I'm not surprised. It's not even on the map."

"How do you know about it?"

"Vicky told me the first night we were out here."

"The *first* night? You went to the cemetery more than once with her?"

"The only night is what I meant to say. God, Lydia! Don't make this any worse than it already is."

Her voice went low. "This night couldn't get any worse."

"Actually, it could. If something goes wrong, it could get a whole lot worse. So we don't need to be fighting between ourselves."

"Okay. So we ditch Tammy's car and walk back to your car. Then you take me home. Right?"

"Right. And we don't say word one to anyone. That means anyone! I can't tell my closest buddies, you can't tell Yolanda."

"Don't worry! I'm not about to tell Yolanda."

"You don't even confess it to a priest."

"I'm not Catholic, Bryan."

"I know you're not Catholic. I'm just trying to make a point. Criminals get caught because they always shoot off their mouths and someone tells the cops."

"I'm not a criminal, either."

"Jesus, Lydia, will you please calm down? I just trying to stress how important it is that we keep quiet. Bigdog calls it the code of silence. After tonight, we shouldn't even talk about it between ourselves."

"Okay, if we're not going to talk about it, I have a question. Suppose something did go wrong. Suppose at some point the cops come to me and ask, 'Where were you on the night of July 20 between the hours of ten o'clock and midnight?' Like in the movies?"

I stole a look at her. "Good question. Let's stick to the truth as much as we can. Anything that's not incriminating, we tell the truth. That way there's less chance of getting caught in a lie."

"So if they asked if he caught us having sex we'd answer truthfully?"

"No, we lie about that because he'd have never let us go. Same with drinking beer. Just say we went to Bigdog's for dinner and watched the Apollo broadcast. Just before ten we drove out to Stubblefield to get a good look at the moon. We were listening to the radio."

"What station?"

I had to pee in the worst way. "XERB. Montrose came by about a half-hour later and told us to leave or he'd write us up for being on private property. Say he put the spotlight on us, just the way he did, and that he got out of his car, but that was it. We left a couple minutes later out Farmer's Road and went by the Phi Delt house. We hung out in the TV room and watched the end of *Abbott and Costello Meet the Mummy*, which ended around midnight. We were the only ones there because the house is shut down for the summer."

"If the house is shut down, how did we get in?"

I downshifted, slowed for a turn. "I have a key to the back door. I'm supposed to go in every couple of weeks and make sure everything's okay."

"Is that true?"

"Yeah, Bigdog has one, too. We each go in about once a week since vacation started," I answered, heading up the incline where Five Mile Road began.

"Why?"

"I'll explain it later."

"Okay, so we watched the movie. Then what?"

"Then I took you home a little after midnight. When I hear about Montrose's death, I'll call you, tell you I read it in the paper, or whatever. That's how you find out. If you find out before I call you, you call me. That's how I found out. We discuss the fact that we saw him alive out at Stubblefield around ten-thirty and that one of us should call the police."

"Really. You think we should call the police?"

I nodded. "Yeah, because that's what we'd do if we were completely innocent. We'd cooperate even if we didn't like the guy."

She bit at a fingernail. "Okay. Which one of us calls?"

"I do."

She wrung her hands, nervously. "What if they follow up and try to trip me up? What if they ask me a bunch of questions about the movie? I haven't seen it."

"Blush. Say Abbott and Costello were these two guys raiding tombs in Egypt, but that we weren't really watching the movie. If we have to, we can say we had sex in the TV room. Just move the sex from the cemetery to the TV room."

I turned left onto Foster Road and soon reached the beginning of Farmer's Road. I nearly missed it because it was no more than a narrow dirt track cutting through a field of wheat. Fortunately, it had been marked by a pair of rusted out oil barrels. Spray-painted in white, one read *No Hunting!* The other, *Keep Out!*

Take no unnecessary chances. Shore up weak squares before they become liabilities. I turned around and parked the Barracuda on the shoulder a quarter-mile away, again wiping down the steering wheel and door handles for prints. "Did you touch anything else in here?" I asked Lydia.

"No, and it wouldn't matter if I did."

"Why?"

"Because I went to the Arctic Circle with Tammy two weeks ago. After school."

"Okay. You can fix your hair if you want to."

She untied her braids and shook them behind her. "Let's get away from here before someone drives by."

"Just a minute." I squatted down, removed the cap and let the air out of the right front tire. The hissing sound startled two horses standing in an unplanted field, no more than twenty feet away. The moon had angled higher and broken free of a solitary cloud, casting ashen shadows all around us. As the horses galloped off, there was enough light to see one was wearing blinkers.

When I finished with the tire I replaced the key in the hide-a-key under the front bumper, again wiping the little magnetic container clean. We ran across the road and headed up the slight incline, my legs burning with fatigue. I felt bad about the damage to the Barracuda, but rationalized that insurance would pay to repair it.

I was certain Foster was almost never used late on a Sunday night. Still, I breathed easier when we reached Farmer's Road, leading up to Stubblefield, high on the hill. We were a third of the way up when a car rounded a corner, its beams aimed squarely in our direction. Lydia reacted first, pulling me down. The earth smelled sweet and the summer wheat stood almost three feet tall, providing a good enough cover that we were sure no one saw us. The car slowed as it approached the disabled Barracuda, but didn't stop.

On seeing the flat tire had had its intended effect, Lydia said, "God, Bryan. Do you think of everything?"

"Let's hope so," I answered in an even tone, but the truth was I was frightened beyond words. Frightened that I'd forgotten something, frightened of how the incident would affect Lydia and me, frightened of going to jail and losing everything.

When we got to the edge of the woods we stopped and peed. I turned my back as Lydia pulled down her pants and squatted. I had made love to her and helped her kill a man that night, but couldn't watch her urinate. We finished relieving ourselves, jogged over to my Chevy and got in. I drove along the edge of the cemetery and headed out Farmer's Road, taking the longer, back way into town. Again, I felt something nagging at me, a detail that seemed as far away as the men walking on the moon. Bone tired, I'd used up my body's supply of adrenaline. Making matters worse, I had a splitting headache, probably from slamming Montrose's car into the bridge and whiplashing my spinal column. I reached into my glove compartment to get some aspirin from a bottle I kept there, but it was empty.

Lydia was quiet, sullen. She didn't ask why I needed aspirin, which was unlike her. I made no effort to engage her, as I was busy running every possible scenario in my head. A new concern emerged. Even if I hadn't been the one to kill Montrose, the cover-up was entirely my doing. That alone could get me ten years in prison.

"I feel dirty," Lydia said, breaking the silence. Her eyes brimmed with tears. "I can't wait to get in the shower."

"I'm sorry . . . about what he did to you."

"He's a pig!" she said, wiping away tears with the back of her hand.

"Yeah, well now he's a dead pig." An image of Montrose came to mind, lifeless in his wrecked car. I wondered how soon they would find him.

"I'm really freaked out, Bryan."

"I know. So am I."

She cleared her throat. "It hasn't really sunk in. What I did."

"It'll take awhile."

"I mean, I did what I had to, but killing a man is . . ." Her voice trailed off.

"I know."

We fell back into silence. I reviewed the moves we'd made and tried to anticipate the type of endgame that could be in store.

"What're you thinking about?" Lydia asked.

"Chess."

"Are you kidding me?"

"No."

Lydia glowered. "After what happened back there, you're thinking about chess?"

"I have been since you slapped me. It's how my mind works."

"Please explain that to me."

"It's complicated."

"Try."

After implying Lydia had done something wrong, I hoped the cover-up would regain me stature in her eyes. "Okay. A chess game is really two games in one. The first is you against your opponent. The second is your opponent against you. Deciding on the best move requires putting yourself in your opponent's position to look for weaknesses."

"So you've been looking for our weaknesses, as if you were the cops."

"Yeah, and then creating a plan that'll win."

"Have you?"

"I haven't been able to keep emotion out of the equation, so I'm afraid I might've overlooked something."

"But you can't think of what it is."

I shook my head. "I can't. The good news is I can't come up with a single way we could get caught. No one saw us kill Montrose. No one saw us stage the accident. No one saw us take the Barracuda, or ditch it. As long as neither of us talks about what happened, we should be okay."

"How many times do I have to tell you I won't talk?"

"I know, and I believe you. I won't talk either."

"The code of silence," she added.

I turned left onto The Gut, planning a brief stop at the fraternity house. If hanging out in the TV room was to be part of our alibi, no one else could be there. It was unlikely anyone was using it, but I had to make sure.

We'd only gone a few blocks when a police car and an ambulance blasted past us, traveling in the opposite direction. Holding my breath, I slowed down and watched in my rearview mirror. Both cars skidded onto Mill Creek Road and headed out toward Kooskooskie, sirens wailing. I glanced down at my car clock. It was midnight, straight up.

Chapter 8
The Broken Taillight

I dreamed Lydia and I were trapped in the back seat of a police car. It leaned precariously to one side, in danger of tipping over. An odd clattering sound drew our attention to the front windshield. I looked up and saw a gaunt hand searching for a way in, long fingernails rattling against broken glass. The hand glided from view and in its place appeared the face of a vampire, as pale and cold as polished white marble. The creature looked at us with glassy metallic eyes, freezing us in a murderous stare. It was Jack Montrose, his corpse covered with blisters and boils, but nonetheless re-animated and recognizable.

I woke with my heart hammering against my ribs. Bolting from bed, I raced to the bathroom. The creaking and cracking of the Zaleski's old house, sounds I usually tuned out, had kept me awake until the first light of morning. I felt wearier than I'd been at the end of Hell Week, after seventy-two hours of sleep deprivation. My injured foot throbbed with every step. Splashing cold water on my face, I tried to rid my mind of the ghoulish image from the nightmare.

The mirror over the sink reflected a chalky mask. My face seemed to have aged several years in the space of a few hours, like Dorian Gray's portrait. A tic quivered below my right eye, a grim reminder of having participated in a homicide. *My life will never be the same!*

I buried my head in my hands and wept as the night replayed itself—Montrose smiling sadistically after putting his fingers in Lydia—Lydia summoning power from the heavens before delivering the fatal blow—the coppery smell of blood as we struggled to lift Montrose's dead body—chasing Lydia in the police car and colliding with the bridge at Kooskooskie—

Reva's voice startled me, mercifully halting the flood of images. "Are you all right, Bryan?" She stood in the open doorway, peering at me over tortoise-shell reading glasses. A look of concern creased her pleasant face.

"Uh . . . I think so."

"I've been calling you."

"Oh, sorry. I'm spaced," I said, shaking my head to get reoriented.

"Vat's wrong?"

"I had a nightmare," I mumbled, self-conscious about the tic under my eye.

"Vat about?"

"A vampire. It was staring at me."

"Should I get garlic?"

"No," I answered, attempting a laugh that hurt my head. I couldn't tell if Reva was serious or making a joke.

"Have you veen crying?"

"No, I'm okay. Just a bad dream."

"Your eyes are red."

"I rub them a lot when I first get up." Like an idiot, I rubbed my eyes to demonstrate. My eyelids felt like sandpaper.

"Breakfast is ready." As she walked away, Reva looked over her shoulder and added, "Zdenek is eager to get going on chess."

"I'll be right up."

Only I wasn't. I sat on the toilet with diarrhea, struggling to process the enormity of what had happened. *We killed a cop. His dead body is . . . somewhere.* Reality had set in, but superimposed on it was a sense of unreality, as if I might awaken from the horror of killing a man the way I'd awakened from the vampire dream. I momentarily wished I could go back to sleep and never wake up.

I shook my head in disbelief. Eight hours before I'd been a straight "A" student at a prestigious college, a national chess hero, a faithful boyfriend, a brother in the best fraternity, a model citizen. My eighteen years hadn't been charmed, by any means, but my life had reached a point where it felt good to be me. That life was over. I'd become an accomplice to murder. I'd orchestrated a desperate and dangerous cover-up. *Not murder . . . self-defense. Stop forgetting that!*

I made it off the toilet and finished washing up. Trudging upstairs, my legs nearly gave out, their weakness telling me: *Everything has changed. Everything has changed* – like a mantra that wouldn't shut off. I picked at my breakfast of scrambled eggs and sausage, barely noticing Reva's looks of concern. Again, I wondered what had become of Montrose's dead body. Had they found him in the dark out at Kooskooskie? Or was he still in the front seat of his squad car, lifeless eyes staring grotesquely into nothingness? By my best guess he'd been found. There had to be a morgue somewhere in Walla Walla. The corpse we stuffed into his car would be as stiff and cold as the metal slab it rested on.

Reva left the room. I closed my eyes. A movie played in my head, a frightful preview of scenes about to unfold. A police detective would come to the Zaleski residence to arrest me. He would show his badge and identify himself, shocking Dr. Z and Reva. "You're under arrest for the murder of Officer Jack Montrose," he would tell me. I'd be fingerprinted like a common criminal and booked into a grimy holding cell that reeked of disinfectant, body odor, urine and feces. A parade of hostile cops would come by and say things like, "You're cute, cop-killer . . . your dance card's gonna be full in the big house." Word would leak out of the police station and KWWA would break the story of a suspect in custody. I'd be given one phone call and would contact my father, who would be stunned into silence. The evening headline in the *U-B* would read: *Whitman Chess Whiz Held in*

Cop Killing Case. My fraternity brothers would be quoted as saying it was all a big mistake, that Bryan Matthews was a regular guy, incapable of committing such a heinous crime. Facing the reality of a life in prison, a life without Lydia, I would contemplate suicide, perhaps devising some clever way of hanging myself in my holding cell. In the end, I'd opt not to do it—

For the second time that morning Reva's hand on my shoulder jolted me into the present. "Vat is wrong, Bryan? And don't tell me is just bad dream." Stone-faced, she looked at me, waiting for a response.

I felt an urge to vomit so I answered, "I think I might be sick."

She pressed the back of her hand to my forehead and said, "You don't have temperature, but skin is, vat you say, clamsy?"

"Clammy," I said, using my napkin to wipe beads of sweat from my brow.

Just then, Dr. Z, who'd been in the study preparing for my morning chess lesson, came in the kitchen holding an empty cup of coffee. "Are you not well, Bryan?" he asked, looking back and forth between Reva and me.

"I didn't sleep well. And I had a nightmare. That's all."

"Dat's not all," Reva insisted. "De boy is . . . clammy, and he von't eat a bite of his breakfast. He just said he vas sick."

"Are you sick?" Dr. Z asked.

I nodded.

He looked as concerned as Reva. "In that case, chess can wait. I was going to show you a variation on the center fork trick, but why don't you go back to bed and rest."

"Probably a good idea," I sighed, relieved to have an out. I'd have been hard-pressed to affect even a semblance of normalcy during my chess lesson.

I went slowly back down the stairs, holding the handrail for the first time ever. When I reached my bedroom I threw myself on the bed. *Maybe I should confess and get it over with,* I thought, rolling onto my back and staring at the ceiling. Tell the truth and rid myself of the horrible dread that gripped me. I considered hiring an attorney. Good legal representation could get me off with a lesser charge, perhaps as little as a suspended sentence. *No, stupid! They'd charge you with being an accomplice to murder, obstruction of justice, tampering with evidence at a crime scene, grand larceny on the Barracuda, impersonating an officer, reckless endangerment, damaging police property, damaging private property, damaging public property, and God knows what else. Fuck the truth! You tried telling the truth after Montrose issued the trumped-up speeding ticket and look where it got you.*

The phone rang, startling me from a fitful, cough syrup-induced sleep. I wanted to answer it, but my body felt straitjacketed to the sagging mattress. Someone upstairs picked up. I heard heavy footsteps on the stairs.

"You up to a call from Lydia?" Dr. Z asked, after peeking his head through the doorway to see if I was awake.

I nodded and lifted the receiver. "Hello."

"Bryan?" Lydia said. I watched Dr. Z leave.

"Yeah. Wait a sec for Dr. Zaleski to hang up, upstairs. Okay?"

"Okay."

The phone clicked.

"Hi, what's up?" I asked, my heart speeding up to double its resting rate.

"You know that cop that told us to leave the cemetery last night. He got killed in a car accident less than an hour after we saw him."

"You're kidding." Lydia acted as if she knew nothing. The way we'd rehearsed it.

"No. Amelia heard it on the radio a few minutes ago."

I sat on the floor, leaned against the bed. "What station?"

"KWWA, I think. She asked me if Officer Jack Montrose was the same policeman bothering you outside the post office before Christmas."

"That's right. Amelia sort of came to my rescue. Where was the accident?"

"Out by the bridge at Kooskooskie. They said he was chasing a stolen car. Maybe we should call the police."

I crouched over the phone. "Uh, I've had . . . I'm not sure that's a good idea."

She paused briefly. "Whatever. Look, I have to go or I'll be late for my shift at the cannery."

"Okay," I replied, affecting a brighter tone. "See you tonight."

"Maybe. I'm not feeling so good."

"What's wrong?"

"I just don't feel good, that's all." She sounded impatient, dismissive.

"Okay, me neither." I said tentatively. "I love you."

"I have to get to work. Bye."

My heart sank. Now I really did feel ill, sick at heart and afraid my relationship with Lydia was over. *I can't live without her.* I stared at the cement floor in numbed disbelief, wondering how a good life could have come so unhinged so quickly.

I stripped down and staggered into the basement shower, getting the water as hot as I could take it before soaping up. Behind the soap was an uncapped half-full tube of Prell. I lathered my hair with green shampoo, the missing cap reminding me that I might've missed some detail out at Stubblefield. I wracked my brain for the next five minutes, but nothing came to mind.

Rinsing off, I realized I'd forgotten to shave before showering. My routine was off. I angrily grabbed my razor and can of shaving cream from the bathroom counter and got back under the water. I shaved and stood there until the water turned cold, trying to sluice away the horror of death. *You could stay under the water for the next twenty-four hours and still not wash away all that's happened.* Stepping from the shower, I stubbed my sore foot on the tile sill. It felt like a mule had kicked it and I swore loud enough to be heard upstairs.

Most of the day I spent ruminating. *Could I have stopped Lydia from delivering the fatal blow? Should I call my father and tell him what had happened? Did the cover-up have a chance of working, or was I just thinking crazy after the shock and ordeal we'd been through?* One moment I would reassure myself, and then a tsunami of free-floating fear would sweep me away. Capital punishment in the State of Washington meant they hung you by the neck until you're dead. And cop killers didn't get off with life sentences.

The *Walla Walla Union-Bulletin* arrived late, a few minutes after five in the afternoon. I'd been checking the front porch every five minutes, eager to know what the police were thinking. I unfolded the paper and stared at the one-inch headline that jumped from the front page:

OFFICER JACK MONTROSE FOUND DEAD, NO SUSPECTS IN FATAL CAR CHASE

By Gene Claghorn
Union-Bulletin Writer

Jack Montrose, a three-year veteran of the Walla Walla Police Department, was found dead behind the wheel of his demolished squad car at approximately 12:13 Monday morning. Officer Montrose had been in pursuit of a stolen car when he was apparently run off Mill Creek Road, crashing into the north end of the bridge at Kooskooskie and overturning as his vehicle rolled down the embankment. Cause of death was not immediately known, but a source close to the investigation said Officer Montrose appeared to have suffered a broken neck in the accident, in addition to severe head injuries. Montrose's untimely death is the first ever for a Walla Walla police officer performing in the line of duty.

Detective Frank Gerritsen, who is heading the investigation into the accident, told reporters the police department has been able to piece together the following bits of information. A few minutes after 11:00 P.M. yesterday, several witnesses saw Officer Montrose traveling at a high rate of speed in pursuit of a 1967 Dodge Barracuda. Nancy Ulrich and her sister, Clara Benton, both from Hermiston, Oregon, saw the high-speed chase from the Chevron station on Isaacs, in the Eastgate shopping area. Mrs. Ulrich said, "When the policeman put on his siren, we thought the driver of the speeding car would stop, but he just kept going. It's a cryin' shame. Kids nowadays don't respect the law, anymore."

The stolen Dodge Barracuda, found abandoned early this morning on the Scenic Loop, belongs to Richard and Audrey Balfour who live on Chestnut Street, near Paine

School. The car is registered in their name, but used by their daughter, Tamara, a junior at Wa-Hi. Mr. Balfour told the *Union-Bulletin*, "It's bad enough to have your car stolen and damaged. We feel violated. But to know it was involved in the death of a policeman who's just trying to do his job is another thing. I hope to God they get the low-life that did this!"

Calls by the police to the nearby Washington State Penitentiary indicate all inmates were accounted for at the time of the fatal accident. "There are more questions than answers, right now," Detective Gerritsen explained. "Whoever dumped the car out on Russell Road seems to have disappeared into thin air. Frankly, we could use some help. If anyone saw anything even remotely suspicious, please call the Walla Walla Police Department as soon as possible." Persons with information have been asked to call Jackson 5-2975. A reward of $1000 is being offered for information leading to the arrest of the driver of the stolen car.

Jack Randall Montrose, twenty-five years old, had been on the Walla Walla police force for three-and-one-half years, following a two-year stint in Vietnam where he served his country in combat duty as an Army infantryman. Those who knew him say he enjoyed a reputation as a hard-nosed cop who believed in the letter of the law. He is survived by his parents, Jim and Marjorie Montrose, and wife of two years, Janice. The couple had no children. Officer Montrose volunteered to coach Little League football and baseball and was himself an accomplished high school football player at Walla Walla High School, where he graduated in 1962. Services will be announced tomorrow.

I forced myself to slow down and reread the article, make sure I hadn't missed something important. The front-page headline intensified my fear of getting caught. Studying the article a third time, I noticed a bothersome rash that had begun to blossom on my upper chest. The police seemed to be buying into the cover-up. The charge would be vehicular homicide, not murder. Lydia and I would be okay unless we could be tied to Montrose out at Stubblefield Cemetery. And how likely was that? What had happened took place five miles out of town in an abandoned cemetery, and on a night when the whole world was glued to their television sets. We were going to get away with killing a cop. Relief washed over me. Then, as quickly as it made its appearance, it disappeared, and I nearly drowned in my own fear.

––––––––––

I phoned Lydia, hoping to get her as soon as she got home from the cannery. I needed to know how she was holding up, but even more I needed to know if she was still speaking to me. Yolanda answered and said her sister hadn't returned. I signed off quickly before she had a chance to bring up the subject of Montrose's death.

The callback from Lydia never came and my sense of desperation metastasized into a frightening mass. At seven-fifteen the phone rang, but it was someone calling for Dr. Z. I waited. Each minute felt elongated, excruciatingly drawn out, like when you're in a desperate hurry and a traffic light refuses to change. At seven forty-five I picked up the phone and started dialing, only to realize Dr. Z was still on the line. I apologized, put the receiver back on the hook and made a fist, ready to punch a hole in the wall.

Half an hour passed and Lydia still hadn't called. I carefully lifted the receiver, relieved to hear a dial tone. Called the Cruz' and got a busy signal. My gut twisted into a hard knot of frustration and fear. She had to be there, which probably meant she'd taken the phone off the hook. I considered driving over but rejected the idea. Instead, I dialed every couple minutes for the next half hour, but got a busy signal every time. I wanted to scream or, better yet, smash windows with a baseball bat. Giving up, I drank some more Robitussin and collapsed into bed.

Feigning nausea, I begged off on breakfast and my morning chess lesson. I padded off in my stocking feet and spent the better part of the day documenting a chronology of the events that had shattered my life. I listed out every conceivable way a clue could emerge and cast suspicion on Lydia and me. Poring over my notes, I examined every event and scene from the perspective of a sharp police detective who might take a fresh look at the evidence (what Dr. Z would've called a "beginner's mind"). When I felt satisfied there was no more information to be gleaned from this examination, I shredded my notes, torched them in a soup can and flushed the ashen remains down the toilet.

Lydia called me mid-afternoon from a pay phone at the cannery. Noise from nearby forklifts, conveyor belts and other machines made it almost impossible to hear, but I gathered she wanted to meet as soon as possible. We agreed I'd walk the half-mile up to Reed and Bell's and meet her at a quarter after five.

I arrived ten minutes early and waited on the sidewalk, guessing at how many cars would pass by before Lydia's would appear. A few minutes later I watched her guide her old Pontiac into an open space at the far end of the drive-in. I'd guessed she'd be the seventh car, but I was off. She was number nine. Like Stubblefield on Slider's map of Walla Walla.

We put in our orders to the carhop, a plain looking girl with radically plucked eyebrows and thin brown hair. Lydia leaned closer. "Smell me and tell me if I smell like mushrooms."

I obliged, grateful for the levity. "Actually, you do."

"That's what Rita said. I've been sautéing mushrooms for eight hours. Now I smell like one. Great!"

Ordinarily her comment would have elicited from me an off-color joke about enjoying mushrooms. Instead I picked at a bleeding hangnail.

She tucked a loose strand of hair behind her ear. "Did you read Montrose's obituary?"

I shook my head. "No, I missed it."

"They always say nice things about people in the obituaries. You know, how much they'll be missed, how much joy they brought to others. What a bunch of bull!"

"Especially in his case."

She blew a long exhalation through her lips and said, "I'm totally freaked out, Bryan."

"I know. Me too."

She paused a long moment, avoiding my eyes. "I can't find the right words."

"For what?" My stomach turned.

Another pause, followed by a sigh. "I need to not be so close for awhile."

"Because of what I said out at Stubblefield?"

"That's a part of it. It's complicated."

I bit the inside of my cheek. "Okay, explain it to me."

"It's not really about you, it's me. I'm all mixed up right now."

"Who wouldn't be? It doesn't mean we have to—"

"It does, though. I can't be with anyone right now." Her voice quavered. "I can't love."

I closed my eyes, searched for the right thing to say. "Then I'll wait till you can."

"You don't understand. The love in me died when I killed Montrose."

"But you'll get—"

A car ground to a stop directly behind Lydia's car, as if to block any possible escape. I turned in time to see two men spill out of a blue sedan, striding purposefully to both sides of our car. They wore suits.

My side arrived first. "I'm Detective Frank Gerritsen," the man barked, flashing a badge. "Are you Bryan Matthews?"

"Yeah. What's this about?" Gerritsen had a broad face and a bent nose that appeared to have been broken more than once. His eyes were clear blue, like Windex.

"Please get out of the car. You're coming to the precinct with me and Officer David." Officer David, who had a hatchet-thin face, had gone to the driver's side door. He stood there like a sentry.

A dark current of dread coursed through my bloodstream. "Okay, " I said, fumbling for the door handle. "What's this about?" The carhop working on our end stopped and stared, her tray heaped up with burgers, fries and root beer floats. A car full of teenagers parked in a red Chevelle convertible craned their necks to see what was happening.

Gerritsen looked past me, ignoring my question. "Are you Lydia Redstone?"

"Yes," Lydia answered, a startled look on her face.

"You'll need to come along too."

"Is this an arrest or something?" Lydia asked in an incredulous tone.

"Not if you cooperate."

"We'll cooperate," I said, looking at Lydia and pleading with my eyes.

"Of course," she seconded.

"Good," Gerritsen replied. "We don't want a scene any more than you do."

We rode silently in the back seat of Gerritsen's unmarked Buick sedan. My mind raced. *Do they suspect Montrose was murdered? Are Lydia and I considered suspects? Will Lydia stick to the story we rehearsed?* Officer David gave me a hostile stare that magnified my fear.

At the police station, Gerritsen and David escorted Lydia and me down a narrow, lime green corridor. I was dropped off in a gray room at the end of a long hallway, the floor gleaming from a thousand layers of wax. The only furnishings were a cheap walnut table and four chairs that didn't match. Gerritsen told me to wait, which I did for over half an hour, watching an old electric clock on the wall. The only sound in the room was the faint flutter of air traveling through the ventilation system over my head. I was pretty sure the wait was intentional, a way to turn up the temperature on my anxiety. I wondered if they were also making Lydia wait somewhere. Anxious people talk. Anxious people confess. Decent strategy. Gerritsen was sharp.

At six o'clock, Gerritsen emerged in the doorway and motioned for me to follow him to another office. He wore a charcoal gray suit with a starchy white shirt and a thin, blue-colored tie, perfectly knotted. David was right behind him, my first real chance to size him up. He was tall and thin with a fair complexion and sandy hair. Mutton-chop sideburns accentuated the thinness of his face and gave him a militant look. He walked like he had a broomstick up his ass. Dark suit, white shirt, thin nondescript blue tie with little white anchors in the pattern. *Navy guy?* He pushed open the door and gestured for Gerritsen and me to go in ahead of him.

A gorilla of a man sat at a small desk, fiddling with the wires on a tape recorder. A yellow legal pad lay face down in front of him. The walls were bare, save a picture of President Johnson.

"We've met," the gorilla said, looking up. "Bud Carter, Chief of Police."

"At the hospital, after my friend rolled his milk truck," I said, shaking his hand.

The Chief nodded solemnly. "Sit down. Watch for the cords." A tape recorder looked ready to go, but hadn't yet been turned on.

Everyone sat at once. I ended up in the flimsiest of the metal chairs, across from Chief Carter. Gerritsen and David bookended the table in sturdy captain's chairs, like castles on a chessboard. David unbuttoned his jacket and exposed a shoulder holster and the black butt of an ugly looking handgun. My stomach did a gigantic flip-flop.

No one spoke and I became aware of the sound of white noise, a faint buzzing from somewhere outside the room. My anxiety mounted with each second, but I was determined not to be the first one to speak.

Chief Parker broke the silence. "There're a few questions we'd like to ask."

"What about?"

"Officer Jack Montrose."

I knew it was coming and yet I flashed back and saw Montrose, lying motionless in the dirt out at Stubblefield, Lydia standing over him. Imagined life in prison. The room spun wildly out of control, like when you've been sitting and you get up too fast. *If I pass out and hit the floor, I might as well confess and get it over with.* "Sure," I managed to say, confused and in a state of semi-shock.

Gerritsen cracked his knuckles. "You all right?"

"I've been fighting off a bug, that's all."

Chief Carter extracted a cassette tape from his shirt pocket, took up the slack with his forefinger and inserted it in the recorder. Looking up, he smiled, flicked a small microphone into the middle of the desk and pressed the record button. "It's Tuesday evening, July 22, 1969." He pulled up the sleeves of his shirt, revealing a plain silver watch and a jungle of dark hair. "It's six-o-five p.m. and this is Chief of Police Bud Carter. With me are Detective Frank Gerritsen, Officer Mac David, and Bryan Matthews, a student at Whitman College. Bryan, speaking clearly for the benefit of the tape recording, would you please state your full name and age?"

"Bryan Matthews. No middle name. I'm eighteen years old."

"Thank you. Bryan, you have the right to remain silent. Anything you say can be used against you in a court of law. Do you understand your rights?"

A clang of fear reverberated in my chest. I swallowed hard and leaned back in my chair. "What the hell's going on?"

Gerritsen answered in a neutral tone. "Chief Carter's reading you your rights. It's a formality. We have some questions."

Chief Carter said, "Mac, why don't you explain to the kid."

David leaned forward, made eye contact. "Couple years ago in Arizona, the good guys forgot to tell some greasy Mexican named Ernesto Miranda that he had the right to remain silent, and the right to get himself an attorney. If we don't apprise you of your rights and then you just *happen* to say something incriminating, we can't use it if the case goes to trial."

I shrugged. "I don't get it. What am I suspected of doing?"

David lapsed back into in hostile silence.

Gerritsen adjusted his position and studied the acoustic tiles on the ceiling.

Chief Carter asked, "Would you like to get a lawyer? Maybe you'd be more comfortable that way, knowing your—"

"I don't want a lawyer. What would I need a lawyer for?"

Gerritsen lowered his eyes and met mine. "We can get you one at no cost. Won't cost you a penny. Might not be a bad idea."

"I've got nothing to hide. I don't want a lawyer," I said, my mouth filled with cotton.

Chief Carter spoke after clearing his throat. "Maybe you'd like to call your parents. Ask them about it."

"That's not necessary."

Chief Carter spoke into the microphone. "Let the record show that Bryan Matthews understands his rights and chooses not to have a lawyer present."

Gerritsen and Chief Carter exchanged glances. I had two impressions. They hadn't contacted my father and they were pleased I refused an attorney.

Chief Carter said, "You're gonna have to sign a form that says we offered you a lawyer, and you refused."

"Am I in some kind of trouble?"

"That's just it," Chief Carter answered. "We don't know. That's why we offer you a chance to get an attorney. Just in case."

"I still don't want one. I'll sign the waiver."

"Your girlfriend didn't want one, either," David added.

If mentioning Lydia was intended to make me more nervous, it worked.

Chief Carter pulled a white sheet of paper from the bottom page of his legal pad and slid it across the table to me. The top line read: *Waiver to Fifth Amendment Rights.*

I made a palms-up gesture. "I don't have a pen on me."

Officer David produced a thin gold pen from his shirt pocket and shoved it in front of me. I signed on the proper line, printed my name beneath my signature and dated it.

"My pen," growled David.

I slid the arrogant prick his pen, wondered if he'd been buddy-buddy with Montrose.

Chief Carter glanced at the waiver long enough to know it was my name I'd signed. He reburied it in the legal pad and continued. "Like I said, we have a few questions. If you change your mind about wanting legal representation, let us know and we'll get you a lawyer free of charge."

"I'll let you know," I said, sounding snottier than I intended.

"Fair enough," he said, ignoring my attitude. "We're investigating the death of Officer Jack Montrose. I'm sure you heard what happened."

"I read about it."

Chief Carter affected a casual tone. "I was wondering if you happened to see him any time last night before he died?"

They knew Lydia and I had seen Montrose. I had no idea how they knew, but I felt certain this was a test to see if I'd lie about it. "Yeah," I answered, trying as best I could to sound matter-of-fact. "I saw him out at Stubblefield Cemetery."

The Chief leaned forward in his chair. "Why didn't you call the station?"

Feigning surprise, I answered, "Why would I?"

He threw his palms up in frustration. "Why wouldn't you? We've been asking for information from anyone who knows anything about what happened last night."

"That's not what the paper said. The paper said call if you saw anything suspicious."

He stared at me and then shrugged a shoulder. "Okay. How did you and Miss Redstone happen to be out at Stubblefield in the first place?"

"We'd had dinner with a couple of my fraternity brothers and watched the Apollo landing on TV. Afterwards, we went out there, kind of as a way to see the moon, but also, you know, to park."

"Who were the fraternity brothers?"

"Oliver Bowens and Spencer Klatt."

"Slider," Chief Carter said, looking up from his note taking. "Both times I talk to you, Slider's involved."

I nodded. "And if we're using nicknames, Oliver goes by Bigdog."

"What time did you get there?"

"At Bigdog's or the cemetery?"

"Both."

"We got to Bigdog's apartment around seven, and left a little before ten."

Chief Carter jotted down the times on the yellow pad. "Did you and Miss Redstone drive straight out to Stubblefield?"

"I pretty much found it on the first try so we got there about ten-ten."

"You two drinkin' beer?"

"No," I lied. "I'm not much of a drinker and neither is Lydia." *That much is true.*

"And how long were you and Miss Redstone parked in the cemetery before Officer Montrose got there?"

"Hmmn. I'd say maybe fifteen or twenty minutes."

"So, Officer Montrose got there around ten-thirty?"

I nodded again. "That's about right."

"And what did Officer Montrose do on arriving?"

"He said we were on private property and told us to get the hell out. He said teenagers had been stealing markers and digging up graves, and if he caught us there again he'd write us up."

Chief Carter set his pencil on the pad. "Did he roll down his window and shout it over, or did he get out of his car and say it close up and personal?"

I tried to work some saliva into my mouth. "First he put his spotlight on us and then he came over to my car. When he saw it was me, he made a snide comment and then he told us to leave."

"What was the snide comment?"

"Something like, 'If it isn't the college boy and his townie girlfriend.'"

"That was the extent of it?"

"Yeah. I guess. He might have said more, but I might not have heard it all."

"And why would that be?"

"We had the radio on when he first walked over. And I was really nervous."

"What station were you listening to?" Chief Carter asked.

"XERB."

"That the one with Wolfman Jack? Comes out of L.A.?"

I nodded. "Yeah."

He glanced at Gerritsen and David and raised his eyebrows. Hopefully Lydia had remembered to tell them the same station. "Tell me why Montrose made you nervous."

"You saw how hostile he was the night I took my roommate to the E.R. Then he wrote me a speeding ticket that was bogus. I challenged it in court and he threatened me outside the courthouse. That was in January. I've been scared of him ever since."

Chief Carter scratched his ear. "Threatened as in 'I'm gonna write you up every time I see you' spit on the sidewalk or—"

"No. Threatened as in 'You cross me again, college boy, and you're dead!'"

David slammed his fist on the table. "That's a crock of shit!"

Chief Carter gave David a sharp look but continued speaking to me. "Officer Montrose said that to you? Those words?"

"Yes, sir. Swear to God. I'm quoting him verbatim." I looked over at David, whose face had turned crimson. *A red hatchet,* I thought.

The Chief took a moment to write another note. "Did Officer Montrose happen to catch you and Miss Redstone in a compromising position?"

"No. We were just listening to the radio and talking."

"What about?"

I shrugged my shoulders. "I don't remember, exactly. Mostly about how amazing it was that men were walking up on the moon. Music, our mutual friends. The kinds of things you talk about when you're a teenager."

"You parked with your girlfriend in an abandoned cemetery five miles outside town and you were discussing the lunar landing and mutual friends? Do you expect us to believe that?"

I forced a self-conscious laugh. "I'm not saying we weren't making out, but nothing else was happening."

Chief Carter gave me skeptical look, but left it at that. "You sure you didn't have some beer with you?"

"If we'd had beer in the car, I can guarantee Montrose would've busted us. No questions asked."

The Chief nodded slightly. "Okay. So you left the cemetery. Did Officer Montrose follow you out?"

"No, he left first, the Reser Road way. And we went out the back way."

The Chief glanced at Gerritsen, but directed his question to me. "The back way?"

"Farmer's Road. It's a dirt road that runs into Russell . . . I mean Foster." Anxiety muddled my thinking. *Careful!*

He paused and licked his lower lip. "You're telling me Montrose left without making sure you left?"

"He didn't have to. He knew we'd leave."

"Why's that?"

"When a policeman tells me to leave a place I shouldn't be in the first place, I leave. I was just glad he didn't arrest us for something."

"But Officer Montrose didn't follow you to make sure you left?"

I gave him a look of incredulity. "Given the man threatened to kill me in January, there's no way I would've stayed. And he knew it."

Officer David squirmed in his chair, barely able to contain himself.

Chief Carter went on. "So you left this back way, a road that's not a real road? Why didn't you leave the cemetery the same way you came in? The Reser Road way?"

"I went out the back way because I was afraid Montrose would be waiting for us on Reser Road."

"What if he was?"

"I thought he might be playing mind games with me. You know, act like he's letting me off easy, and then bust me as soon as I drove out of the cemetery. So I took Farmer's Road just to stay out of his way."

"Why would Officer Montrose want to play mind games with you?"

"For the same reason he wrote me the bogus speeding ticket. For the same reason he threatened to kill me in front of the courthouse. He hates . . . he hated me ever since the night I ignored his siren to rush my friend to the hospital."

The Chief rubbed the stubble on his chin. "Okay, I'm not here to debate that with you. Let's try another subject. How much time elapsed from the time Officer Montrose drove into Stubblefield to the time he drove out?"

I shrugged again. "I'd guess about five minutes."

"Five minutes from the time Officer Montrose drove in to the cemetery till the time he drove out," Chief Carter repeated. "I just want to make sure we're talkin' about the same thing."

"That's right. Five minutes."

"But you said you were guessing. You sure it wasn't longer?"

"No. I mean, yes. I'm sure it wasn't longer."

Officer David snickered, rolled his eyes in disbelief.

Gerritsen's entire demeanor changed. His eyes betrayed excitement, like they were finally on to something.

Chief Carter glanced at his watch. "This is very interesting, Mr. Matthews. You say Officer Montrose was only there for five minutes. But we've been contacted by an eyewitness who says it was more like thirty. How would you account for the difference?"

Since the interview began I'd been wondering how they knew Lydia and I had seen Montrose. Montrose didn't radio in his whereabouts because he told us the dispatcher thought he was ten miles away at the Veteran's Medical Center. The rancher was a long shot because the woods surrounding the cemetery would have obstructed his view. It had to be Vicky Spotts. Leslie Vanzandt had told me of her penchant for following Lydia and me.

Vicky could have followed us out to Stubblefield and then seen Montrose go in a short time later. But then what? Would she have gotten out of her car and hiked up close enough to see what was going on? *Too far to walk and besides, if that were true, we'd already be in custody.* "It's simple," I answered as casually as I could. "Your eyewitness is Vicky Spotts, and Vicky Spotts is so stoned all the time she doesn't know her ass from her elbow."

Chief Carter exchanged glances with Gerritsen and David, and then looked back at me. "What makes you so sure this . . . *Vicky Spotts* is our eyewitness?" He tried to say her name like he'd never heard it.

"As soon as you asked if I'd seen Montrose on the night he died I knew you'd been talking to Vicky. Because she follows us everywhere."

"The point is," Gerritsen interjected, "our eyewitness had Montrose inside the cemetery with you for a full half-hour."

"Proving your eyewitness can't tell time. Montrose drove in, got out of his car, lectured us, got back in his car and left. It can't have taken more than five minutes."

"But if our eyewitness is correct about it being a half hour, a lot of things could've happened. That extra twenty-five minutes is plenty of time for you and Montrose to get in another pissing match."

"That's true, if your eyewitness is correct. But she isn't. The girl's a head case even when she isn't high. Trust me, I know."

"What makes you an expert on this Spotts girl?" Chief Carter asked.

"She was my girlfriend for almost a year. The night I broke up with her she assaulted me in my car, actually drawing blood. And she promised she'd get even with me. That's what this is about."

Chief Carter paused, cleaned his reading glasses with a handkerchief. "If Miss Spotts happened to be the eyewitness, and I'm not saying she is, you're saying she'd exaggerate the time you interacted with Officer Montrose in order to get you and Miss Redstone in trouble?"

"Exactly. She's consumed by jealousy. Oh! She also assaulted Lydia at the Milton-Freewater Drive-in. Ask her shrink how reliable she is. He'd know. She sees him because she cuts on her skin with razor blades. Says it makes her feel better."

"Okay. Let's move on. Where did you and Miss Redstone go after you left the cemetery?"

"We hooked up to the Scenic Loop and drove back to The Gut. From there we went straight to my fraternity house."

"What time did you get there?"

I took a moment. "Sometime before eleven."

"Stop on the way? At Reed and Bell's, or anyplace else?"

"No, sir."

"Any of your friends see you? Honk at you or wave while you were on The Gut?"

"Not that I know of."

"You didn't happen to see Officer Montrose again, did you?"

"No, sir."

"Which fraternity house did you go to?"

"Phi Delta Theta."

Chief Carter turned to a fresh page on his legal pad. "That the big white colonial on Estrella?"

When he looked up, I nodded.

"Answer out loud for the tape recorder." This was Officer David, doing his best to put a little menace in his voice. I was almost certain he was Montrose's buddy.

"Yes, Phi Delta Theta is the big white colonial on Estrella."

Chief Carter looked puzzled. "I thought the fraternity houses had to close down for summer vacation. School rules."

"They do, but I have a key."

"How's that?"

"About once a week I go in and check to make sure everything's okay."

"Any particular reason?"

I nodded. "Two summers ago a pipe ruptured in the second floor head. When they opened the house in September there was water everywhere. They had to replace the carpeting in the living room and it warped the linoleum in the basement."

"So you and Miss Redstone went in the fraternity house to check and make sure everything was shipshape. Is that your story?"

"No. We went there to be alone. Same reason we went out to Stubblefield."

"And were you alone?"

"Yeah, we were alone. Would you mind explaining to me how this is pertinent to your investigation of the accident that killed Officer Montrose?"

Officer David butted in, full of righteous indignation. "Let Chief Carter ask the questions. Unless you want to get an attorney and take the fifth, you answer!"

"I did answer. I *said* we were alone."

David stared me down. Like an idiot, I stared back.

Chief Carter resumed the questioning. "What'd you do once you were in the fraternity house?"

"We went downstairs to the TV room."

"To watch TV."

"That's right."

"Okay. What'd you watch?"

"Some corny movie. At least the last half of it."

"What was it?"

Between nerves and my rising temper, I almost slipped and said *Abbott and Costello Meet Frankenstein*. "*Abbott and Costello Meet the Mummy*."

"What was the movie about?"

"Is this a test?"

"Answer the question!" Officer David boomed.

"Okay." I sighed heavily. "Abbott and Costello are in Egypt. They're raiding tombs and trying to find some temple. I can't remember its name. Kharis, or something like that. I really wasn't paying much attention."

"Is that because you and Miss Redstone were having sexual relations?"

"What?" I blurted.

Chief Carter said, "I asked you if you and Miss Redstone were having sexual relations? It's really a very simple question."

"It's also a very personal question. A very *intrusive* question."

"I don't much care, Mr. Matthews. I ask and you answer. That's the way it works."

I met his eyes. "I was taught that gentlemen don't ask, and gentlemen don't tell."

"I was taught not to ask a question unless I'm willing to get the answer. That's rule number one in interrogating a witness. And since I'm sittin' in the catbird's seat, I'd appreciate it if you'd simply answer my questions without lecturing me on what's gentlemanly and what isn't."

"Do I have to answer?"

"No, you have the right to remain silent. Remember? But if you don't answer, I'll book your ass into custody and ask you the same question tomorrow, and every day until you do."

"Book me for what? I haven't done anything."

"Trespassing, for starters. This tape has you admitting you and Miss Redstone were out at Stubblefield Cemetery two nights ago. That property happens to be owned by one Wilfred Morgan, a personal friend of mine who would be more than glad to press charges. You want me to get Wilfred on the phone?"

I paused a moment. "Okay, we did have sex. Shoot us at sunrise."

It seemed obvious the purpose of the question was to see if Lydia and I would contradict one another, which would mean we were hiding something. We apparently didn't, so Chief Carter moved on. "Let's talk about the bad blood between you and Officer Montrose. I was there when you had your first run-in, the one at the hospital. But I understand there've been several others."

I just looked at him and waited. My rash was acting up and my skin itched with a vengeance.

"You mentioned going to court and challenging a speeding ticket Montrose wrote you, and that there was a bit of a scene in the courtroom."

"Yeah, I fought the ticket because it was completely bogus, but I didn't say anything about a scene in the courtroom."

"That's right. It was Judge Bertram Meyer who called it a scene. He told me over lunch that you called Officer Montrose a liar. Under oath."

"Montrose was flat-out lying and I told the court. That's true. If that's a scene, then I guess there was a scene."

"And then you say he threatened you, outside the courthouse."

"I don't *say* he threatened me, he *did* threaten me. He threatened to kill me."

"You got witnesses?" David snarled.

"Of course I don't have witnesses. Montrose had enough smarts not to threaten me when anyone else was listening."

"Easy for you to say," David countered. "Since Officer Montrose can't be here to defend his reputation."

Chief Carter rolled his pen between his beefy fingers. "Were there other instances of you and Officer Montrose gettin' into it?"

"Just before Christmas. I was coming out of the post office and Montrose ordered me to get in the front seat of his car. He asked me some questions about that flagpole prank at the college. I told him I didn't know who did it and then he said he didn't like me, that he'd have my ass if I did the slightest thing wrong."

"Other than that and the ticket you say was bogus, were there any other incidents?"

"No, things kind of ended after he threatened me in January."

"Okay, out at the cemetery. Did Officer Montrose get a call on his police radio?"

I shook my head. "I don't think so. He just told us to leave and not let him see us out there again."

"Did you have the impression Officer Montrose had been drinking?"

"No." *Better to play it cool, like I have no reason to cast Montrose in a bad light.*

"You didn't smell alcohol on his breath, or notice any signs of intoxication?"

"No, sir."

"Did Officer Montrose discharge his weapon while you were out there?"

"What?"

"Did you not hear the question?"

"I heard it. It just surprised me. No, of course he didn't discharge his weapon. This was no big deal, Chief Carter. He asked us to leave and we left."

"But after he left first."

"Yes! He left first. You keep coming back to that. Was it against police procedure or something?"

"We ask the questions, Mr. Matthews. Is that okay with you?"

I held my breath, then exhaled noisily. "It's fine with me, but you make this sound like we were robbing a bank. Why on earth would a police officer discharge his weapon because two teenagers are parked? And I'm not asking you to answer that."

"Good. Do you know Tammy Balfour?"

A trickle of sweat ran down my chest. "No, but I know of her."

"What do you know?"

"I know it was her car that was stolen the night Montrose . . . uh, Officer Montrose died. A Barracuda. I know it was her car he was chasing."

"And how do you know that?"

"I read it in yesterday's paper."

Chief Carter looked at Gerritsen. "You have any questions, Frank?"

Gerritsen shook his head slowly.

"Mac?"

Officer David stared blackly at me. "Yeah. I got a question. The $64,000 Question. How is it that Officer Jack Montrose, the biggest hardass in the Department, catches you and your girlfriend on private property, in a cemetery that's been repeatedly vandalized, and lets you go scot-free? Explain that to me and I'll feel a whole lot better."

"How could I possibly explain what was in Montrose's mind? I don't know, maybe he had bigger fish to fry."

David countered, "Except that doesn't add up, because you just told us that Officer Montrose didn't receive any calls while you were out there."

"Maybe he'd already gotten a call. Maybe he wanted to go home and pound the suds. Maybe he found God and turned into a human being."

Officer David lunged out of his chair and body-slammed me, leading with a forearm. My metal folding chair collapsed and flew into the wall, making a clanging noise. I went down like a trapdoor had opened out of nowhere, hitting the floor hard, my already sore foot and ankle taking the worst of it. I hadn't seen it coming and offered no resistance. David had a hold of my hair and was trying to yank me to my feet when Gerritsen and Chief Carter pulled him off.

"Jesus Christ, Mac. Wise up!" Chief Carter yelled.

Gerritsen helped me up and folded my chair back into a functional position. "You okay?" he asked.

"Yeah. I'm okay." I flexed my ankle and winced, but mostly for effect.

David adjusted his tie, silently seething with rage.

Chief Carter said, "Do we have a grip on ourselves, Officer David? Or are you going to have to leave the room?"

David said, "Give me ten minutes with this punk and we'll find out what really happened."

"Can he talk to me that way?" I asked, rubbing my ankle and foot.

"Okay, okay," Chief Carter interjected. "Let's all take a deep breath and finish this interview."

"First I want to say something," I said. My eyes were watering from David yanking on my hair.

Chief Carter sighed. "Go ahead."

"Let the record show I was just assaulted by Officer Mac David, and after that he threatened me with bodily harm to get me to change my testimony. The crashing sound on the tape was my chair hitting the wall after he struck me with his forearm. I fell hard onto the floor and hurt my ankle. I may wish to press charges and request that this tape recording not be erased or altered."

"Asshole!" David muttered under his breath.

Chief Carter looked at him and barked, "Shut your pie hole, Mac!" Rubbing his fingertips gently together, he made a church steeple and pondered his next move.

Gerritsen, arms folded, glowered across the table at David. "That was great, Mac. Just great."

Chief Carter said, "I apologize for Officer David's loss of control. It won't happen again. Officer David was a close friend of the deceased. They served in the same unit in Vietnam. Military and police work engender strong loyalties."

"And that gives him the right to rough me up?"

"No, it doesn't. But Officer David made a good point. Officer Montrose was a by-the-book cop, not at all the forgiving type. It doesn't make sense he'd let you go with a warning, you above all people, when he could write you up for criminal trespass. That's just not the Jack Montrose I knew. You agree, Frank?"

Gerritsen nodded and stared me down. "Doesn't figure. Montrose nails you dead to rights for trespassing, but goes all soft and lets you go home. And I don't care what you say about the credibility of our eyewitness, I got a problem with your version of how long he was inside the cemetery."

"Am I being accused of something here? You guys think I bribed Montrose or something?"

They took turns looking at one another. I couldn't read them.

Chief Carter said, "We ask the questions. Remember?"

"I don't get it," I sighed, slumping down in my chair. "I'm getting the third degree because Montrose finally cut me some slack?"

Chief Carter leaned forward and switched off the tape recorder. "You can go for now. Give me a call if you decide to change your story."

If I hadn't fully grasped the magnitude of what Lydia and I had done, I did after the interrogation. A man was dead. The killer or killers had to be found and held accountable. That was the law. Because the dead man was a cop, there was public outrage, and that combined with the unwritten code that cops get cop killers, translated into a manhunt. The pressure crushed me. That night I lay in my bed in my clothes, not moving a muscle and staring at the dark ceiling. I tried to shut off the incessant flow of thoughts, but one question kept jumping out of the hopper. Had Vicky Spotts told the police anything else that might be incriminating?

Unable to sleep or even get drowsy, I got out of bed and tiptoed toward the Zaleski's front door. The grandfather clock in the entryway chimed one in the morning, startling me. Reva had forgotten to turn off the chimes. I knew they sometimes awakened Dr. Z, in which case he'd come downstairs to slide the lever to the "silent" position. Unnerved, I waited for the sound of his footsteps and, sure enough, I heard him coming down the stairs in his bare feet. Not having time to get out the front door unnoticed, I slipped into the living room and quickly lay down on the couch. My heart pounded. If Dr. Z noticed me, I would pretend to have fallen asleep on the couch, thank him for awakening me and shuffle off to bed. But he didn't see me. He merely adjusted the clock and went back up the stairs. I lay on the couch for several minutes, thinking mostly about how deceptive I had become in the space of twenty-four hours.

I arrived at Vicky's house and made my way around to the back basement door that was just off her downstairs bedroom. I tapped on the glass, but no Vicky. The door was locked. I could faintly hear *I Put a Spell on You*, the Credence Clearwater Revival version. Desperate to talk, I knocked louder, risking detection by Mrs. Spotts, or even the next-door neighbor. A few seconds later the lacy curtain on the other side of the window parted. Vicky looked out. "Jesus, Bryan!"

"Sorry," I mouthed through the glass.

She cracked the door. "You scared the shit outta me!"

"Sorry."

"What do you want?"

"To talk."

She looked skeptical. "About what?"

"I think you know."

"I'm not into your games, Bryan, so tell me what you want to talk about or I'm going back to bed."

"About Stubblefield. About what you told the police."

The door opened wide. "I don't know what you're talking about," she said indignantly. She wore only a T-shirt and panties. The T-shirt read *Mallo Cups* and something in smaller script.

"Can we talk, anyway?"

She hesitated. "I'll talk, if you'll listen. You're not the only one with things to say."

"Fine."

"Okay. C'mon in."

I stayed put. "Why don't you put some clothes on and we can walk around the block?"

"No, you come in. I'm stoned. I don't want to walk."

I sighed. "Okay."

I followed Vicky into her bedroom, fragrant with the sweet smell of marijuana and vanilla. A stick of incense burned on her bed table, a tiny pile of ash beneath the glowing ember. Next to the incense were several lit candles, flickering slightly from the displacement of air caused by our entry into the room. The candles illuminated dried wildflowers in a beer bottle and a year-and-a-half old picture of the two of us at the Phi Delt Barn Dance, me with a phony, bleary eyed smile as we embraced atop a hayride. I'd been sneezing and Vicky had made fun of my allergies.

Vicky plopped heavily on her bed, plumped up two pillows behind her and sat cross-legged, very unladylike in her panties. I could read all of her

T-shirt: *Mallo Cups – "milk chocolate with a whipped cream center and a sprinkle of coconut!"*

Vicky spoke first. "Sort of like old times, huh?"

"Sort of," I whispered, choosing my words carefully. I had to be careful not to trigger her temper for fear she'd clam up. There were no chairs in Vicky's bedroom so I sat at the far corner of the bed, which was actually a mattress laying on the floor. The room was trashed, clothes, shoes and magazines everywhere. Her dresser drawers were open, garments spilling out in every direction. On top of the dresser was a green lava lamp and a Hamilton Beach blender filled with water. A solitary goldfish swam claustrophobically in the too-small space. I could only hope the appliance wasn't plugged in.

"You don't have to whisper," she told me. "My mom's asleep. She wouldn't care if you were here, anyway."

"New bedspread?" Opening with small talk, I ran my hand over a thin cotton fabric. The light was dim, but it looked gold and red with an East Indian design.

"You like? I got it at the head shop they opened across from Lutcher's. I think it's supposed to be a very large tablecloth." Pointing to a Grateful Dead poster on the wall behind her, she added, "Got that the same place."

"I like. The poster, too."

She raised her eyebrows. "Maybe you should drop by more often."

"Look, Vicky. The reason I'm here is because I'm getting hassled by the police. And I know you're the one who told them I was out at Stubblefield two nights ago."

"I was partying with Leslie two nights ago. In Milton-Freewater."

"Don't bullshit me. Detective Gerritsen told me it was you."

She picked up a bottle of nail polish and flung it across the room. It hit a large stuffed bear above the eye. "That lying piece of shit! He told me what I said was totally confidential."

"Cool down," I said. "I lied. Gerritsen didn't tell me a thing."

"Then how'd you know it was me?"

"I just did."

She started to get to her feet. "Get out!"

"Vicky, please talk to me. I'm not mad at you. You were trying to be a good citizen. They asked the public for information about Montrose and you had some."

She surprised me by laughing. "I wasn't trying to be a good citizen, Bryan. Don't kid yourself. I was trying to get you and the bitch in trouble."

"Well, I don't want to be in trouble. Especially for something I didn't do."

She smiled. "If you didn't do anything, then you have nothing to worry about."

"Oh yeah? What if they decided I stole that car that ran Montrose off the road? Do you want me to go to jail for fifteen years for something I didn't do? Do you hate me that much?"

She grinned. "I hate Lydia that much."

"Yeah, but this is comin' down on me, not Lydia. I'm the one that had the feud with Montrose."

"You're not the only one."

"What do you mean by that?"

She looked away, lost in her own thoughts. Not a great place to be given the current state of her brain chemistry. "Never mind. I heard about you and Montrose hating each other. But I didn't tell 'em you stole the car."

"Okay, good. What did you tell them?"

She twisted her body and reached into the drawer on her nightstand. I watched her breasts strain against her T-shirt. "Want to share a joint? It's good shit. Acapulco Gold."

"No, thanks. Aren't you afraid your Mom's gonna bust you?"

"Hardly," she laughed. "She smokes it with me." She lit the joint with a metal lighter and clicked it shut. Meeting my eyes she inhaled deeply, an amused smile on her face. "You're just as straight as you always were, aren't you?"

"I suppose."

She chuckled. "Mustn't do anything to mess up that brilliant chess mind."

"Chacun à son goût."

"What's that mean?"

"To each his own. Freely translated."

"To each *her* own!" She sucked in another voluminous hit and blew a cloud of smoke across the bed at me.

I waved it away. "So, what *did* you tell Gerritsen? I need to know."

"You think I care?"

I nodded. "I don't think you'd wreck my life just because I broke up with you. You're too good a person to do that."

She drew too hard on the joint. Coughed. "Okay, I told him I saw you and Lydia go into Stubblefield. I told him I watched a police car follow you in a few minutes later. I didn't even know for sure it was Montrose. That guy Gerritsen told me."

"Where were you that you saw all this?"

She grinned. "I followed you from your friend's apartment and parked a little past the road that leads up to the cemetery. Where Reser turns onto Foster."

"How do you do that? Follow us without our knowing?"

"Trade secret." She laughed again then paused briefly. "I keep my headlights off."

"Would you mind not following us? It's not polite."

"Free country."

I let it go. "So, you parked past the turnoff and then you saw the police car go in. Right?"

She leaned forward and extended her arm, offering me a hit of marijuana. "Sure you don't want some of this? It's Oaxaca tops!" She pronounced it wah-hawka.

"You said it was Acapulco Gold."

"Oh. I guess I'm fucked up! I can't remember what it is." She laughed like she was Johnny Carson's guest and just cracked the drop-dead funny joke of the century. When I didn't join in she slowed herself and said, "You didn't say if you wanted any."

"I don't. What happened after you saw the police car go in?"

"Eight miles high," she muttered, off in her own world.

"And nowhere to touch down," I added.

"Yeah," she laughed idiotically.

I didn't say anything. Just stared at her. Then, "I *said*, what happened after you saw the police car drive in?"

She collected herself and scratched over her eyebrow. "Nothing. I sat on my thumb for a half-hour and then I saw the cop come out."

"A half-hour! It wasn't anywhere near that long." Planting the seeds of doubt.

"Whatever."

"You didn't get out of the car to get a closer look?"

"Too much effort. I was smokin' it."

"And then what? After the cop drove out."

She removed a little weed from the tip of her tongue. "I waited a few minutes. I was royally pissed 'cause you didn't come out after the cop car."

"Why?"

"Because I knew you'd be bangin' Lydia in the back seat and I wondered how you talked him into letting you stay."

"For your information, we left out the back way. You were the one who told me about it."

She looked puzzled, until the light went on. "Oh yeah, the night we met. How could I forget the night I popped your cherry?" Licking her lower lip, she smiled and shook her head.

"So what else did you tell Detective Gerritsen?"

"Lighten up. I only talked to him on the phone, anyway."

"Did he ask to talk to you in person?"

She used an ashtray to break the ember off the end of her joint. "No, but lemme ask you a question."

"Go ahead."

"Was I right? Were you bangin' Lydia in the back seat?"

"Not that it's any of your business, but we were just talking."

A smile creased her lips. "She doesn't take care of you the way I did, does she?"

"No comment."

"You and the bitch gonna get married?"

I paused, considered not answering. "We haven't really talked about it. I'm still eighteen, Vicky. What else did you tell the police?"

She swiped the air between us. "Not so fast. I got a few more questions."

"Okay. I'm in no hurry." Not true. Vicky had been candid, a by-product of the cannabis, but I knew about her volatility and wanted out before the conversation turned sour. I had at least one more question, so I humored her.

She smiled suggestively. "How many times you think you fucked me in this bed? Not in all, counting everywhere, just in this bed?"

I had to suppress a laugh. "I don't know."

"Guess."

I shrugged. "Thirty? Forty? I don't know."

"Try seventy-two. Exactly seventy-two times."

"You kept track?"

"Every time we did it I put a bean in this jar after you left." She grabbed a canning jar from behind the candles and shook it. Dark beans rattled hard against the glass. "We racked up some big numbers the first few months we were together. I was gonna add a ham hock and cook you some beans when we reached a hundred, but you got scared and ditched me."

"I'm sorry it didn't work, Vicky."

She shook her head. "No, you're not. I'm not stupid, you know."

"I know you're not."

"I'm fucked up, but I'm not stupid."

Her behavior was starting to deteriorate. I tried to take over. "Okay, I've answered your questions. What—"

"Don't be in such a hurry," she interrupted, holding up the palm of her hand. She looked ridiculous, like one of the Supremes when Diana Ross sang the word "stop," in *Stop, In the Name of Love*. "There's something I want you to know. I might regret telling you this, but right now I'm so ripped I don't care."

"What?"

"I have a fantasy. Pretty much the same one every night. Makes me feel good."

"Pot doesn't make you feel good?"

She thought for a moment. "It helps. Mostly it makes me not feel at all."

"And that's good?"

"Yeah, it's good not to feel when all you feel is pain. Since I started smoking I haven't cut on myself."

"I'm glad for that."

She leaned back against her pillow. "Want to hear my fantasy?"

"Not really."

Her eyes glassed over. "I go to a party and you're there with Lydia."

"Are you okay?" I asked.

"We see each other, but we don't talk or anything. The music's loud and people are drinkin' and dancin' and after awhile you go to the bathroom. I come in right behind you and shut the door. And you ask what I'm doin' and I do this." Without warning, Vicky pulled her T-shirt up around her shoulders, exposing her naked breasts.

"Vicky, for God's sake—"

"Lemme finish. You start kissing me and pretty soon we're doin' it on the floor, doggy style. I'm watching my boobs swaying in a full-length mirror. We come together and after, we get dressed, taking our sweet time. Then we go back to the party and you tell Lydia you're done with her. And we leave and we're back together. Cool fantasy, huh?"

"Cool. Now pull your T-shirt down."

"Say *please*. What's happened to your manners, Bryan?" She enjoyed my discomfort.

"Okay. *Please* pull down your T-shirt."

"You don't like big tits anymore? You get used to those little mosquito bites Lydia has." She shook her shoulders, made them jiggle.

"I'm leaving."

"Wait! Don't ya wanna put another bean in the jar?"

Wednesday and Thursday dragged on like more bad dreams. Most of the time I spent alone, watching inane daytime television programs and nodding off on the living room couch. The only people I saw were the Zaleskis, and Lydia for a few minutes at a time. Being with her was pure anguish, as she made it clear she'd rather be alone. Our conversations either had to do with her needing space, or what to do if the police called us in for more interviews. We never reconsidered the issue of getting attorneys. Attorneys were for guilty people.

We'd managed to tell virtually identical stories. I hoped that would convince Chief Carter to look elsewhere for information. From what I could gather, Lydia had adopted an even more defiant attitude in her interview. *How would I know why Montrose didn't write us up? How dare three grown men ask a teenage girl questions about her sex life?*

I told her how Officer David had lost his temper. That I'd had the presence of mind to note the assault on the tape recording. I had hoped for her approval, that she'd see I was still on top of things, but instead she got mad about my making another enemy in the police department. Jack Montrose's buddy, no less. We parted on a down note. No way to pretend otherwise, Lydia was slipping away. A massive chunk of grief colonized the area around my heart.

I was waiting when a lanky, longhaired paperboy delivered the evening *Union-Bulletin*. The headline grabbed my attention, forcing me to sit and read on the Zaleski's front steps.

FBI PROVIDES ASSIST IN MONTROSE INVESTIGATION

By Gene Claghorn
Union-Bulletin Writer

An agent of the Federal Bureau of Investigation is now assisting in the investigation of the auto accident that claimed the life of Officer Jack Montrose. On loan from the New Orleans Field Office is Special Agent Dupuy Thibideaux, an expert on forensic evidence and fingerprint identification. Detective Frank Gerritsen, who has spearheaded the Montrose investigation thus far, confirmed the fact that Thibideaux had joined forces with the Walla Walla Police Department as of yesterday, but declined to say how long he would be available.

Montrose was found dead behind wheel of his squad car early Monday morning shortly after being seen in pursuit of a stolen car. Foul play is strongly suspected in that evidence gathered at the accident scene strongly suggests the stolen vehicle was used to run Montrose's car off Mill Creek Road and over an embankment. According to Dr. Owen Johnson, Walla Walla County Coroner, the official cause of death was either a severe closed head injury or a crushed windpipe. The normal sentencing range for persons found and convicted of vehicular homicide is ten to twenty years' imprisonment.

Montrose's funeral took place Wednesday at eleven in the morning, an open casket service at the Mountain View Cemetery. At a graveside memorial service that followed, Pastor Dan Smith from the Glad Tidings Christian Assembly asked mourners to pray that justice be done in the death that has shocked the Walla Walla community. Janice Montrose, wife of the deceased, thanked all those who attended. Also present were Jack Montrose's mother, Marjorie Hansen, currently residing in Twin Falls, Idaho, and his father, Vice Admiral James P. Montrose, Retired Commander, Naval Air Pacific, of San Diego, California.

My exact train of thoughts, in rapid succession: They should've buried the son of a bitch in Stubblefield, right on the spot where he violated Lydia. *Then,* a FBI expert on forensic evidence and fingerprint identification – did I wipe down all our prints? Will they find blood spots in the back seat of Montrose's car that belong in the front? After donning Montrose's shirt, did I leave behind any strands of my lighter-colored hair?

I set the paper in my lap and glanced up. A blue Buick turned the corner, crept down the block in my direction. I froze, then managed to fold and toss the paper onto the porch.

Detective Gerritsen got out first, then a hard-faced man in a tan trench coat. Hard face spoke first. "Special Agent Dupuy Thibideaux," he said, flashing a bright gold badge and holding it in place for a good five seconds. It read: Federal Bureau of Investigation. U.S. Department of Justice. With a name like Dupuy Thibideaux, I'd expected a down-home Cajun accent, but it wasn't there.

My heart stuttered. "I suppose you have more questions about Officer Montrose."

Gerritsen said, "That's right. We'd like you to come with us."

"Sure," I said, relieved that Dr. Z and Reva weren't home.

Gerritsen drove us downtown, Thibideaux riding shotgun and taking in the surroundings like a tourist. I sat in the back seat, next to a stack of black notebooks and some crumpled up fast food wrappers. There was no conversation until we passed the Whitman campus and Thibideaux said, "College looks Ivy League."

Gerritsen responded, "That's what the glossy brochures say, Dupe."

I knew the two of them had been friends for some time.

On arriving at the police station, I was promptly led to the same interview room I'd been in two days before. Chief Carter was waiting. No sign of Officer David, presumably in the doghouse. A glass filled with water waited in front of each of the four chairs.

Thibideaux took the chair previously occupied by Chief Carter, looking confident and claiming authority. They'd given me the same flimsy chair as before, only now it was in even worse shape after Officer David had sent it flying into the wall. I checked out the wall at the point of impact, noticed a shallow indentation.

Chief Carter took a drink of water and led off. "You've met Special Agent Thibideaux of the FBI. He has more experience in cases of this magnitude so he's going to conduct the interview." At that, Chief Carter depressed the record button on the tape recorder, stated who was present and read me my rights for the second time in a week.

I repeated that I had no interest in getting an attorney and nervously scribbled my signature on another waiver. They did their best not to look pleased.

Agent Thibideaux folded his hands and smiled. His eyes were unsympathetic and wary, like a man who'd seen too much over the years. "I've been told you're brilliant."

Poker-faced, I said nothing.

Thibideaux continued. "Detective Gerritsen showed me the newspaper articles on how you took apart Grandmaster Primalov. I'd actually read about it while I was at Quantico. An American kid kicking the snot out of a Russian Grandmaster. It doesn't get much better than that."

"Thanks. I enjoyed it, too." No need to alienate the new guy.

He leaned back in his chair and rubbed the gray stubble on his chin. "Being a chess player myself, I was impressed. Really impressed! I even borrowed a board from one of Walla Walla's finest and played out all the moves. That queen to knight four move that ended it, that was amazing!"

"Thank you. It was actually queen to knight five."

"Right. Right. Well, there you are. I've managed to show my amateur status. I'd be no match for you, that's for sure. Not in a game of chess." He allowed the words hang between us, take their desired effect.

"With all due respect, Agent Thibideaux, I have no idea why I'm here. I've told the police everything I know, and I'm betting big bucks you've already listened to the interview Chief Carter did a couple nights ago."

"Right again." Thibideaux tightened the little muscles around his mouth. "There are still a few unanswered questions, though. New evidence, shall we say."

"Such as?" Fear gave my voice a flat sound. I cleared my throat and took a sip of water.

Thibideaux smiled. "Such as, whoever stole the car wiped down everything imaginable, except for the key he used to start the damn thing. Pretty stupid, huh? We got a nice thumbprint and part of a forefinger."

"So are you going to fingerprint me?"

"We already did," Gerritsen replied in a monotone.

When I looked puzzled Chief Carter added, "You just left a complete set on your glass." Using the butt of his hand, he carefully slid my glass over to Thibideaux.

A feeling of foreboding washed over me. For several seconds, it was almost as if I'd been pushed from an airplane without a parachute. "Good! I want you to have my prints," I finally exclaimed.

Thibideaux rubbed his eyes. "Why do you say that?"

"Because now you can find the thief and leave me and my girlfriend alone."

"You confident the prints on the glass won't match the Balfour's car key?"

"You actually think I stole the car and ran Montrose off the road?" I affected an incredulous look, my mind racing several moves ahead. Thibideaux was right, I'd forgotten to wipe off the key to the Barracuda, but I remembered it as having a good-sized hole at the top and all kinds of ridges. I was no expert on fingerprints, but I questioned whether his lab people could get much of a print off it.

"Well, the thought occurred to us, and you certainly had sufficient motive. The tape you made Tuesday night made it clear there was no love lost between you and the deceased."

"Agent Thibideaux. Let me tell you something these guys won't. Officer Jack Montrose was a real, first-class asshole. Without a doubt, there's a very long list of people who detested the man as much as I did. Probably more."

"Detest is a strong word."

"I'm being candid, Agent Thibideaux. If you listened to the tape, you know he wrote me a bogus speeding ticket and threatened to kill me. Of course I detested him. There'd be something wrong with me if I didn't. But I wouldn't do something like try to run him off the road, because I'm not that kind of a person. And even if I was, I'm not that stupid."

"Stupid for trying to outrun him in a stolen car, or stupid for running him off the road?"

"Take your pick. But playing Ben-Hur in a speeding car is breathtakingly stupid. That's a fifty-fifty chance of getting killed yourself."

"I see. But back to the key to the Balfour's Barracuda. There's a question here I simply can't answer." He paused to affect a baffled expression. "Why would someone steal a car, wreck it, dump it, and then replace the key in the hide-a-key? That's just not the way car thieves work."

"I can't answer your question. I don't know any car thieves." I'd replaced the hide-a-key in the hope the police would think the car was hotwired by a pro. That would deflect suspicion away from anyone who knew Tammy Balfour had a hide-a-key under her front bumper. Like Lydia. In retrospect, I'd blundered.

Thibideaux grinned. "Chief Carter. You know any car thieves?"

Chief Carter scowled. "A lot of 'em, over the years."

"Ever know a car thief to steal a car with a hide-a-key and then replace it?"

The Chief shook his head. "Not a single one."

"What about you, Detective Gerritsen?"

Gerritsen directed his gaze my way. "I've busted a lot of car thieves, but never one that replaced the key he used to steal the car."

Thibideaux smiled at me, like he was letting me in on a secret. "We think the car thief wasn't really a car thief. We think it was someone pretending to be a car thief."

"How do you know the thief didn't hotwire the car?" I asked.

Thibideaux studied my eyes. "Because the thief saw fit to wipe the hide-a-key clean. Just not the key itself."

Thinking fast I asked, "Could it have been some kid who wanted to take a hot car for a joyride and sort of went into shock when the accident happened? In other words, he got all stupid and made a mistake by replacing the hide-a-key."

Thibideaux nodded slowly. "That's not bad. Not bad at all. Some punk gets a hard-on for a ride in a Barracuda, ends up in a ditch with a dead cop and his brain fritzes out." He jotted a note to himself and reached for a manila folder. "As long as you've brought up the subject of the accident, I'd like you to have a look at this picture." He removed an eight-by-twelve photograph and slid it across the table. A black and white photo of Tammy Balfour's Barracuda. Specifically, the damaged right front fender.

I studied it and shrugged my shoulders.

"Come on, Mr. Matthews. You're the brilliant chess player. What's wrong with the picture?"

I picked up the photograph and pretended to reexamine it. I knew what was wrong. The question was whether I wanted them to know I knew. I decided it was okay. "If someone ran Montrose off the road, the damage to the Barracuda would more likely be on the left side."

"More likely? I'd say definitely. If Montrose is chasing a stolen car and he pulls even with them, they ram the right side of his car and damage their left. Only in this case, it's the reverse of that."

Thibideaux was sharp. I pointed to some scrape marks on the Barracuda. "Do these match up with the paint on Montrose's car, or did they come from someplace else?"

"It's white paint from Montrose's Plymouth Fury. No doubt about it. It almost looks like Montrose was the chasee, rather than the chaser."

I went into analytic mode. Thibideaux was too close to the truth. "I can think of another possibility."

"By all means."

"Whoever stole the car might've swerved into the left lane and sort of dared Montrose to pull even with him. If Montrose bit, then the damage to the Barracuda would be on the right side."

"But why would Montrose bite?"

"A chance to run the car thief off the road. Or maybe he was thinking about getting off a shot. I don't know."

He nodded again. "I thought of those possibilities, too. It's also possible the collision was an accident. Officer Montrose is chasing the guy at seventy, eighty miles an hour, one of them loses control for a split second, and whammo, the cars get all tangled up. One man ends up dead and the other guy drives off."

"It's possible."

Thibideaux' hard face turned harder. "Sure it's possible. My question is, are you the other guy?"

My mouth dropped open. "I can't believe this. Is this why I'm here? You guys really do think I'm stupid enough to steal a car."

No one answered until Chief Carter said, "We're not sure."

"Oh, come on! Think it through. I'm a straight 'A' college student with my whole life in front of me. I'm a good citizen who's never committed a misdemeanor, not some idiot criminal who steals a car and gets in a high-speed chase with the cops."

Thibideaux said, "Detective Gerritsen seems to think you're smart enough to steal a car and expect to get away with it. And Chief Carter thinks you've got big enough nuts to try to outrun a cop."

I looked at Gerritsen. "You actually think I'd steal a car?"

"I've seen it all," he replied in a nonchalant voice. "Nothing surprises me any more."

"You think I'd get in a high speed chase and try to outrun the cops?"

Chief Carter jumped in. "That's pretty much exactly what you did when you had your first run-in with Montrose. And, by the way, that was a misdemeanor."

"Oh my God. I don't believe this. How long will it take to verify the prints on the car key belong to someone else?"

"That might be a couple a days," Thibideaux answered. "A week at most."

"Do I get three apologies when my prints don't match?"

No one answered. All I got was three different ways of looking annoyed.

"Think about it," I went on, pleading my case to Gerritsen and Chief Carter. "If someone local stole a car and had to ditch a cop, isn't Mill Creek Road about the last place they'd go?"

"Why would that be?" Thibideaux asked, looking around the room.

Chief Carter answered, "Mill Creek Road dead ends just past the bridge at Kooskooskie, the scene of the accident. There's a dirt road that runs up into the Blue Mountains, but there's only one way in and one way out."

Thibideaux leaned forward and looked me straight in the eye. "Mr. Matthews. You still haven't answered my question. I asked you if you were the driver of the stolen car."

"No, sir. I was not." It helped that I was telling the truth.

"Let's move on," Thibideaux grunted while scribbling a note. He reached into a drawer in the table and removed a clear plastic bag. Taped to the side was a strip of adhesive with the words Exhibit #8 printed neatly with a black felt-tipped pen. Without removing the contents he held it up and showed it to me. A shard of red glass, or maybe it was plastic. "I'm going to leave this piece of evidence in the bag."

"It looks like a piece of broken plastic."

"From Montrose's car. His right taillight to be precise."

"Are there prints on it, too?"

"Very good. Three to be precise."

I folded my arms in disgust. "Tell you what, Agent Thibideaux. I'll bet you a dollar they're not mine or Lydia's. And I'll give you a million to one odds."

"I'm not a betting man, Mr. Matthews. Anyway, it's not so much the prints that interest me in regard to this piece of evidence."

"Okay, I'll bite. What is it?"

"Well, we only found the piece of plastic today. And you know what? We took it to the wrecking yard where Officer Montrose's car is impounded and matched it up with his right side taillight. And voilà! It fit like the last piece of a puzzle."

I shrugged a shoulder. "So?"

"So, we were surprised."

"I don't get it. Montrose wrecks his car. A broken taillight makes sense." I remembered noticing the broken taillight after staging the accident.

"That's just it. We don't get it either. You see, this piece of plastic wasn't found out at . . . what do you call the place?"

"Kooskooskie," Chief Carter quickly interjected.

"Right. It wasn't found at Kooskooskie, the scene of the accident, it was found in Stubblefield Cemetery. The same place where you were seen with Officer Montrose no more than an hour before the accident."

"That's weird," I said.

"So tell me about it."

"Tell you about what?"

"How'd his taillight get broken in Stubblefield Cemetery?"

"I have no idea," I sputtered. "It didn't happen when we were there." My mind flashed on kicking the gun from Montrose's hand followed by a cracking sound. I realized in an instant the broken taillight was the thing that had bothered me, the one thing I knew I was missing every time I'd ruminate over the cover-up.

"That's right," Thibideaux went on. "I remember now. Your version is that Montrose only spent five minutes before sending you and Miss Redstone on your merry way. So it couldn't have happened in such a short period of time."

"That's true, the part about spending five minutes."

"But an eyewitness says it was half an hour."

"That's true, too. And I'm confident you already know my opinion of the credibility of your eyewitness. Oh, and by the way, she was stoned to the gills on the Sunday night in question."

"How do you know that?" Chief Carter asked.

"I talked to her night before last. Asked her to stop following me."

"Still," Thibideaux continued. "It's a big difference, five minutes versus thirty. Six times different! Maybe our eyewitness is a little off. Maybe you're a little off. Let's give you the benefit of the doubt and say it was only fifteen minutes. Ten minutes more than you and Miss Redstone insist upon. Not twenty-five. What happened in that fifteen minutes, Mr. Matthews? What happened that Officer Montrose discharged his weapon and got his taillight broken?"

"First of all, it was five minutes. Period. Exclamation point. Second, this is now the second time I've heard about Montrose shooting his gun so I presume it's something that really happened. But it didn't happen while he was with me and Lydia."

"Did Officer Montrose show off what a good marksman he was? Shoot at a coyote, or whatever kinds of varmints you have around here? Did he fire a warning shot, for some unknown reason? You'd be in no trouble if Officer Montrose did something he shouldn't have. We just want to know what happened."

"I can't help you. He didn't so much as touch his gun in our presence."

"You're a smart kid, Mr. Matthews. Brilliant, according to these fine police officers. When do you think it happened?"

"Are you serious? You want my opinion?"

"Yes, please."

I suppressed a smile. "Montrose was a cowboy. If he fired his gun, I'd guess it was during the car chase."

Thibideaux, Gerritsen and Chief Carter took turns looking at one another. I had the impression my theory was identical to someone else's, which told me they were still guessing. I was the only one in the room who knew for certain the gun had been discharged in the cemetery.

Thibideaux rubbed the side of his nose. "I'm not up on West Coast slang. What exactly do you mean when you say Montrose was a cowboy?"

"I meant a redneck with a wild streak. The kind of cop who would write a bogus ticket and threaten to kill a person for calling him on it. The kind of cop who would shoot his gun in the middle of a car chase."

Chief Carter spoke up. "Did Officer Montrose shoot his gun at you when you failed to pull over on your way to the hospital, the time with your injured friend?"

"No, but I wasn't in a stolen car."

Chief Carter said, "Officer Montrose would've had no way of knowing the Barracuda was stolen. I'll grant you he could be gung-ho, but not reckless like you'd like to paint him. So keep your theories to yourself. "

"Sorry, I seem to recall someone inviting my opinion."

Chief Carter looked away, fed up.

Thibideaux said, "Okay, so your story is that Montrose didn't fire his weapon during the five minutes it took to tell you and Miss Redstone to leave the graveyard."

I unfolded my arms. "It's not my story. It's a fact."

"Final question, Mr. Matthews. It's a chess question, so it should be easy for you." He paused, set down the pen he scribbled notes with. "At your level of play, do you ever make a big mistake? A blunder, I believe it's called. End up with a losing position?"

"Not really. I mean, I make mistakes and so do Grandmasters. But we don't really blunder the game away the way amateurs do."

He adjusted himself in his chair. Made himself bigger. "Maybe I'm not asking right. You ever make a move and wish you could take it back?"

"Sure. That happens all the time."

He nodded, pleased with himself. "I thought so. Make any bad moves last Sunday night? Moves you'd like to take back?"

"Yeah."

"What?"

I scowled. "I wish Lydia and I hadn't gone out to Stubblefield. I wish we'd have stayed put at Bigdog's apartment."

Thibideaux glanced at Chief Carter and then at Gerritsen. "You know, we're not to happy about this, either. A cop is dead and we can't say for certain what happened. At least, not yet."

I waited.

"It's almost as if someone deliberately made the case confusing. The damage on the wrong side of the Barracuda, replacing the hide-a-key, the plastic from the broken taillight in the wrong place, the fact that only one fingerprint was left in the stolen vehicle."

I shrugged, resisted the temptation to talk.

"I'm thinking whoever's throwing us off is one smart customer. Maybe even brilliant."

"I disagree. Anyone dumb enough to steal a car and get in a high-speed chase with a cop is an idiot."

"Not necessarily. For instance, that Russian Grandmaster you beat. Primalov. Ranked right behind Bobby Fischer and the other guy. He made maybe one bad move and you took advantage. Doesn't make him dumb."

"But he didn't really make any bad moves. I just made better moves."

"That's what's got us worried, Mr. Matthews. You're capable of making the kind of moves that we could only dream of. Make us look like the Keystone Cops."

"I've told you the truth. You'll find out when the print comes back."

Thibideaux nodded enthusiastically. "Yes we will. Yes we will."

"Am I in custody or something?"

"No, but don't leave town."

"Why?"

He thought for a moment. "Because a cop is dead and you have a lousy alibi."

"I don't need an alibi, but if I do, I was with Lydia."

"And she was with you. Too convenient."

I made a sweeping gesture. "What about the five thousand people in Walla Walla who have no alibi at all?"

"They weren't seen with Officer Montrose right before he died. That's called opportunity."

"We weren't with him right before he died, either."

"I'm not going to argue with you. Just don't leave town."

"I have no intention of leaving town. I just want to know why I shouldn't."

Thibideaux growled, "Because you're a suspect. How's that?"

I took a deep breath. "Now I'm confused. What exactly do you suspect me of doing?"

Thibideaux stared at me, exhaled noisily through his nostrils. He was debating. The roll-the-dice part of him won. "I'll tell you what I think," he said. "I think something went down at the cemetery. I don't know what it was, but it might've caused Montrose to fire a shot, and it definitely got his taillight broken. I think sometime later you maybe stole the Barracuda and lured Montrose into chasing you. I think you figured you could outrun him in a hot car, and then it went bad out by Kooskooskie."

I looked at Chief Carter and Detective Gerritsen. "If you guys believe this, you really are the Keystone Cops."

"I'm ending this interview," Thibideaux announced, without looking at me. "You're free to go."

This time I kept my mouth shut.

———————

Gerritsen offered me a ride back to the Zaleski's but I refused, my expression letting him know I'd rather have a root canal. I walked up Second Avenue and cut over to the railroad tracks, my mind replaying the interview as I stepped from one railroad tie to the next. I followed the tracks north and east about a mile and peeled off at Ninth to get to the Cruz' house.

Lydia saw me coming from her front window. Why she was looking out at that exact moment I don't know. Maybe she expected me. She held up a finger to say just a minute and emerged from the house a short while later.

I'd sat down and waited on the curb. She walked several steps past me and into the street, turned and faced me.

"I might be in trouble," I said, looking up. "I'm not sure."

"What's wrong?" Her eyes looked lifeless, depleted.

I wanted to put my arms around her and comfort her. Comfort myself. "I just had a second interview at the precinct."

"Me, too. They picked me up an hour and a half ago."

"What'd you tell your parents?"

"Just that we saw Montrose an hour before he died. Amelia's buying it because she thinks I'm perfect. Hector wants to know why they'd take me downtown. He says I can't talk to them again unless he's in the room." She eyeballed a crumpled Dixie Cup that someone had tossed in the street. "Tell me why you might be in trouble."

"The FBI guy says they got a fingerprint off the key to the Barracuda. And it's possible. I forgot to wipe it down."

Her eyes came to life. "So mine would be on it, too. And they got my fingerprints off a glass of water I touched."

I stood up. "Don't feel bad. I fell for the same trick. But the key would have Tammy Balfour's prints and anyone else's who might've driven it recently, which means it's probably one big smudge in a very small area."

"Let's hope so."

I took a deep breath and blew the air through pursed lips. "Did they show you the piece of broken plastic from Montrose's taillight?"

She nodded. "Yeah, but I just shrugged it off like . . . how would I know anything about that?"

"Same here. I knew there was something important I was missing. That was it. I vaguely remembered the sound of something breaking when I kicked the gun from Montrose."

She lightly touched my arm. "Don't worry about it. We left the cemetery as soon as Montrose told us to and that's that."

Her touch felt heavenly. I wanted to return it but knew not to push my luck. "Right. All we have to do is stick to the story."

"Yeah. Did Thibideaux tell you about finding one of my hairs in Tammy's car."

"No, he didn't mention that. What'd you say?"

"I told them about going the Arctic Circle with her a couple weeks ago and they backed off. I don't even think they could prove it came from my head. Tammy runs around with a lot of Indian and Mexican girlfriends and we all have long black hair."

"Did you tell 'em that?"

She nodded impatiently. "Of course."

"Want to go for a walk?"

"Not really. I'm wiped out."

I kicked a rock down the street. Too hard. It bounced up and nicked a parked car. "They seem to think we stole the Barracuda and lured Montrose into chasing us. But they're not sure. At least that's the impression I got."

"Me, too. It's like they were fishing."

"Right. Trying to get us to contradict ourselves."

She tucked her hair behind her ears. "Are they going to figure out what happened?"

"I don't think so, but we have to be careful."

She gazed skyward at the gleaming underbelly of a commercial airliner, just taken off from the Walla Walla City-County Airport. "I wonder if anyone in that plane ever killed a person."

"Don't torture yourself, Lydia. You did what you had to do."

"That's not what you said when it happened," she snapped.

A door slammed across the street. Slim, Lydia's retarded neighbor, loped off the steps of his front porch and promptly punted a deflated basketball into the weeds. He wore shabby jeans and a red, short-sleeved western shirt. Looking up, he waved. "Hi Lydia."

"Hi Slim."

"I know you, too," he said, making his way over with an uncoordinated gait. He stopped alongside Lydia, wiped his nose with a skinny forearm.

"Hi Slim." I wished he'd leave, but didn't want to be rude.

"I forget yer name," he said, blinking rapidly.

"Bryan."

Lydia showed surprise. "How do you know each other?"

"We met the first day I came out here," I answered.

"You did?"

"Over by the refinery," I added.

Rocking from foot to foot, Slim looked at Lydia and mumbled, "He gave me money."

Lydia gave me a puzzled look.

"Slim noticed my gas cap was open and he closed it for me. It could have been dangerous so I paid him for his services."

"That's right," Slim said excitedly. "I gave the money to Gladys. She's saving it for a trip to Tahiti. I get to go, too."

"How much did you give him?" Lydia asked with a quizzical expression.

"Two dollars."

"Gladys was mad. She threw a can of peas at me." He rubbed his side, presumably where she hit him.

I winced in sympathy. "She threw a can of peas at you because I gave you the money?"

"No, 'cause I told you about Lydia's momma bein' an Injun whore."

"I beg your pardon?" Lydia said.

Slim went on, oblivious to the impact of his words. "I saw pictures of Tahiti in a magazine. It's real pretty there."

"I'll bet," Lydia said. "You told Bryan my mother was an Indian whore?"

"Yep, an I know what it means, too."

Lydia turned to me, hands on her hips. "He told you about my mother the first time you came out here? The day after Slider rolled his milk truck?"

"Yeah."

She frowned. "And you've never asked me about it?"

My body tensed up. "I wasn't sure Slim knew what he was talking about."

"You knew and you pretended—"

"Come on, Lydia. What was I supposed to do?"

"You could have told me what you heard. Given me the chance to say it was or wasn't true."

"So we just meet and I'm supposed to ask you if your mother was a prostitute?"

"In Tahiti they cook whole pigs on the beach."

"That's great, Slim. I wonder if Lydia and I could be alone for a few minutes. We have something—"

"No!" Lydia exploded. "Slim stays. This is his neighborhood. *You* go."

My shoulders slumped. "Give me a break, Lydia. I didn't want to embarrass you. Is that so bad?"

"Honesty would've been nice."

"Honesty's the best policy," Slim lectured.

"Lydia, please. Let's talk. I apologize—"

"Save it," she said, storming into the house. "I don't even know you."

Slim swallowed hard and then swallowed again, his Adam's apple bobbing up and down in his scrawny neck. "Did I say something bad?"

I waited a moment before answering. "No, Slim. I did."

"Are you Lydia's boyfriend?"

"Good question."

The next evening I excused myself from supper and went for a walk, ended up in the alley behind the fraternity house. I debated and let myself in. The emptiness of the place amplified my sense of desperation. I went downstairs to the TV room and collapsed on one of the couches. I turned on the light and then turned it back off.

I switched on the TV set. A show I'd never seen had just started, the opening scene showing a brightly-lit amusement park at night. The Ferris Wheel, the roller coaster, all the rides were going full-bore, but there was not a soul in sight. I thought of little Lydia, trapped on the Gravitron. Changed the channel and came in on the middle of a jingle, " . . . wonder where the yellow went, when you brush your teeth with Pepsodent." Changed to the local news, a station broadcasting out of Spokane. A theme song faded out and a voice over informed me I was watching Q8 Eyewitness News, the "Eyes of the Inland Empire."

A Cessna with two passengers, a young physician and his wife, had crashed in the Selkirk Mountains north of Spokane, near Waitts Lake. A camera panned a densely forested area and settled upon the twisted wreckage of a small yellow airplane, a crash no one could possibly have survived. It reminded me of Montrose's car after pushing it down the embankment, so I switched to *"What's My Line?"* The first guest signed in – a distinguished looking woman who manufactured dynamite. I left the room and went to get a Coke from the machine at the bottom of the stairs. Sat on the bottom step and fought back tears. Lydia wouldn't return my calls. I was losing her. An odd queasy sensation settled in the pit of my stomach.

I forced myself back into the TV room and turned back to the local news. A high school student taking a Driver's Ed course had hit a woman pedestrian in a crosswalk and broken her leg. Then a bar at the bottom of the screen read: BREAKTHROUGH IN COPKILLER CASE? I froze as an attractive thirty-something newswoman with heavy makeup and platinum hair faced the camera. Her expression was grim, but affected. "Police in Walla Walla may finally have a suspect or suspects in last Sunday's car chase accident that claimed the life of a young police officer."

A picture of Montrose flashed on the screen. Dressed in uniform, he looked young and wholesome, like a good cop. Had I never seen the man or known he was a psychopath, I'd have felt a mix of compassion and outrage. Just like the media wanted.

The newswoman reappeared and glanced down at her notes, exposing dark roots. When she realized she was on camera she said, "Earlier today, Bob Reilly, our roving reporter, was outside the Whitman County courthouse."

The picture wobbled, cut to the steps of the courthouse where a lean, casually dressed man held a microphone in one hand and what looked to be a stack of note cards in the other. A box popped up in the upper right hand corner of the screen and, inside it, the words RECORDED EARLIER.

Bright afternoon sun shined directly in Bob Reilly's eyes, causing him to squint absurdly as he began his report. "Only minutes ago, Q8 Eyewitness News learned of a possible break in the nearly weeklong investigation into the violent death of local policeman, Officer Jack Montrose. FBI Special Agent Dupuy Thibideaux, speaking to this reporter, and others, acknowledged there might be a suspect or suspects in the case that has thus far baffled local authorities." He went silent and stood awkwardly for several seconds, waiting for a clip filmed earlier.

The picture changed again to show Thibideaux standing in the lobby of the police station and about to speak with several reporters. He appeared impatient with Q8's Reilly, who had shoved a microphone into his face.

"Agent Thibideaux," Reilly said excitedly. "Could you begin by informing our viewers in what capacity you've become involved in this case?"

"Certainly," Thibideaux responded. "The FBI is the main arm of investigation for the United States Department of Justice. We have the responsibility and the authority to help other law enforcement agencies investigate crimes such as the death of Officer Jack Montrose."

"Has the FBI has taken over the investigation into the suspicious death of Officer Montrose?"

"No," Thibideaux answered, grimacing. "The Walla Walla Police Department is in charge of the investigation. We're here to help the locals investigate and solve a complicated case."

"And are you any closer to solving this case?"

"It would be premature for me to comment on that at this time."

Reilly ruffled his notes. "Our station, Q8 Eyewitness News, received an anonymous phone call this morning. We were told two teenagers have been interviewed in connection with this case, and that they interacted with Officer Montrose prior to the fatal car chase. Can you verify this information?"

Thibideaux said, "I can only say we're investigating all possible leads."

"Are these teenagers in police custody?"

Thibideaux shook his head. "No one is in custody. We don't have sufficient evidence to charge anyone with a crime. No charges have been filed."

Reilly looked frustrated. "But these teenagers are considered suspects?"

Thibideaux looked away, tugged at his ear. "I have to go."

"Thank you Special Agent Dupuy Thibideaux, on loan from the New Orleans field office of the FBI. This is Bob Reilly, Q8 Eyewitness News, reporting live from Walla Walla."

I cocked my arm, poised to throw my half-full bottle of Coke through the television screen. Instead, I jammed it into a corner cushion and raced to the first floor head with imminent diarrhea. The same first floor head where I'd once taken Vicky Spotts on a night she'd become ill after having had too much to drink. The same Vicky Spotts who was the unidentified source for Q8 Eyewitness News.

————

Most of the next day I mulled over the TV interview with Thibideaux, trying to read between the lines. Then, late in the afternoon, the Zaleskis' doorbell rang. I panicked, yelled that I'd get it and raced upstairs. *Please don't be the police. Please don't tell me my fingerprint showed up on the Barracuda key. Please don't be Gerritsen or Thibideaux with a warrant for my arrest.*

I inched the door open and peeked out.

Bigdog leaned hard against a pillar, panting from the exertion of negotiating the eight steps that went from sidewalk to porch. "Got a minute?" he wheezed.

"Sure. What's up?" I stepped outside and gently closed the door behind me.

"What's up is this cop named Gerritsen?"

"I take it he asked you some questions?"

"For the last half-hour." Bigdog coughed and tried to catch his breath. "Corralled me coming out of my apartment."

"What'd he want to know?"

He coughed again and thumped his corpulent chest with a fist. "What time you and Lydia came over Sunday night, what time you left . . . what time we saw your car in the Phi Delt parking lot. Lots of stuff."

"What?"

"Lots of stuff," he repeated.

"No," I shook my head rapidly. "Just before that."

"He asked what time me and Slider saw your car at the house."

"You saw my car at the fraternity house?"

Bigdog nodded. "Yeah, and you owe me big for not coming in. Slider wanted to play Ping-Pong in the worst way, but I told him you might be, shall we say, getting intimate with Miss Lydia."

"What time was it?"

"Eleven-fifteen."

I took a moment. "You told Gerritsen you saw my car at the house at eleven-fifteen?"

"Yeah," he answered, mopping his brow. "Is that a problem?"

"No. It's good. Better than good."

"What the hell's goin' on? I know this is the guy investigating the Montrose case, but why's he interested in you?"

I looked up and down the street, checking for police surveillance. "It turns out Lydia and I were the last ones to see Montrose alive. Out at Stubblefield."

"Yeah, he asked about that. I told him you guys were intending to go out to Stubblefield. That you left right before the start of the ten o'clock movie."

"And then what?"

"That Slider and I gave up on the movie and went to the house to play some Ping-Pong. Slider bet me a case of Coors he could beat me. Anyway, we got to the house and I saw your car in the alley so I kept going."

"What did Gerritsen say when you told him it was eleven-fifteen?"

"He asked how sure I was."

"And then he dropped it?"

Bigdog shook his head. "No. He asked me the same question about five different ways. I showed him the Bulova my parents gave me for Christmas. Told him it's accurate to the second and that I checked it on Sunday night. That it was exactly a quarter after eleven."

"Did he accept that?"

"I think so," he answered.

I wanted to smile but restrained myself. "Good."

"Why is the exact time so important, anyway?"

"Gerritsen wants to be sure we weren't the ones that stole the car Montrose was chasing when he hit the bridge."

Bigdog laughed. "Because you and Lydia are such big time car thieves."

"Right."

"What a bunch a shit-for-brains! And to think we pay their salaries."

I allowed myself a smile. "Did you tell Gerritsen you kept on going after seeing my car?"

"Yeah," he chuckled. "I told him it was the brotherly thing to do."

I nodded. "It was downright brotherly."

Bigdog hawked up some phlegm and spit it into the bushes. "So it helps, my telling Gerritsen you were at the house at eleven-fifteen?"

"Bigtime. If Slider tells him the same thing, we're golden."

"He will. I called him as soon as Gerritsen left."

"You did?" I asked, surprised.

"Yeah. He's expecting a visit. Told him what I said so he could say the same thing. Truth is, Slider was too drunk to remember a thing about Sunday night. That's why you owe me for not coming in the house. The case of Coors was a lock. He couldn't even have seen the Ping-Pong ball, much less hit it."

"I owe you big."

"Pizza Pete's," he grinned. "Friday night. A large with extra cheese and the works and we call it even."

"Deal."

Bigdog flashed me an odd smile and proceeded to skip down the steps. He could be remarkably agile for someone carrying close to three hundred pounds. Stopping at the sidewalk he turned and said, "Oh, Gerritsen wanted to know if you and Lydia took beer with you when you left my apartment."

"And you said?"

"You kiddin'? Tell a cop a minor had beer in his car?"

"The code of silence?"

"Right on, brother!"

He drove off, a plume of white smoke spewing from the tailpipe of his '57 Mercury, the slanted taillights lighting up as he braked for the corner. I sat on the top step, dumbstruck with my good fortune, but also baffled at what made Bigdog think he saw my car at the fraternity at a quarter after eleven on Sunday night. At that time, Lydia and I had just staged the accident at the bridge. By the time we left, dumped the stolen car, retrieved my car from Stubblefield and drove back to the fraternity house, it was several minutes past midnight – not even close to eleven-fifteen. Then it dawned on me. Bigdog had lied to the cops.

———————

Gerritsen showed up mid-afternoon the next day. The Zaleskis just had left to go antique shopping in Milton-Freewater. I'd lost track of time perusing chess books in the library, finally settling on an interesting game to study – as if I could purge my mind of Lydia, stop thinking about Stubblefield and what would happen if the police managed to put two and two together. I showed the detective in and asked him to sit down, my heart pounding. He took the seat across from me at the chessboard.

"What do you have going here?" he asked, looking over the board.

"This is the Stonewall, my favorite opening. I've been reading up on what to do when Black gets White's light-squared bishop off the board."

"So tell me, what's interesting about this position? In lay terms."

"This is what the board looked like after fourteen moves when Sultan Khan played Mattison in 1931. What's interesting is how Khan left his king exposed. Castling wasn't a legal move in his native India, so Khan's games often show his king remaining in the center for the entire game."

Gerritsen let slip a sly smile. "Isn't the king afraid of getting caught out there? I mean, I'm not the best player in the world, but he looks awfully vulnerable. One wrong move, he gets captured and the game's over. Right?"

"Right. Only a player as accomplished as Sultan Khan doesn't necessarily make a wrong move. He was a genius. Besides, in this game, his king's better off smack dab in the middle of things than he would be hiding on the usual wing squares."

"So Khan wins this game?"

I nodded. "Black resigns on the twenty-second move."

"Does Khan always win?"

"Nope. The Persian rug under our feet used to be his. Dr. Zaleski won it from him in a game in the early thirties."

Gerritsen glanced at the carpet, wriggled the soles of his shoes to test the nap. Satisfied, he cleared his throat. "The fingerprint evidence came back from the FBI lab."

"And?"

"Thibideaux' people couldn't get a good print off it. Not even a partial."

"Too bad."

Gerristen leaned back and folded his arms. "Because?"

"Because now you're always going to wonder if my print was on it."

"I suppose I will," he replied with a series of barely perceptible nods.

"You guys are way off on that. What about that piece of broken taillight? Any prints on it?"

"Lots of 'em, but not yours or Miss Redstone's." He reached under his jacket and removed a little spiral notebook. "I talked to your buddies, Bigdog and Slider." He paused and stared, watching for my reaction.

I shrugged my shoulders and waited.

Gerritsen flipped open his notebook. "They both say they saw your car at the fraternity house on Sunday night. At eleven-fifteen, which fits with what you told us."

"But you still have questions, because they didn't actually see me and Lydia, they just saw my car. And you wonder if I told them what to say."

"Did you?" he asked, cracking his knuckles.

"No. I talked to Slider briefly on the day I was so sick. Monday. He called to tell me about Montrose being dead. I told him I'd heard, and then we talked about doubling to the movies with our girlfriends. That was it."

"What about Bigdog?"

"I talked to Bigdog earlier this afternoon. He came by to tell me you'd asked him a bunch of questions. First time I've talked to him since Sunday night when Lydia and I went to his apartment for dinner."

Gerritsen thumbed through his notes. "Another thing. It turns out that eleven-fifteen is just about the exact time Montrose crashed his car."

I feigned a puzzled expression. "How do you know that?"

He paused before answering. "He phoned in a few seconds before he crashed. Against procedure . . . to phone in during a high-speed pursuit. The dispatcher actually heard him slam into the bridge."

"Did he say anything about who he was chasing, or what the hell was going on?"

"I'm not going to answer that."

"Suit yourself."

He paused again. "I will tell you a woman who lives on the other side of the alley saw you and Lydia leave the fraternity a few minutes after midnight. She had just come home from her Bridge club meeting and checked the clock on her kitchen stove. So I guess your story holds up."

The grandfather clock chimed, provided a temporary distraction. "Are Lydia and I free to leave town now?"

"You planning on leaving Walla Walla?"

"I'm giving it some serious consideration."

He glanced at the chessboard before meeting my eyes. "Mind if I ask why?"

"Are you kidding me? After what you've put us through?"

"We've interviewed a lot of people."

"Did you go on TV and talk about them, like Thibideaux did?"

"You saw that?"

"Unfortunately."

He shrugged. "Okay, so what about it? That reporter mentioned two teenagers. You weren't named."

"Oh, come on, Detective. The Montrose case is Walla Walla's crime of the century. How many cops have already told their wives that Lydia and I were in for questioning? That the prime suspect is the Whitman kid that beat the Russian chess player. How many wives told their friends? You know how Walla Walla is. By now a hundred people know. Tomorrow, it'll double. In a week, it'll be half the town. Our reputations are totaled, thanks to you guys."

"But if you're innocent—"

My voice rose. "That doesn't matter and you know it. People are always going to wonder if we were the ones that ran that poor cop off the road."

"You know what? I'm going to wonder, too. Despite your alibi, I think there's a chance you're getting away with murder. You *and* your girlfriend."

"You have any evidence?"

He closed his notebook, put it in his shirt pocket. "Not a shred."

"Then leave us alone," I said, sounding bolder than I felt.

Gerritsen stared at me through icy blue eyes, reached out and plucked the black king from the board. "I wouldn't have resigned like Khan's opponent." He leaned forward and pointed the chess piece like a miniature pistol. "I'd have waited for him to make that one wrong move, then I'd nail the bastard."

I made a brief stop on the way to the cannery and waited for Lydia to get off her shift. She was almost to her car when she saw mine. I saw confusion, then a pained expression as she walked over to my window.

"Something good happened." I'd scripted my first few lines in the conversation.

"What?"

"Hop in," I said, trying to sound upbeat.

"I don't want to."

"C'mon Lydia, it's important."

She moved slowly around the car and slid into the passenger seat. "What's that smell?"

"Calamine lotion. I have a rash."

"Sorry. So what's important?" she asked in flat voice.

I noticed a faint tinge of purple beneath her eyes, presumably from poor sleep. "Gerritsen interviewed Bigdog today. Bigdog told him he saw our car at the fraternity house. At eleven-fifteen."

"He couldn't have. We didn't get there till midnight."

"I know. But he told Gerritsen eleven-fifteen."

She stared at me. "Did you tell him to say that?"

"No, I never even talked to him."

"How would he know to say that? It backs our alibi perfectly."

I nodded. "I know. We're golden."

"Okay, help me think. Did the paper say what time Montrose hit the bridge?"

"I think it said he sped past the gas station at eleven, or a few minutes after. The implication was he wiped out about ten minutes later."

She smiled. "That *is* good news."

"Yeah."

"How could Bigdog be so far off on the time?"

"You tell me."

She gazed out the window, tilted her head ever so slightly. Ten seconds later she said, "He lied to the police?"

I nodded. "Must have."

"But how would he know to say we were at the fraternity house? How would he know that's what we told the police? And how would he know what time to say he saw us there?"

"I have *no* idea."

"And you're not going to ask."

"No, ma'am."

"Wow! Bigdog comes through."

I looked around, as if someone might be within earshot. "It gets better."

"What?"

"The fingerprint evidence came back negative. No usable prints."

Her body straightened. "Does that mean we're in the clear?"

I nodded, suppressed a strong urge to reach out and hold her to me.

"God, what a relief," she said to herself.

I reached into the back seat and handed her a paper bag. "I got you something." I'd picked up Buffy Sainte-Marie's latest album on the way to the cannery.

She removed it slowly and read the title aloud, *"I'm Gonna Be A Country Girl Again."*

"Cool, huh?"

Her eyes darkened. "I can't accept it."

"Why?"

She reached behind her and set the album gently on the back seat. "I'm leaving."

"What do you mean?" I asked, dreading the worst.

She took a deep breath and braced herself. "I'm leaving you, leaving Walla Walla, my family . . . everything."

I slumped against the steering wheel. "Look, I'm sorry if I said the wrong things out at Stubblefield. I'm sorry if I should have told you what Slim said about your mother."

"It's not that. It's me. I can't love. I tried, but I got it wrong."

"It felt like love to me," I muttered.

"Maybe it did, but it wasn't real. I'm too messed up by the stuff that happened in my childhood."

The tears started coming and I covered my eyes. I could play it tough with the cops, but the thought of losing Lydia turned me into a frightened child.

She placed her hand on my knee, gave me an ever-so-gentle squeeze. "I'm sorry," she whispered. "I didn't mean for it to end like this."

"It doesn't have to end. I could leave with you."

She shook her head. "I'm going by myself. Up to B.C. to look for my mom. I have to see her before she dies."

"We could go together. It'd give us time to work this stuff out."

"I don't want to work it out. I want to be on my own. I'm better that way."

"I'm not," I told her. It felt like I had a boulder in my chest.

"You'll be okay," she reassured me. "You'll forget me and find someone better."

"No I won't," I said, unable to hold back the tears.

She met my eyes. "I'm sorry, Bryan. I don't want to hurt you."

I leaned back in my seat, stared at the cannery workers weaving their way through parked cars. "Can't you think about this for awhile? When things get back to normal, you might change your mind."

"Normal? You think things are going to get back to normal? Bryan, wake up!" She lowered her voice. "I'm running away. I killed a man."

I stopped crying. "A man who was raping you."

"That's true, but it doesn't matter. I feel different inside. I killed someone. Nothing can change that."

"But you might change your mind about us."

She shook her head slowly. "I'm not going to argue. Say goodbye to me, Bryan."

"I can't."

"You have to. I'm leaving town, tomorrow." She patted the front pocket in her jeans. "As soon as I cash my paycheck."

"Have you told Hector and Amelia?"

"I haven't even told Yolanda. They'll try to talk me out of it."

"Yeah, because it's a bad idea."

"I have to leave, Bryan. I killed a cop. If Gerritsen or the FBI figure it out, they'll lock me up for life. Why would I stay and take a chance on slipping up?"

I sighed. Arguing with Lydia was pointless. "So it's Canada."

"Yeah."

"Then what?"

"I don't know, but I'm not coming back here."

"Could you call me, or write? Tell me what's happening with us?"

"Nothing's happening with us. It's over. I need to make a clean break, end up somewhere where I can start over."

"I'll find you. We're supposed to be together."

"Don't try to find me. And don't ask Yolanda where I am. Or Hector or Amelia."

"I don't want to lose you," I pleaded.

"Let me go."

"I can't."

She straightened in the car seat. "I'm sorry, I have to go now. This is too hard." A tear spilled down her cheek, lost momentum and stopped at her jaw line. "Goodbye, Bryan. I wish you all the best." She kissed her fingertips and tenderly touched my cheek. After a long look, she let herself out of the car. The door closed with a decisive thump.

I watched her walk away. A shimmer of tears blurred my vision. Her hair spilled over a tattered, threadbare red sweater. I'd never seen her wear it. Something about the sweater made her unbearably sweet, made me long for her with a passion I would have never imagined possible. My soul ached. I cried harder. Deep, wracking sobs. "I'll find you," I said, choking out the words. She didn't hear me.

———————

I telephoned my father from the Zaleski's basement phone. Maybe I just wanted to hear a familiar voice, get some support. He answered on the third ring.

"Hi, dad." My voice sounded shaky, so I upped my volume. "How've you been?"

"Good. Cat and I were hitting golf balls at the driving range."

"The one next to the old dump?"

"Yeah. It's actually on top of the old dump."

"Remember how you used to take me along with you?"

"Of course I remember. The seagulls fascinated you. So did the fires. I had to explain everything from chemical changes that release heat and light, to combustible substances. But that was before chess. After you discovered chess, or chess discovered you, the dump came in a very distant second."

I managed a sad laugh. "So how'd you hit 'em?"

"My slice is worse than ever. Cat said it looks like a warped banana."

"Maybe you should get a lesson."

"Right. That reminds me. Cat wanted to know what to get you for your birthday."

"Oh." I closed my eyes, saw Lydia walking off in the red sweater.

"Well, any ideas?"

I blinked back tears. "I'll think of something and let you know."

"You call for any particular reason?"

No, other than to say that I helped kill a man. I could feel the pull in my chest to tell him everything. Lydia killed a cop. I covered it up. She left me. I could be charged with murder, go to prison. I wanted to be held. There was a second, maybe two, where the door cracked open between us, between father and son, and then I heard myself say, "No, I just called to say hi." The door snapped shut, like when Lydia said goodbye.

"Everything okay? You're voice sounds funny."

I cleared my throat. "Lydia and got in a fight. I guess I'm bummed."

"What're you fighting over?"

"I don't know." Another chance to unload, get my father to help carry the burden. "Something happened, and she thinks I wasn't supportive."

He chuckled, which bothered me. I heard ice cubes clinking in a glass, which bothered me even more. "Women. Can't live with 'em. Can't live without 'em." Cat said something in the background and he laughed outright.

"You got that right," I said, trying to manufacture some semblance of closeness.

A pause in the conversation, then he asked, "How's the weather on your side of the mountains?"

"Hot. How's it there?"

"In the sixties. Rained most of yesterday."

"Amazing."

Silence for maybe ten seconds, and then, "How's the chess game?"

"Pretty good. Look, I better get goin'. My buddy Slider and I are going to a movie." Another lie. So easy.

"You sure you're okay? Need any money, or anything?"

"No, I'm fine. Really."

I went the night without sleep, got to morning with a headache tight across my forehead and eyes so swollen and red, I went out of may way to avoid the Zaleskis and the sympathy I knew they'd extend. With nothing to lose, or so I told myself, I dressed in a hurry and rushed over to Lydia's. *Maybe I can talk her out of leaving.* Her Pontiac, usually parked out front, was nowhere to be seen. Panicked, I ran up the walkway and pounded on the front door.

Yolanda answered the door in a robe, red-eyed and sullen. "She's gone," she told me before I uttered a word.

"To Canada?"

"I guess," she answered, holding up a crumpled letter. "She says she wants to find her mother. Before it's too late."

"How long ago did she leave?"

"We don't exactly know. Hector found this goodbye letter when he got up. He and mom went after her in the Malibu, but I think she had too much of a head start."

"Probably."

"Why'd she break up with you, Bryan? What happened?"

"I don't know," I answered. "I tried to talk her out of it, but she wouldn't listen."

"I don't get it. You were Lydia's life until a week ago. She was always talking about how wonderful you were, how much she loved you. Then everything changed. Poof! All at once! At first I thought she was just bitchy because of her period, but . . ."

"I don't get it either." I halfway expected Yolanda to say something about Stubblefield, or the police interviews, but it was clear Lydia hadn't confided in her.

"Hector thinks you got her pregnant?"

I shook my head. "No, that's not it."

"I didn't think so."

I sighed. "I might not see you again."

"Of course you will," Yolanda countered.

I struggled to contain my emotions. "No. I'm leaving town, too. For good."

She bit her lip and paused. "Don't do it, Bryan. Don't throw away your education."

Sadness overwhelmed me, but I attempted a smile. "Tell Hector I loved hanging out with your family. Tell Amelia I'll miss her cooking. Please tell them."

She wrapped her arms around me and began to cry. Her embrace was soft and warm, like a blanket just out of the dryer. "I'm losing all the people I care about."

"Me too," I told her.

"How soon are you leaving?"

I broke the embrace and took a deep breath. "As soon as possible."

"You can't be talked out of it?"

"No."

"You're stubborn like Lydia. I'll miss you. A lot."

I took a last look at the Cruz' living room. Taco, the family cat, was sleeping in his favorite spot on the couch. It hurt to think I wouldn't see him again. "You know what, Yolanda? If I hadn't fallen so hard for your sister, I'd be in love with you."

Tears streamed down Yolanda's chubby cheeks. She threw herself into my arms a second time. We held each other for a long time.

I drove back to the Zaleskis', parked at the curb and sat in a moody silence. Not having to face Hector and Amelia was a relief, but I still had more goodbyes to do. Bigdog and Slider I would write from Seattle. I was so messed up I didn't even think about Ethan. Dr. Z and Reva I had to see in person. Mom Waters, too. *Get it over with. If you're going to amputate a hand, you don't do it one finger at a time.* I glanced at my wristwatch. It was not yet noon. I restarted the car and drove over to Mom Waters' apartment.

My head hurt from the combination of skipping breakfast and all the crying, so I stopped at Safeway and got pre-packaged egg salad sandwich from the deli section. After washing it down with a quart of milk, I walked over to Mom's, directly across the street. She didn't answer on the first knock so I knocked louder. Still no answer. I scribbled her a goodbye note on the back of the grocery bag and returned to my car.

Dr. Z and Reva were out, attending a seminar at Professor Ryan's about planting vineyards in the Walla Walla valley. Dr. Z had left me a note on the kitchen table: "Please call us if you need anything. We're worried about you."

I loaded the car with my few possessions, then trudged back inside and collapsed on the living room couch. Closed curtains made the room dark and depressing. My head spun. I considered telling Dr Z. and Reva the truth, tried to imagine their reaction. The air was stale from lack of ventilation. I dozed off and woke up maybe half an hour later to the sound of muted voices on the back porch. A key jiggled in the lock and I heard the door open. The Zaleskis came in the back door conversing in Russian, something they'd never done in my presence. "Hello, there," I called out. My voice sounded dull and lifeless in the warm, soft air.

I heard footsteps moving through the house. Dr. Z and Reva entered the living room holding hands, like a young couple. I felt the sting of envy, longed for the security they'd found in one another.

"Bryan, you look positively forlorn," Dr. Z commented. He released Reva's hand and took a chair on the opposite side of the room.

I sat up, cleared my throat. "Lydia broke up with me. Yesterday. This morning she left town."

"Oh dear," Reva muttered. She came over to the couch to sit with me. "Is lover's quarrel, or is permanent?"

"Permanent." To my surprise, I didn't dissolve into tears.

"Will she be coming back to Walla Walla?" Dr. Z asked.

I shook my head. "She says she's never coming back. And I believe her."

He exhaled audibly through his mouth. "What's going on, Bryan? You've been acting strangely ever since last weekend."

I hesitated, felt an impulse to spill part of the secret. I was dog-tired from an overdose of adrenaline and too little sleep. Massaging my temples, I calculated risk versus benefit and gave in. "If I tell you guys something, do you promise not to say anything?"

"Of course," Dr. Z told me.

Reva put her hand on my shoulder.

I took a deep breath. "Okay. Here's the deal. I can't tell you everything, but Lydia and I know something about that police officer's death out at Kooskooskie."

Dr. Z tensed. "What is it that you know?"

I shook my head. "I can't tell you that."

He stared at me like I was a complicated board position. "Are you in trouble with the law?

"No, not now, but we were. The police have interviewed me twice and a detective was here yesterday, while you were out."

"What did the detective say?"

"That they suspect we had something to do with the car wreck that killed Officer Montrose, but they're dropping it for lack of evidence."

"Is it true? Did you have something to do with the accident?"

"I don't want to answer questions about it." I took turns looking them in the eye. "I can only assure you we didn't do anything wrong."

Dr. Z rubbed the underside of his chin, making a scraping sound as he went against the grain of his whiskers. "Do you need to get an attorney?"

I shook my head. "No."

"Have you shared this with your father?"

"No, and I'm not going to so don't bother trying to talk me into it."

He went silent for a long moment. "So the situation with the police is resolved, but it has something to do with Lydia leaving town?"

I swallowed hard. "Right. And I'm leaving, too."

Dr. Z shifted in his chair, became agitated. "Leaving Whitman?"

"I have to."

"But if you didn't do anything wrong—"

"No, I have to go. I can't live in a place where I'll always be looking over my shoulder."

Dr. Z adopted a pleading tone. "You shouldn't have to leave town if you didn't do anything wrong. These kinds of things die down. People forget and life—"

"Only the police won't forget. I'd be a constant reminder of an unsolved homicide. No, I have to leave, and I have to do it right away."

"Homicide?"

If I had any doubts about the need to leave Walla Walla, they disappeared with that one slip of the tongue. I dissembled. "The authorities suspect me and Lydia stole that car and ran Montrose off the road out at Kooskooskie. I can tell you this. We didn't do it."

Dr. Z stayed silent. I had the impression he wanted to ask a series of tough questions, but rejected the idea. "Obviously, I want you to stay at Whitman. But I know you, Bryan, and it's clear you've made up your mind. When will you leave?"

"First thing in the morning. The car's already loaded."

"You *must* stay in touch."

"Yes, please," Reva seconded.

"I will. I promise."

Dr. Z picked up the briar pipe I'd given him for Christmas. He'd left it on the end table next to his chair. He studied it for a moment and set it gently down. "It's going to be difficult not having you around."

"For me too," Reva chimed in. She straightened her spine and managed a smile, but tears gave away her sadness.

My heart broke open. "I know. I'd give anything if things could be different."

Dr. Z's expression turned stony. "Under no circumstances can you allow this tragedy to derail your chess career. Do you understand?"

I nodded. "I'm too upset about Lydia to think about chess right now, but . . ." The tears materialized, gradually at first and then harder, like the arrival of a long-awaited weather disturbance. Reva put her arms around me and held me for what seemed a long time. I thought about all the mothering I missed out on.

Chapter 9
The Empty Years

Getting out of Walla Walla did nothing to relieve my longing for Lydia. And flashbacks came in droves, triggered by a myriad of innocuous experiences. I'd look across a room and see a dark-skinned girl—a police car would pull alongside me at a stoplight—I'd hear *Unchained Melody* on the radio—a letter from the Zaleskis—all would transport me back in time. A path formed in my brain, leading always to the same horrific image: a wild-eyed, half-naked Lydia raising her handcuffed fists to the night sky and delivering the deathblow to Jack Montrose's throat. My life had divided itself into "before it happened" and "after it happened." Stubblefield came to define a moment before which my life was good and full of promise, and after which it seemed pointless. I cursed God for the randomness of the universe.

Returning home to Seattle, I tried immersing myself in chess. An effective defense, chess, but like an infected splinter, the ugly memories worked their way toward the surface, always, and with them came the iron chain of misery. Nighttime proved a special kind of torture, when the slowly descending darkness snuffed out any foothold of normalcy I might have gained over the course of the day. I'd twist in anguish beneath my covers, whirlwinds of grief propelling my body. Several times I got out of bed and wrote love letters to Lydia, but they ended up shredded in the trash.

Sleep offered no respite, as I suffered a recurring nightmare. Lydia and I kiss in a field in the Blue Mountains. Without warning, fat, speckled rattlesnakes infest the grasses. Lydia bolts to safety and calls after me, but I can't move. I'd wake up with my heart pounding, the night closing in on me like the vipers in my dream—buzzing, treacherous, ready to inject me with deadly venom.

I stayed with my father and Cat less than a month. My father seemed oblivious to my grief and I resented his irate appeals to finish my education at Whitman. It was partly his lack of emotional support that sent me packing. In his defense, I allowed him to believe dropping out was solely motivated by despondency over losing Lydia, which made no sense to him.

What made no sense to me was the fact he received no notification of the Montrose investigation. I was a minor who'd been formally questioned in the death of a police officer and yet no one contacted my only living parent. Maybe they feared I'd report Officer David for roughing me up. Maybe it was "the Walla Walla factor," Slider's reference to a small town that follows its own rules.

One morning, in the car, my father seemed unusually quiet. I volunteered, "Don't worry, Dad. I'll eventually finish my education."

"It's not that," he replied.

"What's wrong then?"

He hesitated, turned off the car radio. "Did you read the paper about the little boy who drowned over by University Village?"

"Huh uh." I hadn't so much as glanced at a newspaper since reading about Montrose in the *Walla Walla Union-Bulletin.*

"A one-year-old boy drowned in a pool. Last week, in an apartment complex in the U District. His mother's a student I've had the last three years. One of my favorites."

"I'm sorry. How'd it happen?"

"That's what bothers me so much. Verna, that's her name, told me she decided to have a second cup of her morning coffee. In the time it took to go into the kitchen and brew a second batch, her son managed to open a door and make it out to the swimming pool. It was the first time he'd ever even tried to open the door. She found him floating face down a few minutes later."

"God, that's horrid!"

"Here's what gets me." Our eyes met as he slowed for a stop sign. "She told me she almost never had that second cup of coffee. If she'd settled for one cup like she usually did . . ."

"Why does crazy stuff like that have to happen?" I asked, thinking about Stubblefield. "Why would a benevolent God let it happen?"

"Don't ask me." He shook his head in sympathy. "Poor Verna. She loved that kid like you wouldn't believe. Never saw anyone so depressed."

At that precise moment I knew I couldn't stay with my father. I was dying inside, strangled by grief. I needed someone to comfort me, someone to put me back together, and he barely noticed. I know, a mother lost a child. I lost a girlfriend. But I felt like a guy with a broken toe who isn't supposed to be in pain because someone else has a broken leg. I had to leave, be on my own. Like Lydia.

––––––––––

Two weeks later, in the parking lot of the Seattle Chess Club, I rolled down the window of my Chevy to let out the stifling afternoon heat. Paul Berliner flagged me down in the parking lot. "Bryan!" He smiled, walking over. "Are you coming or going?"

"Going,' I replied. "Is the summer tournament schedule out yet? No one inside knew."

"It comes out this weekend."

"Oh." I shifted my position to get my legs unstuck from the vinyl seat.

He smiled again, putting his gapped front teeth on display. "It seems strange to see you behind the wheel of a car. How old were you when we started our lessons together."

"Six."

He shaded his eyes from the bright sun. "Hard to believe. When do you go back to Whitman?"

"I'm not going back."

His smile disappeared. "What?"

"I'm not going back. It didn't work out."

"But your game took off under Dr. Zaleski's tutelage. You beat Vladimir Primalov."

I put the key into the ignition. "I know. But I can't take Walla Walla."

He tilted his head at an odd angle. "What are you going to do?"

I shrugged. "I don't know."

He paused to reflect, rubbing the top of his balding and sunburned head. "I have an idea," he told me. "IBM is teaching a computer to play chess. You might be just the guy they're looking for." He opened his over-stuffed briefcase, ruffled some papers and handed over an advertisement from a chess newsletter that came out of Los Angeles.

> *Seeking consultant with tournament chess experience.*
> *Must have background in higher mathematics, especially*
> *linear algebra and algorithm design. Excellent compensa-*
> *tion and benefits package.*

I read it twice and smiled inwardly, knowing the fusion of chess and computer programming would churn my mind into a machine. Machines being immune to grief, I wanted the job. "Thanks Mr. Berliner. Do you need this back?"

He was smiling again. "Keep it. If you get the job you can send me a palm tree in the mail."

In 1969, the computer chess field was barely twenty years old, and the best programs occasionally lost to players of average ability. IBM, collaborating with a group of computer geeks at Cal Tech, had started work on a project they dubbed Endgame. They wanted someone to develop their opening book and consult on questions regarding strategy and tactics. A number of brilliant minds already worked on the project, but none of them fully understood the fiendish complexity of chess.

Two days after running into Mr. Berliner I flew a nonstop to Hollywood-Burbank Airport, rented a car and drove to Cal Tech in Pasadena. Toward the end of my interview, I set up a chessboard and did a demonstration, borrowing a portable blackboard to explain the math. I showed the Endgame team how at any given time a player has approximately forty possible moves. Say he moves, followed by his opponent. Just one move each creates the possibility of about 1000 different board positions. By the time each player makes a second move, the board can take approximately one million possible positions, and after both move a third time, a billion! The permutations and combinations made them dizzy. I then promised I could raise Endgame to a Grandmaster-level ranking in a decade. They hired me on the spot.

After passing a routine physical, I rented a tiny, furnished house in Sierra Madre canyon, not far from the Cal Tech campus. I spent two days buying necessities, then hurled myself at the task. I began by outlining twenty-two classic king pawn openings, starting alphabetically with the hypermodern Alekhine's Defense and ending with the seldom-seen Vienna Game. I included the first dozen moves of every known variation, as well as hundreds of practical and idea variations of my own. The computer geeks generated a new program from my detailed notes, including my observations on key positions. I worked twelve hours a day, seven days a week and took a year to complete the king pawn openings.

Work became my salvation and the higher-ups at IBM considered me indispensable. Unaware of the demons that drove me, they awarded me with a sizeable bonus. I used it as a down payment on a one-bedroom cabin in Topanga, a charming and remote little town north of LA in the rugged Santa Monica Mountains. A haven for musicians, actors, painters, sculptors, and intellectuals, Topanga might have been the hippest place in all of Southern California. But it was the sense of isolation that appealed to me, allowing me to disconnect from the world of people and relationships.

My cabin hid at the end of a dirt road in steep Greenleaf Canyon, its terrain inhospitable to more than a few small houses. I took to working almost entirely from home, mailing in volumes of notes and phoning in ideas. Even on those days I drove in to work, I felt invisible, like ink that required special treatment to be seen.

In my second year I covered twenty-six queen pawn openings, filling six notebooks on the Indian Defenses alone. When the computer programmers couldn't keep pace, my project leader encouraged me to enter the West Coast Open Chess Tournament, a yearly event that drew an impressive international field. I balked at first, not wanting to risk losing my status as the invisible man. Besides, I expected to be rusty from lack of play and didn't welcome the idea of losing to lesser opponents. I held out for a month before caving in to pressure from my co-workers, some of whom goaded me by hinting I was only good on paper.

The tournament was held at the handsome and spacious Huntington Library and Botanical Gardens in San Marino. The Huntington, as it was called, was less than a mile from Cal Tech and without doubt the most stately, impressive and gloriously beautiful place I'd ever seen. To my surprise, my eighty-hour workweeks had actually sharpened my play, and I won my first four matches. In my fifth match I went up against Alexander Karnauktov, a forty-year-old Russian Grandmaster who'd somehow gotten out of his homeland and taken up residence in Chicago. He played a Russian variation of the Grunfeld, which began with an early queen sortie by White. I allowed him to take complete control of the center and paid for it, resigning on the forty-fourth move.

When the final standings were in, I'd amazed my co-workers and myself. The results were published in *Chess Digest,* along with a brief article that plugged me in the second paragraph: *"The promising Bryan Matthews finished in a tie for second place. Matthews, who has apparently been in hiding, is the former college student from Washington State who less than two years ago trounced World Championship Contender Vladimir Primalov in an exhibition match. Matthews' fine showing will raise his Elo rating close to the Grandmaster level. Regrettably, he refused interviews following the tournament."*

A postcard arrived a week after the article appeared, an aerial photograph of the snow-capped Blue Mountains. I couldn't help but flash on the Phi Delt cabin and my first glimpse of Lydia at the kidnap party. I flipped the postcard and saw Dr. Zaleski's distinctive printing and his "Z" signature. It read: "Bryan, Congratulations on your second-place finish in San Marino. I was delighted to see you'd entered a tournament. You might be the only player in the world who could take two years off and actually improve his game. Apparently, rust does sleep! There is still time to become the next great American player." Reva added a P.S. to let me know they missed me. I intended to write back, but three attempts convinced me it would be too painful. I knew literally hundreds of the most complicated chess openings ever devised, but didn't know how to open a letter to people I loved.

The third year after Stubblefield I devoted to openings that began with moves other than either pawn to king or queen four. I also included a number of offbeat patterns, some of which my co-workers had never even heard of: the unorthodox Paris Opening, the esoteric Orangutan, and the preposterous "Spike." I completed the opening book between Thanksgiving and Christmas, giving IBM the most up-to-date, in-depth and exhaustively analyzed computer chess program in the world. The *Los Angeles Times* ran an article, calling Endgame "a supercharged system of intelligence that responds expertly to the most difficult opening positions." The lead writer invited me to write a weekly piece for the newspaper's Sunday *Games* section. I accepted, welcoming the added commitment of time. An editor dubbed the column, "Move by Move by Matthews."

I spent my fourth year at IBM working on Endgame's evaluation function, the part of the program that tells the computer whether its position is good or bad. Borrowing the concept of point count from the game of bridge, I dreamed up a method (literally, it came to me in my sleep) that weighed the strategic advantages and disadvantages inherent to any given board position. Now the computer could "call" the evaluation function and compare the scores of all possible positions, then choose the candidate move that had achieved the highest score. The team was ecstatic and invited me to a celebratory dinner dance at the prestigious California Club in downtown Los Angeles. I politely refused, having become as boring as the computer.

Four years had passed. Four years. A procession of overlong workdays that felt like all the time that ever was, interspersed with surges of memory that made it seem like my college days had just happened. My job enabled me to live and breathe chess, to stay in my head and safeguard what was left of a mangled heart. I let my brain swim with chess concepts that would be lost on all but one person in ten million.

There were times when I felt like I'd actually become a chess piece, a wooden object in a convoluted game. While other young men in their early twenties were pursuing women, I ruminated about the mysteries of the chessboard and documented the list of imbalances that lead to favorable situations. Yet I played in no more tournaments and nothing of any significance happened outside of my work. Then I let down my guard and everything seemed to happen at once.

In the fall of 1973 I got in a dispute with my neighbor, Bob Darrow. A Bible thumper who lived in a rambler one hundred feet away, Bob not only disliked my long hair, but also seethed over the fact I hadn't served my country in Vietnam (I'd drawn a favorable lottery number). The argument was over the squirrels that feasted on his black walnut tree. Bob, a realtor who liked to think of himself as a farmer living off the land, protected his harvest by trapping the squirrels in a clamp-like steel device that crushed their hind legs. On one occasion, I pried open the trap with a pair of screwdrivers (risking a bite from a frightened animal), only to realize the squirrel would soon die anyway. Acting on impulse, I confiscated Bob's traps and tossed them in a burn barrel during a morning run. When Bob found his traps missing he confronted me, and my refusal to confirm or deny his suspicions convinced him of my guilt. When I attempted to explain the cruelty of a steel trap, he threatened to "kick my hippie ass."

Later that day, I visited a fruit stand in Malibu and bought a fifty-pound bag of organic California walnuts. I had just set them on Bob's squeaky front porch when he marched though the front door.

"What the hell are you doin'?"

"I got you a bag of walnuts. To replace the ones the squirrels are taking."

He eyed the bag and gave it a probing kick with the toe of his cowboy boot. "You're missing the point, Matthews."

"The point is, this way the squirrels don't have to die a slow, painful death."

"No, the point is it's my tree and my property. And you're lucky I haven't gotten the police involved for stealing my traps."

I tried to ignore the thinly veiled threat, but the mere mention of police brought up bad memories and high anxiety. "So, if it was a cherry tree and the birds were eating the cherries, would it be okay for you to poison them?"

He squared his jaw. "Absolutely. God gave us dominion over the animals."

I moaned. "Dominion doesn't mean extermination. It means control."

"The squirrels are taking the fruits of my labor. I have a right to exterminate them."

"I don't buy that. The squirrels were here before we were."

"Big deal. So were the Indians."

I flashed on Lydia and her people, considered decking the son-of-a-bitch. A deep breath kept me from exploding. "Look, Bob. They're just being squirrels. Squirrels eat walnuts. They're doing what they need to do to survive."

"So am I."

"You need the walnuts to survive? Then take these, and when you run out, I'll buy you some more."

He sneered and puffed up his chest. "Get off my porch, Matthews. And take the bag with you."

"Keep 'em, Bob. They're organic. Better than yours, anyway."

This time he kicked the bag hard, knocked it over.

Marge Darrow stepped through the doorway and deliberately slammed the screen door, disgust written all over her face. "Would you two stop arguing over a bag of walnuts."

Bob gazed in the direction of the walnut tree, folded his arms across his chest. "The whole thing's a mute point, anyway."

"Why's that?" *And the word is 'moot,' Bob, not 'mute,' you ignoramus!* I thought.

He clenched his jaw, didn't answer.

Marge sighed, looked at me. "We're moving out the end of the month."

"Where to?" I asked, as if I cared. I could've danced a jig.

Again, Bob ignored my question, looked at Marge.

"We bought a house just off Old Canyon Road," she answered.

I tried to make my voice friendlier. "I didn't see this house for sale."

"Because it's not *for* sale," Bob replied in a condescending tone.

"Our daughter is moving in," Marge told me. "With our granddaughter."

"Enough talk," Bob declared. "Get the bag off my porch. Now."

I tossed the bag over my shoulder and carried it up the hill to my cabin.

Several weeks later I passed the Darrow residence and caught a glimpse of a young woman lifting a cardboard box from the back of a Volkswagen van. She appeared to be my age, maybe a little older, and cute in a tomboyish, athletic-looking way. I piloted my car around the switchback and up the hill to where I always parked, under the oak trees. Not wanting to appear rude, I walked down the incline with the intention of introducing myself. As I came into view, a little girl darted out from behind a stand of bamboo and ran to her mother's side.

"Hi," I announced from a distance of thirty feet. "I'll bet you're my new neighbors."

The woman brought her eyes up from her daughter and flashed an inviting smile. Her sun-streaked brown hair was short and bobbed. It seemed a practical, low maintenance cut. With nice cheekbones and freckles dotting her nose, she also had the natural, no-makeup look I found attractive. She wore short cutoff jeans, frayed at the hems and a sleeveless, tight-fitting T-shirt that read, "Viva Zapata!" under a picture of the handsome Mexican revolutionary. "I'm Annie Darrow," she said, extending her hand, "and this is my daughter, Kaalaea."

"I'm Bryan Matthews." It had been a long time since I'd attempted to socialize with a woman and I found myself staring at her.

She lightly touched her daughter's head. "Can you say hello, Kaalaea?"

Kaalaea smiled shyly but didn't speak. A towhead with creamy skin and unusually large brown eyes, she looked about three, though I wasn't the best at guessing children's ages. The expression "cute as a button" came to mind. "Hi, Kaalaea. How old are you?"

Her face turned bright pink, but she managed to hold up three fingers.

I kneeled in a catcher's stance. "I *thought* you were about three. How'd you get such a pretty name?"

This time she grabbed her mother's leg and hid.

"Kaalaea is the town where her Mommy made her. Huh, Peanut?"

I stood, scanned my memory for geography. "Hawaii?"

Annie nodded. "Ten miles north of Honolulu."

Good thing you didn't conceive her in Kalamazoo. I used my unspoken joke to wrench my face into what might pass for a relaxed smile. "Well, welcome to Topanga."

"Do you like it here?" Annie asked.

"I like it okay." *Better with your father gone.*

"My dad told us to watch out for rattlesnakes."

"You'll be okay as long as you don't step on one. But I wouldn't go tromping around in the sagebrush without boots. Or in the ivy." I motioned behind me and to my left. A tangle of dust-covered ivy overgrew the hillside.

Annie skittered her eyes in the direction of Kaalaea's bare feet. "We're not used to worrying about anything more than garter snakes."

"Where're you from?"

"The Bay area. My parents moved here after I graduated from high school, but I stayed in the city. How about you?"

"I grew up in Seattle and went to college in Walla . . ." I stopped myself. "I moved to Southern California four years ago."

"Cool. What do you do? I asked my parents and neither one of them knew."

"I'm a chess player," I answered, a bit awkwardly.

She looked surprised, a common reaction when people learn my occupation. "Is that how you make your living?"

"Yeah. I work for IBM on a project that's teaching computers how to play. And I write a monthly chess column in the *LA Times*."

"Whoa. You must be *really* good. I'll have to tell dad." Her expression turned gleeful. "It'll piss him off."

I chuckled. The idea of irritating Bob Darrow appealed to me, but I felt pretentious and averted my gaze. A horse trailer had been parked in front of the tack house, partially obscuring the corral. "Do I see a horse?"

"He's mine," Kaalaea answered, peeking out from behind her mother with a quick giggle. Until then, I wasn't sure she could talk.

"What's his name?" I asked her.

"Popcorn."

"Wow! That's a *great* name. Is he the color of popcorn?"

Kaalaea nodded. No blushing, this time.

"With or without butter?"

She looked up at her mother.

Annie said, "Tell him, Peanut."

Kaalaea squirmed. "*With* butter, 'cause he's gold."

"He's a palomino," Annie added, with a smile.

I smiled back, allowed myself the unfamiliar tug of sexual attraction. Annie wasn't beautiful like Lydia, but nice-looking in an earthy way. *Stop making comparisons.* "Need help moving stuff in?"

"We really don't have much stuff, and anyway, my parents left it furnished."

"Cool. I don't have much stuff, either." I'd run out of small talk and, antsy to leave, shifted from foot to foot.

Annie hoisted her daughter, slung her on her hip. "We're going to the swap meet on Saturday? In Woodland Hills. Want to join us?"

"I'm gonna get a Barbie," Kaalaea informed me, her face lighting up.

The old Bryan, the Bryan before Stubblefield, would've acted silly and come back with, *Maybe I could get a Barbie doll, too!* Kaalaea would have giggled and playfully corrected me, formed the beginning of a bond. Annie would've enjoyed my sense of humor, the way I connected with her daughter. Instead, I said, "Thanks, but—"

"You can get some great deals," Annie added.

"Let me think about it. Okay? I'll see you around."

"I hope so," she replied.

I retreated, trying to decide if Annie was coming on to me, or just being neighborly. My radar for women had been out of order for so long I honestly couldn't tell. Regardless, I didn't want to encourage her, so when Saturday came around I left a note on her door saying I had to drive over to Cal Tech in Pasadena. Over the course of the next eight weeks, I also refused Annie's occasional dinner invitations. I realized I was terrified of infecting her with bad energy that felt strong enough to be contagious. More importantly, though, I had to remain faithful to Lydia.

———

Annie knocked on my door late one morning. I was at the kitchen table writing a chess column for the *Times*. After an awkward moment, I pushed back my chair and invited her in.

"Is it a bad time?" she asked.

"No, not at all. I was bored, anyway." My eyes slid over her blue running shorts and white tank top, UCLA written in powder blue.

She glanced at my notes and smiled. "Is this your next article for the paper?"

"Yeah. Believe me, it's boring."

"What's this one on? I read the last one."

"Oh, come on. You read my column on the Schara Gambit?"

She let out a self-conscious laugh. "I did, but I have a confession."

"Let's hear it. You'll feel better."

"I read it 'cause I liked the name. I thought it was the *Sahara* Gambit. But why are gambits riskier for Black? I forget."

"You really did read it." I felt pleased. "Okay, a gambit is usually the offer of a pawn. It's riskier for Black because you're not only down a point, but you also lose something in developing your pieces—"

"Since White got to move first."

"Right. I didn't know you played chess."

"Dad taught me when I was little. I'm not good at all."

"But, do you like it?"

"Yeah, I like the challenge of it. That's why I read your column."

"Cool."

She smiled and waited. "So, I think you were going to tell me what this one's on."

"Oh, sorry." I glanced at my notes, as if I needed to remind myself of the subject matter. "This one is about a quote attributed to Grandmaster Siegbert Tarrasch."

"What'd he say?"

I chuckled. "Tarrasch said the opening was a way to establish the reputation of being a dashing player at the cost of losing the game."

"Well, I'll look forward to reading it," she said, smiling. Annie smiled a lot. Then her expression changed and she seemed all business. "I came up to ask a favor."

"Sure."

She cleared her throat. "It's okay if you say no, 'cause it's a big one."

"Okay." Butterflies flitted in my stomach as I imagined she was about to ask me to baby-sit Kaalaea.

"I was wondering if I could plant a vegetable garden on your property." She looked out the big window over my brass bed. "Up on the hillside. My place doesn't have a spot that gets full sun."

"I don't—"

"Wait, let me finish." Her voice sped up. "I've been thinking about how it could work for both of us. I'd grow the vegetables and give you half the produce. You wouldn't do have to do anything. And I've got a green thumb, so you'd be getting vine-ripened organic tomatoes and zucchini, and all kinds of stuff for free."

"I guess it'd be okay."

Without warning, Annie put her arms around my neck and hugged me close to her body. "Thank you, Bryan. Thank you so much."

I actually stopped breathing, not having felt a woman's embrace in four years. The effect stunned me. It was like Annie had found something lost in me, however brief, and it gave me a feeling of being connected. When I finally inhaled, I caught the scent of lemon in her sun-bleached hair. I panicked and pulled away. "I learned a little about gardening from an older couple I used to live with. I could turn the soil and do some of the grunt work part."

"That'd be fabulous. Come on, I'll show you the spot I had in mind." She took my hand and led me out the front door.

Feeling awkward, I released her hand, but followed her up the hill. "Here?" I asked.

"Yeah, it's perfect. Full sun, good soil, and we could use the water from your overflow tank. If we terrace the hill a little bit, the water won't run off." She was smiling again, excited.

Annie emitted a combination of excitement and vulnerability that drew me in, made me want to help. "When do we start?" I asked.

"Now would be good. Kaalaea's at my parents' house for the day."

"We're going to need a fence around it. To keep the rabbits out. Deer, too."

"We get deer?"

"Deer, coyote, foxes, raccoons, bobcat, possum, tree rats, you name it."

Her brown eyes went wide. "What in God's name are tree rats?"

"Like regular rats, only a lot bigger and with a pretty coat."

She made a face. "Yuck! I don't want rats in our garden."

"Me neither." I glanced back at the cabin. "Look, why don't you run down to the hardware store and pick up four fence posts and enough chicken wire to do the job. I have to get this piece for the *Times* in today's mail."

"I can get the vegetable seeds, too. What do you want to plant?"

"You decide," I told her. "It was your idea. Oh, and we need at least fifty feet of hose."

I hurried back inside and came out with two fifties to give Annie for our supplies. I wasn't sure about her finances, but she had a nonpaying job as a mom and I had more money than I needed. I finished my article by the time she returned and we spent the rest of the afternoon working in our garden.

We started by aerating the soil, tossing the larger rocks into a small pile (Reva had taught me to leave in a few small ones to conserve heat). For compost we mixed in several wheelbarrows full of soft, crumbly, well-cooked horse manure, courtesy of an Arabian horse named Gypsy that'd lived in the corral before Popcorn. After digging two-foot holes and placing our pressure-treated fence posts, we anchored them using the pile of rocks, then strung the chicken wire until we had a reasonably taut fence.

Our planting space ended up about fifteen by twenty feet, so with terracing, there was plenty of room to plant Beefsteak tomatoes, green onions, snow peas, leaf lettuce (eventually to be shaded by a row of corn), zucchini and yellow squash. Annie's hands were so fast and skillful in placing the seeds, it looked as though she was buttoning Kaalaea's blouse. I connected the hose to the overflow tank (our houses were on a gravity-flow water system from an underground spring) and Annie soaked the soil until it was soggy and black.

"Done," she announced with a satisfied smile. "This soil has a good heart."

"That's a nice way of saying it."

Our eyes met, then we looked down at our own bodies, filthy with dirt and sweat. Annie's eyes lit up; she jammed her thumb into the end of the hose and squirted me. I took the stream of water on my bare chest, dodged to the right and crimped the hose to stop its flow. Taking up the slack, I wrested the hose from her grip and squirted her back. She fought for maybe ten seconds, but I was dousing her good, so she ran down the hill screaming. "Truce," she yelled from a safe distance, laughing and raising both hands in surrender.

"Okay, truce. But keep in mind I still have the hose." I set it down, hiked up to the overflow tank and turned off the faucet.

Annie watched me walk back. Her wet tank top was plastered to her chest and I could see the shape of her breasts. She wiped a strand of hair from her forehead and admired the garden we'd created.

"It looks good," I told her, feeling awkward again. *And so do you.*

She nodded. "By the way, you're filthy."

I looked at myself and cringed. "I better head in and get a shower."

She hesitated a second, bit her lip and flashed a tentative smile. "Want to make it a buddy shower? Save water for our new garden?"

I stopped breathing again, the same as earlier in the day when she hugged me. I started to say something, I don't remember what, but the words got strangled in my throat.

Annie's face flushed pink. "I'm sorry. God, what an idiot I am."

I thought of Kaalaea blushing on the first day we met, wondered if it was hereditary. "No, don't be sorry. It's just that . . . I guess I'm not really available."

Annie gave me a confused look. Her lips pouted faintly. "I see you coming and going all the time, but I never see you with anyone."

"I know. It's complicated." I would offer no satisfactory explanation and left it at that.

"I'm sorry, Bryan. I haven't been with anyone for a long time and . . . oh, God, I'm sorry." She marched down the hill and broke into a run when she reached the road.

I watched her disappear, already imagining what it would have been like to accept her offer. With no way to deny I wanted to make love to Annie Darrow, I felt like I'd betrayed a sacred trust. I picked up a rock from the garden and fired it at my house. It landed with a thud on my flat roof.

Annie and I colluded to avoid one another for the next couple weeks. Except for one occasion, we managed to stay out of each other's space. That time, I was coming in slowly from a run while she was putting out flakes of hay for Popcorn. We froze like statues until I managed a question that had been on my mind: "Is Popcorn safe for Kaalaea to ride?" Annie smiled and said the horse was "half-dead and bomb proof," which I took as a yes. I laughed at the appropriate time and continued on to the cabin.

Several days later I drove in after grocery shopping and saw Annie watering the garden. "Hi, stranger," she called out as I was about to slip into the cabin.

"Oh, hi," I answered, acting as if I hadn't seen her. I set my bag on the front step and walked up the hill.

She gestured to the garden with an air of pleasure. "Everything's coming up." Any residual embarrassment seemed to have disappeared.

"You really *do* have a green thumb."

She smiled, kneeled in the rich soil to soak the tomato mounds without getting water on the leaves. "I have to thin out the lettuce. We planted some of the seeds too close together."

"Need help?" I felt confident she'd say no.

She set the hose aside and brushed dirt from her arms. "What I need is company for dinner. I made enough soup for an army."

"What kind?" I asked, feeling the flutter of anxiety in my chest.

"Chicken with vegetables. Kaalaea's favorite, only she calls it her *flavorite*."

"I can help with chicken soup. What time?"

"It's still cooking. How about seven-thirty?"

"Sounds good to me."

I showed up at her back door at the appointed time, after making a trip to the Topanga Market for a loaf of sourdough and a good bottle of red wine. I wasn't sure what the wine meant. Was I hoping to throw off my guilt and get Annie in bed, or merely trying to be a well-mannered dinner guest? Probably the former, knowing how I kept visualizing her wet tank top after the water fight.

Annie greeted me wearing cutoff jeans and a white blouse with red, heart-shaped buttons. She'd taken a shower and her hair was still damp. I handed her the bread, which she accepted with a sheepish smile. "I can't have any wine,' she said, "but there's a corkscrew in the top drawer if you want some."

"You're—"

"Mommy can't drink wine," Kaalaea interrupted from the kitchen table. "She's allergic."

Annie shrugged. "It's fine with me if you want some. Really." She stood in front of the stove and tested the soup. My eyes strayed to her shapely legs and a very sexy bottom.

"I'll have whatever you're having," I told her.

"That'd be water from the tap." Annie poured me a glass from a pitcher in the refrigerator, handed it to me. As always, her hair smelled fresh and lemony.

I took a seat next to Kaalaea, who was coloring. "What're these?" I pointed to a row of nondescript geometric figures that appeared suspended in thin air. A stick figure stood alongside them.

She pointed with a red crayon. "That's Mommy putting clothes on the clothes line."

"Why these clothes look wet," I commented.

Kaalaea laughed. "Of course they're wet, you silly. That's why Mommy's hanging them up."

Annie smiled from across the room. I watched her as she tossed a salad in a large wooden bowl, a sense of curiosity blooming in me. *Why no wine? What's her story?* She finished the salad and summoned Kaalaea and me to the dining room where a table had been set. Kaalaea said a cute grace and Annie ladled her hearty soup into three bowls. We ate slowly, talking mostly about Kaalaea's preschool and how our garden was doing. When the meal was finished, Annie told Kaalaea to get ready for bed. "First I want to show Bryan my stuffed animals," she protested.

"Okay, Peanut. But first you have to get on your jammies and brush your teeth."

Kaalaea bolted from the table. I looked at Annie and shook my head. "Boy, is she a cutie."

"Best thing that ever happened to me. That's for sure."

I buttered one last piece of sourdough. "Can I ask a nosy question?"

"Sure."

"Is her dad in the picture? You've never mentioned him."

Annie lowered her voice. "He's out of the picture. And I prefer it that way."

I took the cue and whispered, "Does he live around here?"

"No. Last I heard he was up in Alaska. He's heavy into drugs. He wasn't there when she was born, wasn't there on her first birthday, doesn't even send her a Christmas card."

"Bummer."

"Yeah." She took a deep breath, exhaled slowly. "I've got bastard radar. If there's ten guys in a room and one of 'em's a bastard, that's the one I fall for."

"At least you got Kaalaea out of it," I said, convinced her attraction to me qualified me as a bastard.

She chuckled. "I remind myself of that whenever I think about the support payments that never come."

Kaalaea burst into the room wearing a pair of pink flannel pajamas. "I brushed really good, Mommy!" She opened her mouth wide and showed us.

I laughed and followed Kaalaea into her bedroom, with Annie a few steps behind. The walls were done in light blue wallpaper with red and yellow kites trailing long white tails. Kaalaea introduced me to Vanilla, a pint-sized green dinosaur; Snuggly, a floppy white rabbit with a zippered back; and her very favorite, "Dougie Lamb," a sad-faced little fellow who rattled with movement. I scratched my head and affected a puzzled expression. "I could guess how Snuggly got his name, but how did Vanilla and Dougie Lamb get theirs?"

Kaalaea answered, "Vanilla 'cause he's sweet, and Dougie 'cause where we found him."

Annie picked him up and filled in the story. "We found him in Laguna Beach on Douglas Street. Someone must've either dropped or thrown him in the gutter."

"He was all dirty, but Mommy tied him up in a pillow case and washed him in the washing machine," Kaalaea added.

"Wow! That's quite a story. I wonder why anyone would throw away a great guy like Dougie?"

"Maybe because they didn't know he was great," Kaalaea explained.

"I think you're probably right," I told her.

Annie smiled at Kaalaea and said, "Weren't you going to ask Bryan something?"

Kaalaea blushed. After several false starts, she stammered, "Would you teach me to play chess when I get older?"

"Sure. You're a smart cookie, so we can start tomorrow if you want."

"I'm not a cookie!"

I feigned gobbling her arm, said goodnight and returned to the living room. Annie stayed behind. They recited "Now I Lay Me Down to Sleep." I'd developed a stomachache that wasn't from anything I'd eaten. I felt conflicted about being alone with Annie and emotion had written itself in the sand of my body. I wanted her in the worst way and, at the same time, feared how I'd feel afterwards.

Annie returned a minute later. She sat at the opposite end of the couch, leaned back and closed her eyes. "Okay, here's the deal. Just before I moved in I was in drug rehab in Santa Monica. For cocaine addiction. I'm not supposed to have any alcohol because it might trigger a relapse. I told Kaalaea it's because of an allergy."

I didn't know what to say. Women in California seemed so open and disarming. Different boundaries than in the Pacific Northwest. I told her, "I don't care if you had a problem."

"I *have* a problem. Present tense. It's part of my program to own up to it."

"Okay. How're you doin'?"

She smiled without conviction. "Clean for eleven weeks and feelin' pretty together. But I have to stay away from the scene in Laguna." I must have looked puzzled because she quickly added, "Too much blow in Laguna, and I know *all* the wrong people."

I wondered how she'd react if I told her I'd been involved in the death of a cop, that I wasn't a saint, either. Instead I said, "Sounds like your treatment's working."

"It has to, 'cause if I screw up I could lose my Peanut." Her eyes swung in the direction of Kaalaea's room.

"Did your ex-husband get you into drugs?"

"No." Annie laughed quietly. "I got *him* into drugs, but he gets the credit for going hog wild. And he's not my ex. We were only together for a couple months."

"Oh."

"My drug counselor told me that coke's a substitute for being in a relationship. That connecting is way better than the high you get from using."

"Do you agree?"

"I do." She chuckled. "But coke's easier to find, and it works faster, too."

I wasn't sure if I agreed or disagreed, but had no experience with drugs so I kept quiet.

A half-minute elapsed and Annie broke the silence. "There was this girl in treatment, a groupie doing the rock scene, and she had to have Teflon implanted in her nasal passages. She was seventeen and she'd burned out the lining of her nose. Maybe that's how treatment works; you listen to other people's stories and it scares the shit out of you. I don't want to end up like she did."

"I'm glad you're doing so well."

She fidgeted with a button. "Now can I ask you a question?"

"Sure." My stomach tied an extra knot.

"The other day you mentioned an older couple that taught you about gardening. Who were they?"

I'd feared something going back to my comment about not being available. "Zdenek and Reva Zaleski. He's an International Grandmaster from Poland. My chess coach for two years." I omitted the *in college* part.

"Did you tell me you lived with them, or did I make that up?"

"No, I lived with them over a summer. So Dr. Z could train me every day. That's what I call him: Dr. Z. Reva liked to cook, and I liked to eat, so we hit it off. Great people." I felt a swell of guilt for not writing.

"Wow! An International Grandmaster. Did you ever beat him?"

"Once or twice, but only because he's in his late sixties. In his prime, he'd have kicked my sorry butt."

"Oh. You mean like Vladimir Primalov did?"

I froze, stared at her. After a long pause, I asked, "You know about that?"

She nodded slowly. "The jig's up, mister."

"How did you—"

"My dad came by last week to fix the water heater. We got to talking and I told him you're a professional chess player. He said you were bullshitting me, so I showed him one of your columns from the *Times*. The next day he went to the library in Woodland Hills and did a little research." She got up, crossed the room to a cinderblock bookshelf and came back with a Xerox copy of an article from the *Los Angeles Herald-Examiner*.

I read the headline: American Teen Trounces Russian Grandmaster! "People sent me a lot of articles, but I never saw this one." I set it down, closed my eyes and flashed back on the moment when I realized Primalov had no way to escape checkmate. Remembered how I felt as I looked into the audience and met Lydia's eyes. *Before it happened.*

"You should read it."

"I was there, Annie. I know—"

"Jesus Christ, Bryan. It says you were *eighteen years old* and you beat the third best player in the world. It says you totally dominated a World Champion contender."

I fought back the strongest urge to cry. No idea where it came from. "I got lucky. Besides, it's old news. I've only played one tournament in the last four years."

"Yeah. I read about that one, too." Her voice switched from supportive to accusatory. "You came in second in an international field that included six Grandmasters."

There was a small decorative pillow between us. I picked it up and clutched it to my chest. "Somebody's been doing her homework."

"I wasn't snooping, if that's what you think. My dad dug up this stuff. I didn't ask for it. By the way, he's in total shock. He thought you were a total loser."

"I *am* a loser." The words flew out my mouth before I could censor them.

"What are you talking about? You're a genius!" She had raised her voice, but now she lowered it. "And you're cute, too."

I rolled my eyes, felt my stomach tighten another notch. My mind traveled back to age six when Grandpa Matthews called me a prodigy at the family picnic. I remembered the sheer excitement of learning chess and the feeling of competence that came with excellence. *Before it happened.*

" . . . doesn't make sense." Annie was talking to me. "You were supposed to be the next Bobby Fischer."

I shifted my position, willed myself back to present time. "Let me tell you a dirty little secret only the chess world knows. There is no *next* Bobby Fischer. And there never will be."

She shrugged her shoulders. "Maybe not. I don't know about that. But why would someone with your potential essentially retire at the age of eighteen?"

"I haven't retired."

"You said it yourself. One tournament in four years."

I felt caught, off balance, unable to think. My brain switched to automatic pilot and I got defensive. "It's all downhill after you beat someone like Primalov."

Annie's jaw jutted out. "You know what, Bryan? In treatment they taught us to call bullshit on each other when we were conning ourselves. It's a way of helping a person heal. I'm calling bullshit on you."

It took me awhile to respond. "Not to be rude, Annie, but my stomach doesn't feel so good. I better call it a night."

She frowned. "So I confront you and you have to go home?"

"No, that's not it. My stomach's really hurting. Honest." I pulled myself to my feet and headed in the direction of the back door.

"Don't forget your wine." Annie caught up with a burst of speed, handed me the unopened bottle from the kitchen counter. "A night like this and I might be tempted."

I grimaced. "Don't say that. I really enjoyed myself."

"No you didn't. You don't let yourself. You never do." She folded her arms and glowered at me.

I felt a mix of distress and guilt. "Sorry if I've been a bad guest." I closed my eyes and forced myself to say something honest. Annie deserved as much. "I really do appreciate your friendship."

She studied my eyes. "Then answer me one question."

"What?"

"Are you available, or aren't you?"

I puffed my cheeks and blew out. "I don't have a girlfriend, if that's what you mean."

I'd taken precisely three steps out the door. Annie's words stopped me in my tracks. "She must've really done a number on you."

"What?" I turned and faced her, straining to understand the full meaning of what she'd said. Moths with feathery antennae swarmed around the light bulb above our heads, their stout bodies controlled by forces the human eye can see but not explain. "What did you say?"

"I *said,* 'she must've really done a number on you.' The one that broke your heart."

"You have no idea." I took the shortcut up to my cabin. I'd forgotten to leave a light on and it was pitch black inside.

I got up early the next morning, padded barefoot to the kitchen sink to get a drink of water. A simple glass vase filled with brightly colored wildflowers rested on my front porch. I opened the French door, picked up the flowers and looked around. Scotch-taped to the side was a folded note card. It read: "Did I blow it again? Sorry, Annie."

I set the vase on the kitchen counter next to a stack of dirty dishes. A sharp pain stabbed at my forehead. Annie had tripped a switch in my mind and activated the fierce, bone-penetrating anguish I still felt over Lydia. It had made for a rough night. I ended up opening the bottle of wine I'd taken to dinner and poured myself a tall glass. Slumped in a chair at the kitchen table, I wondered where Lydia was living and if she ever thought about me. I poured a second glass and imagined Lydia being sexual with other men, considered the possibility she might even have a child. Less than an hour later I sloshed the last bit straight from the bottle and cursed Jack Montrose for ruining my life. The alcohol worked like truth serum and made it impossible to deny my feelings for Annie Darrow. I felt the beginning of hope and asked myself if I could possibly connect with someone besides Lydia. Hope was a big feeling, maybe the biggest feeling of all, and it frightened me. Drunk, I thought about going back down to Annie's house and asking to spend the night. I actually thought I would do it, but in the end I chickened out and masturbated, allowing myself the rare pleasure of fantasizing about Lydia's naked body.

I pulled myself back to the present moment, gazed at the wildflowers. They drew me in no matter where I went in the room. I imagined Annie walking the mountains in the early morning light, picking them for me. It touched me that she cared and I felt my heart open, but only a little.

Shortly after noon, I set aside my chess notes and started in on the dirty dishes, again admiring the flowers' uncultivated beauty. As I looked out the window, I saw Annie hanging clothes on the clothesline. I quickly wiped my hands and walked down the hill to join her.

She saw me rounding the thicket of bamboo that marked the corner of her property. "You still speaking to me?" she asked.

"Please, I'm the one that should be apologizing."

She pinned Kaalaea's pink blouse to the line. It was tiny, like doll clothing. "I had no right to say what I did."

"Even if you hit the bulls-eye?"

She smiled. "I wasn't sure what you meant by 'You have no idea.' I thought it meant I was right, but then I thought it might mean I was way off."

"It meant you were right. I had a girlfriend. She broke up with me and it really messed me up."

"Can I ask what happened?"

I looked away. "It's a long story. She left me."

She reached into a yellow plastic basket and pulled out another garment to pin to the clothesline. When she finished, she said, "Foolish girl."

I shrugged.

"What was her name?"

"Lydia." It pained me to say it.

"When did you break up?"

"In college. It's been four years."

Annie folded her arms, like she had the night before when she became irritated. "Four years?"

I nodded, kicked a smooth stick into the tangle of bamboo. A tiny lizard scurried for cover under some dried leaves.

"Have you been with anyone since?"

I shook my head.

She looked bewildered. "Jesus, Bryan. Four years is a long time to hold on."

"I know." The more she looked at me the more nervous I became. "I told you. It messed me up."

"You want to talk about it?"

I frowned, shook my head.

She reached into her basket and pulled out a large patchwork quilt. "Could you give me a hand with this?"

I grabbed an end. It was heavy from being wet, cool to the touch. Together, we draped it over the remaining six feet of sagging clothesline. "Nice quilt," I told her.

"I got it in North Carolina." Her mood brightened. "I call it my trust quilt. There's a story behind it."

"Tell me," I said, grateful for the change of subject.

She put her hands on her hips. "Okay. The year before I met Kaalaea's father I went back to Charlotte, North Carolina, for a wedding. My cousin Sarah and I were driving to Greensboro to go to a rock concert and we saw this cardboard sign out in front of a little rundown house. It said 'quilts 4 sale,' with the number four instead of the written word. So we stopped and knocked on the front door. This tiny little Black woman answers the door and before we can introduce ourselves, she says, "I just know the Lord sent you two girls to me because you're hungry.""

I laughed. "That would've been if it was two guys."

"Yeah. I told her we'd actually stopped to see her quilts and she invited us in. She showed us about twenty quilts. She'd picked the cotton herself and stuffed them. Anyway, I chose this one and asked her how much it was. She said they were all ten dollars. Sarah and I were shocked, 'cause they were so beautiful, but anyway I got out two five-dollar bills and handed them to her. She took 'em from me, but kept looking at my eyes."

"She never looked at the fives?"

"No, she just looked at me and said, 'Is this ten dollars?' I said it was and she smiled and said, 'I don't understand money.' Sarah bought two quilts and gave her a twenty. She asked if it was the same as two tens. She just totally trusted us."

"That's cool."

"Then she invited us into her kitchen and served us chicken and dumplings, hot off the stove. Collard greens, peach cobbler for dessert . . . mm! I never decided what was better. The meal or the lesson."

I stayed away from Annie for the next few days, but Kaalaea came up on her own for her first chess lesson. She'd brought along Snuggly the rabbit and the three of us went over the basic moves. In twenty minutes we consumed her attention span and put an ever-so-slight dent in what remained of her grandfather's fifty-pound bag of walnuts. She ran off then, saying she wanted to see her Mommy and tell her about the chess piece that looked like Popcorn, her horse. Late in the afternoon, I noticed Kaalaea had left Snuggly on her chair. I unzipped his back, crammed him full with walnuts and a bag of M&M's and took him home. I knocked on the back door, feeling a tad foolish with a stuffed animal in my arms.

Annie answered the door and invited me in. She wore two-piece swimsuit, bright pink with white daisies and yellow centers. Her delicate skin was blotched with heat.

"Kaalaea left Snuggly in my kitchen chair," I told her.

"Oh, thanks. My mom took her to see *Mary Poppins*, but she'll be glad her pal got returned. Looks like he might've put on a few pounds." She zipped down the back and smiled. "M&M's. I might have a few of these myself."

"Have you been working in the garden?"

"No, I was lying out in the sun," she answered. "If you'd gotten here ten minutes sooner, you could've seen me naked."

"Really?" Her candor caught me off guard. Turned me on, too.

"Yeah, I was lying on a towel out by the bamboo. Too bad for you, you missed the show."

"I never have any fun."

"Poor baby." She smiled provocatively and reached behind her back, unfastening her top. It fell to the kitchen floor, revealing small and firm breasts, tiny pink nipples.

I stepped towards her. She tilted back her head to receive my kiss. Our mouths pressed together. Annie smelled of patchouli and the faint tang of sweat. I trailed my hand over the smooth curve of her breast.

Her eyes widened. "You sure you want to do this?"

"Yeah." My body had already decided.

She took my hand and led me to her bedroom, pulling off her bottoms along the way. "Bryan," she said in a pleading voice. "Please don't let it be a problem, but I'm having my period."

"I couldn't care less." I stumbled out of my clothes as Annie went in the bathroom. Seconds later she returned and joined me in her bed. She touched her lips to mine. I let my tongue stray down her freckled neck and onto her nipples.

She moaned. "Don't make me wait."

My hand found the wetness between her legs. "I love your body," I told her. It had been a long time since I'd touched a woman.

"I love yours!" She spread her legs and guided me inside her with an urgency that matched mine. "Oh God. I've wanted you so bad," she whispered in my ear.

We found a fast rhythm and stayed with it until we both came, Annie's muscles quivering with strain and me nearly blacking out. I pulled out and flipped on my back, my penis bright red with Annie's menstrual flow.

"That was wonderful," she murmured.

I looked around the room, took a moment to catch my breath. A Meher Baba poster told me "Don't worry, be happy!" The adjacent wall featured a map of Middle Earth and a black and white Jefferson Airplane ad for a gig at the Filmore. Framed pictures of Kaalaea on the dresser, along with an incense holder, some jewelry and a short pile of unopened mail. An unwanted image bubbled up from my subconscious telling me how unlikely it was that Lydia went as long as I did without sex. *It doesn't matter. That was before it happened. She's gone. She's never coming back.*

"You okay, Bryan?" Filmed in sweat, Annie brushed a strand of hair off her damp forehead.

"Yeah. Just out of practice."

"Whoa! In that case, I can't wait till you're *in* practice."

Something bothered me, something more complicated than guilt over sleeping with another woman. I couldn't quite pull it into awareness, only knew it felt bad.

"Bryan. You're thinking too much. I can tell."

"Sorry, I've been known to do that." A thread of melancholy wove its way through my words.

Annie laughed. "Between your four years and my two, I think this qualifies as what my friend Sunshine calls a mercy fuck."

I felt myself begin to pull away. The loner part of me wanted the privacy of my cabin, but I forced myself to stay in the conversation. "You went two years without sex?"

"Uh huh. It's weird. The girls I know do coke and get horny. With me it's just the opposite."

I rolled on my side and looked at Annie. She had blood smears on the insides of both legs and the perfect outline of a crimson finger on her belly. A curled and accusing finger. "We should clean up," I told her.

She laughed. "Let's take that buddy shower."

I nodded, saw it as a way to get out of Annie's space, escape the maelstrom of emotion developing in my psyche. I told her that after the shower I had to drive some notes over to Cal Tech, to meet a deadline. We rolled off opposite sides of the bed and tramped self-consciously into the bathroom. I tried not to look at the blotches of blood that streaked our bodies and was all business in the shower. Afterwards, I toweled off and hurried into the bedroom to retrieve my clothes. A dark pool of blood stained the middle of the white sheet. Annie's patchwork quilt from North Carolina lay crumpled on the hardwood floor. The trust quilt.

Lying in my bed that night, I figured out what had gone wrong at Annie's. It wasn't so much that I'd been unfaithful to Lydia, but that I had severed the last connection to her. Four years had passed, but I never let go of the hope that someday I might get her back, and I held on like a drowning man to a passing raft. Being intimate with another woman meant the death of hope.

I avoided Annie for a week, which took some doing given the proximity of our houses. One afternoon, returning from the outdoor fruit market in Malibu, she waved me down from her front porch. I stopped and she approached my open passenger window. "We need to talk," she told me.

"Okay. Let me park and I'll be right down."

"Now's not good, 'cause Kaalaea'll interrupt us a hundred times. Come down after I put her to bed. Say, nine o'clock?"

"Okay." She walked away without saying anything else, which, in my mind, spoke volumes.

At three-thirty my postal carrier knocked on the front door, interrupting me. A large woman with a single braid that went past her waist, she normally left the mail in a box a quarter-mile away. Resting on her knee was a good-sized cardboard box, and a clipboard on top of it.

"Hi," I said, wishing I could remember her name. "I hope you didn't carry that all the way down the road."

"Drove." She motioned with her head. The ropelike braid swung like a pendulum. "Parked by your corral. Need a signature."

Whatever her name was always spoke in incomplete sentences, which on this day I found annoying, though in the past it had been a source of amusement. After signing, I carried the box inside and set it on the kitchen table. A letter had been sealed in clear plastic and taped to one side of the box. The return address indicated it came from Walla Walla. Though I didn't know the sender, Hammett & Kane, P.S., I recognized the ring of a law firm. A sick feeling turned my stomach.

I tore open the envelope and unfolded the letter. It read: LAST WILL AND TESTAMENT of Cecelia Dorothy Waters. "Oh, no." I slumped on the kitchen table and let in a tender sadness. After a moment of reflection I began reading. "I, Cecelia Dorothy Waters, a resident of Walla Walla County, State of Washington, being of sound and disposing mind, memory and understanding, do hereby make and declare this my Last Will and Testament, hereby revoking all wills and codicils previously made by me." I skipped to the bottom of the page to a passage highlighted in yellow. "I wish to leave to my friend Bryan Matthews the crystal he so admired (tagged item number 4)."

I cut the packing tape and folded down the flaps on the box. The crystal had been safely packed in the center, surrounded by tightly wadded newspaper (a Sunday edition of the *Walla Walla Union-Bulletin*) and several chunks of Styrofoam. It was the size of a large cantaloupe and felt unusually heavy. Stripping away silver duct tape, I unwrapped a blue bath towel and removed the crystal, which had the number 4 Scotch-taped to the bottom. I peeled it off and set the crystal on the table where the box had been.

Annie appeared at the open front door. "Kaalaea's napping. We can talk now. Oh, are you okay?"

I wiped away a tear. "A friend died."

"Who?" Annie let herself in.

"My housemother in college. Mom Waters. A really neat lady."

"I'm sorry." She put her arm around my shoulder.

Her touch made me want to cry, really let go. I bit my lip and looked out the window at the comical scarecrow Annie had placed in the corner of our garden. Attached to his shoulders were brightly colored pinwheels, revolving hypnotically in a gentle afternoon breeze. "She willed this to me." I turned the crystal so Annie could read the inscription.

"'*Chance cannot change my love nor time impair.*' Oh, Bryan. This is absolutely beautiful."

I nodded. "I loved it the first time I saw it."

"You must've been very special to her."

"I didn't realize . . . I should've written her."

"What was she like?"

"Like a mother, I guess. Patient, kind, loving." I smiled. "She gave good hugs."

"She sounds sweet."

I nodded. "Not just to me. To everybody."

"Yeah. But she didn't leave everybody the crystal."

I just looked at Annie, unsure of myself. "Her late husband had given it to her for an anniversary, or maybe for their wedding. I can't remember."

"How'd she die?"

"The letter doesn't say, but I know she had high blood pressure." I brushed the will with the back of my hand. "Maybe I'll call her attorney."

"I'm really sorry, Bryan. You want me to hold you?"

I wanted to be held, but felt a pulling away sensation in my body. No one had ever offered so directly. I forced a nod.

Annie took my hand and led me over to the bed. We lay down and she wrapped me in her arms. I felt no pressure to talk about Mom or how I felt and treasured Annie's willingness to allow my silence. Her hair had its usual lemony smell. We lay there for almost an hour and I fell asleep. When I awakened I rose up in bed. Annie had gone home to Kaalaea. I looked outside. A crow landed on the fence post, a few feet from our scarecrow. Its glossy black head bobbed as it let out a raucous call. Crows meant imminent danger. Lydia taught me that.

The next morning Annie drove Kaalaea over to her parents so she could join me on my morning run. She said I shouldn't be alone after a loss and I didn't argue. We started out on the road that ran along the high side of the corral, slowing down to watch Popcorn playfully roll on his back.

Annie kept up with a seven-minute-a-mile pace, even on the steep fire roads that striped the ridges of Greenleaf Canyon. I was used to running by myself and worried she'd want to have the talk we never had, but she didn't utter a word. We ran five miles, approximating a large circle back to her front porch. I offered her a thankful hug, which led to her initiating a kiss. We ended up having sex against the side of the house, Annie dripping sweat like a broken faucet.

Annie and I made love every day for the next three weeks, usually more than once. She called it skin hunger. I wasn't sure if she meant a strong desire to be touched, or the uncomfortable sensation that comes from years of deprivation. I suffered from both. Our lovemaking excited me during the act itself, but after each encounter I felt lonelier and emptier. One night, after sex on her living room couch, Annie told me, "This is getting confusing. The way we are."

"What do you mean?" I asked, hiding behind a question. I knew exactly what she meant.

"I don't know. We just have sex. That's all we do."

"I thought you liked it."

"I do like it. I love it. But I don't want to feel like we're just bed partners and nothing more."

I nodded, tentatively. "Okay."

"Maybe we should start dating. You know, go to a movie or something. Dinner out. Not just sleep together."

I balked, long enough to expose my ambivalence.

Annie read my face. She'd been lying on top of me, but sat up and folded her arms across her breasts. "You don't want to go places with me?"

"No, it's not that."

"What is it then?"

"It's hard to explain," I offered, punished by the wounded look in Annie's eyes.

She brusquely pulled a T-shirt over her head. "Get dressed. I can't have this conversation naked." After putting on her cutoffs, she left the room to check on Kaalaea, or maybe to give herself time to think. I dressed, suppressing the urge to run through the kitchen and out the back door. Annie returned and said, "That was a perfect example of what's wrong with us. I make a simple suggestion about dating and you freak out."

"I didn't freak out. I just didn't know what to say."

"Couldn't you just say, 'Yeah, I'd love to take you to a movie'?"

I fixated on a blue sweatshirt she'd draped over the back of a dining room chair. Its color lured out the memory of a dream in which Annie had handed me a series of photographs of Hawaii. Picture after picture of electric blue sky, transparent blue-green water, dark green foliage, orange and purple sunsets. When I touched the pictures, the color disappeared. I returned them to her and she wept.

A hand squeezed my forearm. Annie's hand, summoning me to the present. "What're you thinking? You were like light-years away."

"Oh, I spaced on a dream I had last night."

"You do that more than you realize," she said with an irritated tone. "You tune me out."

"I don't mean to, it's just what I do. I think constantly."

"Why? What good does it do?"

I met her eyes. "If I stop thinking, I start feeling, and then it catches up to me."

"What? What catches up?"

"The past."

"Lydia?"

I nodded. "Lydia's part of it. But there's more. It's all tangled up together."

"Tell me about it. I'm your friend. I want to know."

"I can't talk about it, so don't ask."

"You *won't* talk about it. There's a difference."

"Maybe so. It doesn't feel like a choice."

She sighed and laid her hand over mine. "Okay. Tell me your dream."

"It was about you, when you lived in Hawaii. You showed me some really colorful photographs." I left out the important part.

She pressed her back against the couch, showing surprise. "You had a dream about me?"

"Yeah."

She drew a deep breath through her nostrils. "Bryan, could you please tell me where I stand with you?"

I took a moment to reflect. "I don't know. We've only known each other a couple months."

She hesitated, looking unsure of herself. "Did it take you months with Lydia?"

"That's not a fair question." The words shot out angrily from some hurt place deep inside.

"In what way?"

"I was different then." *Before it happened.*

"How?"

"That gets into what I don't want to talk about."

"Suit yourself. But you need to tell me where I stand."

"I can't, Annie. I don't know."

"Well, until you do, I'm not sleeping with you." Tears welled up in her eyes. "It hurts too much the way it is."

"I'm sorry."

She let out an exasperated sigh. "Something's been trying to happen between us, and I'm coaxing it along and you're not."

My body tightened. "I'm sorry."

She slapped her bare thighs, startled me. "You act like you like me . . . I don't know, it's confusing."

I searched for the right words. "Before you moved in, I was numb. No. Dead is a better word. But that was okay, because I didn't want to feel anything. After being with you I'm alive again and I remember why I preferred to be dead."

"Meaning you can feel again."

I closed my eyes and nodded. "Yeah."

"And what's so bad about that?"

"You said it yourself. It hurts too much."

"That's life, Bryan. It's a risk you take. You don't think I hurt when you get close and then pull away?"

"I'm sorry."

We sat in silence. Annie asked me to leave. I traipsed home, feeling guilty for hurting someone so vulnerable. Annie wanted to be a couple, probably wanted to live together and find a father for Kaalaea. *Poor Annie,* I thought, and the movie *Poor Cow* popped into my mind. Carol White played Joy, a young mother whose no-good husband was in prison. Desperate to find happiness, she got into a physical relationship with another loser and ended up heartbroken.

That weekend, bored, I browsed an old chess text and happened upon Amelia Cruz' guacamole recipe. Seeing her handwriting left me feeling out of sorts and I decided the right thing to do was to prepare a batch. I had ripe avocados on hand and spring onion from the garden, but needed to make a run to get Anaheim chilies, cilantro and a lime.

I drove into town to the Food Chakra, the only place in Topanga to get organic produce. A stereo behind the counter played *Hotel California*, midway through the classic Joe Walsh/Don Felder guitar duet. Looking past a row of red and green apples, bright yellow bananas and purple plums, I watched a heavyset, perspiring woman sniff scented candles. She smiled engagingly and asked me if a man would prefer blueberry or vanilla. I told her the latter and thought of Kaalaea's little green dinosaur.

I was choosing a lime when raucous laughter spilled out the back room. Annie's laugh, but distorted in some way. I considered leaving without my ingredients. Shrugging off my discomfort, I made my way down the aisle past see-through bins of fructose, flour, rice and beans, past the riot of color that made up the vegetable section, and peeked in.

Annie and her friend Sunshine, who worked at the Chakra, sat crosslegged on the floor. They were leaning against several fifty-pound bags of carrots, next to the bulk honey barrel. A broken spigot had overflowed and Sunshine was smearing spilt honey on Annie's face. They giggled like teenage girls. "Speak of the devil," Annie said, seeing me in the doorway.

"Hi." I forced a smile.

"You know Sunshine, don't you?"

"Hi Sunshine." I'd seen her in the store but we'd never been introduced. "What're you guys doing?"

They exchanged glances and giggled some more. "What does it look like? We had a little spill and I'm putting honey on Annie's face."

"I can see that. But why?" Something felt off.

Annie answered. "It's an astringent. It tightens wrinkling skin." Again, they looked at one another and snickered.

"Does it work?" I tried to keep the conversation going, as if smearing honey on one's face and acting foolish was normal behavior.

Annie smiled at me. "It gets rid of the lines I've gotten from too much sun."

I gave them a curious look, considered excusing myself. Sunshine finished smoothing the sticky stuff under Annie's eyes, got to her feet and went to a large sink where she washed up. Then she pranced out of the storeroom, presumably to look in on her customer.

"What's her trip?" I asked.

"What do you mean?" Annie asked in a too-loud voice.

"I mean what's going on?"

"None of your beeswax. No pun intended." She laughed, again in an odd way.

I changed the subject. "How'd you get here? I didn't see your van out front."

"I walked. My clutch is shot."

I leaned against the door casing. "Bummer. Need a ride?"

"Yeah. Could you run me to my parents to pick up Kaalaea?"

"Sure. Are you going to wipe the honey off your face?" I took several steps into the room, intending to sit on the floor, in the spot Sunshine had vacated. Annie moved her body and then her fringed leather purse, trying to hide something on the floor. The strange behavior suddenly made sense. On the floor, in the space between where Annie and Sunshine had been sitting, were a pocket mirror and a razor blade. A single line of white powder bisected the surface. I heaved a weary sigh. "Oh, Annie. What're you doing?"

She got to her feet. "I don't have to answer your questions."

"What the *hell* are you thinking?"

Sunshine peeked into the storeroom and whispered, "Do you mind? I have a customer out here."

I grabbed Annie's purse, took her by the arm and marched her through the store. Sunshine shot me a dirty look. So did the heavyset woman, mopping at her brow with a handkerchief. Once in the car I jammed the key in the ignition and stared at Annie. "Aren't you supposed to call someone, or do something to stop yourself?"

"I did. I called my sponsor."

"And?"

"She told me to write down all the reasons I shouldn't use."

"Did you?"

She looked away. "Yeah. I could only come up with one. Kaalaea."

"And Kaalaea wasn't enough?"

"I don't need your guilt trip, Bryan."

The lid was off, her anger about to boil over. I put on my sunglasses, started the car and pulled onto Topanga Canyon Boulevard. "Okay," I said, trying to contain my disappointment and salvage something. "One slip-up doesn't mean—"

"This is my third *slip up* in the last four days, Bryan."

"What happened? You were doing so well."

"You happened."

I shot her a sideways glance. "What?"

"Forget it."

"No, tell me what you mean."

We passed a longhaired hitchhiker holding a case for an electric guitar. Annie turned and shouted a greeting out the window. Her face flushed with excitement, she said, "I know that guy. He used to play with Sky Saxon."

"Wonderful! What did you mean by 'You happened'?" I took a left onto Old Canyon Road, knowing approximately where her parents had moved.

She didn't answer right away. "After our conversation the other night I got really depressed. When I get depressed, I start wanting some coke."

"Like coke's going to make it better?"

"Don't preach. You play chess to cope. I do drugs. You're just as addicted as I am."

"Bullshit! It's not the same and you know it. Drugs are illegal and they fuck up your brain. Not to mention your life."

"Oh, like your life isn't fucked up?! You lost a girlfriend four *fucking* years ago and you're still so depressed you can't even talk about it. Much less give another girl a chance."

I'd have asked her to get out of my car had I not been certain she'd walk straight back to the Chakra and snort that last line. "Did Sunshine give you the coke?"

"No," she replied, all attitude. "Other way around. I scored it from one of my connections in Laguna. That's when my clutch blew out. On the way home from Orange County."

"So where's your car?"

"At a shop in Santa Monica. Sunshine picked me up." She laughed. "We had a nice talk about you on the ride home."

"You talked about me?"

"Yeah. Girl talk."

"What'd you say?"

"Let's not," Annie answered.

"Tell me. You brought it up. I want to know."

"No, you don't."

"I do. That's why I'm asking."

"I told her about us."

I slowed down for a dog running on the side of the road. "That's pretty vague."

"I told her how good our sex life was in comparison to our love life."

"What does that mean?" *You know precisely what she means.*

"Take the next right and wind up the hill till it flattens out." She looked askance at me. "I don't think we should get into this."

"We're already into it. It's filling up the car."

Annie sighed, folded her arms. "It means we fuck, but we don't make love. It means we're together, but we're not a couple. Story of my life." She pointed to the right. "Park behind that car."

I pulled in behind a blue, beat-to-hell Opel Kadett, removed my shades and placed them on the dashboard. We sat in silence. The conversation wasn't working anyway, so I said, "Get Kaalaea and we'll go home."

"I'd rather finish talking, now that we've started."

"Go ahead," I told her, thinking how ridiculous she looked with honey on her face.

"Sunshine thinks you've been taking advantage of me for sex."

A pang of guilt wormed its way into my stomach. "Is that what *you* think?"

She turned to face me directly. "I think you're a head case. Maybe you didn't know you were using me, but that's exactly what you were doing."

A firecracker of guilt exploded in my gut. "If all I wanted was sex, would I have waited four years to get it?"

Annie began to weep. "I don't know, but I fell in love with you and all you did was push me away." She dabbed at her wet eyes with a shirtsleeve, now sticky with honey.

I withdrew inside myself. I wanted to say something supportive, but nothing came out.

Annie stared at me, her eyes desperate. "Look, Bryan. I'm weak. I act like I've got it together, but I'm weak when it comes to coke. I know all the reasons not to use, but they just fly out the window as soon as I start feeling bad. And now I'm on a run and I don't think I can stop on my own."

The blood drained from my head. I felt weird, wrongheaded, like I'd been snared in a complicated checkmate with no way out. "I can't make you stop."

She stared at me. "Of course not. All you can do is fuck me!"

I had to get away. "Get Kaalaea and we'll talk more tonight. After we've both had time to think." I watched her open the car door. Some honey had melted and run down her neck, blotchy with emotion. I added, "I'm sorry, Annie. You're a neat lady. Really."

Her eyes swung to mine as she slammed the door. "That's what you said about your dead housemother!"

Shame swelled up inside me, shaping a perfect wave I would ride . . . where? I watched Annie walk under an old olive tree and past a row of dust-covered jade plants. She looked over her shoulder before knocking on the front door. It opened and she walked slowly inside, allowing me a glimpse of Marge Darrow and Kaalaea, who hugged her mother's leg. I loved Kaalaea. Why couldn't I love Annie? *Because you're defective, that's why!* I grabbed my sunglasses from the dashboard, snapped them in two and gouged my forearm with the jagged plastic. An ugly red welt sprung up. *Remember how you judged Vicki Spotts for mutilating her skin? You're no better than she is!*

I stared through my dirty windshield, rich with self-loathing. Annie loved me, something I'd known before she said the words, but I couldn't return her love, or for that matter, the love of any good woman. My heart had dried up for anyone but Lydia. I started the car and sped off, made a screeching U-turn halfway down the block. I would not inflict myself on Annie again. Or anyone else.

I hit my brakes at the bottom of the hill, gravel spitting out from under my tires. Left would take me home. *Home to what? Chess books and computer programs? Amelia Cruz' guacamole and other painful memories?* A steady, churning sense of desperation seized me. I shook my head and closed my eyes, heard the words my mother had spoken just before leaping from the Aurora Bridge. "If you come with me, we'll always be together . . . just us two in a place where there's no more pain." Hopelessness forced a decision, a resolution with some real energy behind it. There would be no emotional goodbyes, no suicide letter to justify my final move.

Taking a hard right onto Old Canyon Road, I took off with the idea of reaching the mountain roads that crisscrossed Calabasas. Once there, I would get the Chevy to its top speed, drive off the road and into oblivion. No one could survive a headlong plunge into the deep, rocky canyons of the Santa Monica Mountains. I heard myself crying and turned on the radio to drown out my own sound. I punched a preset and landed on KRLA:

"Sitting on a park bench, eyeing little girls with bad intent . . . "

Jethro Tull. A hit song about a pedophile. It's a fucked-up world! I smashed my fist into the dashboard and rammed the accelerator to the floor, desperate to complete the job. A car whizzed by from the opposite direction, a man and a woman in the front seat, both following me with their eyes. I backed off, slowed to forty miles an hour. *Don't take anyone with you! You've hurt enough people as it is.*

It took five minutes to get to Mulholland Drive and another five to reach the part that's well away from civilization, where the highway doubled back on itself, like the lateral looping motion of a desert sidewinder. I got my speed up, flew around a corner at sixty and passed a biker on a Harley with a suicide clutch. *How apropos!* I barely looked at him as a succession of rapid-fire images shot through my mind—*mother stepping off the Aurora Bridge when I was six—Montrose's corpse staring lifelessly into the night—Lydia leaving me, walking away in the red sweater—the bloody smudge on Annie's sheet.*

I gripped the wheel and fixated on the cement in front of me, my eyes strained and unblinking. A straightaway of several hundred yards stretched out ahead. I gunned the engine. A road sign cautioned to slow to 35 miles per hour for the sharp right that would end my suffering. A guardrail curved around the outside of the turn, but a quick calculation told me I would hit it doing at least ninety, more than enough speed to take it out. This was it! I reeled in the road, remembering something Grandpa Matthews taught me about letting road come to you. *This time a canyon's coming to me, Grandpa!* I braced my body against the back of the seat and pushed the accelerator into the floor with all my strength. My last thought: the photo of Lydia stashed on page 235 of Horowitz' *Chess Openings* – the one of us holding hands and smiling in the gazebo in Pioneer Park. I screamed from my gut and as the wail turned itself into a strangled cry I yelled, "I love you, Lydia!"

I glanced down at the speedometer, saw the needle fluttering just this side of a hundred. Looked up and saw it. An animal had darted in front of my car, wolfish gray and large. I only caught a glimpse, but it registered as the biggest coyote I'd ever seen. I jammed on my brakes and went into a long, sideways skid, but a fraction of a moment too late. My front bumper clipped the animal's hind end, spinning it into the air. The side of my car slammed against the guardrail and screeched to a stop. I slammed the car into reverse and backed up a hundred yards, the smell of burnt rubber stinging my nostrils.

I found the animal on the opposite side of the road, lying motionless on its side. *Oh God, what have I done?* I threw open my door, sprinted over and found a dog that had to weigh a hundred pounds. It appeared to be a female and she was alive, her deep chest heaving as she stared at me through terrified eyes. I squatted down, heard the throaty hum of the Harley I'd passed. The biker downshifted through the gears and pulled off the road on the far side of my car. I watched him kill his engine, lower a kickstand and quickly dismount. He had a beard that was going white and a single gold earring in his left ear. "You all right?" he asked in a hoarse voice. Dried beige paint covered most of his hands and forearms.

"I'm okay, but she isn't."

"Man, you were flyin'!" He stood over the fallen animal, took a hasty step back when she silently bared her teeth.

"I have to get her to a vet," I said, swallowing hard. "Would you help me lift her into my back seat?"

"You sure? She doesn't look too happy."

"I'm sure. I have to save her."

He cocked his head. "You know what? This dog's one of those wolf hybrids. Guy I ride with had a male. Couldn't housebreak it."

I knelt three feet from the animal's face, looked for a collar with a nametag. There was none. "Gotta get you to a vet, Girl." I reached out to pet her, drew back in response to a low, guttural growl.

"Careful, Man." The biker motioned for me to get away. "She's lookin' to settle the score."

I rubbed my forehead, straining for a clear thought. "I'm gonna bring my car over so we don't have far to lift her." I ran over to the Chevy, pulled it across the road and lined up the back seat a few feet from where the animal lay. Though I pulled close, she made no attempt to move. I got out and tried to think of the best strategy for getting her into my back seat.

The biker shook his head. "You thinkin' we can lift this beast without gettin' ourselves bit? Because those chompers can definitely do some damage."

"Let me see what I can do," I replied. I lay down in the road, on my back, positioning myself so my neck was close to her head. Dangerously close. I scooted closer yet, fine-edged bits of gravel digging into my scalp.

"What the hell you doin?"

I didn't respond, and he added, "You're fuckin' crazy, Man."

"It's okay. I'm showing submission, so she won't be so scared. I saw it in a *National Geographic* article on timber wolves."

The animal growled again and the biker said, "Maybe she don't read *National Geographic*."

I actually smiled. *You were seconds from death and now you're smiling. You are 'fuckin' crazy'!* Trying to keep things calm, I used a gentle voice. "I'm not going to hurt you, Big Girl. It's okay, Big Girl. I just want to get you to a vet." She moaned and stopped growling. I rolled on my side, got close enough to move my hand in and scratch her chest. Her entire body tensed, but then she relaxed and even whimpered a little.

"I'll be damned," the biker said.

There was no blood on her, but she appeared to guarding her right hind leg. I also wondered about the canine equivalent of shock. No time to waste. "What's your name?" I asked the biker.

"Leroy. People call me Lee."

"Okay, Lee. We're going to lift this dog into my car. Put her in the back seat. There's a vet at the bottom of Topanga Canyon Boulevard."

"If I get bit, you gonna pay the doctor bill?"

"Deal. You take her rear."

"Good, 'cause your end's gonna bite you, sure as hell."

"Yeah, well, I'd probably feel better if she did."

"An' I thought my buddies were nuts," Lee muttered.

We kneeled simultaneously and got our arms in position to slide under the injured animal. Given her size, I knew this would be difficult, even if she wasn't in pain. Also knew it could go bad if she turned on one of us. "On the count of three," I said. "One . . . two . . . three." I carefully slid my hands under her shoulder and watched Lee slide his under her hips. But then, just as we began to lift, the animal staggered to her feet and wobbled onto the highway on her three good legs. She had an inch-long Z-shaped scar between her eyes.

"Good girl!" I turned to Lee. "We're still gonna have to lift her into the back seat."

"I was afraid you were gonna say that."

A red convertible came around the bend, the one where I was supposed to nose-dive into the canyon. With the dog still in the road, I waved my arms to get the driver to slow down. As it rolled to a stop, the driver, a woman with frizzy black wind-blown hair, asked what was happening.

"I hit this dog," I explained. "We're trying to lift her into my back seat without getting bit."

"I have a blanket in my trunk," she said. "Maybe you could get it under her chest and stomach, wrap her up a little before lifting her." She pulled her car to the shoulder without waiting for a reply.

While she was getting into her trunk, I walked in front of the dog and extended the back of my hand. She sniffed, somehow managing to stand still. I gently stroked the top of her broad head.

The woman handed me a folded pea-green blanket and asked, "Are you sure that's a dog and not a coyote?"

"It's a wolf-hybrid," Lee answered, sure of himself.

"She's beautiful," the woman gushed. "But you better be careful, in case she's not tame."

I made my voice gentle again and said, "Okay, Girl. Easy now. We're not going to hurt you." I carefully worked the blanket under the animal's torso and, with Lee's help, hoisted her into my back seat.

"Thanks, Lee," I said, once she was in. I handed the blanket to the Good Samaritan and thanked her, too. When she said she'd beam up a prayer I thought of Lydia praying over Ethan after Slider rolled the milk truck.

I started my car, tried to collect myself.

Lee walked over to my open window. "What were you thinkin,' drivin' like that?" He didn't appear to be angry, just curious.

I put the car in gear, noticed the acrid smell of burnt rubber. "Sometimes I just like to go fast."

He shook his head and laughed. "You need to get yourself a Harley, man. You're seriously crazy."

Chapter 10
Tuna

I drove fast to the Valley Veterinary Hospital in Woodland Hills, a place I'd passed hundreds of times on my way to Cal Tech. The injured dog sprawled helplessly across the length of the back seat, whimpering on the sharp turns that gave Mulholland its reputation as a road-racing venue. I tried to reassure her, using the calmest voice I could summon.

I pulled into an almost empty parking lot and, using every bit of my strength, lifted the dog carefully from the back seat. She was a big brute, heavily boned and muscled, and I barely managed to get her out. I set her on the pavement, thankful once again for her lack of aggression, as my jugular vein ended up precariously close to the largest and most impressive set of canines I'd ever seen. With a bit of coaxing, she hobbled at my side and together we entered the building, finding ourselves in a brightly lit waiting room.

A matronly woman with a tiny gold-colored Pomeranian in her lap greeted us from one of the waiting chairs. "A dog that size should be on a leash," she asserted, her eyes saucer-sized.

"Sorry. I don't have a leash." I used my body to gently guide the limping patient toward the reception desk.

"Well, you certainly should," a second woman told me in a lecturing tone. "There's a rule." Tossing aside a magazine, she pointed to an easy-to-see sign. Indignantly, she stuffed an enormous tabby into a portable carrier. Both the woman and her cat were morbidly obese.

The receptionist, a young woman not quite my age, hurried around the counter and efficiently slipped a rope-like yellow leash over the dog's head. "What happened?" she asked with appropriate urgency.

"I hit this dog with my car. I think her leg's broken."

"Poor girl," she cooed, bending down and feeling around the dog's neck. "Did her collar come off in the accident?"

I spaced out. "What? Oh . . . I don't think she had one."

"She looks like she's got some wolf or coyote in her." A look of concern creased the receptionist's face. "Look, Dr. Norman can't treat her unless the payment is guaranteed. So many people bring in injured animals and—"

"I'll pay whatever it costs. It's not a problem."

"Oh. Good." She retreated behind the counter and came back with a clipboard and a pen. "Fill this out. I'll go tell the doctor there's an emergency. We'll get you in next."

"Thanks." Using the leash, I carefully steered the dog across the room.

Traction was poor on the shiny linoleum, but she made it without slipping. I took a seat directly across from the Pomeranian, bug-eyed and trembling. The owner, holding her charge like a halfback trying hard not to fumble, said, "Sorry I was cross with you. I just assumed the dog was yours."

"That's okay." The dog continued to stand on her three good legs, holding the damaged hind leg a few inches off the floor. Strangely, she wouldn't take her eyes off me, having the unwelcome effect of magnifying my guilt.

A minute later, the receptionist returned and asked me to follow her. With the dog limping gamely, we ended up in a small examining room that reeked of pet odor. "I'm Angela," she said, spraying a disinfectant on the table and wiping it off with a thick wad of paper towels. "Dr. Norman's putting the final stitches in a Collie that ran into a barbed wire fence. They're not the brightest breed, you know."

"Oh." I remembered Lassie rescuing Timmy and performing amazing feats, wondered if Angela knew what she was talking about.

"Anyway, he'll be in in a couple of minutes."

"Thanks for not making us wait." I handed her the clipboard.

She smiled, patted the dog on the head and left.

I sat in a white plastic chair, noticed a print on the wall. Dogs playing poker. I looked at the dog I'd nailed. She held my gaze with intelligent eyes. I reached down and stroked her back. "I wish you could talk, Big Girl. I'd love to know what you're thinking." She pricked her ears and moaned. I apologized profusely, felt criminal.

A few minutes later a tall, balding man in a white jacket entered and introduced himself as Dr. Julius Norman. "Angela was right," he said, with an air of surprise. "This *is* a wolf hybrid. Probably mixed with Malamute, to get this kind of size in a female. Tell me what happened?"

I explained how I'd barely clipped the animal's rear end, but hard enough to send her airborne. He looked me over as he listened. I was dressed in T-shirt and jeans and, with all that had happened, looked almost as sorry as his new patient. "If I have to do surgery, she could easily rack up a three hundred dollar bill," he said in a cautioning tone. "Can you afford that?"

I nodded. "I work for IBM. I can afford it."

"Okay." He looked mildly surprised by my report of gainful employment. "Do you think she'll let us put her on the table?"

"Yeah. She's not aggressive at all."

We lifted her up and he noticed the fresh gouge on my arm. "She scratch you?"

My face reddened over my self-inflicted wound. "No, that happened earlier."

He gave me a curious look. "Wash it in the sink over here. Use the antibacterial soap in the dispenser. It looks likes it wants to be infected."

I complied while Dr. Norman directed his attention to the dog, gently palpating various parts of her body and speaking in a soothing, reassuring voice. He had uncommonly long and graceful fingers that made me think of Chopin, who composed piano music no one else could play because their hands weren't as large as his. "Is her leg broken?" I asked, wiping my arms and hands on a couple of paper towels.

"I don't think so." He stuck his head into the hallway and summoned an assistant. A large woman in aqua scrubs appeared, older than the receptionist, but still in her twenties. She and the doctor carried the patient to another part of the clinic for a series of X-rays.

I picked up a tuft of gray-white hair the dog had shed and prayed for her to be okay, pleading with God and promising I'd do whatever was needed to restore her to health.

Fifteen minutes later, Dr. Norman returned alone. Miraculously, the dog had no broken bones, but did have a dislocated kneecap that would require surgery to fix. When I told him I didn't even know dogs had a kneecap, he removed a notepad from an inside pocket and illustrated what the procedure would entail.

"Can you do it, or do we need to take her someplace else?"

Dr. Norman smiled. "I can do it. I'm a board-certified surgeon and it's a procedure I've done many times. It's usually smaller dogs. They seem to have a congenital predisposition for this problem."

"How soon can you operate?" I asked, my eyes burning from animal dander.

"Do you have any idea who the owner is? I'd rather not work on her without informed consent. There's always a risk when you put a dog under anesthesia."

"I have no idea. I hit her up in Calabasas." I sneezed, apologized.

"Bless you. There're no vets in Calabasas, but there's one in Agoura. I'll give her a call. Dog appears to have had good care. And there're only a few of these hybrids around. If she's up on her shots, there'll be a record."

I pictured the dog in a cage. "Will her injury get worse while we wait?"

"It won't hurt her to wait a day. Let me call Dr. Meyers and I'll be right back."

He returned in a few minutes. "Dr. Meyers hasn't treated any wolf hybrids. But there was no collar, and I can tell the dog hasn't been wearing one, so we can go ahead with the surgery first thing in the morning. Meanwhile, why don't you run a 'found' ad in the paper?"

I drove home from the vet's and collapsed on my bed, trying to come to terms with the ambivalence of a failed suicide attempt. Turning the day over in my mind amplified my despair. A hard knock at the door startled me. I sat up in time to see Annie let herself in. "Thanks a bunch for ditching me!"

I heaved a weary sigh. "What can I say? I should've waited."

"Well, why didn't you?"

I closed my eyes, struggled for the truth. "I kind of lost it after you went inside your Mom's house. So I took off. I apologize."

"I had to wait for Dad to come home with the car, and Mom figured out I was high."

"It was pretty obvious, Annie."

Annie's eyes filled with tears. "Yeah, well, my parents threatened to take Kaalaea. Dad says he might hire an attorney."

I got up and walked over to her. She let me hug her. I whispered, "They aren't going to take Kaalaea. They just want you off drugs. So do I."

"I know, but it still scares me. *I* scare me."

"That's probably good. You need to clean up your act."

She pushed me away. "It's not as easy as everyone seems to think."

"Okay, it's not easy, but you can do it. You've done it before."

"Have you been crying?"

"Allergies."

She softened a little, noticed the gouge on my arm and did a double take. "God, what happened to your arm?"

"Long story." I hid my arm behind my back.

She squinted at me. "What happened?"

"If you have to know, I broke my sunglasses and gouged my arm."

Her mouth dropped open. "You did that to yourself?"

I nodded. "Pretty stupid, huh?"

"After leaving me at my parents'?"

"Just before I left."

"Because of what we talked about?"

"Because I was mad at myself. Because I felt . . . overwhelmed."

"Are you okay? Now?"

"Not really. But I'm done doing stupid things, if that's what you're worried about."

She stared into my eyes, compassion pushing aside her anger. "I should apologize, too," she said. "Especially for the 'all you can do is fuck me' comment. That was cocaine talking."

"Don't worry about it."

"I'm not worried about it. I just want you to know I didn't mean it. I was coked up and angry at the same time. Bad combo."

I nodded again. "Look, something happened after I drove off. I hit a dog and took her to that vet at the bottom of Topanga Canyon Boulevard. She's going to have to have surgery tomorrow."

Annie looked puzzled. "Is she going to be okay?"

"I think so. She has a dislocated tendon in her knee, but the vet says the surgery should fix it."

"Topanga dog?"

I shook my head.

"Where'd this happen?"

I tried to keep my expression neutral. "Calabasas."

"Calabasas! What were you doin' out there?"

"Just drivin'," I answered, too embarrassed to tell the truth.

"Who's the owner of the dog?"

I shrugged my shoulders. "No collar. But the vet thinks we can find the owner 'cause she's a rare breed. I have to call the *Times* and put in a Lost and Found ad."

"What kind of dog is she?"

"The vet says she's half wolf and half Alaskan Malamute. You should see her, Annie. She's huge, and beautiful like you wouldn't believe."

"God. I hope she's okay."

"Me too. I feel terrible." Feeling the push of tears, I looked out the window.

Annie touched my shoulder. "Bryan? What were you doing in Calabasas?"

I bit my lip, covered my mouth with my hand.

"Were you up on those hairpin turns on Mulholland?"

Closing my eyes, I realized how close I'd come to ending my life. In my mind I heard the awful sound my mother made as she hit the water two hundred feet below the Aurora Bridge.

"I knew it," Annie said. "I knew it. Ever since you got that crystal thing from your housemother, I thought you might try something."

I opened my eyes. "You did?"

She nodded slowly. "God, Bryan. Please don't kill yourself. Our therapist in treatment told us suicide is a permanent solution to a temporary problem."

"Well, my *temporary* problem has lasted four years, and it's goin' strong."

"You should get a therapist. There're a lot of good ones in Santa Monica."

I nodded to placate Annie, but knew I wouldn't.

"Are you going to try it again?" she asked, in a strained voice.

"No. I guess it's not my time. Maybe that's why I hit that poor dog."

She looked puzzled. "Like it was God's way of stopping you?"

"I know it sounds stupid, but I was literally seconds away from death when I hit her. I suppose it could just be coincidence—"

"God, are we messed up, or what? I'm on drugs and you're suicidal. What a pair!" She laughed. "You sure we shouldn't be together?"

"I'm not sure of anything," I told her.

"Tell you what. I'll promise not to do coke, if you promise not to off yourself."

"Deal."

Dr. Norman called mid-morning to tell me the surgery went well. He said he chiseled a V-notch in the dog's knee bone and set the wayward tendon where nature intended it to be. The deeper notch ensured the tough band would stay in place, connecting muscle to its bony attachment. Just like the drawing he'd shown me.

I arrived late in the day to visit the big girl, who'd tipped the scales at ninety-eight pounds. She was groggy from the effects of anesthesia, but I was allowed to sit with her, just outside her cage door. I scratched her chest and tried to speak in reassuring tones. I'd already fallen in love, but when she plopped her massive head in my lap and gazed at me with those large, soulful brown eyes, I was a complete goner. I'd sat with the animal for an hour when Angela the receptionist brought me a handful of multi-colored dog biscuits.

"For me or the patient?" I asked. Angela was what the guys at IBM called "a looker," with a wide mouth, full lips and gleaming teeth. I hadn't noticed before. With high cheekbones and straight black hair, she looked to have some Indian blood. Lydia popped into my mind and I panicked when I couldn't immediately recall her face.

"They're for the patient, but it wouldn't be the first time someone ate one by mistake."

"Thanks." I fed the dog a biscuit, which she chewed indifferently.

"Don't get too attached," Angela warned. She'd spent more time on her makeup than the day before, giving her a slightly exotic look.

"I'm trying not to—"

"But it's not easy. Tell me about it. I work here every day."

I nodded my understanding. "I put an ad in the paper, but I hope to God no one answers it."

"Yeah. Usually they don't, but this girl's a specimen. She had to cost somebody a lot of money."

"I figured that." I offered her another biscuit, but she turned her head away.

Angela cleared her throat. "Hey. Change of subject. You know the group Icarus?"

"I've heard *Wings of Fire* on the radio, and I know they live in To-panga."

"Well, they're friends of mine and they're opening for Credence Clearwater at the Anaheim Convention Center Saturday night. You want to come? I can get us backstage."

"Thanks, Angela. But I've got a ton of work to do."

She looked disappointed, but recovered quickly with a dazzling smile. "Cool. Maybe some other time. I'd better get back to the front desk."

"Thanks for the invite." *Maybe Lee the biker was right. Maybe I am seriously crazy.*

————————

The veterinary clinic, a converted rambler, had a back porch that led to a small, fenced area with a carpet of dichondra, a substitute for lawn grass in parched Southern California. Two days post-surgery the patient and I were given permission to go there after a promise to take it easy. We sat in the shade of an old ficus tree, its shiny leaves fluttering in the breeze. Though limited to the use of three legs, she played with a partially deflated basketball Angela had brought out. To our surprise, the dog picked it up in her enormous mouth, tossed it ten feet in the air and caught it before it hit the ground. "Whoa! Nice catch!" I said. She appeared to smile.

Angela left as Dr. Norman appeared in the doorway, wiping his hands on a white towel. He shook his head at what he saw. "I've never seen a dog recover so quickly from that surgery. She'll be fine to go home tomorrow."

"If only we knew where home was."

He ignored my comment. "Ever have a dog of your own?"

"Not really. When I was five, a puppy followed me home. A black mutt I called Lucky. We kept him for about a week and my mother got rid of him."

"How come?"

"Let's just say my mother was low on coping skills. If he'd come housebroken, it might've worked out."

"So why didn't you get a dog when you moved to Topanga? Seems like most people up there have two."

"I've noticed. I guess I was too busy playing chess, working on my project at IBM. How about you? You have a dog?"

"Four," he laughed. "Angela calls 'em 'The Fearsome Foursome' after the Rams front four."

"How'd you end up with four?"

"Easy. People don't come back and I don't have the heart to send them to the pound. I don't suppose I need to explain why."

I nodded and said, "Bless your heart." I'd never used the expression and it sounded odd. But I meant it.

Dr. Norman stepped into the yard, shaded his eyes from the sun. "You remember I asked Dr. Meyers in Agoura if she knew anything about a wolf hybrid?"

"Yeah."

"Well, she happened to mention it to another vet and he knew who the owner was. Turns out the dog lives all the way out by Lake Sherwood. What is that? Twenty miles?"

"It's a ways," I said, my heart sinking fast.

"I just got off the phone with her owner. He bought her as a puppy on a hunting trip in Alaska. Got her before her eyes were open, which helps explain why she's so friendly."

"Are you sure it's the same dog?"

"Yeah. He described the "Z" scar between her eyes. He was horseback riding in Camarillo and she tried to make friends with a bobcat."

"What's her name?"

"Tuna."

The dog dropped the basketball and looked at Dr. Norman.

"Tuna?" I repeated. She looked at me and tilted her head. I met her eyes and bit my lower lip. *I'm going to have to give her up.*

He nodded. "All dogs like tuna fish, but this one goes bonkers over it. At least that's the story. By the way, she's just a little over a year old, younger than I'd estimated from the size of her teeth. That means she'll fill out a bit, which seems hard to believe."

I nodded, braced myself for the inevitable.

"Anyway, I told the guy how you hit her and brought her in . . . explained the surgical procedure. He was pleased to hear you've paid all her medical bills." A strange smile crossed Dr. Norman's face.

I froze. "What?"

"He asked me if I thought you'd want her. And if I thought you were the responsible sort."

A rush of excitement tickled my back, radiated down my arms. "What'd you tell him?"

Dr. Norman seemed to pause for effect. "I told him you're a fine young man. And that you love the dog so much you're losing I.Q. points by the minute."

"What'd he say?"

"He said you can keep her if you want. Free of charge if you give her a good home."

"Are you kidding me?"

"I wouldn't do that, Bryan."

"God, yes, I want her!" I jumped to my feet and thrust a fist in the air like I'd just defeated Bobby Fischer for the World Chess Championship. Then I rushed over and hugged a startled Tuna, who made a quick recovery by licking my face and neck.

"You can take her home. I'll play go-between and have the guy mail me something that shows he's transferring ownership. Just to be on the safe side."

"Thanks." I looked down at Tuna, barely able to contain my joy. "But why's this guy willing to let her go?"

"He says she keeps running off and not coming back. This time she'd been gone for over a week. Same day you brought her in, his wife went out and bought a Golden Retriever puppy."

I glanced down at Tuna, watched her lick a gray paw as big as my fist. "You think she'll keep running away?"

"When her cast comes off in a month, bring her in and I'll spay her. That'll keep her from straying."

I nodded. "Thanks, Dr. Norman. For everything. Thank you *so* much."

"You're welcome, and congratulations. I've seen a few of these wolf hybrids, but they were all high-strung and unstable. Tuna's mellow. She'll make a good pet once you get her spayed. She'll live longer, too."

"I can't believe I get to keep her."

Dr. Norman smiled. "You'll believe it when you get her food bill each month. You should've seen what she put away for breakfast."

"You think she'll forgive me for hitting her?"

"Dogs are forgiving creatures. Way more than we are. The way she looks at you, I'd guess she's already over it."

"I hope so."

Dr. Norman smiled. "The previous owner said they call her the 'wonder dog.'"

"Why's that?"

"Everyone wonders what kind of dog she is." He chuckled again and walked back into the building.

I flopped on the ground alongside my new companion. "Good girl, Tuna! You're a good girl. You saved my life."

She stretched her long body and licked the steady flow of tears from my cheeks.

As Tuna healed, so did I.

Brimming with energy, she accompanied me on short walks, ignoring the full-length cast on her hind leg. By mid-October we began navigating the sun-scorched hills and waterless creeks behind my cabin, stopping occasionally to roughhouse in fields of sagebrush or sit on the fire roads and watch red-tailed hawks gliding on the thermals above our heads. With Tuna in tow, an emerging will to live replaced the grief and shame that led me to suicide.

It didn't happen all at once, but by degrees the desperate feelings that had darkened my soul began to lift. Annie noticed the change, and went out of her way to comment. "You seem so much *lighter* since you got Tuna," she explained. I realized she was right whenever I caught myself staring in wonder at the hummingbirds that fed outside my bedroom window. In the past I'd barely noticed these tiny creatures, sometimes allowing their feeder to go empty for weeks at a time. Now I was awestruck by their brilliant, iridescent plumage, flashing in the morning sunlight.

The Blurs, as I called them, were friends with whom I could be silent. Each bird was unique, dancing in the air and producing wondrous displays of lustrous, rainbow-like colors. I named the regulars who appeared daily at my feeder – the final stop after extracting nectar from the fuchsia, honeysuckle, lilac and bee balm the previous owner had planted around my cabin. I christened my favorite The Leaner, an especially slender female who would zoom in at breakneck speeds, dip her long bill in the feeder, then lean back so far she seemed destined to tumble backwards from her perch.

One afternoon, having just replaced the plastic bee guards on each of the individual feeder tubes, I took one step away and stood perfectly still. The Leaner flew in, unconcerned by my presence. She hovered motionless a few inches from my face, emitting a continuous low drone. Feeling the wind from her wings, I smiled like a happy child. The humming ended as she landed on the feeder. Drawing nectar from the feeder's imitation red flowers, she began her impossible, idiosyncratic leaning. I would have laughed if not for the fear of interrupting her gravity-defying acrobatic act. Then, as abruptly as she'd arrived, she zoomed off around the corner of the cabin.

I followed her with my eyes and saw Annie approaching from the driveway. "Something weird happened," she said, bounding up the stone steps.

"What?"

"Sunshine just called. From the Food Chakra. She said there was a girl in there asking about you."

I did a double take. "Asking about me? What was her name?"

"Kitty. She said she was an old friend." Tuna came through the front door to greet Annie, who took a knee and gave her a scratch behind the ears.

"Did Sunshine get a last name?"

"She just said Kitty."

"The only Kitty I knew eloped with a fraternity brother."

"Maybe it was her."

I shook my head. "Doubtful. We barely knew each other. Besides, last I heard they're in Africa doing graduate work in paleontology."

She frowned. "You should call Sunshine. Something wasn't right about this girl."

"What do you mean?"

"She made a scene."

My gut registered a bad feeling. "You know the number at the Chakra?"

"Huh unh."

I dug out my phone book, found the number and dialed it.

"Food Chakra, hello," a bright voice answered.

"Sunshine?"

"She's unpacking stuff in the back. You want me to get her?"

"Please." I waited, listened to their stereo playing *Mechanical World*, by Spirit. A Topanga band doing an eerie meditation on death.

Tuna rolled on her back to expose her tummy. Annie asked, "When did Tuna get her cast off?"

"Couple of days—"

"This is Sunshine."

"Hi. It's Bryan. Bryan Matthews. Annie's here. I'm told I had a visitor."

"That's right. A rude one."

"What happened?"

"Just a sec." I heard the sound of a cash register closing followed by muffled voices. "Girl came in by herself and filled a shopping basket. When she got in the checkout line, she asked if I knew 'Bryan Matthews, the chess player.'"

"And you said?"

"I said, 'Sure, it's a small town.'"

"Then what happened?"

"She laughed and said that's the way it was where she grew up. All nice and friendly, at that point."

"And she said her name was Kitty?"

"Yeah. Didn't give a last name. You know her?"

"I used to know a girl named Kitty, but she's out of the country. And she'd never be rude in a million years." I gazed at the ceiling and wondered about Vicky Spotts. Four years had gone by, but she was more than capable of tracking me down and intruding on my new space. I took a flier. "Did she have bleached hair?"

"Yeah. Come to think of it, she did."

My pulse quickened. "A little overweight, on the busty side?"

"No. This girl was thin. *Rail* thin." Sunshine's voice turned acidic. "As far as her bust size, I really didn't check out her out."

I ignored the snide remark. "Is that all she asked? If you know me?"

"No. She wanted to know where you lived."

"Did you tell her?"

She hesitated. "Sorry if I screwed up, but I told her you live up Greenleaf Canyon. I got a weird vibe when she asked for directions, so I asked her to write down her name and number and told her I'd get the message to you."

"I take it she refused."

"First she said she was staying with friends and didn't know their number. That's when I asked her her last name. She said that would ruin it, that she wanted to surprise you. She more or less insisted I should tell her how to find you. When I told her I wouldn't do that, she slammed her shopping cart into our incense display and stormed out."

"She left without paying?"

"Yeah. I had to put a ton of groceries back on the shelf. You sure you don't know this girl?"

"It sounds like a girlfriend I had a long time ago, but she was on the heavy side. And you wouldn't have had to check out her chest to know she was busty."

"This girl was skinny. Like a speed freak."

———

Annie stayed long enough to ask a few questions about the "old girlfriend," curious if the reference was to Lydia. I told her Lydia had been my second girlfriend – that my first had been jealous and unstable. Annie scowled and left, assuring me she'd keep an eye out for anything unusual.

I stayed up late, but before getting in bed I walked around the cabin, stopping every few feet and listening for God knows what. All I could hear was the wind, which happened to be gusting up from the ocean that night. I went back inside, turned out the lights and crawled under the covers. The wind whistled under the front door and through a crack. Tuna fell fast asleep on the couch, snoring lightly. I looked at the clock. Not quite two a.m. I lifted the velour curtain Annie had made and peeked out the window. The night was clear, but the moon was little more than a sliver. I saw vague outlines, nothing moving.

I awakened to the sound of Tuna growling. I sat up and looked around, trying to orient myself. If anything, the wind had picked up. I listened to the window rattling and then the yipping of a lone coyote, a long way off. I was about to lie back down when I heard what sounded like a car door being shut. Fear entered through the little "O" my mouth made and wound its way to my stomach, shivering and alive. Spacey, I reached for the flashlight I'd placed so carefully alongside my bed. It wasn't there. *God damn it! Where's my flashlight?* I groped in the dark, knocked it over. The sound was loud enough to alert anyone outside that I was awake.

My eyes adjusted to the dark. Tuna slid off the couch and moved stealthily to the front door, her nails clicking lightly on the wood floor.

"What is it, girl?" I whispered, swiveling off the bed. I fell in step behind her, flashlight in hand. On reaching the door, I aimed the flashlight through the glass and switched it on. My heart nearly burst. Frozen in the beam was the ghostly face of a startled woman, her face a wide-eyed glare of fear and aggression.

"It's me, Bryan! Open the damn door." Vicky Spotts threw up an arm to shield her eyes from the harsh light. Her previously plump face had been hollowed out and a more prominent jaw line altogether changed the shape of her head. The once voluptuous body seemed to have been divided in half. Her eyes sunk into her head but were otherwise unchanged.

I opened the door without thinking, took two steps back and switched on the kitchen light. "Jesus God, Vicky! You scared the living crap out of me!"

She stepped into the cabin and into the light. "You scared *me!* I was just about to knock."

"What're you doing? It's the middle of the night."

"Nice to see you, too." She lunged forward and gave me an awkward hug.

Hackles bristling, Tuna growled louder, this time like she really meant it.

Vicky jumped back, clutching a large purse to her chest. It looked like a carpetbag. "What's his problem?"

"What's *his* problem? What's *your* problem? It's the middle of the fucking night."

"You already said that. I'm sorry. Now will you call him off?"

"Call *her* off."

"What?"

"She a female, Vicky. And stop staring at her or she'll think you're trying to establish dominance. Trust me, you don't want to do that." I reached down and tousled the hair on the back of Tuna's neck. "It's okay, girl," I said halfheartedly.

"Does she bite?" Vicky asked, forcing her eyes away from Tuna's gaze.

"Yeah, she's trained to be a guard dog." *A lie, but good strategy under the circumstances.*

Vicky stole a glance. "God damn she's big! She looks more like a wolf than a dog."

"She's half wolf," I said, folding my arms. My heart pounded against my chest, but with less urgency.

"What's her name?"

"Tuna." *Why are you answering her questions?*

Vicky wiped a runny nose with the back of her hand. "Could we sit down and talk?"

My instincts told me no, but I didn't want a scene. "You promise to behave?"

"Cross my heart."

"Since when did you get a heart?"

"Same old Bryan, huh?"

I motioned for her to take a chair at the kitchen table. She smiled and set down her purse, which clunked on the hardwood floor. I remained standing and didn't speak. Tuna sat close to my side, ears pricked and eyes vigilant.

"Can you make her stop looking at me like that?"

"Not really, she doesn't like you. Can you tell me what you're doing here?"

"In Southern California, or on your property?"

"Both." The reflection in the glass door reminded me I was in my shorts. I walked over to the couch, grabbed my jeans and pulled them on.

"You looked cuter in your shorts."

I shot her a dirty look. "Are you going to answer my question?"

"I just finished up some business in Venice, or was it Marina Del Ray? I don't know where one ends and the other begins. I asked my business partners how far Topanga was and they said fifteen minutes. So I decided to drop in and see you."

"How'd you know I was living in Topanga?"

"Your pal Slider. But don't be mad at him, I sort of tricked him into telling."

"You saw Slider? I thought he was back East, pitching for some team in the Pirates organization." I'd seen his name in a *Sporting News*. He played for Batavia and had a decent earned run average in the high threes.

She nodded. "He was, but they made him . . ." she shook her head. "What's the guy that comes in later on in the game?"

"A relief pitcher."

"Yeah, and he threw his arm out. He was in Walla Walla resting up. Now they've sent him to Puerto Rico where he can pitch in warm weather."

"I hadn't heard that."

"Because you don't keep in touch with anyone. Not even your best friends."

I ignored the dig, shook my head in amazement.

"What?" Vicky asked.

"If I hadn't had advanced warning, I wouldn't have recognized you."

She laughed. "So, your spies told you I'd be paying a visit."

"No. My spies told me it was someone named Kitty, and that she was rude as hell."

"Bad Kitty!" She grinned maniacally.

"It's not funny, Vicky. You said you're a friend of mine and then made a scene. That's not cool."

"Sorry. If that girl would've told me how to find you—"

"No. That's no excuse for being rude."

"Sorry." She sniffed again, like a person fighting a cold. "I've had a lot of shit comin' down on me."

I didn't ask what she meant. "Want some tea?"

"Got anything stronger?"

"No." Another lie. I had an unopened bottle of Southern Comfort a co-worker had given me for Christmas, but knew better than to serve Vicky alcohol.

"Okay, I'll take the tea. Tons of sugar." She plucked a black knight from the chessboard, examined it and set it back down on the wrong square. A subtle smile made the mistake appear deliberate.

I put a pot of water on the stove, turned the burner on full. "It's been a long time."

She nodded. "Almost five years."

"You okay?" She didn't look okay. With chalky skin and vacant eyes, she had the haggard look of an addict.

"Not bad. How about you?"

"I'm okay."

"Hmmm. How's your chess game? You beat Bobby Fischer yet?"

"Chess game's fine, and no, I haven't beaten Bobby Fischer."

"Knowing you, you'll probably do it someday."

"How's your Mom?"

She shrugged a shoulder. "Still drinks too much of that cheap plum wine."

"That's too bad."

"I just bought her a cute little turquoise and white Nash Neapolitan. I'm drivin' a hopped-up '65 GTO. Got a Shaeffer racing clutch put in for this trip."

"GTO, huh? Dealing coke is lucrative, I take it?"

She flashed a big grin that reminded me of a jack-o-lantern: no one behind the eyes. Then she blinked rapidly and answered, "Easiest money in the world."

I shook my head in disgust. "You'll get busted."

"Not in Walla Walla. The cops aren't that smart." She smirked and added, "You, above all people, should know that."

I got a queasy feeling in my stomach. The water on the stove was boiling. "You'd be smart to stop dealing. Before it's too late."

"I'm not worried." She reached into the carpetbag purse, took out a can of shaving cream and handed it to me. "Check this out."

"It's late, Vicky."

"C'mon. Check it out."

It was red and white, a 79-cent sticker on the plastic cap. I shook it without thinking and shrugged.

"Try it," she said.

I removed the cap and pressed the center of the top. A small amount of lather oozed out. I shrugged again and wiped my hand on my jeans.

She reached across the table and took the can. With a sly smile, she began unscrewing it at the bottom. To my amazement, the bottom portion came off neatly at the seam. The can had been converted to a container, and in the space intended for shave cream was a clear plastic bag with white powder. "No way the cops will figure this one out," she gloated.

"Whoa," I said. "Is that coke?"

"It ain't baking soda. Want to try a little?"

"No, and I don't want that stuff in my house, either."

"Yup, same old Bryan." She placed the bag of cocaine back in the container and screwed the bottom back on.

"Seriously, Vicky—"

"Relax. If the cops came through the door right now, it's just a can of shaving cream." She held it up and smiled seductively, like a television actress doing a testimonial.

The can was clever ruse, but hardly foolproof. "As soon as you sell a few of these cans, the word will be out. The first person to get busted will point the finger back to you."

"I don't *sell* these cans. I just use 'em to move my products from point A to point B."

I finished making a cup of green tea, spooned in sugar and set it next to her. "You can't move much product in a can that size."

She laughed. "You'd be surprised. In the trunk of my car is a scuba tank with ten pounds of pure Peruvian coke. I pay five thousand dollars a pound, and sell it for twenty. Do the math, Bryan."

"The scuba tank's full of coke?"

"No, it's full of coke *and* compressed air. The same guy that makes the shaving cream can puts the tank on a lathe and machines out exactly ten pounds of metal. When he puts the bottom back on, he color-matches the paint so no seams or threads show. Then he puts a plastic cap on the bottom and seals it with a good glue."

"Isn't the plastic cap on the bottom a give-away?"

"No, because an aqualung needs a plastic bottom."

"Why's that?"

"So the metal doesn't damage the boat you're on. Once a year I go to

Peru with my scuba diving club and pay up the ying-yang to get the empty part filled with high-grade cocaine. Customs weighs it on my way back into the country, but it looks ordinary and weighs exactly what it's supposed to."

I shrugged. "Okay, so you've got a good scam. But you're also addicted to cocaine."

"No I'm not." She gulped her tea. "I just use a little when I need to."

"Right, Vicky. Look at your body. How much weight have you lost, anyway?"

"From one-sixty something to ninety-eight pounds. How much is that? You're the math whiz." She stood suddenly and pirouetted to show off her new figure.

Tuna growled, low, eyes darting back and forth between Vicky and me. Vicky froze and sat back down.

"That can't be good, to lose that much weight. You don't even look like you."

"I don't get any complaints," she said in a defensive voice. "Can I have some more sugar?"

I handed her the sugar bowl and a spoon. "Dealing's a dangerous business. You could get yourself killed."

"I'm not scared. I've got bodyguards."

"I don't see 'em."

"Smith and Wesson." She glanced down at her purse.

"I think it's time for you to leave."

"Mellow out, Bryan. God, you are even more uptight than you used to be."

"Oh, is that a fact? You come in my house in the middle of the night with hard drugs and a gun, and I'm not supposed to react? Get real, Vicky!"

"It's not a big deal. Besides, I need to ask a favor."

"Forget it."

"Come on. I need to spend the night."

"Uh unh. I just asked you to leave."

"Please, Bryan. Pretty please! I won't come on to you, if that's what you're afraid of."

"Sunshine told me you were staying with friends."

"Was that her name? *Sunshine?* Oh God, how California!"

"I'm not going to let you spend the night. Period."

"Why not?"

"Because you make me nervous. Because I don't trust you enough to let myself fall asleep." *Because I don't want your cocaine anywhere near Annie.*

"Okay. We could stay awake. Maybe rack one off for old times' sake."

I shook my head. "Nice to know you're still you. You just look different."

"Be cool, Bryan. I'm in a jam. A guy in Venice thinks I stepped on some coke I sold him."

"Stepped on?"

She rolled her eyes. "Diluted. He thinks I stretched it with cornstarch."

"That's great, Vicky. Some drug-crazed cokehead thinks you ripped him off, and you want to hide out at my place with your gun ready."

"No one could find this place in a million years."

"You did."

"I'll pay you." Again, she wiped her nose with the back of her hand.

"I'm not interested in money."

"How 'bout a blow job? You seem like you could use one."

"Leave, Vicky."

She sighed and pushed her chair away from the table. "Okay, but first answer me one question." Her knee had been going up and down a mile a minute, siphoning off nervous energy. Suddenly, it stopped, as if the moment for her visit had arrived. "You ever think about me?"

I considered the Smith & Wesson in her purse, decided to answer. "I can't say I never do. But I've sort of blotted out Walla Walla. Nothing personal."

"You blot out Lydia, too?"

"That's more than one question."

She grinned. "Humor me."

I drew a deep breath, blew out through my lips. "I try to blot her out, too."

She shook her head slowly. "If I live to be a hundred, I'll never understand why you chose that girl over me."

You'll be lucky to make it to thirty. "It's been real, Vicky." I walked briskly to the front door and held it open. Tuna got to her feet, came over and stood at my side like a sentinel.

Vicky hoisted her purse and passed close, stopping inches from my face. "Since you're so big on giving advice, I'll give you a little."

"I can't wait."

"If I were you, I wouldn't be visiting Walla Walla anytime soon."

"And why's that?"

"Remember Gerritsen, the detective?"

"Of course I remember Gerritsen." Hearing his name activated a cold fear in my gut.

She smiled, enjoying her regained sense of control. "He questioned me about a year ago. A dealer from Yakima bought a large quantity of Thai weed, then stole back the money he'd paid and got an ice pick in the temple."

"He got murdered?"

"No. The lucky bastard lived. Anyway, Gerritsen came by to ask me some questions. No big deal. As he was about to leave, he turned around and asked if I ever heard anything about Bryan Matthews. I said 'no' and he said, 'Someday I'm gonna figure out how that kid got away with murder.'"

I tried acting unruffled, but the anger in my voice gave me away. "I shouldn't come to Walla Walla because some idiot detective can't accept the fact that Jack Montrose died in a car accident?"

"That's just one reason." She kissed me hard on the mouth and walked into the shadows. The wind had completely disappeared.

Chapter 11
The Slide Show

Annie pretended to faint when I agreed to be her "date" on New Year's Eve, especially since the party would take place at The Corral, an infamous watering hole known for its rowdy patrons. "I'm not sitting home on New Year's Eve," she announced, and I consented to go along. What Annie didn't know, and I didn't bother to tell her, was that I'd never set foot inside a bar.

Tucked inconspicuously into the side of a hill along Topanga Canyon Boulevard, The Corral was considered the place to go for live music, cheap beer and shootin' pool with your buddies. Having driven past their outdoor sign almost daily for four years, I knew they'd played host to all the great Topanga bands – Spirit, Canned Heat, Jo Jo Gunne, Spanky and Our Gang, Taj Mahal. Even the late Jimi Hendrix had jammed there on weekends (his house, between Topanga and Malibu, resembled a Spanish castle).

Annie drove, I suppose because the night out was her idea. She looked great in tight jeans and a sheer chocolate brown blouse, but she was still off limits and I intended to keep it that way. We arrived at The Corral around ten, squeezing her V-Dub van into one of the last parking places.

Tacked to the side of the building, a glossy promotional photo announced the evening's headliner would be 1313 Blueview Terrace. They sounded good enough from a distance and we queued up in a short line. Annie tugged at my arm and said, "Okay, Bryan Matthews. Here's the deal. If I meet someone cool, I can ditch you without feeling guilty. Okay?"

I smiled. "Sure, as long as the door swings both ways."

She rolled her eyes. "Yeah. Like you're gonna pick up a girl."

We headed up a wood ramp to the main entrance. A bouncer carded a drunk and a skinny black-haired woman who had on more makeup than clothing. They made a strange couple, he wearing a plump blue parka and her almost nothing. Their I.D. was good and then we were up. Taking me by the hand, Annie said, "Cliff. This is my friend Bryan. I'll vouch for him."

"Still have to see I.D.," Cliff shouted over a high decibel guitar solo. He resembled an ape with long hair.

I showed him my California driver's license. He looked at the picture, pierced me with his gaze and gave us the go-ahead. *Weird game,* I thought to myself. *All this display of control when everyone knows the whole point is to get hammered and lose control.*

Once inside, I reeled from the smell of cigarette smoke and spilt beer. Annie dodged several dancing couples and guided me toward the tables farthest from the stage and off to the side of the speakers, which was good because the thump thumping from the bass was hurting my ears and making my scalp vibrate. Through a series of hand gestures, Annie got permission to join two couples at a table just in front of the pool and foosball tables.

I scooted my chair in close and yelled in Annie's ear. "Is it always this loud?"

"What?" she said, pretending not to hear me. Then she laughed. "You'll get used to it."

Our waitress, twenty-something with smooth olive skin, wore a low-cut blouse that framed six inches of cleavage. I ordered a pitcher of beer to share with our new tablemates. Annie, sober for seven weeks and working her program, ordered a ginger ale with a twist of lime. When the waitress disappeared into a hanging curl of blue and red smoke, Annie leaned in close and asked, "Did you like the view?"

"I liked it," I answered. "And you know the rule."

"What's that?"

"Anything I can see I can touch!"

Annie slapped the back of my hand and scanned the crowd.

A surfer-type with curly blond hair yelled across the table. "My roommate just put down his *seventh* margarita!"

His roommate grinned through an alcoholic haze. "Seven's gotta be the record."

"Are you college students?" Annie asked, cupping her hands like a megaphone.

He nodded, with an air of pride. "Pepperdine Waves."

"The record's nine," I shouted back.

Annie elbowed me in the ribs. "You're evil," she said, but she couldn't help but laugh.

Our drinks arrived and I paid, looking away from the waitress' cleavage. Not that I was above taking a peek, but all that female skin made me feel uncomfortable. I downed half a glass of beer and wiped my mouth. Annie asked if I wanted to dance and I did, for the first time since leaving Whitman. We danced okay together and, after two songs, the lead singer, a good-looking guy who pinwheeled the microphone à la Roger Daltrey, announced a ten-minute break.

On the way back to our table, Annie was telling me about her day with Kaalaea, who'd engaged a friend in a tug-of-war over a plastic baseball bat. As the story went, Kaalaea abruptly let go and her little friend fell on her bottom, sending Annie and some other grownups into peals of laughter. I was about to ask how the kids responded when I heard a female voice say, "Bryan?"

I looked next to me and saw Angela, the receptionist from Valley Veterinary Hospital. She looked terrific in a short jeans skirt, cowgirl blouse and hand-tooled western boots.

"Hi Angela," I said, louder than necessary now that the band was on a break. "This is my friend Annie."

"Hi," she said. "And this is Brad. Oh! How's Tuna?"

"She's great. She's up to a hundred twenty pounds."

Angela's eyes lit up like the pinball machine directly behind her. "You're kiddin'!" She turned to Brad and said, "Tuna's the wolf hybrid I told you about. She's such a sweetheart."

"Tell Dr. Norman she's running without a limp," I added.

"I will. Hey. Remember I told you I know the guys in Icarus? We're about to leave for a party at their road manager's house. A guy named Big E. Why don't you follow us?"

I looked at Annie and shrugged my shoulders. "You want to?"

Annie looked at Angela. "Is it cool? We don't want to crash someone's party."

"It's cool," Angela assured us. "Big E's gonna do a slide show. He'll want a big audience, believe me."

"Slides of what?" I asked.

"The band's first road trip. They opened for a lot of big groups. It'll be fun. You should come."

"I wouldn't mind going somewhere where the air's better," I told Annie. My eyes stung and we hadn't been there half an hour.

"Sure," she shrugged. "Why not? Let me get my purse."

"We'll wait for you out front," Angela said.

Annie retrieved her purse. I followed her to our table and confessed to the college students that I'd been kidding about the record for margaritas. They looked pissed until I told them they could finish off our pitcher.

We followed Angela and Brad to a house near the top of Glen Trail, a steep and winding road on the other side of the canyon from my cabin. Annie parallel-parked on an incline, wedging between a Chevy pickup truck and an old bullet-nosed Studebaker covered with rain-splattered dust. Fireworks echoed through the canyon, the acrid smell of gunpowder mixing with the leftover aroma of waterlogged sage. "Good thing it rained yesterday," I mentioned. Annie nodded. Topanga residents shared a dread of fire in the same way Texans dread killer tornadoes.

Angela pointed out Big E's and we made our way up a stone path, catching a whiff of marijuana along the way. I felt a vague discomfort, like a premonition, but quickly dismissed it. Big E's house reminded me of Annie's, ranch style with a long front porch for families to sit out on at night and talk. The door had been propped open with a ceramic Emperor penguin. Neil Young's first solo album spilled out on the best home stereo system I'd ever heard.

"Round and round and round we spin, to weave a wall that hems us in, It won't be long. It won't be long."

We entered a spacious kitchen with pine cabinets and gleaming Formica countertops. Big E (or so I presumed) leaned against a timeworn
butcher-block table. He went about six-five, two-thirty, with long black hair
tied back in a ponytail. He gestured widely with his hands, " . . . so the signal went from the slide guitar, an Armstrong, to the Wah-Wah pedal, to
the Echoplex, to the phase shifter, to the Marshall amp—" He spotted Angela, stopped mid-sentence and came over to give her a bear hug. "Angela.
What's happening?"

"Not much," she answered.

"Hey! Did you get that part in the Dennis Hopper movie?"

"I did, but I don't have any speaking lines," she replied. "And I'm not
willing to sleep with Dennis to get a better part."

"It's not who you know, it's . . . " Thankfully, Big E left the rest unsaid.
Noticing Annie and me, he said, "Hey, introduce your friends."

Angela, who seemed to know everyone, made introductions all around. I
could feel butterflies at the prospect of meeting so many people. I fixed on
Angela, a face I knew. "I didn't know you were an actress."

"I've only been in one movie," she said in a sunny voice. "I played a
teenage runaway in a movie called *Book of Pages*. Did you see it?"

"No," I answered, "but I don't go to movies much."

"Me neither," Big E seconded, "better things to do. But stay for my
slide show. It starts in a few minutes." Smiling, he reached into an ice filled
tub and handed me a beer.

I took a swig, hiccupped. My eye caught a spectacular mural painted on
the kitchen wall. "Wow!" I said to no one in particular. The painting de-
picted a beautiful red-haired, green-eyed angel plummeting toward water
with one wing on fire. The angel made me think of my mother falling silently from the Aurora Bridge. Not a pleasant thought. *Was this why I felt
uncomfortable before coming in?*

Big E watched my reaction. "You know Icarus, from Greek mythology?"

"Yeah. He flew too close to the sun and melted the wax that fastened
his artificial wings to his body. Fell into the Aegean Sea."

"Very good," Big E said. "Icarus is the band I work for. This mural is
the cover of our first album. Actually, our only album."

"It's powerful," I commented. "But Icarus was a man."

"The artist's a Jungian. They think men have a feminine inner
personality."

"The anima."

"What?"

"The anima. That's what Jung called it."

"Oh, I thought you said *enema*." He laughed too hard and I realized he
was stoned.

"Anyway, it's fabulous."

"What do you do, Bryan?" Big E asked.

"I work for IBM."

"Really. What do you do?"

"I program computers to play chess."

"So I guess I shouldn't play you a game for high stakes."

"Probably not." I forced a smile to hide my nervousness.

Annie stepped in close to me, drinking from a bottle of sparkling cider. New Year's Eve seemed perfect for a relapse and I'd decided to keep a close eye on her. "Bryan is being modest. He once beat the third best player in the world."

"You must be kidding," Big E replied.

She smiled impishly. "No, seriously. He beat a Russian Grandmaster named Vladimir Primalov."

Big E looked stunned. *"Vlad the Impaler!* I've read about him. He's the guy that wanted Fischer after Fischer beat Spassky."

"That's him," I said, blushing.

"Far out! You beat him?"

"He beat him when he was eighteen years old," Annie answered, her eyes mischievous.

"Whoa! Could I get a lesson sometime?" Big E asked. "We take a portable board on road trips and I keep losing my per diem to our lead singer."

"Sure." I tried swallowing a gulp of air to stop the hiccups. "Maybe I could help."

"That's great." He glanced at a clock on the kitchen wall. "Oh, time for the slide show."

We made our way into Big E's living room, memorable for having an entire wall of record albums. Annie and I sat on the floor, leaning against a scuffed-up brown leather couch. I said, "Hey, thanks a bunch, Annie."

"You loved it," she replied with a grin.

"Right." Funny thing, she *was* right. I'd surprised myself by letting in the admiration. Something I wouldn't have done before—

Annie clinked her bottle to mine. "Cheers. Thanks for being with me tonight."

"Cheers. Thanks for asking me." *I wouldn't have let it in before Annie . . . and Tuna.*

Maybe fifteen people crowded into the small room, noisy with music and dope-induced merriment. Next to me, a doe-eyed girl in her late teens offered me a hit off her joint. When I refused, she asked, "Are you a nark?"

Her question caught me off-guard. "No. I just don't smoke it."

She studied my face. "Oh, I know you," she said. "You're the guy with the wolf dog? I saw you outside the Smoothie Bar."

I hiccupped again, excused myself. "That'd be me."

She flashed a high-voltage smile, made her large eyes larger. "He's scary! I saw him stand on his hind legs and put his paws on your shoulders. Out in the parking lot. He's taller than I am."

"It's a she. And she's sweet. Not a mean bone in her body."

"Really? Could I meet her sometime? I like wild things."

"Tuna's pretty domesticated." I kept wishing the slide show would get under way. Conversing with a girl I didn't know made me all jittery.

"Tuna?" She laughed, covered her mouth when she began coughing. "That's a great name. What's yours?"

"Bryan. And you are?"

"Cindy. Maybe I could come by your place some time. Meet Tuna. If it's okay with your girlfriend."

"Oh." I glanced over at Annie, talking to a chubby guy with apple cheeks and compassionate eyes. "She's a friend. I don't have a girlfriend."

"Cool." Cindy smiled, took a long drag and scooted closer. With her came the sweet smell of marijuana and the warm press of her thigh.

Someone turned off the lights, and then the stereo. People scurried to get seated. Big E switched on a projector and inserted the first slide. It showed Big E himself, at the wheel of a truck and wearing a gas mask. "This is me in Elizabeth, New Jersey," he said. "You think L.A.'s got bad air?" Everyone laughed and, on cue, one of the pot smokers had a coughing fit.

The second slide showed a police officer, head tilted down in concentration as he wrote out a traffic ticket. It appeared to be taken from the cab of the same truck as in the first slide. Big E deadpanned, "This is me getting a speeding ticket in Elizabeth, New Jersey." Another wave of laughter.

The next slide showed Big E bending over the innards of a grand piano, an enormous and colorful crowd of people in the background. "This is me putting on the 'Countryman' in Gaelic Park in New York. We opened for Yes."

Someone called out, "Hey, Earnest! Are all the slides about you?"

"No," Big E answered. "Just the best ones."

"What's a 'Countryman'?" someone asked.

"It's an electrostatic piano pickup," Big E explained. "Basically, it turns a piano into an 88-string guitar." He put in the next slide: a rock group playing on an outdoor stage at night, multi-colored spotlights illuminating the stage. The skin of the bass drum read: Icarus. "Ah! Here we have the lads at the Mississippi Mud Festival in front of 30,000 fans. ELP headlined, but the highlight of the evening was when Bobby backed the equipment truck into a trailer and knocked it off its blocks." A ripple of laughter. Several partygoers razzed a guy standing in the doorway and the closest gave him a good-natured shove. It had to be Bobby, from his show of embarrassment.

The slides continued, professional quality and showing an excellent eye for composition. Big E had roughly organized them into categories. For the next ten minutes we viewed slides of rock groups Icarus had played with over the past year of touring. Most were name groups: Rod Stewart, Jethro Tull, Sly and the Family Stone, Bad Company, Humble Pie. Big E narrated, sharing some great stories: how he got drunk with Bad Company and rode around Memphis singing "Hail Britannia" in a limo; how a Humble Pie cigarette accidentally burned down the Whisky-A-Go-Go on Sunset Strip;

how Bobby saved a coked-out Sly Stone when he fell off a stage in Charlotte. I was on my second beer, but couldn't seem to loosen up.

Big E moved on to a rapid-fire sequence of well-known groupies. The infamous Connie in Little Rock, smiling while holding up a bumper sticker that gave out her home phone number. Then the sultry Cinnamon in Chicago, at a dressing room mirror applying lipstick to her generous lips. Tiny Sparkle Plenty in Minneapolis, sitting on the lap of an aging, bespectacled hippie with straggly gray hair.

After the groupies came an assortment of interesting people and places.

Traffic's Stevie Winwood scowling as he played a Steinway onstage at Winterland in San Francisco. The opening act had broken a piano string.

A morbidly obese teenager devouring a Twinkie at an outdoor concert in Wisconsin. At his feet lay a guitar case with a sticker that read: *After flushing your Nixon, wipe your Agnew.*

A tough-looking black biker wearing shades and a studded leather jacket. Comically, a store sign behind him advertised panty hose for 76 cents.

A hump-shouldered bag lady in New York City giving cameraman Big E the finger.

The next slide had everyone helpless with laughter. A Holiday Inn sign read: GOOD FUCK, PAT AND MIKE, THEY DONE IT! Big E chuckled as he explained how he and Bobby the roadie liked to pull into the local Holiday Inn, read the current greeting on their outdoor sign, then change the letters around in the early morning hours. On this particular one, they only had to change the "L" in "LUCK" to an "F," and they were done. *A prank Bigdog himself would have appreciated,* I thought.

The room had become too loud, the hilarious patter closed in on me. I wanted to go outside, breathe fresh air and feel some space around me. But, too self-conscious to get up and move, I stayed put and told myself to relax.

The next slide showed Andy Matson from Icarus, onstage with Sly and the Family Stone. "You won't believe this story," Big E told us, as a rowdy cheer died down. "Sly's lead guitar player got caught in a snowstorm and couldn't make it to Charleston, so Sly asked Andy to sit in for the guy. The gig's in this old theater and about ten of us are in a little viewing room right over the stage and a joint's gettin' passed around. Just as I'm takin' a hit, the door flies open and this big-ass West Virginia cop is standing there with a scowl on his face. I'm thinkin', 'Marijuana possession in the South, ten years in prison.' So the cop steps into room and orders me to hand over the joint. I think about eating it, but give it to him. He smiles, pauses for effect, and then takes a big hit off it. After he exhales, he says, 'Round here, kids call me Smokey the Pig!'"

As the group belly laugh died down, Big E inserted his next slide. "Here we have War Dance at a sound check in Rapid City, South Dakota." Dressed in all black were three tough-looking Indian men with waist-length braids.

My heart stalled. "Oh my God!" I gasped aloud. In the slide, leaning against a light standard on the far side of the stage, was a long-legged Indian girl. She looked exactly like Lydia.

"What is it?" Big E asked. Everyone had stopped talking.

I strained my eyes to be sure, shook my head in disbelief. "I think that's my old girlfriend. She ran away from home . . . up in Washington. I haven't seen her for over four years."

"That's Lydia?" Annie asked, sounding annoyed.

"I'm pretty sure," I replied.

Big E said, "The girl by the lights? She was the bodyguard for War Dance."

"Bodyguard?" Annie again.

"Yeah," Big E explained. "War Dance is known for being militant. Billy White Wolf, the lead singer, pulls in death threats from rednecks. I was told the woman in the picture knew karate."

"Then it has to be her," I said, my heart pounding hard enough to produce a coronary. "She's Indian and she has a black belt in karate."

Annie tugged at my arm. "Are you sure, Bryan? I mean, from that distance . . ."

I nodded, whispering, "Lydia Redstone." Saying her name gave me a strange feeling, like what was happening wasn't real.

"Oh!" Big E exclaimed. "I've got a close up of her. I left it out 'cause it's overexposed." He jumped to his feet and strode purposefully from the room.

"I don't believe it," I muttered.

"Are you okay?" Annie asked, her face now creased with worry.

I nodded. But I didn't feel okay. Shock waves pulsated through my body. The only girl I'd ever loved stared at me from the screen. I could barely draw a breath.

Bobby the roadie said, "I know how you feel, man. We did a gig at a county fair in Buffalo and I ran into an old girlfriend from Pasadena. What was weird was she had this ferret with her. And she'd named it Bobby, after me." Comic relief, for everyone but me.

Big E rushed into the room holding a slide between his thumb and index finger. He inserted it without fanfare. Lydia's mesmerizing beauty jumped from the screen to a chorus of "Wows!" Momentarily, I smiled at the sight of her—Lydia of the amazing cheekbones—standing alongside a set of drums and grabbing for the outer edge of a bronze cymbal. The prairie wind whipped her glossy black hair as she smiled at someone not in the picture. She wore tight-fitting, bleached-out blue jeans and a white peasant blouse with gathered sleeves that showed off her long, lean arms. Though the photograph was slightly overexposed, her nut-brown skin appeared as dark as I'd ever seen it.

"I wanted to take a whole roll of pictures," Big E said, directly to me. "But she caught me taking this one and ordered me to stop. The way she said it, well, let's just say I didn't take any more pictures."

Next to me, Cindy twisted her baby face into bewilderment. "She's beautiful. I can't imagine her working as a bodyguard."

"I can," I murmured, remembering what she did to Jack Montrose. Then I looked at the slide more closely and felt my stomach drop, as if I was standing in an elevator and it suddenly dropped ten floors. On the ring finger of her left hand, the hand reaching for the cymbal, Lydia wore a gold band.

After declining Annie's offer to run me home, I left Big E's with the two slides in a manila envelope. The rush of adrenaline on finding Lydia had dissipated and I needed time alone to sort things out. That she had a gold band on her ring finger seemed incomprehensible, a cosmic error of the cruelest proportion. I jogged the mile to my cabin in the dark, half wishing to get hit by a drunk driver as I crossed busy Topanga Canyon Boulevard.

I reached my front door at the stroke of midnight, hailed by an explosion of fireworks from up and down the canyon. The clamor didn't faze Tuna, who greeted me with a joyous hug (standing on hind legs, tail wagging frantically, paws grasping my shoulders). Dodging her kisses, I told her something amazing had happened. She cocked her head and lowered herself to the floor, sitting attentively at my feet.

The next ten minutes I spent holding the close-up of Lydia to the light over the kitchen table. Something about her smile triggered the memory of a time we made love while left alone in Bigdog's apartment. Afterwards, we got in the shower and took turns soaping each other's bodies beneath a strong stream of piping hot water. We were kissing and laughing, incredibly in love, our bodies luminous from sex. At that moment, I believed I'd been placed on Earth to look at Lydia, caress her, worship her. Looking at the slide, I felt that way again. I leaned it against the white queen on my chessboard and buried my head in my hands. *I love you so much,* I whispered, in awe of her amazing presence and beauty. Unable to even consider sleep, I asked Tuna if she wanted to go for a walk. She bolted to the door and spun in rapid circles.

We wound our way up a favorite path that led to the main fire road. A bomb of a firecracker echoed through the canyon and seconds later a spooked coyote darted in front of us, running into a thicket of scraggly, stunted shrubs. I grabbed Tuna by her leather collar before she could take chase.

The night soon quieted, but not my mind. I'd endured over four years with no idea of Lydia's whereabouts and now I had a chance of contacting her. I marveled at my own dumb luck, yet realized it came with some frightening possibilities. Doing nothing was not an option. One way or another, I had to get word to Lydia. Whether she reciprocated was another story. I felt like a jittery rat in a maze, waiting for the shock that comes with taking a wrong turn.

I stopped, squeezed back my shoulders and massaged my neck. Tuna sniffed at the damp earth. The slide show came to mind. The scene in South

Dakota looked as though it'd been taken in the summer, so I guessed the image of Lydia was less than half a year old. Half a year. I wondered where I had been at the exact moment Big E had taken the picture of Lydia—wondered if I'd been thinking about her—wondered if she'd been thinking about me or remembering some shared moment in our past.

Tuna and I ended up walking for the better part of an hour. I narrowed my options to three. Call Hector and Amelia Cruz in Walla Walla, tell them I knew Lydia's approximate whereabouts and ask for an address or phone number (since I'd eventually find her anyway). The second option, fueled by desperation and more than a tinge of anger, had me showing up unannounced in South Dakota. I knew this strategy would backfire and quickly dismissed it. The final possibility: simply write Lydia a tell-all letter, mail it to the recording company that produced War Dance, and ask them to forward it to her. This one seemed less intrusive, but required me to wait on tenterhooks with no way of knowing the letter actually reached her.

We returned to the cabin, my brain churning out questions like monster waves in an unexpected storm. *Was the gold band a wedding ring? What would happen once I'd contacted her? Would Lydia want to see me? Would rejection push me over the edge?* I took another look at the slides, this time remembering the premonition I'd had before entering Big E's house. I forced myself to get in bed around one-thirty and coaxed Tuna into sleeping next to me. Nerves jangling, I never really fell asleep. Instead, I ruminated to the rhythmic pattern of Tuna's breathing and the off-and-on hum of the refrigerator. By the first hint of dawn, I'd made my decision.

———

By noon the next day I had the slides in the hands of Steve, a USC film major who worked part-time for a place called ProLab Imaging. He'd explained on the phone that it was New Year's Day and they were closed, but $50 off the books for two color photographs convinced him to wait the half-hour it would take me to get to Culver City. While Steve converted the slides into glossy 8x12 prints, I walked to a nearby Orange Julius to kill time. I was too anxious to eat, but enjoyed watching Tuna charm the girl behind the counter for not one, not two, but three free hotdogs, hold the onions.

The prints turned out to be an improvement on Big E's slides. Steve did something to darken-up the one that was overexposed, restoring Lydia's skin to a close likeness of its natural color. On the slide of War Dance at the sound check, he enlarged the portion showing Lydia in the background. He also gave me duplicate prints from each slide. As I handed Steve a worn fifty-dollar bill, he said, "If you don't mind my asking, is this your wife?" He must've noticed the gold band. "Former girlfriend," I answered. He sighed and said, "Too bad."

———

Annie dropped by that afternoon. Seeing the prints spread side by side on my kitchen table, she commented, "You didn't waste any time."

"No fleas on me."

She picked up the one that had been enlarged. "How'd you get prints on New Year's Day?"

"Bribed a struggling college student at a place in Culver City."

Tuna ambled over and bumped Annie playfully, getting a dismissive pat on the head. Annie set down the print and examined the one of Lydia reaching for the cymbal. "I've got to admit, she *is* beautiful."

I nodded. "Yeah, she is, but the thing about Lydia is that she's doesn't know it. And she doesn't try to capitalize on it like most girls. She's just totally down to earth." When Annie didn't respond, I added, "Maybe because she's Indian."

She squared up the two prints. "Why would that matter?"

I thought about the best way to say it. "Indian girls were second class citizens in Walla Walla."

"Oh. So the girl's beautiful and humble. I guess that makes her perfect."

"I didn't say that. Actually, she's just as mixed up as anybody else."

"That's comforting," Annie said, sarcastically. "What're you going to do?"

"Call her parents. Tomorrow night. See if they'll play go-between."

Annie hesitated. "You'd take her back in a minute, wouldn't you?"

I felt caught and couldn't reply.

"Good luck." She turned on her heel and left with a sour expression.

Amelia Cruz answered on the third ring.

I swallowed hard and almost hung up. "Hi Amelia. It's Bryan Matthews."

Slight pause. "No! Bryan. Is it really you?"

"It is." I'd rehearsed a script, but a lump in my throat stopped me from launching into it.

"You won't believe this, but just this weekend Yolanda was talking about you. I served chicken enchiladas for dinner, you're old favorite, and she said, 'I wonder how Bryan's doing?'"

I smiled a little at the thought of Yolanda. "Tell her I'm okay."

"Good. Good! My goodness, Bryan, it's been what . . . four years?"

I went blank for a moment, then recovered. "Four and a half."

"Well, it's good to hear your voice. We felt terrible that we never got to say goodbye to you."

"That was my fault. I had to get out of Walla Walla."

She let it go. "Did you transfer to the U.W.?"

"No. I moved to Southern California about a month after leaving town. I'm working for IBM, teaching a computer how to play chess."

"That sounds interesting. Do you like it?"

I noticed my hand was shaking. "It's challenging. And it keeps me busy. How're you? How's the family?"

"I'm good. Oh, there's so much catching up to do. A year ago, Yolanda married a nice boy from Soap Lake and she's six months pregnant. They're going to have a baby in April."

"Did she move to Soap Lake?"

"No!" she exclaimed. "They live in an apartment a few blocks away, near the train station. Ramon works for Village Hardware and Yolanda's selling the clothes she makes."

"Wow. That's exciting, but it's hard for me to think of you as a grand-mother."

"Me, too. My baby is making a baby. Hector's fine, too. He's become quite the long distance runner. He's training for a marathon that goes from Walla Walla to Waitsburg and back. And . . ." her voice faltered. "I'm sorry, Bryan. I really am. But you know I can't talk to you about Lydia."

I bit my lip. "Actually, Lydia's the reason I called."

The line went momentarily silent. "But Bryan. We're sworn to secrecy. If—"

"I know. I'm not going to ask you to betray Lydia. Just hear me out." I cleared my throat and glanced down at my speaking notes. "By accident, I found out where she's living. It happened last night, at a New Year's Eve party. Only I don't know how to get in touch with her. And I wouldn't ex-pect you to tell me. But I am asking you to get a hold of her and see if it's okay for me to write her a letter."

"You were at a party . . . and you found out where Lydia's living?"

I nodded as if we were talking face to face. "I know. It's the weirdest thing that ever happened. I met someone who saw her at a War Dance con-cert last summer. He took a picture of her. Two pictures. And I know she's living somewhere in South Dakota." *I don't really know that, but if you let it go, I'll assume I'm right.*

Silence again. This time I thought the line had actually gone dead. Then, "How on God's green earth did this person know that you knew Lydia?"

"He didn't. He works for a rock group named Icarus and he was show-ing slides he'd taken on their road trip. One of the pictures he took was of War Dance and Lydia was in the background."

She took a moment, presumably to digest what I'd said. "So you want me to tell Lydia you know where she is and ask if it's okay for you to write her a letter? And that's all?"

I nodded again. "That's all. That way, you don't have to tell me a thing."

A short pause. "I don't know if she'll go for it."

"She probably won't."

Audible sigh. "Well, I don't see the harm in telling her you called."

"There isn't any, or I wouldn't ask you to do it. I'll give you my address and phone number and she can make the first move. If she doesn't want to hear from me, she doesn't have to do anything. And that'll be it."

Long pause. "Why exactly do you want to get in touch with her?"

I'd anticipated this question. "Because I still love her and I want to know how she's doing. You know, what's happened in her life."

"A lot has happened, Bryan."

I woke the next morning feeling frightened and alone. After Stubblefield, my life had been on hold, a careful routine intended to ward off intense feelings. I couldn't let go of Lydia because losing the possibility of being together meant losing what was left of me. The slide show had stripped me defenseless and released a flood of anxiety.

I spent some time studying the prints of Lydia, then tried writing a column on the Trompowsky Attack, a popular opening for club players. Unable to concentrate and looking for an excuse to be around people, I herded Tuna into the car and drove over to Big E's to return his slides.

Doe-eyed Cindy answered the door with a welcoming smile. Even with no makeup and disheveled hair, she looked every bit as cute as she had on New Year's Eve. On seeing Tuna she squealed with delight, not at all intimidated by her size. After answering the usual question about how I'd acquired a wolf hybrid (I owned up to hitting her, but omitted the part about being suicidal and driving like a fool), Cindy led me through the house and into Big E's backyard.

Big E sat at a badly warped picnic table and spooned wildflower honey onto Ak-Mak crackers. "Is this your dog?" he gushed.

"Yeah, this is Tuna." As if on cue, she loped over to Big E, who carefully extended the back of his hand to be sniffed.

"She's half wolf and half Malamute," Cindy explained. "Isn't she beautiful?"

"For sure! Hey, man," he said, turning to me. "You missed the end of the slide show."

"Sorry. I had to go. Here're your slides." I set them on the table.

He licked his fingers and grinned. "Thanks. Don't think I've ever gotten such a big reaction from one of my photos."

I smiled, embarrassed. "I wouldn't think so. Speaking of which, I don't know if you noticed the gold band on my old girlfriend's finger, but I was wondering. Did you get the impression she was married to one of the guys in the band?"

He looked away for a moment, shook his head slowly. "I didn't get that impression, but most of the time I was pretty busy setting up for the show and all."

"Okay. I was just wondering."

"Hey. Mind if I take some pictures of you and Tuna?"

"Sure. Could I get copies?"

Big E broke into a lopsided smile. "Of course." He rose up from the table and took a few long strides into the house.

Cindy followed him in with her eyes then looked at me. "Are you going to try to find the girl in the picture?"

"Yeah. I already called her mother."

She nodded, approvingly. "Good move. Fate has to be involved when you find an old girlfriend in such an unlikely way."

I drew a deep breath. "If she's married, fate screwed up."

She shrugged. "Maybe. Maybe not. Things happen for a reason."

"Well, I hope it's a good reason."

"How'd you meet her?"

"On the way home from a keg party in the mountains. Some friends of mine rolled their truck and she stopped to help." I thought about Ethan and Slider, a gnawing emptiness developing in my chest.

Cindy smiled knowingly. "That sounds like fate, too."

Tuna placed her gigantic paws on top of the table and snuffled the box of crackers. Cindy spread a liberal amount of honey on a cracker and fed it to her.

"Now you've got a friend for life," I said.

"Yeah,' she giggled, as Tuna accepted the treat. "Look at those teeth! I think I'd have named you 'Teeth.'"

I smiled. Cindy had good feminine energy.

Big E reappeared with a camera around his neck and an assortment of lenses cradled in his long arms. He stopped, set his equipment on the table and surveyed the yard. "The light's really good over there," he told me. He gestured toward the dappled shade of a California pepper tree, its trunk heavy and fantastically gnarled. "Could you get her over there?"

"Sure," I answered. "Give me a cracker."

The phone was ringing when I got back from Big E's. I dashed inside and picked up, but no one was there. "Shit!" *What if it was Lydia? Why couldn't I have gotten here five seconds earlier?* I beamed up a prayer for Lydia to call me and resolved to sit near the phone for the rest of the day.

By suppertime I'd finished my article on the Trompowsky Attack and made myself two peanut butter and sweet onion sandwiches, sharing the second one with Tuna (after plucking off the onion, which Annie swore was bad for dogs). By eight o'clock I was seriously considering calling Amelia Cruz to see if she'd succeeded in relaying my message to Lydia. Then, the phone rang.

"Hello."

"Bryan?"

"Yeah. Who's this?" A voice from the past. I couldn't quite place it.

"It's Yolanda."

My voice brightened. "Oh, God. Yolanda. How are you?"

"Good." She laughed. "Really good, now that the morning sickness is gone."

"Your Mom told me the good news. When are you due? I forget."

"Mid-April. But I'm already big as a house, so I think it might be sooner."

I imagined chubby Yolanda with a huge tummy. A female Buddha. "That's great. Are you happy?"

"Very happy. My husband, Ramon, he's really cool. You'd like him. And I'm selling some of my swimwear to Nordstrom's up in Seattle."

"Fabulous. Lydia always said you'd be a famous designer."

A brief pause. "Mom hasn't been able to reach Lydia. The band she works for, War Dance, is on a road trip for three more weeks."

"Oh."

"That's why I called," she explained. "I didn't want you to read too much into not hearing anything."

"Thanks, Yolanda. I appreciate it."

"Mom told me how you found Lydia. Pretty incredible."

I closed my eyes. "Yeah. I'm still in shock."

Another pause. "Do you still love her?"

"I do." *Take a chance.* "Is there any reason for hope?"

Yolanda sighed. I heard a TV in the background, canned laughter. "I can't answer that without giving stuff away. And I—"

"I understand. I just want Lydia to know we can be in touch if she wants."

"She's probably not going to get your message for awhile. When they go on tour they're basically incommunicado till they get back. It's the Indian way, if you know what I mean."

"Free as the wind?"

She chuckled. "Yeah. If I had quintuplets tomorrow, we still couldn't get word to her."

"Okay," I said. "I'll try to be patient, but it's not my long suit."

"Oh, I don't know about that. I remember watching you play chess."

"Chess is different. When I'm playing chess I'm in control."

"I'll tell you this much, Bryan. No one's in control when it comes to my sister. The last time you saw her, that's the last time I saw her, too."

Time did not fly over the next three weeks. Not over the fourth, either. I stayed as close to the phone as my life would allow, always disappointed when the rare call I received had nothing to do with Lydia. Every day I checked the mailbox with the same outcome. I sank into a bog of pessimism.

During the first week of February, I was watching TV. The Lakers were playing a road game at Madison Square Garden and play-by-play man Chick Hearn had just announced " . . . Jerry West faked his man into the popcorn machine." I jumped up, remembering the bag of carrots I'd bought for Popcorn. I was halfway to the corral when the phone rang. I dropped the bag and sprinted back inside, my hopes running wild with possibility. "Hello, this is Bryan," I half shouted into the receiver.

"Hi Bryan. It's Amelia. Have you been running?"

"Not really. I was on my way to the corral. That's all."

"You have a horse?"

"My neighbor does. What's happening?" I pressed the receiver to my ear.

"Lydia says you can write her."

My heart skipped a beat. "She does. Really?"

"Really and truly. I'd left a message with John, uh . . . I left a message to have her call me as soon as she got back from the road trip. And she just called a half-hour ago."

Who's John? I wondered, thinking of the gold band. "Did you tell her how I found her?"

"I did. She remembered Icarus. Did I say that right?"

"Yeah—"

Speaking faster than usual, Amelia said, "She even remembered the fellow that took the picture of her. Said he was a big guy."

"Yeah. They call him Big E." *God bless his soul!*

"So anyway, I told her that you wanted to write. Do you—"

"How'd she react?" I asked.

She paused briefly. "I don't know. At first she thought she might like to write you first, but then she thought it over and said it was okay. To tell the truth, I'd have expected more of a reaction."

"Me, too."

"Do you have a pencil handy?"

"Yeah, go ahead."

"Her address is 144 Feather Road, Kyle, South Dakota. It's on the Pine Ridge Reservation."

I wanted to ask a hundred questions, starting with "who's John?" Knowing better, I said, "I really appreciate this. It means a lot to me."

"It's not a problem. Hey, Hector wants to say hi. Take care of yourself."

She put the phone down and a moment later Hector came on. "Bryan. How the heck are you?"

"Pretty good, Hector. I heard you're training for a marathon. Twenty-six miles, right?"

"Twenty-six *point two* miles. They say it's the point two that hurts the most."

I forced a laugh. "No doubt." My mind was elsewhere.

"Hey, when you write that daughter of mine, tell her to get her rear end off the rez. I don't care how tough she thinks she is, it's too danger-ous."

February 5, 1974

Dear Lydia,

I hope you're not angry with me. I guess Amelia told you how I found you, though I know it's hard to believe. So you have the story straight, I went with my neighbor to a bar on New Year's Eve and we ended up at someone's house for a slide show. This happened in Topanga, California, which is where I've been living the last four years. The guy that gave the slide show is the road manager for Icarus and something of a photographer. Anyway, he was showing us slides of their road trip and it was almost over when he put one up of War Dance at a sound check in Rapid City—and there you were, standing alongside an amplifier in the background. I couldn't believe my eyes. He also had a close up of you, laughing with the wind in your hair. I was stunned by how beautiful you are.

I've thought a lot about what to say in this letter and decided to make it short and as honest as I know how to be. There's no point in telling you what I've been doing if you still want me out of your life. If nothing's changed. But a few things must be said to be true to myself. The first is I still love you. I love you every bit as much as I did when we were teenagers. I love you with all my heart and soul and nothing will ever change that. It's been hard knowing you're out there, but not knowing where. It felt wrong. I never got used to the idea of not being together, and I'm not sure I ever will. Often I would catch myself thinking . . . Lydia is laughing with a friend, or Lydia is listening to a Buffy album, or Lydia is braiding her hair, or Lydia is having trouble falling asleep. Then it would hit me that I don't even know where you are and my heart would break. When you left me you said I'd forget about you and find someone else. Someone better. You couldn't have been more wrong.

I apologize again for the jerk I was after Stubblefield. My first reaction was out of shock and I made your burden worse. I'm very sorry. I wish I could take my words back and do it over again, get it right. It took a long time but I finally realized what you did was the right thing—that you saved our lives. And now I think I know the price you paid in the process. You said I let you down when you needed me most, and you were right. I only hope you can someday forgive me.

There's so much more I could say. More than four years has passed. You may have a man in your life, maybe even a husband or children. Your family hasn't told me a thing. If you choose not to answer this letter, I won't write again. I'll leave you alone if that's what you want. I'm praying you'll write me back—even if it's to tell me not to write you again (not my favorite outcome).

Love always, Bryan

I mailed the letter and endured two weeks of a low and anxious feeling that gained momentum with every passing day. The path I'd chosen seemed flanked by despair on one side and rejection on the other. My life turned into a mass of longing that could only be relieved by Lydia. I chastised myself for daring to hope, for dreaming of eternal love, for being a sentimental fool, for swerving from the relative safety of chess. Unexpectedly, I wished my love would begin to retreat. I considered trying to make it work with Annie, but images of Lydia intruded on me like a migraine.

Then, a blessing I could scarcely believe – a letter from Lydia found its way into my mailbox. My heart nearly stopped as I recognized her graceful handwriting and sniffed the envelope for her scent. I wanted to hold myself back before opening it, maybe go for a run and try to convince myself I'd be okay regardless of what she said. But instead I tore it open and read it right there.

February 26
Dear Bryan,

I don't know what to say. The way you found me was so weird I almost didn't believe you at first. Then I remembered the big guy that took my picture. I guess I'm surprised you still love me after the awful way I ended things. We both did badly. I felt really bad when Yolanda told me you'd dropped out of Whitman. I know how much you loved your fraternity brothers and Dr. Z and that you'd have never left if I hadn't left you behind. And I'm sorry for telling my family not to talk to you. Looking back on how crazy things were at the time, we did our best, but we were too young to handle what happened. Way too young. Even if we were older we would have been overwhelmed. It took me a long time, but I came to forgive you for anything you might have said. We're both sorry, so let's call a truce.

What has happened with your chess? Amelia said something about teaching computers to play. Anyway, I wouldn't be surprised if you're one of the top players in the world by now. We're kind of isolated here and maybe I should've read something about you, but I haven't.

Momma died shortly after I last saw you, and I got to see her before she passed. Not too long after, I ended up on the Pine Ridge Reservation, where I've been ever since. I got a part-time job teaching karate to a bunch of junior high kids who reminded me of me at their age, only they're wilder and angrier and drink like maniacs. Then I got a job working as a bodyguard for War Dance. People either love or hate Billy White Wolf, the lead singer. The FBI is out to get him because he's vocal about them interfering with our affairs. Billy gets a lot of threats, and not just from rednecks, but from Indians on the rez, too. In case you don't know, it's very violent here and even more complicated. Tomorrow we go to Chicago for a recording session, which is good. I feel safer when we're on the road.

Hearing from you is confusing, to say the least. I'm going to need awhile to sort out my feelings. I was okay when Amelia told me you found me, but it scares me to think about you. There are a lot of memories and only you know how bad some of them are. What does it mean if we resume a friendship? I honestly don't know, but if you want to write me again it's okay. As the Sioux say . . .

Walk in Beauty, Lydia

P.S. After Chicago we have a gig at Chuck Berry's farm outside of St. Louis. I'll be riding in a helicopter for the first time. Egad! I'll be gone at least two weeks so if you write back, don't expect a return letter right away.

A gust of relief swept over me. No word on whether she was with someone, but no news could possibly mean good news. Or, maybe not, given that I'd hinted about a man in her life and she'd chosen not to respond. *Because there is someone, but it's none of my business? Could it be John . . . the name Amelia accidentally dropped on the phone? Maybe Lydia's unattached but still not interested in me.* My brain swam with possibilities, some depressing, some too exciting to be considered for more than a fleeting moment. I ran to the cabin, reread her letter and wrote back immediately.

March 3, 1974
Dearest Lydia,
Alas, my chess is a bit of a sore subject. After Stubblefield my game took a turn for the worse. I study chess every day, but seldom play and don't have the passion I once had. I did play in the West Coast Open a couple years ago and finished second. Another good showing in tournament play and I'll have my Grandmaster rating. So that's good. Amelia's right, I work for IBM and teach a computer named Endgame how to play. I'm proud to say it can already beat good amateurs. I also write a monthly column for the Los Angeles Times.
Guess what? I have a dog. Her name is Tuna. You'd love her. She's half-wolf, half-Malamute and weighs 120 lbs. She has the disposition of a Malamute but every once in awhile she weirds out and does something that's neither wolf nor dog—like when she sleeps on top of my neighbor's car and won't budge till the car moves. I've enclosed a picture of Tuna and me that was taken in January. Ironically, it was taken by Big E, the guy who took the pictures of you in Rapid City.
How was the helicopter ride? Did you meet Chuck Berry? I've heard he's a letch.
Oh God, Lydia. I can't do this. Making small talk and acting like old friends catching up. I have to be real. How could you be surprised I still love you? I don't get that. Did you think I didn't mean it when I said I'd always love you? Remember my housemother at Davis-Jacobs, Mom Waters? Remember the beautiful crystal she had in her room? I know I mentioned it to you because you told me you wrote it down in that journal you did for English class. Anyway, Mom passed away not too long ago and left me the crystal in her will. It's on my bookshelf. I'm looking at it as I write and it expresses exactly what I feel about you. "Chance cannot change my love nor time impair."
The truth is you took the best part of me with you. I've been floundering ever since we've been apart. I even tried being with someone else, an experiment that failed miserably. I felt sick to my stomach when I saw the ring on

your left hand. Please tell me if you have a husband or a boyfriend. If you're committed to someone, it's better for me to know now and let you go—once and for all. If there's any chance at all we could try to put it back together, I'll walk to South Dakota to see you.

Love always, Bryan

March 14

Dear Bryan,

Thank you for your brave letter. You're still honest about your feelings. I always liked you for that. Some things never change. Sorry to hear about Mom Waters. I remember how she was special to you. I was also sorry to hear you've lost your passion for chess. But you'll get it back.

Thanks for the picture. Tuna is gorgeous. So are you. My God, Bryan, your hair is way past your shoulders. I love it! Where did you get those curls? And you're so tan from living in California that I can't call you Paleface anymore. What's the world coming to when a nice Indian girl can't tease a white boy about the color of his skin?

I'm not ready to tell you all that's happened to me, but you deserve some answers. No, I don't have a boyfriend or a husband, or a child. I went with Billy White Wolf, the lead singer for War Dance, for almost two years. I met him at his thirtieth birthday party. The band gave him a harmonica as a gift. He'd never picked one up but by the end of the party he could play it as good as Magic Dick in J. Geils Band. Everyone was blown away, including me. I fell for him right there. Billy's like an angrier version of Buffy. Listen to the lyrics on "Trail of Tears," you'll see. Unfortunately, he got a big head when the "Warpath" album made the top ten. He started doing cocaine and I caught him cheating on me. That was it. I haven't been with anyone the last two years and I like it that way. The gold band on my finger? I started wearing it when I was with Billy because guys were always hitting on me and it made him crazy jealous. I still wear it because being on the road with a rock group is weird. When I take it off I get the kind of attention I don't want.

As far as trying to put things back together, it wouldn't work. I still care about you or I wouldn't be writing, but that's different than trying to rekindle romantic feelings. Besides, it's been a long time and you're a couple thousand miles away. Remember what happened to me at the Pendleton Roundup as a kid. I've decided that being in love is like being trapped on the Gravitron—feeling totally out of control. Being alone is so much easier.

Walk in Beauty, Lydia

I sat with Lydia's letter for a week, rereading it over and over, my heart wrenching in response to her turning away from love. Like never before I saw myself as flawed, yet our exchange of letters had amplified my longing. The best moments I spent running or playing with Tuna, activities that temporarily got me out of my head.

One afternoon the phone rang while I was outside chopping wood. I got it on the sixth or seventh ring. "Hello," I answered.

"Bryan."

Instant goose bumps. "Lydia?"

"Hi, Bryan."

I pushed aside an impulse to cry. "Oh, God. It's good to hear your voice. Really good."

"Am I calling at an okay time?"

"Yeah, I uh . . . I just had a cord of orangewood delivered and I was outside splitting it up."

"You burn orangewood out there?"

I felt my heart pounding at the back of my throat. "Yeah. It's got to be the hardest wood in the world."

She paused. "I started writing you another letter, but . . . it just seemed easier to call."

I untangled the phone line and sat on the edge of my bed. "I'm so glad you called. Just . . . surprised. How are you?"

"I'm okay. Cold. It snowed about four inches today. I stayed inside and watched *The Wizard of Oz* on TV. I'd never seen it before."

"Oh. It was in the seventies here," I said, fighting a queasy, hyperventilating kind of feeling.

She chuckled. "If you're trying to make me jealous, it's working."

I let out a little nervous laugh, tried to think of something else to say. "Thanks for being so honest in your letter."

"We were always honest with each other."

"We were," I agreed. "Even when it hurt." *You're doing okay so far.*

"That was good. Especially considering how young we were."

I realized I'd been holding my breath. "Yeah," I answered, exhaling.

"It feels strange to be talking again."

"For me too. But good strange."

She went silent for a moment. "Strange and confusing."

"That doesn't surprise me. I sort of reappeared out of nowhere." I looked out the window, saw Tuna gnawing on an orangewood log. "I was afraid you'd tell me to bug off."

"The thought crossed my mind. But I'm not going to do that."

I looked up and silently thanked God. "Maybe we could just play it by ear? See what happens?"

"Playing things by ear scares me. I need to plan things out."

"Okay. What's the plan?"

She chuckled. "I wish I knew. Hey, do you keep in touch with the old crowd. What's Slider doing? And Ethan?"

"I haven't kept up very well. Slider's in the minor leagues in the Pirates organization. I guess he's playing winter ball in Puerto Rico. At least that's what Vicky Spotts told me."

"Vicky?! God, there's a blast from the past."

"Yeah, she paid me an unexpected visit a couple months ago. You'd barely recognize her she's so skinny from doing coke."

"Doesn't surprise me in the least. The coke part, anyway. What was she doing in California?"

"Drug deal," I answered. "I made her leave after ten minutes."

She laughed. "You should've let me beat her up at the drive-in. Remember that?"

"Of course. It was our first date. She made you spill our popcorn and Cokes."

"Worse. She called me a 'skinny Indian bitch.'"

I closed my eyes. "That was almost five years ago. Do you believe it?"

"Not really. It doesn't seem possible. What's happened with Ethan?"

I felt exposed for losing track of such dear friends. "I think he's at M.I.T. Starting graduate school in engineering."

"Is he still playing chess?"

"I'm not sure. I think he kind of gave it up after leaving Whitman. The head injury took away some of his competitive fire."

"I hope he's happy," she told me. "Slider, too."

Happiness. What's that? I shook my head to clear the negative thought. "So, I hear you're going to be Aunt Lydia."

She laughed. "I always said it'd be Yolanda before me."

"Did you? I don't remember that." *I remember making love—*

"It's true. Yolanda used to complain 'cause I had more boyfriends. And I told her she'd be the first to marry and first to have kids. Turns out I was right on both counts."

Thank God, I thought. "Have you met her husband?"

"Ramon. No, but Hector and Amelia say he's cool. If he can get past Hector, he's got to be okay."

I smiled. "That's for sure."

"That's sort of why I called."

"What is?"

"Yolanda. She wants me to be with her when she delivers. When we were little, even before we were sisters, we pretended our dolls were our babies. And we promised to be there when the other became a mommy."

My jaw dropped. It seemed unthinkable. "You're not going back to Walla Walla."

"I *am* going. At first I said I wouldn't and Yolanda was really hurt."

"Because she doesn't understand—"

"Right. I never told her about what happened. But there's another reason to go."

"What?" I asked.

She took a second. "I've been seeing a Sioux Medicine Man on the rez. His name's Marvin Tall Bear. Listen to this. He's one of the fifty that survived the massacre at Wounded Knee."

"Wow! That was a long time ago."

"1890. Tall Bear was only five, but he remembers the machine guns shredding the teepees."

"Not to mention men, women and children," I added.

"That, too. He's eighty-eight, but his mind is sharp as a tack and you wouldn't want to fight him."

"Cool," I said, wondering where she was headed.

"Tall Bear says I should go back to Stubblefield and perform a healing ritual."

"You told him what happened?"

"I did. I couldn't sleep." She lowered her voice. "And Bryan, be careful what you say. There's always a chance the FBI is listening to us."

"Are you serious?"

"Absolutely. They open our mail, too."

"Pigs!"

"You got that right. Anyway, Tall Bear says a dark wind blew over us. That it's still affecting me and I need to do a healing ritual to cleanse my body and make myself whole again."

"To cleanse your body?"

"Yeah. I don't always know what he means, but I'm still haunted by what happened. It's what I see when I close my eyes at night. Then I fall asleep and have nightmares."

"Me too," I said. "It's like watching a horror movie and the scariest scene just keeps playing and playing."

"Really? That happens to you?"

"All the time. Flashbacks, full-blown panic attacks, you name it." My hands had gone cold. I jammed the phone between my shoulder and ear and tucked them under my armpits for warmth.

"Tall Bear wants me to take sacred soil from Wounded Knee . . . the 'dust of our ancestors,' he calls it, and sprinkle it out at Stubblefield. I'm supposed to burn some plants, too. It probably sounds hocus-pocus if you're not Indian."

"And you're going to do it?"

"Yeah. Tall Bear says he can see holes in my spirit body, which means my energy is draining away. That if I don't do it soon I'm going to die before I get old."

A momentary panic seized me. "Then you should."

"I know, but I'm scared. What if I run into Detective Gerritsen? What if I get out to the cemetery and flip out?"

"You won't," I reassured her. "You were strong enough to survive it the first time, you can certainly handle it now."

Silence. "Thanks, Bryan. That really helps." She paused again. "The first time I saw Tall Bear was a couple years ago. I told him about Stubblefield and he told me you should be there when I do the ritual. And I had an excuse. I said I didn't even know where you were."

I put the receiver back in my hand. "Only now you do."

"And I told him that a couple days ago. He told me our energies are woven together by what happened, like different colored threads making a pattern in a blanket. That if I do the ritual without the Wasichu boy, I'll only undo my half of the pattern."

"I'm surprised he'd want you to involve a white man."

She chuckled again. "Tall Bear says there are some good Wasichu. There just weren't any at Wounded Knee."

"I'd be honored to go." *Hell, I'll show up in a clown costume and crawl over broken glass if it means I get to be with you.*

She cleared her throat. "But I'm not sure it's a good idea to see you."

"Why? It's not like we're getting back together." A hummingbird rocketed in to the feeder just outside my window. The Leaner. I tuned her out.

"I know. But I don't want you to get your hopes up and get hurt again."

"I don't see how going to the cemetery to do a healing ritual—"

"It wouldn't, but we'd be together, and your letter said you think you still love me."

"I didn't say I *think* I love you. I said I love you. There's a difference."

Her voice softened. "I know, Bryan. That's what makes me think you could get hurt again. But I've given it a lot of thought and it's your call. I'm going to Walla Walla to be with Yolanda when she delivers. Then I'm going out to Stubblefield. If you want to join me, it's okay."

"Do you want me to?"

"I do," she answered without hesitation. "I want to do it together. But I don't want you to read anything into that."

I looked out the window. The Leaner, perched at the feeder, leaned way back and appeared on the verge of tumbling backwards and crashing to the earth. I swallowed, willed myself to speak. "Lydia. Tell me you have no feelings for me. Tell me there's no chance of us getting back together."

There was a long pause, followed by an audible sigh. "I can't say that, Bryan."

With wings supplying lift but not propulsion, The Leaner backed slowly away from the feeder, then zoomed upwards into the brilliant sunlight.

Chapter 12
The .38 Special

Lydia planned to drive to Walla Walla, arriving no later than April 10. I would drive up Highway 395, skirt Reno, and continue north through eastern Oregon. Pretty much a straight shot. My twenty-year old Chevy had had a succession of engine problems, so I traded it in on a like-new Volvo 122S. I expected to reach town the same day as Lydia.

I paced the cabin for an hour before phoning the Zaleskis to tell them I'd be visiting in less than two weeks. Dr. Z recognized my voice immediately and called Reva to the phone. Though excited at the prospect of talking chess, he was curious about my reasons for coming. I told him it was a chance to see Lydia and he let it go, though I could sense his unease and felt certain it had to do with my having referred to the Montrose case as a homicide before leaving Walla Walla. Reva spoke up, insisting I stay in my old room in the basement. I warned them I'd have Tuna with me, but both professed to be dog lovers. I accepted their invitation, vowing to myself to make amends for my years of selfish withdrawal.

Early on the morning of April 9, I set out for Walla Walla. The night before Kaalaea had given me one of her stuffed animals as a good luck charm, the little green dinosaur named Vanilla. She told me Vanilla would keep me from forgetting her and her Mommy and when I looked over at Annie clearing dinner dishes I noticed her eyes had filled with tears. I stored the critter in my glove compartment not only because Tuna would chew it up, but also because the sight of it touched off sharp pangs of guilt.

I drove fourteen hours straight, obsessing about Lydia. *Will she want to hug me or declare all touching off limits? Will I know what to say or be stricken dumb? Will she be open to the possibility of getting back together?* I considered every possible thing that could go wrong—saying something that would brand me as weak and desperate—touching her in an unwelcome way and watching her recoil in disgust—being seen out at Stubblefield and inviting the attention of Detective Gerritsen.

Tuna and I spent the night in the Wagon Wheel Motel just outside Burns, Oregon. The woman behind the counter, busy smoking unfiltered cigarettes and painting her fingernails hot pink, insisted the dog would have to sleep in the car. A brief introduction and a ten-dollar tip changed her mind.

Our room had a western motif with lodgepole pine furniture and beige wallpaper that showed a cowboy lassoing a running calf from his horse. Its downside was a wall-mounted deer trophy (a buck with a handsome rack of antlers) that agitated Tuna, who alternately growled and whimpered for

twenty annoying minutes. Unable to reassure her, I covered the dead in-
truder with a wool blanket from the bed. It worked and Tuna fell asleep,
exhausted from having spent the entire day watching the road pass by.

I myself didn't so much sleep as enter a weird trance, ruminating about
the prospect of seeing Lydia and warning myself not to blow it by coming
on too strong. I longed for real rest, but the act of racing toward Walla
Walla had set off an avalanche of fearful imagination and bright, concentrated passion. At one point I even considered going out to the car to get
Vanilla the dinosaur to comfort me. Instead, I rolled over and followed my
breathing, registering the occasional sound of a car whizzing by on the
highway.

We were back on the road by seven a.m., winding our way through first
the Malheur National Forest and then the Umatilla in northeastern Oregon. The dim gray light of early morning gave way to dazzling sunshine and
spectacular mountain views, but I couldn't get my mind off Lydia.

Five hours later we passed the Milton-Freewater Drive-In, one of my
old haunts. I thought about the time Lydia and I went there to see *Little
Big Man*, one of the first and few movies where Hollywood showed any
sympathy to the Indians. I smiled, remembering a scene where Chief Dan
George turns to the Dustin Hoffman character and says, "My heart soars
like an eagle." I still felt queasy, but knowing I'd soon see Lydia made my
heart soar like a dozen eagles.

The spring wheat shimmered under bright sunlight as I wove my way
through the fields that separated Oregon and Washington. Minutes later I
found myself driving through downtown Walla Walla, which proved to be a
nerve-wracking task. My eyes flitted right and left and I almost choked
when I saw Leslie Vanzandt, Vicky Spotts' best friend, coming out of the
Baker-Boyer National Bank. She was stuffing papers into a pocketsize
purse and momentarily looked up, but Tuna was riding shotgun and
blocked her view.

I chastised myself for a close call and took the next right to get off the
main drag, as left would've put me too close to the police station. I drove a
back way to the Zaleski's, my stomach churning as I got closer. Turning
onto Alvarado Terrace, I caught a glimpse of the Phi Delt house and felt a
bittersweet longing for the innocence of my college days. It evaporated as I
set eyes on the Zaleski's home, the place where I'd spent the best and worst
summer of my life. Tuna, who somehow sensed we'd reached our destination, squeezed her way through the bucket seats and turned circles in the
close confines of the back seat.

I parked at the curb and took a deep breath, then marched to the front
door with Tuna in tow. Dr. Z answered my knock, stepped onto the porch
and locked me a bear hug that literally lifted my feet off the ground. Tuna
watched from ten feet away, sniffing at Reva's springtime flowerbed of brilliant orange, yellow and red primroses.

Stepping back, Dr. Z sized me up and said, "I didn't think I'd ever see
you again." His eyes were moist.

Feeling both awkward and touched by his uncharacteristic display of emotion, I replied, "I wouldn't have let that happen."

He cleared his throat. "And this must be Tuna. My, you weren't kidding, she *is* a big girl." Tuna bounded up the porch steps and greeted Dr. Z like he was her new best friend.

A moment later Reva rushed into the entryway, looking no older than the last time I'd seen her. "Ah, Bryan. My goodness is good to see you. Vat beautiful hair!" We embraced and kissed each other's cheeks.

"Bryan's or Tuna's?" Dr. Z deadpanned.

We laughed and went inside, Dr. Z carrying my new canvas duffel bag while Reva oohed and aahed over Tuna's beauty and size. It took but a few minutes to get situated, then I phoned the Cruz' to see if Lydia had arrived. She hadn't, but Amelia said she'd called several hours earlier from Idaho Falls, which would put her in Walla Walla between eight and nine that evening. Amelia could barely contain her excitement. "I have one daughter delivering a baby and the other home for the first time in five years," she gushed. "Life is good!"

I went upstairs and listened to the Zaleskis apologize for the unseasonably warm weather. Permission was granted to bathe Tuna in the backyard. Reva assisted by carrying one bucket of warm water after another from the kitchen sink. After extracting the last residue of shampoo from Tuna's thick coat, I brushed her out, leaving giant mounds of white and gray hair. Reva said it looked like they'd had a late snowfall and suggested we leave the hair for the birds to use for nest building. Tuna looked magnificent. Dr. Z took pictures with the same camera they'd always had.

I took a much-needed nap for the rest of the afternoon. I woke up groggy and disoriented, but startled to my feet on realizing Tuna had left the room. I ran upstairs and found her in the kitchen eating Reva's corned beef and cabbage from a large metal bowl. "I hope that was light on the cabbage," I told Reva. She smiled impishly.

During supper, I told the Zaleskis the slide show story and how Lydia and I agreed to meet while she attended Yolanda's delivery. I left out any discussion of the healing ritual at Stubblefield Cemetery. Then Dr. Z and I retired to his study for a game of chess. I felt grateful to have something to do while waiting for Lydia's phone call.

As we set up the board we discussed game twenty-one from the 1972 Fischer-Spassky World Chess Championship in Reykjavik, Iceland. Spassky had inexplicably blundered twice in the endgame, allowing Bobby Fischer to end twenty-four years of Russian domination of the title. Dr. Z wondered aloud if Bobby had lost his grip on reality despite playing brilliantly and winning the match. I drew White and opened pawn to queen four, then followed with the early development of my bishop.

"Ah, the Trompowsky," Dr. Z commented as he moved his knight in response. "A most complicated opening. Like the Stonewall without the bad bishop. I'm not surprised you'd take it up."

The game progressed quickly. Dr. Z played aggressively, placing me in check with his queen on the fourth move and forcing me to abandon the usual outposts for my knights. After seventeen moves his center began to fall and I was able to use an open queen file to good effect. Unable to save the game, he resigned.

"Reva, come look at this," Dr. Z hollered.

Reva came into the study with Tuna on her heels. "Vat?"

Dr. Z shook his head. "Bryan beat me in twenty-six moves."

"Good boy, Bryan," she laughed, slapping my back. "For putting old man in his place, you vill get delicious dessert."

"Amazing," Dr. Z said. "My current crop of students can't touch me. You hand me my head before my seat is warm. I'll show them this game so they'll know what inspired chess looks like."

"Thanks," I said. "What ability I have, I owe to you. I mean it."

He placed his hands over his chest. "Thank you, Bryan. The work you've done on the Endgame project has paid great dividends. You should enter the U.S. Chess Championship in the fall. Go head to head with Bobby Fischer."

"Actually, I got an application in the mail. I'm thinking about entering."

The phone rang in the kitchen. We looked at one another and I rushed in to get it, like I still lived there. "Hello . . . Zaleski residence." My heart was in my throat.

"Bryan?"

I lowered myself to the floor. Now my heart pounded, not just in my chest but in my throat and temples and groin. "Hi Lydia."

"Guess what? I'm right across town."

"Wow! How're you doin'?" I glanced at the clock on the stove. Nine-thirty. *Probably too late to see her tonight.*

"Pretty wiped out from the long drive. I'm going to catch up with the family and go to bed. How about we get together tomorrow about noon? I need to sleep in."

I tried to tune out my mind's uncontrollable anticipation of the longed-for moment. "Fine. You want me to pick you up?"

"Let's meet at Pioneer Park. It'll be more private. There's some stuff I want to tell you."

Is she going to give us a chance or end it forever? "Okay. At the gazebo?"

"Perfect. Do you have Tuna with you?"

"I always have Tuna with me."

"Good. I'll see you guys tomorrow."

I placed the receiver on the hook, turned around and looked into the concerned eyes of Dr. Z and Reva.

I reached Pioneer Park a few minutes early. After slipping a choke chain over Tuna's head, we walked through the parking lot in the direction of the grassy lawn. The sky was clear, the temperature more moderate than the day before, perfect for spring. Tuna struggled against the leash, which she hated with every ounce of her being, but it was a Saturday and the park bustled with activity. Her size and wolfish appearance frightened people, especially other dog owners and parents with young children. We passed a convertible with the top down, radio booming Country Joe McDonald's anti-war anthem, *I-Feel-Like-I'm-Fixin'-To-Die.*

> *Well, come on mothers throughout the land,*
> *Pack your boys off to Vietnam,*
> *Come on fathers don't hesitate,*
> *Send 'em off before it's too late.*
> *Be the first one on your block*
> *To have your boy come home in a box.*

I shook my head in disgust. The war was over, but only because Congress had cut off funding. Nixon would've kept on sending troops till another 50,000 died. *And Vietnam was what pushed Montrose over the edge. Why couldn't he have come home in a box? My life . . . Lydia's life, would've been completely different.*

I headed over to the pond. A grade school boy with Buddy Holly glasses fed the geese and ducks from a paper bag full of breadcrumbs. The kid showed off a good arm, reminding me of Lydia throwing balled-up Wonder Bread on our first trip to the park. *I can't believe I'm going to see her in a few minutes.*

My longing was as visceral as it was intolerable. I recalled the fresh scent of her hair, like black satin against my cheek, the way she pressed my arm to her side when we walked together, the pear-shaped birthmark on the inside of her thigh. Unintentionally I made the mistake of thinking of Lydia in her nakedness, the responsiveness of her nipples, the wetness between her legs, the many remembered sensations of lovemaking. My mind became a whirlwind of memories, all intensifying an insatiable hunger.

I walked to the gazebo and climbed the steps, Tuna still straining against the leash. I checked my watch and waited for fifteen minutes. Lydia was late and getting later. Gazing out over Pioneer Park, I was afraid I'd gotten the time wrong or, God forbid, that Lydia had had second thoughts about seeing me.

Tuna licked on a paw, bored. We were alone so I removed her leash and threw a stick that someone left sitting on top of the handrail. Tuna would never play retriever – the wolf in her wouldn't allow such submissive behavior. Her idea of fun was to pick up the stick and entice me to chase her until I dropped from fatigue. I obliged and soon was running all over the gazebo, laughing and lunging as Tuna darted to and fro. She was amazingly agile for her size, but at one point I anticipated her move and almost caught her. As I spun around to grab at the stick in her mouth, I noticed someone in the periphery of my vision.

I stopped to catch my breath. There stood Lydia, who'd apparently been watching. She looked an inch taller, though it might have been my imagination. More beautiful than ever, her hair was parted in the middle with two long braids. She wore faded blue jeans, neatly pressed, a plain white blouse and black boots. Her belt was black leather with a shiny silver and turquoise buckle, cinched tightly in a way that accented her slim waist. She carried a small hand-tooled black leather purse in her hand. My heart thumped like a jackhammer. I took a step back and leaned against the railing for support.

Smiling, Lydia walked the thirty feet that separated us and put her arms around me. We hugged a long time, like our bodies would die a sudden death if we broke contact. The smell of her hair and her body came back to me in a rush. I inhaled her scent, savoring the moment. I felt her breasts against my chest and no resistance as I held her to me. I wanted to say something to lighten the moment, struggled to find anything that would make sense to tell her, but my mind went utterly blank and failed me. Speechless, I just stood there, choked with almost five years of backed-up emotion. Tears started despite a promise I'd made to myself.

Lydia took a step back and looked me over, still beaming. Behind her, the flaring sun gave her hair an aura of purple. "It looks like you have a girlfriend," she joked.

I don't know why I'd never thought of it before, but her voice made me think of the colors orange and yellow. Lost somewhere in time, I shook my head and bit my lip to get control of my emotions. "She doesn't know any better."

"Are you going to introduce me?"

I cleared my throat. "Lydia, this is Tuna. Tuna, Lydia."

Lydia took a knee and playfully boxed Tuna's ears. "Wow! You're a pretty girl, Tuna. Do you know that?"

"Careful. She'll think she's hot stuff."

"She *is* hot stuff. Look at this coat!"

"Yeah, she got a bath yesterday."

"Well, you always wanted a big dog. Now you got one, and then some."

I nodded, feeling a flush of pride. "That's for sure."

She got to her feet. "Hey, sorry about being late. I slept till after eleven."

"It's okay." *I'd have waited forever for a hug like that.*

She slowly shook her head. "Do you believe it? By chance you see a picture of me taken by a guy neither of us knows, and three months later we're back in Pioneer Park."

I could barely look at her, though nothing in the world could have enticed me to look away. She looked more confident. Her eyes were large and alive and focused on me. "I know," I told her. "I can't quite believe it, myself."

Lydia fiddled with the latch on her purse. "It's weird how things play out."

"That's for sure." My mouth had gone so dry I feared I'd sound strange and different from the Bryan she'd once loved.

She smiled again. I could tell she was checking me out, maybe looking to see how much I'd changed. Having her eyes on me felt like being caressed by a lover. "You look good, Bryan. I love your long hair."

"Thanks. You look good, too." I winced from my lack of originality. My throat constricted in a spasm of nervousness. A thousand times I'd wondered how it would feel to be close enough to touch Lydia. Now that the moment had arrived I felt riddled with insecurity, an awkward teenager all over again.

But Lydia didn't seem to notice. "You should see Yolanda. She's huge. If she sneezes that baby's gonna come out. She wants to see you, by the way."

"Cool. I'd like that."

She paused a long moment. "I was thinking about something on the way over. I never told you this because I didn't understand it myself, but I was in awe of you, Bryan. You were so incredibly bright . . . it just took my breath away."

"Oh, come on." This was not false modesty. I never felt superior to Lydia. I was book smart, but considered her wiser in the ways that really mattered. Stubblefield proved the point.

"Think about it. We were eighteen and I watched you destroy the third best chess player in the world. You should have seen yourself!"

I couldn't help but smile at the memory. "Yeah, that was pretty neat. I got lucky and beat a Russian Grandmaster."

"In front of God and all your friends."

"In front of you, Lydia. Know what stands out most about that night?"

"What?"

"I remember the exact moment I realized I had Primalov beaten. I smiled at you in the first row and you smiled back. I think it was the sweetest moment of my life."

Her voice softened. "It was sweet for both of us." There was something about the way she was looking at me that told me there was something she had to say. I could still read her. She drew a deep breath. "God, Bryan. There's so much to tell you. When you first wrote me, I wasn't ready to share it all."

"Are you now?" I asked, hopeful I was reading her correctly.

"Yeah. Talking on the phone did it. When you said I survived Stubblefield the first time so I could do it again, it *really* helped me. I remembered how supportive you could be."

"Thanks," I said softly.

Lydia went momentarily silent. Children squealed with excitement from over by the wading pond. The interruption made me realize our eyes had been locked for some time. Finally she said, "I used to think Walla Walla was hard, but living on the rez is absolute hell."

"That bad, huh?" I asked.

She nodded. "At first it was good. I mean, God bless Hector and Amelia, but I'm an Indian girl who was raised by Mexicans in a white man's town. Being with my people just felt right. Like I belonged for the first time in my life."

"That sounds good."

"It was, but it didn't last."

I looked at her inquiringly. "What happened?"

She sighed. "I got tired of it all. The drunks, the car wrecks, the murders, the suicides, the politics, you name it."

"That's a long list. How'd you end up at Pine Ridge, anyway?"

"That's what I didn't want to talk about over the phone. Something amazing happened." She lowered herself to the floor and sat cross-legged.

"What?" I put Tuna back on the leash and sat facing Lydia, close but not too close. I wondered if she'd reach over and touch me every so often as she spoke, the way she used to – more or less decided she'd keep her hands to herself, that touching would convey an intimacy she didn't feel.

"When I left Walla Walla I drove to Vancouver to find my mother. To see her before she died. I found her in a government sanitarium near the border. She had bad TB and the doctor told me she was at death's door."

"Was she glad to see you?"

She nodded. "Really glad. But she wanted Jimmy to be there, too. I called a number she gave me in Seattle. The Lockspot Tavern. Jimmy happened to be there and he drove up right away. I was holding Momma's hand when he came into the room. She was so broken and pathetic from all the years of abusing her health that all my hatred was gone."

"Did she know she was about to pass?"

"Yeah. Jimmy asked if he could have a minute alone with Momma so I went down the hall to look for a Coke machine. When I came back, Jimmy said my mom had something she wanted to tell me." Unexpectedly, Lydia's eyes filled with tears.

"Here," I said, producing a handkerchief like a magician. "I brought this for me."

She half-smiled and dabbed at her eyes. "Momma said there was something she needed to say to me before she passed to the Spirit World. She told me she'd made up a big lie and let me believe it my whole life. And the big lie was that my father died in a car accident."

My jaw dropped. "That was a lie?"

She nodded again. "She made up the whole thing. Remember the story? That he hit black ice and wiped out on Deception Pass? She said she did it because she figured we'd never see him again. I sort of fainted and Jimmy had to splash cold water on my face."

I shook my head in disbelief. "Deception Pass."

"Yeah. Momma's little play on words. Anyway, she told me my father's name was John Numa. She was too weak to tell the whole story and it was hard to hear her because of the mask they made her wear, but Jimmy kind of filled in the blank spots."

"Did Jimmy know your father was alive? When you were growing up?"

"He knew. But Momma had sworn him to secrecy."

"Did she say anything about her time with John . . ."

"Numa. It's an Indian word for Comanche. She said he was this handsome guy she was with about a month. That he was tall and thin and athletic like me. He worked as a mechanic at a wheat ranch out by Lowden."

"So the part about him being full-blooded Comanche was true?"

She nodded. "Yeah, that part was true."

"Did he know he got your mom pregnant?"

"No. I asked her the same question. It sounded like he was gone even before Momma knew."

"Why'd he leave?" I asked, always curious why relationships end.

She shrugged a shoulder. "He had the wanderlust. Said he was too young to settle down, and that he was messed up." She leaned forward and tousled Tuna's mane. "Sound familiar?"

I left the comparison alone. "How old was he?"

"Nineteen. Knowing my mother, she probably scared the shit out of him."

"Nineteen's young."

"For sure. Momma had no idea where he was, but said he'd be somewhere making hunting knives because that was his passion. I guess he made Momma a beautiful knife by carving a deer antler for the handle."

"What happened to it?"

She frowned. "She threw it in the Snake River after he left town."

I looked away, wondered what it'd be like to be lied to and then learn your deceased parent might be alive. "How'd you react to all this?"

"It was overwhelming. I remember staring out the hospital window, trying to make sense of something that seemed so senseless. The big lie, I mean. Then Momma asked me to forgive her and I squeezed her hand and told her I forgave her for everything, not just lying about my father."

"That's wonderful. For both of you." I admired Lydia's ability to forgive, made an invidious comparison to myself.

She nodded, shyly. "Momma cried and then she kind of faded out for a while. Fessing up took a lot out of her and she didn't have a lot left. An hour later she woke up coughing blood and when that ended she started breathing really fast and shallow. I started to leave to get a nurse but Jimmy told me not to and a couple minutes later she drew her last breath, right in front of us. She's in the Spirit World now with Big Momma, her Cayuse mother."

I took a moment to find something to say. Not necessarily the right words, but anything. "Where'd you bury her?"

"A social worker at the sanitarium told us there was an Indian burial ground nearby. It was mostly for people from the Lummi tribe, but Jimmy and I thought it was right to put her there. At the gravesite, Jimmy told me Momma thought Lummi women were ugly and that it'd make her happy to be the prettiest one in the area. Then he apologized for never telling me the truth about my father."

"Did you accept it?"

She gave me a consenting nod. "I did because Momma said she'd shoot his balls off in his sleep if he ever told me the truth about John Numa. I can just see her saying that."

"I'd call that a good reason for keeping your mouth shut."

She sat slightly more erect. "When we got back to Jimmy's truck he opened the glove compartment and handed me an envelope. I asked him what it was and he said, 'open it.' It was a black and white photo of Momma with John Numa. And Bryan, you won't believe this. It was taken right here, in the gazebo at Pioneer Park." She flipped the latch on her purse and produced a dog-eared photo, its colors more umber and tan than black and white. It showed an attractive young Indian couple, slightly out of focus, both squinting slightly on a bright day. The young man had his arm around her waist while she smiled seductively at the camera.

I got a chill. "This is uncanny. They're standing by the rail, right where we've been a hundred times. I have a picture of us in almost the same place."

"I know. Right over there by the top of the steps." She motioned to the spot. "Read the back," she said.

I turned it over, glancing first at her expectant eyes. "Myrtle and John, Pioneer Park, December 1950."

She gulped a little breath and nodded. "Jimmy found it in a shoebox Momma left behind when she moved to B.C."

"Wow! Look how pretty your mom is. And your Dad's really handsome."

"I was so happy to know my father was alive and to have a picture of him that I couldn't be mad at Jimmy. After the burial, I followed him back to Seattle and stayed at a boarding house for about a week. I was crazy about what happened at Stubblefield and I wasn't sure I'd done the right thing in leaving you, but now I had a mission in life. A quest to find my father. I started calling sporting goods stores and gun shops that sell knives, but no one had heard of John Numa. Jimmy said Momma had never mentioned where my father was from, so I decided to start looking in Oklahoma."

"Why Oklahoma?" I asked, wondering how she made the leap.

"That's where the Comanche ended up."

I handed back the picture. "You just took off for Oklahoma?"

She placed it carefully in her purse. "Yeah, but my Pontiac threw a rod in Northern California. I called Hector and Amelia and told 'em about Momma dying and how I was searching for my father. They tried to talk me into coming home but ended up wiring me three hundred dollars. A junk-yard gave me fifteen dollars for the Pontiac and I took a Greyhound bus the rest of the way to Oklahoma. The next day I bought a Buick out of the newspaper. An elderly lady owned it and she'd had a stroke and couldn't drive any more so she gave me a good deal. She'd been a librarian and told me how I could search the whole state by checking phone books at the main branch in Oklahoma City."

"Did it work?"

"I found a couple Numas and a couple different spellings, but no one knew John Numa the knife maker, or John Numa who'd be in his early for-ties and might be working as a mechanic. But then a miracle happened. I was in a pawnshop in Norman and I found a knife just like the one Momma described. And guess what?" She reached over and briefly laid the palm of her hand on the back of my hand.

A thrill raced up my arm and settled deep in my heart. That simple act drove home the feeling I could never survive without her. I made myself respond. "John Numa made it."

"Yeah," she said. "His initials were carved into the handle. Just touch-ing it made me closer to my father than I'd ever been in my life."

"God, Lydia. That's exciting."

She nodded. "I bought the knife for twenty dollars and asked the owner where he'd gotten it. He said he won it in a poker game from Roy Bird, an old Indian who made knives on the Tenkiller Reservation, near Muskogee, a hundred fifty miles east. So I went there and found the guy in a little machine shop off the highway. He was suspicious of me and wouldn't talk, but I could tell he knew something about John Numa."

"So why wouldn't he talk to you?"

"I don't know. Indians are suspicious. He left the room. I started crying and his wife came out from a back room. I told her I'd just buried my mother and was trying to find a father I'd never met and she took pity on me. I showed her the picture of Momma and John in the gazebo and, right away, she said John Numa apprenticed with Roy Bird in the spring of 1950, the same year the picture was taken. She remembered the year because it was the year she lost her younger brother in the Korean War. Anyway, the old lady said she thought my father might have kin in a town called Tahle-quah."

"Is that in Oklahoma?"

She nodded again. "Yeah. I drove there and found my father's first cousin, a tall, skinny man named Early Numa. I followed him to the trailer where he lived and he showed me a knife my father had given him when his own father had died, two years before. It had been mailed from somewhere in South Dakota, but he couldn't remember where."

"What'd you do?"

"This time I got smart and drove straight to the Pine Ridge Reservation in South Dakota. I stopped in Oglala and talked to a man who happened to be whittling on his front porch. He'd never heard of John Numa, but when I mentioned he made hunting knives he said he'd heard of a good knife maker in Kyle. So I drove to Kyle and approached an old Sioux woman who was coming out of a grocery store. She asked me what I wanted with John Numa and I told her I wanted to buy a knife. She could tell I was lying and she walked off, so I caught up and told her he might be kin. She looked me over from head to foot and started laughing."

"How come?"

"She said, 'I'd guess you're John's kin, all right, 'cause you're the spittin' image.'"

"Wow."

"She gave me directions to his house and I went straight there and knocked on the door. No one answered so I walked out back where there was a shop with a sign that read, Numa's Custom Knives. The door was open. I looked inside and saw this tall, good lookin' guy with braided hair as long as mine. He was washing his hands in a big cement sink. A grinding machine was on and he didn't hear me coming so I just stood there and stared at him for the longest time. Finally he noticed me and turned off the machine."

"What'd he say?"

"I spoke first. I said, 'Are you John Numa?' and he nodded his head. Then he asked me my name and I said 'Lydia Redstone.'"

"Ring any bells?"

"Yeah. He wiped his hands on his jeans and said he used to know a Myrtle Redstone, a Cayuse girl in Walla Walla, Washington. I told him, 'She got T.B. and died a month ago. She was my mother.' And then I kind of choked up because my emotions were just too much for me."

"What'd he do?"

She fought back tears. "He just stood there and didn't say anything. I told him my whole life my Momma told me my father was a full-blooded Comanche who died in a car wreck before I was born. But on her deathbed she admitted she'd made it up and that his name was John Numa. And that he made knives. I handed him the picture and he looked at it and started shaking his head."

"Like it wasn't him?"

"That's what I thought at first. That he was going to say I had the wrong person. But instead he smiled and said his buddy Pete took the picture. That Pete was with a girl named Marla that day and that later on my Momma got drunk and threw the camera at Marla. He said the camera broke but that Pete must've salvaged the film."

"So he'd never seen the picture?"

She shook her head slowly. "Huh uh. He told me he and Momma were together for a month at most, that they'd spend nights together in the bunkhouse at the ranch where he worked. He wanted to know how she could be sure he was the one who got her pregnant. I told him she swore he was the only one she was sleeping with at the time."

"Did he accept that?"

"I guess he did 'cause he asked me how old I was and when I told him I was eighteen he did the math and said I might just be his daughter and damned if we didn't bear a resemblance."

"What about getting blood tests?"

"Yeah, it was expensive but the next day we drove to Rapid City and did just that. He said he didn't take fatherhood lightly and wanted to be absolutely sure I was his daughter 'cause he knew he'd get attached to me. The clinic called a week later and said they were ninety-nine percent sure he was my daddy, but the truth is we already knew it."

"Because you look so much alike?"

She smiled, knowingly. "That, but also because . . . I guess it's hard to explain."

"So that's how you got to Pine Ridge."

"Yeah. I moved in at John's suggestion. That's what I call him: 'John.' I've lived in Kyle ever since. He's a good man, Bryan. Can you believe it? I have a father and he's a good man."

I felt tears of joy well up. "I'm *really* happy for you."

She smiled again. "Cool, huh?"

I nodded. "Does he know why you're here? I mean, does he know about Stubblefield?"

"I told him about a month after I moved in. We'd go on long walks and talk for hours at a time. I was totally moody and he wanted to know why."

"So what'd he say?"

She grinned. "At first he refused to believe I was a black belt in karate. So I kicked a fencepost and knocked it clean out of the ground and that was that. Then he told me how sorry he was for what I'd gone through, but that I did the right thing."

I bowed my head. "Which is what I should've said."

"Yeah. I told him my boyfriend at the time let me down. John said it was easy for him to say the right things because he wasn't there when it happened. That it's easier to answer the quiz show questions when you're watching at home. He's big on quiz shows."

"I like your dad."

"There's something else he said."

"What?"

"He said the cover-up you orchestrated was brilliant. That it kept us from going to prison. On the rez, you sneeze and you get locked up. He wanted to thank you for preventing a miscarriage of justice. He made me realize I never thanked you, so I'm doing it now."

I felt a surge of emotion. "I never expected—"

"No, no. Don't do that. I was all over you for letting me down. We both got it wrong so let's not ever question each other again."

"Thanks, Lydia. That means a lot." I longed to hold this kind woman, close my eyes and merge with her like when we used to make love.

Tuna began twitching and whimpering in her sleep. Lydia smiled and said, "Chasing rabbits, Big Girl?"

"That's funny," I said. "That's exactly what I call her. Big Girl."

"Really?"

I nodded. "So what does your father think of you coming back to Walla Walla?"

"He told me to be careful, but he was all for it. Not only to do the healing ritual, but to be there for Yolanda. And to honor Hector and Amelia for raising me in his absence. He thinks they did a good job." She leaned over and gave me a playful elbow to the ribs.

I held my side in mock pain, feeling remotely normal. "Your father sounds very wise."

"He's a pretty together guy . . . which makes me a lucky girl." She stood and stretched. "Let's walk around a bit? My butt's sore from sitting in the car for three days."

"Good idea," I seconded. I roused Tuna and the three of us walked down the steps. We headed over by the pond, me sneaking sideways glances and marveling at Lydia's beauty. The kid with Buddy Holly glasses was holding a Frisbee and I asked him if I could borrow it. I filled it with water from a nearby drinking fountain and set it at Tuna's feet. When she finished lapping it up, I flipped it to Lydia and she tossed a strike back to the kid. We walked some more and I said, "You mentioned the politics on the reservation. What are they?"

She half-snorted, half-laughed. "Got a year?"

"Actually, I do."

"Watch yourself, mister," she said, smiling. "Have you heard of AIM?"

I nodded. "The American Indian Movement. There was an article about Dennis Banks in the LA Times."

"Right. Dennis and George Mitchell and Clyde Bellecourt founded AIM. Right away they made noise about issues like returning ancestral lands and treaty rights, even reparation for genocide. Needless to say, the government is trying to destroy the movement."

"Hence the presence of the FBI?"

"Yeah, the rez is crawling with FBI agents. They act like they own the place, pushing people around, pointing their guns and scaring everyone, even kids." She narrowed her eyes. "And then there's the Goons."

"Goons?" A woman sitting on a bench turned and gave me a disapproving glance, as if I'd uttered a swear word in front of her two young children.

"Also known as the Guardians of the Oglala Nation. A bunch of thugs."

"How do they fit in?"

"They're a paramilitary group that opposes AIM. Some of 'em are actually off-duty policemen from the Bureau of Indian Affairs."

"Does the FBI hassle the Goons, too?"

She stopped in her tracks and shook her head vehemently. "The FBI *trains* them. With money from the federal government! To say the Goons are violent would be the understatement of the century."

"Bummer. Why are Indians fighting Indians?"

She gave me a curious look. "Like white people don't fight white people. Did you forget about Kent State?"

"Good point," I replied, sheepishly.

"Indian way is to speak your piece, but the violence on the rez is out of control. I'm sick to death of it."

"Ever think of moving?"

She nodded and resumed walking. "I'd have already moved, except I want to live with my father. He's AIM and he won't leave the People behind. He says, 'What would Crazy Horse think of me if I walked away?'"

"Are you in AIM?"

"I am, but politics are the fool's hope. Who said that?"

"John Ciardi."

She smiled to herself. "Know what I'd really like to be doing? With my life, I mean."

"Yeah. Of course."

She looked off in the distance. "I'd like to become a history teacher. Tell kids what was done to the American Indian. Teach 'em about Geronimo, Crazy Horse, Chief Joseph."

"On the rez?"

"No,' she answered, in a jaded voice. "The kids on the rez know what happened. They live the consequences every day. I'd teach white kids. Raise consciousness."

"That's a great idea. You should go for it."

She folded her arms. "Let's talk about something else. Okay?"

"Sure."

A warm breeze rustled the trees, causing Lydia to stop and take notice. "Maybe we should go out to Stubblefield and do the ritual, get it over with. Then go back and check on Yolanda."

I stole a glance at my wristwatch. "Okay with me. Do you want to take one car or two?" I desperately wanted to ride together, but preferred that Lydia make that decision.

Her voice brightened. "Let's go in one so we can keep talking. It's weird. We haven't seen each other for almost five years and it's like we picked up right where we left off."

"That's ironic."

"What do you mean?"

"We left off at Stubblefield."

———

We climbed in Lydia's car, a Ford station wagon that belonged to the band she worked for. I rolled down the back windows for Tuna, gave her a doggie treat I'd been carrying in my pants pocket.

Instead of starting the car and leaving for the cemetery, Lydia surprised me by saying, "Tell me about the girl."

"What?"

"The girl you were with in Topanga."

I took a measured breath, tried to steady my nerves. "That was Annie,
my next-door neighbor. The short version is we grew a vegetable garden
together and I started hanging out with her and Kaalaea, her little daughter. At first it was just a friendship, but Annie's a good woman and
eventually we got sexual. But for me that's all there was."

"You were with her just for sex?" she asked, taken aback.

I shook my head. "No. I was with her because I was lonely. What I
meant was it didn't go anywhere, and that made me feel even lonelier."

A car pulled in next to us and a woman with two young children piled
out. "In your letter you called it a failed experiment. I think that's what
you said."

I nodded in agreement. The car felt suddenly hot. "Yeah. I guess I
wanted to see if I could fall in love with someone besides you."

"You can't try one time and then give up if it doesn't work."

I met her eyes, puzzled. "How many times should I try?"

"I don't know. You only have to get lucky once."

"I know. I did."

She gripped the steering wheel. "Oh, Bryan. I worry about you."

I shook my head again, this time slowly. "Don't. My worst days are behind me."

"Are they really? Or are you just saying that?"

"Really. I bottomed out a few months ago." I drew a deep breath and
veered into dangerous territory. "But on the phone you said there might be
a chance for us."

She started to say something, stopped herself and restarted. "What I
said was, I couldn't say there's no chance."

I gulped some air. "So is there a chance or isn't there?" A short, simple
question with my life hanging in the balance.

She fiddled with a button on her blouse, her fingers caressing its
smooth, pearly white surface. "There's stuff in the way, Bryan. Stuff that
goes way back."

"Stubblefield?"

"That's part of it." Her voice went low and somber. "The truth is, I look
at you and I see bad memories. I see someone who's not Indian. I see someone who loves me more than I love myself. I see someone who lives half a
continent away. It all adds up."

"Okay. I get the point." Her words felt like barbells fastened to my
heart.

She started the car, ending the conversation. We pulled out of the parking lot, heading in the direction of the neighborhood where we stole Tammy
Balfour's Barracuda.

"Is Tuna okay back there?"

Tuna had her head out the window, content to watch the scenery and breathe in the smells. "She's fine," I answered. "Tell me about the healing ritual."

"It's a smudging ceremony where we burn sacred sage. I'll tell you what to do as we go along." She withdrew back into herself, either talked out or thinking about God knows what.

After taking a left at Reser Road, we went up over a rise. Like Mother Nature's bosom, the Blue Mountains swelled up from the floor of the Walla Walla valley. Two minutes later we came up on Stubblefield Cemetery, just our side of the lush green foothills. *How could something so ugly have happened in such a beautiful place?*

Lydia hadn't noticed the cemetery, high on the hill and easy to miss. Pointing, I said, "Take the dirt road on your left. There."

She slowed and took the turn, which led us uphill toward a stand of trees in the middle of a wheat field.

"It looks different," Lydia commented.

"It *is* different. This road used to be lined with trees. I remember them brushing against the windshield. And someone removed the stone pillars, too."

She focused on the road, swerving to avoid a pothole. "Yeah. It's not as spooky as it used to be. Maybe because it's daytime."

We reached the top of the hill and entered what had once been the cemetery proper, surrounded by the same kind of scraggy trees that once bordered the road. A flock of starlings scattered like a handful of thrown seed, first due north and then, in response to an unseen signal, due east. Lydia parked the car and we got out beneath an immense arc of agate blue sky. Neither of us spoke. I checked to see if we'd drawn any attention from the ranch house a half-mile away. If we did, there was no sign. Tuna bounded out of the back seat and headed straight for the woods, excited to be running off leash.

Lydia looked at me and smiled reassuringly. "I've got some things Tall Bear gave me," she said, opening the back gate of the station wagon.

A distant dog barked incessantly. "Tuna. Stay close!" I yelled, wandering into the cemetery. I stopped in front of a light-colored granite marker, overgrown by weeds that made clusters of tiny white flowers. Using my hands, I pushed aside enough weeds to read:

Elijah S. Pomeroy
Dearly Beloved Son
1894 – 1898

The inscription depressed me. I did an immediate about-face back to the station wagon. "Can I help?" I asked, watching Lydia take out two cedar boughs, a clay pot and two pouches.

"In a minute," she answered, as she hung the smaller pouch around her neck on a string of rawhide. "Where exactly did . . . the incident happen?"

"Over here." I walked thirty feet to my right, stopping before the edge of the clearing. "We stayed back from the trees."

"So we could see the moon," Lydia added.

I nodded. "We parked my Chevy here, off the gravel road, and Montrose pulled in next to us, right about here." I made a mark in the dirt with the toe of my sneaker, remembering how his tires made a crunching sound that ended as he skidded to a stop.

Lydia squeezed her eyes shut. "Is this where he tried to rape me, where his car was?"

I nodded again. "Yeah." It pained me to hear that vile word. Without intending to, I momentarily relived the moment of Montrose sticking his fingers in Lydia.

Dead silence for a few seconds, then she opened her eyes. "And we fought in the space between the two cars?"

"Right."

"So I guess it was right about here that I broke his windpipe." Her voice quavered.

"More like here." I indicated a spot ten feet from the one Lydia had indicated. "He was where you said, then he crawled over here where the dirt is softer."

She shrugged nervously. "I'll take your word for it."

"You okay?" I asked, wishing I could hold her, be a comfort, erase the bad memory from her consciousness.

"A little shaky. Does it show?"

"A little."

"Thanks for asking. Are you okay?"

"Yeah," I answered, but my eyes darted nervously about the cemetery.

"Good. By the way, don't worry about being seen. Tall Bear says we'll be invisible."

I felt a measure of relief. "Cool."

Lydia handed me the largest of the cedar branches. "Okay, brush the ground with the cedar. Go clockwise. We're supposed to make a big circle around the area it happened."

"Could you explain that to me?"

"The Power of the World always works in circles. That's why our people made our teepees circular and then set them in circles. Tall Bear says to circle the space where the dark wind blew over us. That releases the past and gets us back our power."

I nodded my understanding and brushed the ground mindfully, kicking up billowy puffs of dust. Lydia followed me in the same direction. We'd almost finished when Tuna ran into the circle with a stick in her mouth. "Not now, girl," I said. She cocked her head, paused and loped off toward the dense underbrush at the far end of the cemetery.

Lydia poured what looked to be dried grasses into the clay pot, the size of a cereal bowl. "These are the sacred herbs."

"Sage?"

"Sage and sweetgrass. We burn them and work with the smoke."

I shrugged. "What's sweetgrass?"

"It grows on the Plains. I got ours behind my father's shop, then I braided it and let it dry out."

"What does it do?"

"It invites positive vibes." She lit a wooden match with her thumbnail, touched it to the small pile in the bowl and blew gently. A thin trail of smoke wafted up.

"And this is called smudging?"

She nodded. "It's been a sacred Indian ritual for thousands of years. When the incident happened, this place captured a lot of negative energy. It gets absorbed into the rocks and the earth. Literally. Smudging will cleanse the space. Our bodies, too."

"Did Tall Bear teach you how to do this?"

"Yeah. He taught me some prayers, too. That reminds me. There's an eagle feather in the back of the station wagon. Will you get it?"

I walked briskly back to the car, saw Tuna a hundred feet away, squatting and urinating at the edge of the woods. Since she preferred the woods to the abandoned cemetery, I decided to let her roam. I removed a magnificent eagle feather from a paper bag and took it to Lydia without comment.

She thanked me and walked the circle in a clockwise fashion, carrying the smudge pot and fanning the thick smoke with the eagle feather. As she walked, she recited:

> Oh Great Spirit. Sage Plant Spirits.
> Let the Sacred Sage cleanse and heal this troubled place.
> Let the Sacred Plants teach this place to be free from evil.

She made gradual spirals inwards, making four revolutions in ever decreasing concentric circles. When she finished, she moved close to me and smudged my body by fanning me from head to foot. I closed my eyes and inhaled the pungent, earthy smell of the grasses as she moved clockwise around my body saying something about the sacred hoop of life. This time the prayer went:

> Oh Great Spirit. Sage Plant Spirits.
> Let the Sacred Sage cleanse and heal our troubled bodies.
> Let the Sacred Plants teach us to be free from pain.

Her voice soothed me. I felt a hand over my heart and opened my eyes. She said softly, "Do it for me. I'll recite the prayer to myself."

I took the bowl and feather and brushed the smoke over Lydia's body, from head to foot. She inhaled deeply, closed her eyes and smiled. I had the distinct impression of fluffing up the energy in her body. Her shakiness disappeared entirely and she looked radiant, like a woman in love. *In love with whom?* I wondered. After a minute she opened her eyes and told me to set the bowl in the middle of the circle. When I did she said, "Now I'm going to sprinkle sacred soil over the area of the circle."

"The dust of your ancestors." I remembered the words Lydia used when she called me in Topanga.

"Right. Tall Bear collected it at Wounded Knee. The day before I left." She removed the pouch from her neck and poured about half the contents into her left hand.

"After this we'll be done?"

She smiled again, confidently. "Better than done. Healed."

I wanted to take her in my arms and never let go. She meant everything to me, nothing else seemed remotely real or meaningful. "I'm really glad I get to be here with you," I said.

"I'm glad you're with—"

The sound of an approaching car startled us. We looked at one another and swung our eyes to the road leading into the cemetery. A silver '65 GTO appeared at the crest and veered toward us, a roostertail of dust in its wake.

"Do you know who it is?" Lydia asked with a pained expression.

I nodded. "Unfortunately."

Vicky Spotts swung in alongside the station wagon and skidded to a stop. Curiously, she leaned forward against the steering wheel and twisted from side-to-side. A moment later she stepped from her car.

So much for being invisible. "Vicky," I said, taking two steps in her direction. "I don't know what the hell you're doing, but you are *really* not welcome here."

"You're not welcome here, either," she snapped back. "I warned you about coming to Walla Walla."

I tried staring her down. "How about you leave and we discuss it later?"

Vicky sneered and moved closer, to within twenty feet. "Chance to see the bitch, huh?"

"Hello, Vicky," Lydia said, her voice calm. "It's been five years."

"That it has," Vicky smirked, right arm bent behind her back. "I've lost sixty pounds and you . . . you still look like an Indian."

"Thank you," Lydia replied.

"Up yours!" Vicky swiped at her runny nose with the back of her hand.

Lydia's eyes went icy cold. "Look, we're in the middle of something. You need to leave."

Vicky noticed the smoking bowl that rested on the ground midway between us. "Are you guys sending smoke signals or burning pot?"

Lydia shook her head in contempt and glanced at me like, *how do you want to handle this?*

I took another step toward Vicky, fists balled in anger. "It's none of your business what we're doing. Get the hell out of here!"

With surprising quickness, Vicky produced a handgun from behind her back, its nickel-plated snub nose glinting in the sunlight. "Don't take another step," she warned. "This is a Smith & Wesson .38 Special. Fires five shots. I'll use it."

A jab of terror jerked me backwards. I saw Vicky cradle the belly of the gun with her left hand. She looked like she knew what she was doing. Summoning the gentlest voice possible under the circumstances, I said, "Easy, Vicky. Easy."

Lydia grabbed me by the elbow and pulled me another step back. Her own voice was eerily calm. "Vicky. Please don't point that at us. Guns—"

"Shut the fuck up, you bitch! If I want you to talk, I'll rattle your chain."

Lydia continued in the same calm voice. "Okay, I'll shut up. And we'll leave, if that's what you want. If you want us to leave Walla Walla, we'll do that too."

"We will," I seconded, thinking I might have more influence. "We'll leave right now. Just take it easy and don't do anything you'll regret."

Vicky's eyes glassed over, like she'd been transported to another time and place. A moment later she said, "There's that word again. Regret. As in, I *regret* the day I met you . . . right here in Stubblefield Cemetery."

I wanted to say something that would calm her down, but no words came out.

"Just tell us what you want us to do," Lydia said, raising her hands to show they were empty.

Vicky moved the gun slightly to the right, sighting down the barrel at Lydia's chest. "Okay," she said, her voice rising an octave. "I want to know why you came out here. I want to know what happened here five years ago. How you guys killed Officer Montrose."

"What are you talking about?" I imitated Lydia by spreading my arms wide, palms up. "Jack Montrose busted us for being parked in the cemetery and then he left. Don't you remember? You saw him leave with your own eyes."

Vicky squeezed the trigger, fired a warning shot over our heads. She smiled, a dissociated grin, and aimed the gun back at me. I could see the little black hole in the short, shiny barrel. The gun had seemed small when she first whipped it out from behind her back, now it looked big. Big enough to take a life. When she spoke again, her voice carried some real menace. "I'm asking what happened after—"

There was no time to stop it from happening, no time at all. In a blur, I watched Tuna charge Vicky from behind. Running at full speed, she launched herself from ten feet away, striking Vicky high in the shoulder. The roar from the second gunshot dissipated into the afternoon sky as a battering ram hit me in the stomach. I staggered backwards, struggled to stay upright, then let go and watched the ground rise up to me, like I'd been tackled from behind, only in slow motion.

"Oh, Jesus," Lydia shrieked.

Warm, slippery blood gushed over my hands as I instinctively covered the wound, just above my navel and slightly left of midline. Blood pulsed out, pressured by every thump of my heart. I rolled onto my side and pulled up my knees to lessen the ache, but a searing poker of pain probed me from the inside. With my cheek pressed against the ground, I watched Tuna drag Vicky away from me and toward the two cars. She had her jaws clamped down on Vicky's arm and jerked her back and forth like a weightless cloth doll. Vicky howled in pain, kicking helplessly and begging for someone to call Tuna off.

Lydia knelt at my side. Inexplicably, she had Vicky's gun in her right hand. She set it down even with my face and gently pried my hands away from the hole that gaped in my stomach. "Let me see it, Bryan," she commanded, eyes wide with fear. "Let me see how bad it is."

Contorted in pain, I let one arm flop to my side and, with tremendous effort, worked the other under my head. Vicky sobbed hysterically in the distance, saying over and over she didn't mean to shoot me, that she just wanted to scare us. I sensed that Tuna had let her loose. Then my bladder emptied and I recalled Montrose wetting himself just before he died. "Damn," I whispered, feeling a moment of unexpected compassion for the man who'd cost me everything.

"Bryan. Listen to me. Bryan. Listen to me! We're only ten minutes from the hospital. You just hang on!"

Burnt powder mingled with the smell of sacred sage. The earth cradled me as my muscles went slack, soft dusty soil somehow finding its way into my mouth and nostrils. A flicker of awareness told me I lay a few feet from where Montrose had taken his final breath, and a few feet more from the gravesites of people who'd died a hundred years before. I imagined what it would feel like to sleep beneath the earth for eternity.

"We have to get you to—"

I must've blacked out for several seconds because I dreamed about Vanilla, the little green dinosaur Kaalaea had given me, all alone and unable to breathe in the airless glove compartment of my car. I awakened to Lydia's tears splashing wet against my face and Tuna licking them off. Ignoring the buttons, Lydia tore off her blouse, wadded it up and pressed it hard against my stomach. Again, she pleaded with me to hold on. "Don't die, Bryan! Don't you die on me!"

I glanced at Lydia's white blouse, soaked with blood. The pain in my gut flowed out of me, like boiling water down an open drain. Summoning all that remained of my strength, I mumbled, "I wanted to show you what I was made of."

"Do it!" Lydia ordered, her voice strangled by panic. "Show me what you're made of!" But the words sounded frightened and far away.

I could feel Tuna's warm breath on my shoulder and the grit of dirt against my cheek. I wanted to tell Lydia how much I loved her. Tuna, too. But my body seemed to swallow itself from the inside and I couldn't hook up with whatever it is that allows a person to organize a thought and speak. In all my life I'd never known so much love – it poured forth from my body like soft flowing water from a broken vessel. Lydia's long black braid swayed in and out of my field of vision, bound in powder blue felt and strips of otter fur. My eyes rolled back in my head and I felt an overwhelming urge to die. Just before entering a silent and velvety blackness, I thought I heard her say she loved me, that she'd really never stopped loving me and that she promised to never leave me again if only I'd fight and stay alive. I felt as close to heaven as I'd ever be, but I might have been dreaming. And then, I dreamed I heard the roar of three more gunshots, each one punctuated by a sharp splat.

Chapter 13
Sister Morphine

I came to in a brightly lit hospital room, my mind stupefied by morphine. Adding to my daze, I found myself in a half-sitting position with a broad-faced, bent-nosed man no more than twelve inches from my face. His breath smelled of coffee. I turned away and explored the tubing that pumped clear fluids into the veins of my elbow. An IV bag hung from a curled steel stand, confusing me with its upside-down writing.

"What do you mean the shard of plastic is the final piece of the puzzle?" the man demanded, his voice matching his expression in intensity. He looked familiar, a thicker version of someone I'd known in the past.

"What?" I croaked. My tongue felt like a lump of chalk.

"You *said*, 'The shard of plastic is the final piece of the puzzle.' What did you mean by that?"

"I said that?"

"Yes, you did. Tell me what you meant."

The Windex-blue eyes. I remember those eyes. Am I dreaming? I blinked repeatedly and the chemical fog lifted a little. "You're Gerritsen, aren't you?"

"Yes, Bryan. Now tell me what you meant by, 'the shard of plastic is the final piece of the puzzle. Put the shard in its proper place and solve the murder.' Tell me now before you forget."

"I don't know what I meant. I don't even know where I am."

"You're in Walla Walla Memorial Hospital. Intensive Care Unit. You were brought here two days ago after being shot in the stomach. Now, you have to tell me. What did you mean?"

Anxiety lurked in the back of my mind, dulled by painkillers but shaping up like an ominous shadow in a lifting fog. I shook my head to clear the image, heard a rubbery footfall. A tall, light-skinned black nurse entered the room. "Who are you?" she demanded.

"Bryan Mat—"

"Detective Frank Gerritsen."

"How long has he been conscious?" The tone of an irritated woman, one used to being in charge.

"A couple minutes. I jostled his arm and he woke right up."

"I've got to get Dr. Benjamin, and you have to leave!" she barked. "No visitors except close family."

"I'm with the Walla Walla Police Department," Gerritsen replied. He reached into his suit jacket and produced a shiny silver badge.

"The orders say no visitors. This boy has been in a coma . . . never mind, just leave." She elbowed Gerritsen out of the way, lowered my bed and took my hand. "Welcome back, Bryan. We've been waiting for you."

Her hand felt warm to the touch. "Huh?"

"Could I have *one* minute with him?" Gerritsen inquired from the foot of my bed. "I just need him to answer one question."

"No, you may not have one minute with him. Not now, anyway. Now, please leave, and tell someone at the nursing station to send Dr. Benjamin. Stat!"

Gerritsen stormed out, muttering obscenities.

The nurse pressed a button on the side of my bed and a light appeared directly above me. I shielded my eyes to block the glare. My arm felt like a massive block of wood. "I've never seen a black woman with freckles."

Chuckling, she plumped my pillow. "Someone's got a load of narcotics on board."

I read her plastic nametag. Irene Williams.

A minute later, after I answered questions like who's the President and what month is it, a middle-aged woman burst into the room, smiling broadly. "Bet you don't remember me," she said cheerfully. "I'm Dr. Nancy Benjamin. I treated your friend after that milk truck rolled. Years ago."

Even snowed with drugs, I remembered her. "I do. Sort of," I said, my voice slipping away.

Dr. Benjamin seemed to glide to the edge of my bed. A mind trick of the medications, it looked like she was coasting on roller skates. "What's happening, Irene?"

"Vitals good. Pain under control. Oriented to person and place, but not time. A policeman woke him up. I had to shoo him out."

"A policeman? How did he get in here?" Dr. Benjamin removed a penlight from her jacket and shined it in my eyes. I had to fight to hold them open.

"I don't know. I came in to check on Bryan and he was asking him something about something." Irene stepped closer and stroked my forehead. My head suddenly weighed a ton. I felt myself fading away, like a radio station losing its signal. Her hand felt blissfully soft and soothing. I gave in to sleep.

I dreamed a set of eyes stared at me over the edge of a blue-green surgical mask. The eyes looked deep into my soul, producing a swell of strange energy in the area around my heart. Then Lydia floated into the room and began caressing my forehead the way Nurse Irene had.

I opened my eyes and watched the room swim into focus. Lydia stood at the side of my bed. "Is this a dream?" I asked, befuddled.

She stroked my forehead. "No. I'm really here. And so are you." Her dark eyes shined with tears.

It was definitely Lydia's voice. I said, "You're still here." I loved her so much it hurt.

She nodded. "We're both still here."

"Good. Can I have a sip of water?"

"Here." She held a glass in front of me.

I drew weakly from a flexible straw. When I finished, she fished a thin ice cube from a plastic container and placed it tenderly in my mouth, like a priestess offering a wafer at communion. The cube melted and I said, "Vicky shot me."

Lydia nodded again. "She didn't mean to, but she's an idiot. You never point a loaded gun at someone."

"Jesus. Did you see the look in her eyes before the gun went off?"

"Yeah," Lydia said, shaking her head in disbelief. "Like one of the Manson women."

I nodded, tried to get my bearings. My eyes moved from a cheap print of a sailboat on the wall to my IV drip and back to Lydia. "Aren't they going to operate on me?"

"They already did. They removed a bullet and part of your spleen. You've been out for two days."

I frowned at her. "I'm not afraid, if that's what you think. Tell the doctors to do the operation and get it over with."

She threw back her head and laughed. "Honest, Bryan. They operated as soon as I brought you in. Look." She peeled back my covers.

I raised up a few inches and yelped in pain. "Give me a hand, will you?"

Lydia worked an arm behind my back and ever so carefully helped me up. A clean white bandage circumnavigated my stomach. "But I don't remember—"

"You were unconscious."

"Am I going to be okay?"

She smiled. "Yes."

"Why are you crying?"

She wiped her eyes with a napkin from an untouched meal tray. "Because at first the surgeon told us you might not make it."

"Who's us?"

"Me and Dr. Z and Reva. They've been here both days. The hospital staff thinks they're family."

"Oh." I yawned. "Who do they think you are?"

"I guess they let me in because I brought you here."

I took a moment to think. "Does my Dad know I got shot?"

She shook her head and frowned. "Huh uh. He and Cat are ocean fishing somewhere near the tip of the Queen Charlotte Islands. There's no way to reach them till they come back."

"Is that Canada?"

"Between Canada and Alaska. It's pretty remote. They're trying to get a message to them on short-wave radio."

An unintelligible announcement over the hospital P.A. temporarily distracted me. "Oh. Is Tuna okay?"

"Oh yeah! She's with the Zaleskis. Don't worry about Tuna. Reva fixed her a flank steak last night. She says she's going to fatten her up."

I started to laugh and paid for it with a stabbing sensation in my lower rib cage. "Can I have another sip of water?"

"Sure. You can have all you want."

I closed my eyes and drew on the straw. The scene at Stubblefield came back to me. "Tuna mauled Vicky, didn't she?"

"Yeah. I brought Vicky in, too. They treated her in the ER and then they took her straight to jail. Do not pass go, do not collect two hundred dollars."

I smiled but managed not to laugh. "Don't make me laugh, okay?"

"Sorry."

I licked my lips, cracked and dry. "Is Vicky okay?"

"Except for two hundred stitches in her arm and scalp."

"Ow!" The image of Tuna attacking Vicky elicited another memory, but this one hid behind a curtain of drug-induced repression. "Something else happened. At the cemetery . . . but I can't remember it."

"We were just finishing the healing ritual when Vicky showed up. Remember? She pulled a gun and fired a shot over our heads. Then the gun went off a second time, when Tuna attacked her. I got you both in the station wagon and brought you here."

Gunshots. That's it. "Were there more gunshots after the one that hit me? Or did I dream that?"

"No. That really happened. I had to get you help and I didn't want Vicky around a loaded gun, so I fired the remaining shots into the ground. I could've just emptied the chambers, but I wasn't thinking."

"Oh." Another memory was right there. Something Lydia had said to me as I lost consciousness. So tantalizingly close and yet unreachable. I bore down till my brain ached, but the memory eluded me.

Lydia squeezed my arm to absorb my attention. "Bryan. Listen carefully. Detective Gerritsen was here. Earlier today."

"I know. A nurse kicked him out."

"Right. I'd left you alone to go see Yolanda and her baby in Maternity. When I got back, the doctor told me Gerritsen had spoken to you—"

"Yolanda had her baby?"

"Yes, a boy. Emilio. Seven pounds, eight ounces. But—"

"Good name. Like Zapata." I visualized Annie in her Zapata T-shirt, felt an unexpected wave of emotion.

"Bryan, listen to me. You told Gerritsen something about the broken taillight being the final piece to the puzzle. Are you following me?"

I nodded, tentatively.

She glanced at the door, leaned forward and whispered. "If Gerritsen comes back, *when* Gerritsen comes back, you absolutely can not talk to him about the broken taillight. Or anything to do with the death of Jack Montrose. You'll have to answer his questions, but don't give anything away. Do you understand how important that is?"

"I think so." The same morphine that smothered my pain had reduced me to a dolt.

She rolled her eyes and lowered her voice. "Remember, Bryan? You kicked the gun out of Montrose's hand. It hit his taillight and broke the plastic. They found the shard of plastic in the cemetery, not out at Kooskooskie where we staged the wreck. If Gerritsen figures out why that's the key, it might dawn on him that we killed Montrose in the cemetery and moved the body. Then he'll reopen the case and charge us with murder."

"That would be bad."

"That would be *very* bad. So don't talk to Gerritsen anymore about the broken taillight. Or anything to do with what happened five years ago at Stubblefield. Okay?"

"Okay."

Nurse Irene entered quietly, light on her feet for a large woman. "How's the patient feeling?" She held a metal clipboard in one hand and small paper cup in the other.

"Better," I answered, looking to Lydia, as if she'd either confirm or deny my self-report.

"I've got some medicine for you. To keep you comfortable."

"If it's a painkiller I don't want it."

"You'd rather have the pain?"

I nodded. I was used to pain.

———————

I woke up the next morning in a different room. Less shiny equipment, no glass window between the hallway and my bed. The mattress was lumpier. A dish of wobbly green Jell-O sat untouched on a scarred metal tray. Lydia was asleep in a padded vinyl chair in the corner of the room. Sunlight streamed through open Venetian blinds, amplifying the luminous quality of her complexion. She made a tiny sound with each inhalation, the same little click I recalled fondly from the times we'd slept together. I smiled, wished she was next to me in the hospital bed.

As discreetly as possible, I rolled on my side and relieved myself in a urinal bottle, careful not to rile my stitches. Then I set it aside and watched Lydia. She was wearing the turquoise ring I gave her to commemorate our fourth date, since she always broke it off with guys after three. It touched my heart, but I knew better than to assume it meant anything momentous. *Don't get carried away. Don't be a fool.*

I derailed that train of thought and glanced out the window. I couldn't quite see my old fraternity house on the edge of the Whitman campus, but thought I could make out the crown of the giant Catalpa in the front yard. I half-smiled as I unspooled memory of the good times with Ethan, Slider and Bigdog. How could I have turned my back on my friends? I loved all three and didn't even know where they were. I sat with that awhile, the realization leaving me feeling less worthy of Lydia's love.

She stirred and I looked back at her, the only one still in my life. Barely. I imagined her living in Topanga with me. Going for runs with Tuna and me, cooking meals together and sleeping in the same bed. Shopping trips to the outdoor fruit stand on Pacific Coast Highway, dinners at the Charthouse in Malibu followed by a walk on the beach. I wanted to struggle out of bed and touch her but knew it would be a mistake. I cleared my throat to wake her up, but mostly to get my mind off the terrible longing.

She stretched her long neck. "Good morning, Sleepybones Jones."

"You should talk. I woke up before you did." My voice was still hoarse. It felt like I'd swallowed a nail file.

She smiled and yawned. "I don't get twenty-three hours like some people."

"Don't Hector and Amelia let you sleep at home any more?"

"I sleep better here," she replied, rubbing her eyes.

I sat up and flinched, a razor-sharp pain shooting through my gut. "Ooh. Maybe cutting down on the painkillers wasn't such a good idea."

"Does it hurt bad?" she asked, her eyes full of compassion.

"I'll be okay."

"Dr. Benjamin said the bullet sort of ricocheted around in there."

"Wonderful. When did they move me?"

"Last night. Don't you remember? You complimented Nurse Irene on what a pretty yellow dress she was wearing."

I took a moment, scanned my recent memory. "I *don't* remember. And I've never seen a nurse in a yellow dress."

She chuckled. "That's because she was wearing white. But don't feel bad, we all got a good laugh out of it."

"Nice to know I'm providing the entertainment."

She scooted to the edge of the chair. "You seem more with it this morning."

My turn to yawn. "Yeah. Not so dopey. Hungry, too."

"That's a good sign." She got to her feet, moved to the side of my bed. "Look, Bryan. Gerritsen's sure to come by as soon as he hears you're off intensive care. He has to investigate the shooting and decide how to charge Vicky Spotts."

"Only I told him something about the piece of plastic that broke out of Montrose's taillight."

"Right. You were babbling a lot yesterday. There's no telling what you told him."

"Bummer."

"Yeah, but all you have to do is say you're all drugged up and you don't have a clue what you were talking about."

"Okay. Could you help me sit up?"

She found the button and raised the head of the bed electronically. "I'm staying with you until he comes. I can help handle him if you need it."

"Has he already questioned you?"

She nodded. "Naturally, he wanted to know what we were doing in the cemetery. And Vicky had told him we were burning something, so I had some explaining to do."

"What'd you say?"

"I had to make up something quick."

"And?"

"I told him Stubblefield is where we broke up and that we'd gone out there to try and work things out. That the sage was part of an Indian reconciliation ritual I learned on the rez."

"Good thinking. Did he buy it?"

"He seemed to. But that was before you mentioned the taillight."

Dr. Benjamin came by mid-morning, accompanied by Nurse Irene, who seemingly worked every shift. This time they were all business. After her usual spate of questions, Dr. Benjamin surprised me by asking if I felt up to getting out of bed. Before I could answer, she lowered the metal guardrail and put herself in position to steady me if I faltered. "Scoot over to the edge of the bed and put both feet on the floor," she said.

I swung around, placed my bare feet on the cold linoleum and rose up to my full height. "Shit!"

Nurse Irene scolded me with her eyes, a reminder I was in a Seventh Day Adventist hospital.

"It felt like I tore a stitch," I explained, trying to cover my faux pas.

"Let me see." Dr. Benjamin reached inside my hospital gown and carefully pulled back a thick wad of sterile bandages. "It looks good. Dry, no sign of infection. But you're going to have a nice scar for your efforts."

I shrugged. A scar was the least of my worries.

Lydia asked, "How long will Bryan have to stay here?"

"The gunshot wounds I've treated were hunting accidents. But I'd estimate a couple of weeks."

"A couple weeks? I don't think so," I protested.

She gave me her best *I'm the Doctor* expression. "Afraid so."

Nurse Irene left, but stopped abruptly at the door. "Oh. That Detective Gerritsen called the nursing station. He said to tell you he'd be by at three o'clock. Sharp."

Dr. Zaleski stopped by shortly before noon. He sat on the edge of my bed and plopped down a grocery bag filled with clean underwear and several shirts. "We're still trying to reach your dad," he said. "No luck, so far."

I shrugged it off. "Let him fish in peace. There's nothing he can do, anyway."

Dr. Z looked momentarily puzzled, but then smiled. "You look pretty good for a guy who just took a shot in the stomach. They're the worst."

"You sound like you're speaking from experience," I said in an offhand way.

"More or less. I took some shrapnel in the gut in World War II. Got shot down over the English Channel."

"You got shot down over the English Channel?"

He nodded. "1941. I managed to crash my plane in the south of England. They thought I was dead and took me to a morgue. Woke up in a room full of dead soldiers."

Lydia's mouth fell open. "My God! That's freaky."

"I didn't even know you served," I told him.

"I don't usually talk about it."

"What kind of planes did you fly?"

"I flew Spitfires for the R.A.F. Two missions a day over Nazi Germany. And before that I flew PZL-11's for Poland."

"PZL-11's?"

He nodded again. "It was 1938. They were already obsolete, but the best we had."

I sat up as straight as my ailing body would allow. "I want to hear about this," I said, imagining Dr. Z in a dogfight with the Red Baron.

"It's not a coincidence this came up," he explained. He got off the bed and pulled up the smaller of the room's two chairs. His expression turned grave. "I think it's time I told you a few things. Both of you. When I was an officer in the Polish Air Force I was taken prisoner."

Lydia slid her chair closer. "By the Nazis?"

"No, by the Russians. My squadron had orders to go to Romania where we were to pick up some British aircraft. Hurricanes, if my memory serves me. We were supposed to fly them back into Poland. To make a long story short, we commandeered a bus and headed toward Romania but found ourselves facing a line of tanks belonging to the Soviet Army."

"I thought the Russians were our allies," I said.

"The Russians had signed a non-aggression pact, but they weren't considered allies until the war started in 1939. Anyway, using loudspeakers, they ordered us out of the bus."

"What'd they say?" I asked.

"'We're friends. We are brother Slavs. We'll keep you free!' They spoke pretty good Polish and fooled us. We got off the bus and were marched to one of two tables. Enlisted men were told to go home. Officers, like myself, were taken prisoner and loaded onto a freight train, no questions asked. The Russians locked the doors and we started moving. We were cramped like cattle and had no food or water. Several hours later, men started urinating and defecating in the corner and the stench became unbearable. But I escaped on the second night."

"How'd you do it?" This was Lydia.

"My crew chief was a weightlifter, almost as wide as he was tall. As an enlisted man he could have gone home, but he stayed with me to protect me. He insisted on it. Using his hands he started working on one of the floorboards in the train car. It took him two days, but he managed to pry loose one of the planks. The train was just creeping along so he told me to lower myself down and keep my head down until the train passed by."

"You went through the floorboards and lay on the tracks?" I asked, incredulous.

He nodded. "The train was barely moving. It wasn't as difficult as it sounds."

"He didn't join you? Your crew chief?"

His expression saddened. "No. I went alone, but I'm sure others went later. At least the thin ones."

"What did you do then?"

"I walked for almost two weeks, moving only at night and navigating by the stars. My orders were to get to Romania so that's the direction I headed. I was starving so I ate some grass, which was stupid because I almost died from diarrhea. Then, one night I heard dogs barking and followed the sound to a small village. I peeked in the window of a little cottage and saw an elderly woman. It looked safe enough so I tapped on the glass."

A noisy gurney in the hallway distracted me. "Did she feed you?"

He chuckled. "Not right away. My presence caused her great consternation. I spoke a little Romanian in those days and told her I'd escaped from the Russians. That I was starving. I asked her for a piece of bread. She came over to the window and said, 'Go away! Go away!' So I asked her how a beautiful lady like herself could refuse a starving young soldier."

Lydia laughed. "You're a charmer, Dr. Zaleski."

He beamed. "Well, it worked. She gave me a toothless smile and handed over an entire loaf of potato bread and a big hunk of cheese. The next night, I swam across a river into Romania. Unfortunately, my luck ran out. The border patrol was waiting for me with guns. They loaded me into the back of a truck and took me to what amounted to a concentration camp."

"That's horrible," I said. I thought about the Washington State Penitentiary, no more than a few miles away. How I would fare as a prisoner.

"Yeah. They fed us a horrible slop but at least it was something. I regained some of my strength and escaped again about a week later."

"How'd you do it this time?"

"I just went under the wire early one morning when no one was on guard. Half the soldiers were barefoot, a real ragtag outfit, so it wasn't hard. But I foolishly went to the nearest village and they were waiting for me. They brought me back and beat me within an inch of my life. As soon as I was better I escaped again. But this time I was smarter. I'd befriended a guard by asking about his family and children. When he asked about mine I told him I had to get out and find what had happened to my wife. We identified with one another. In the end, he gave me his rifle and the only round of ammunition he had."

"Why would he give away his rifle?" Lydia asked.

"I don't know. Maybe it would identify him as a soldier gone AWOL."

"So then what happened?" I asked.

"I went in one direction and he ran off in the other." Dr. Z stopped talking. His eyes went icy cold.

"What?" I asked.

He took a deep breath. "This is the point of my story, Bryan. That night I hid in the ladies room at a train station. I waited until early morning, thinking the guards would either be gone or asleep. I was wrong. A soldier tried to recapture me as I was hopping the train. I don't know if he was German or Romanian. I shot him in the chest."

No one spoke while we assimilated the enormity of his words. The room was quiet except for extraneous sounds from the hallway. "Did you kill him?" Lydia asked in a whisper.

"Oh, yes," he answered, decisively. "I had no choice. I didn't think I could survive another beating."

I nodded my understanding. "I know why you're telling us this."

Dr. Z got up and closed the door to the room. "I should've told you before you left Walla Walla . . . when I realized the two of you had something to do with the death of Officer Montrose."

"How'd you know that?" Lydia asked, her eyes showing surprise.

He looked at her and made a slight head gesture toward me. "Bryan hinted at it. Without actually saying what happened."

She nodded solemnly and met my eyes. Several moments passed. "I think we should tell him."

I nodded back, knowing Dr. Z would take our secret to his grave. Keeping my voice low I said, "The short version is this: Montrose caught us parked out at Stubblefield Cemetery. Instead of just giving us a ticket or a lecture, he went psycho. He handcuffed both of us and tried to rape Lydia in the back seat of his squad car. We got the upper hand and killed him."

"We had to," Lydia jumped in, her voice a little too loud.

I cautioned her with a finger to my lips.

She grimaced, lowered her voice. "After what he did to me and after what he was about to do, there was no way he was going to let us go back to town and report him."

Dr. Z paused to think. "How did you get the upper hand, as you put it?"

Lydia cleared her throat. "Montrose had his penis out and was about to violate me. He'd already used his fingers. Bryan started shouting insults, really raunchy stuff about Montrose's mother. He pulled his pants up and walked over and threw a punch at Bryan. Bryan was handcuffed to his car but he managed to kick him and he spun around and I knocked him down with him a karate kick."

"Then he pulled his gun on us," I added.

"He pulled his gun?" Dr. Z asked, his eyes widening.

I nodded. "I was close enough to kick it out of his hand."

Dr Z went silent and stroked his whiskered chin. I'd seen him do it a hundred times over the chessboard, assessing a complicated position. "But I thought Montrose died in a car wreck. Out at Kooskooskie."

I shook my head. "We staged it. He was already dead when we rammed his car into the bridge and pushed it over the embankment."

Dr. Z looked even more confused. "But . . . the newspaper report. A number of witnesses saw Montrose speeding through town just before the accident, trying to catch some guy in a stolen car. I distinctly remember reading about it."

I met his eyes. "That was me wearing his uniform. People just assumed it was Montrose 'cause it was his squad car. He was dead in the back seat. And Lydia was the one driving the stolen car. It was all part of our cover-up."

He nodded slowly as understanding sunk in. He fastened his eyes on Lydia. "If Bryan was handcuffed to his car I'd have to assume it was you who delivered the fatal blow."

She held his gaze but didn't respond. When she did, her voice was clear and remorseless. "That's right. I hit him in the throat with all my might and crushed his windpipe. And if I had to do it over, I'd do it again."

Dr. Z's eyes softened. "Good. You both did what you needed to do to survive. He'd have never let you leave Stubblefield alive."

Lydia's shoulders relaxed. She walked around the bed and gave Dr. Z a long hug. "Thank you," she whispered. "I know I did the right thing, but it helps to hear it from someone I respect. Someone who understands."

I looked at Dr. Z. "You know, they could throw you in jail if they found out you were hiding the truth about us killing Montrose."

He sneered. "Fuck 'em!"

Lydia sat smiling in the chair vacated by Dr. Z.

"What is it?"

"When Dr. Zaleski said 'fuck 'em,' I felt like I'd received a blessing."

"Me too," I said, smiling back. "It's the first time I've ever heard him swear."

"He's a good man." Lydia's smile disappeared. "I wish Gerritsen would get here and get it over with."

My stomach felt instantly queasy. "Yeah. God, I hope to hell I didn't blow it."

"You didn't," she reassured me, glancing over her shoulder at the door. "Just remember to say you were all doped up. Can't even remember talking to him."

"Okay."

She grabbed the bag of clothes Dr. Z left and began rummaging. "Yikes," she said, pulling out a Hawaiian shirt with a loud floral print. "Where'd you get this?"

"Birthday present from Dr. Lawrence Grove," I answered, relieved to be off the subject of my drug-induced blunder.

"Who's he?"

"My neighbor in Topanga. Great guy."

She looked puzzled. "I thought Annie was your only neighbor."

"She's my only close-by neighbor. Dr. Grove lives in a commune at the top of the canyon."

"What kind of doctor lives in a commune?"

I fluffed my pillow, tried to get comfortable. "A hippie psychiatrist doctor. Only he's more or less retired."

"Because of age?"

I grabbed the handrails and sat up straighter. "No, because he got in trouble for his views on drugs."

"What do you mean?"

"He went on television and argued that man's desire for altered states of consciousness is a fourth drive. A craving as powerful as hunger, thirst or sex."

She set the shirt in her lap. "Isn't he entitled to state his opinion?"

"Yeah, but he also talked about doing magic mushrooms and peyote with some of his patients. The State of California disapproved."

"Sounds like this Dr. Grove's a character."

I laughed, paid the price with another reminder of Dr. Benjamin's stitch work. "Like no one else I've ever met."

"Should we call him and tell him what happened? Or call Annie?"

"Why?"

"When you go home to Topanga. You might need some help."

I felt like I'd taken another bullet to the stomach.

"Bryan, wake up. Detective Gerritsen's here."

I opened my eyes and scanned the room. Groggy from sleep I replied, "No he isn't."

"He is. I told him to come back in fifteen minutes. You've got to wake up."

"Oh, okay. Help me to the sink. I'll splash some water on my face." The cold water stung, but not like what Lydia had said before my nap. *She's going back to the rez and I'm going back to Topanga. And that'll be that.*

I was back in bed when Gerritsen entered the room, scowling and agitated. He produced his small spiral notepad and a ballpoint pen. "You ready to answer some questions?"

I met Gerritsen's eyes, but inside I could feel my nerves buzzing. "I'm up to it. They took me off the painkillers so my mind's a lot clearer."

"Good," Gerritsen said. "You can start by telling me what happened with Vicky Spotts."

"Didn't Lydia already do that?"

Lydia leaned forward from the corner chair. "I did, but—"

Gerritsen interrupted. "She did, but there's this new police procedure called interviewing the victim."

I took a deep breath. The air smelled antiseptic. I heard the slow scrape of a walker in the hallway. "Fine. Lydia and I went to Pioneer Park and then out to Stubblefield. My dog Tuna went with us. We were in the cemetery talking when Vicky Spotts showed up. I asked her to leave and she pulled a gun and started asking some stupid questions. Then she pointed it at me. That's when my dog attacked her and the gun went off. It looked accidental to me."

"Is your dog attack-trained?"

"No, but Vicky had just fired the gun and Tuna's protective. Also, she'd met Vicky down in California and took a real dislike to her. Vicky threatened me at that time, too."

"Okay. What kind of threat did Miss Spotts make in California?"

"She alluded to the fact she had a gun and told me to stay away from Walla Walla. That sort of thing. I didn't take it too seriously."

"Maybe you should've."

I shrugged my shoulder on the side that didn't hurt.

Gerritsen cracked his knuckles. A woman's voice came over the intercom. When she'd finished informing us that a Chevrolet license number HDM205 had an engine fire in the parking lot, Gerritsen asked, "What kind of 'stupid' questions did Miss Spotts ask you?"

"First she asked if we were sending smoke signals or burning pot. That was because we had some ceremonial sage burning. Then she wanted to know what happened with Officer Montrose five years ago. At the cemetery." I paused to think. "That's all I can remember."

"And what'd you tell her?"

"I told her it was none of her business what we were burning. In regard to the question about Montrose, I don't remember exactly what I said. Something like, he ordered us to leave the cemetery, we left, end of story."

Lydia cleared her throat. "You reminded her that she saw Montrose leave."

"Right," I said, grateful for Lydia's presence.

"Did she appear to be on drugs?" Gerritsen asked.

Lydia and I looked at one another and nodded. "She looked pretty coked up to me," I answered.

"Definitely," Lydia added. "She didn't lose all that weight on a diet."

Gerritsen riffled the pages in his little notebook. "Needless to say, we're pressing charges against Miss Spotts. As soon as you're up to it, I'll need a written statement."

I winced from a sharp pain in my side, gently massaged a spot over my hip. "What's going to happen to her?"

"Well, she's damn lucky you lived; I can tell you that. As it is, she'll probably only face reckless endangerment on the shooting charge."

"Is there another charge?" Lydia asked.

Gerritsen looked surprised. "Didn't you read the morning paper?"

Lydia shook her head. "I've been with Bryan all day."

"We found an ounce of cocaine under her car seat. Made it look like she was dealing so we got a search warrant and went through her house. Found a scuba tank in the garage with three pounds of coke in a hidden compartment. We'd have never found the stuff, but Miss Spotts had left the false bottom screwed off the tank. She's in for some serious time at Purdy."

"Good!" I blurted out, a bit too gleefully. "How the hell did she know we were in town, anyway?"

He paused. "A friend of hers saw you as she was coming out of the Baker-Boyer bank."

I looked at Lydia, shook my head in disgust. "Leslie Vanzandt."

Gerritsen scribbled a note and looked up. "Okay, let's talk about our conversation yesterday morning."

"I didn't know we had one."

Though barely audible, he snorted dismissively. "Well, let me refresh your memory. I woke you up and asked you to tell me what happened out at Stubblefield. Only you thought I meant what happened *five years ago*. And you said," he licked his thumb and flipped several pages, "and I quote . . . 'the shard of plastic is the final piece of the puzzle. Put the shard in its proper place and solve the murder.' Mind telling me what you meant?"

I shrugged and held his gaze. "Your guess is as good as mine."

He stared me down. "Oh, come on, Matthews. Try a real answer. An honest answer."

"Sorry. I have no idea what I was talking about."

He clicked his ballpoint pen several times in succession. "Know what I think, Matthews? I think your guard was down and for the first time ever you were telling the truth."

I gave him a little headshake. "Jesus, Gerritsen. I was in a coma. You woke me up—"

He studied me with an unblinking gaze. "And caught you with your guard down. Next best thing to truth serum."

"Oh, give me a break. I'd just been shot in the stomach and operated on. Then they loaded me up with morphine. I was babbling my brains out."

Gerritsen set his jaw. "Didn't sound like babble to me. I've been around awhile. It had the ring of truth, especially when you used the word 'murder.'"

Lydia chimed in. "He also complimented one of the nurses on what a pretty yellow dress she was wearing. Only she was wearing white."

Gerritsen stuffed his notebook inside his suit jacket. "You know you two *really* piss me off! You're just as evasive as you were five years ago."

Lydia looked down, smoothed a wrinkle in her jeans.

I tried switching tactics. "I don't understand your anger, Detective."

"Well, let me explain. Five years of an unsolved case can do that to a guy. I'm trying to find out what really happened and all I get is the runaround."

"We can't help it if you don't like our answers."

"That's bullshit, Matthews. I know it and you know it. You're hiding something about Montrose and yesterday you admitted it."

"I'm not hiding a thing. I apparently blathered something about a shard. I remember the FBI guy, Thibideaux, showing me an evidence bag with a piece of red plastic from Montrose's taillight. I suppose I was referring to that. But I was delirious."

Gerritsen's eyes became fierce, steady as gun sights. "I think Thibideaux had it right. Either you or Miss Redstone drove the Barracuda that ran Montrose into the bridge. I'll be goddamned if I know why the piece of plastic is important, but I'll get it, eventually."

I felt a sizzle of fear, chose to stay on the offense. "Isn't it enough that you wrecked our lives? This is even more insulting—"

"I'll tell you what this is. This is personal, Matthews! A young cop got killed on my watch. I happen to think his life was worth more than a wreath and a few minutes of bagpipe music. Jack Montrose may have been in his grave for five years now, but all the files from the investigation are very much in my study at home. It's just a matter of time till I figure out how you killed him and then I'm gonna put you two behind bars, where you belong."

Chapter 14
The Manzanita Seed

The phone rings and I stop talking. It doesn't so much startle me as break a trance.

Annoyed at the interruption, Dr. Grove reaches behind him. "I should've unplugged this," he grumbles before lifting the receiver. "Hello."

Tuna gets to her feet and stretches, arching her back and groaning. I thought she was outside, running with the commune dogs. Our eyes meet and she walks over for some attention. I scratch her behind the ears, glance at the cheap wristwatch I wear when I go for runs. I realize I've been telling Dr. Grove my story for over three hours. Which explains why I feel exhausted.

Dr. Grove rubs his nose and smiles. "Yeah, he's here." He looks at Tuna and adds, "She's here too." After a short pause he says, "No, everything's fine. He was just telling me an interesting story and we lost track of time. He should be home pretty soon." He says goodbye and sets the phone back on the cradle.

My glass of lemonade has some slushy ice at the bottom. I swallow the last of it and look at Dr. Grove. "Man. I've never talked so much in my life."

His expression is that of a confidant. Reassuring. "It's an unbelievable story, except I believe every word you said."

At first I don't know what to say, then I realize there was really only one reason for speaking the unspeakable. I take a deep breath and brace myself. "Do you think we got away with murder?"

He presses the tips of his fingers together and taps them three times. "You didn't get away with anything. And you've paid for it with five years of needless suffering."

"Needless?"

"Because it should've never happened in the first place. This Montrose was a loose cannon. A psychopath with a badge."

"You got that right."

He nods. "Your friend Dr. Zaleski was right on. If Lydia hadn't killed the cop, he'd have murdered her, made you watch and then done the same to you. And he'd have gotten away with it, too."

"But Vicky Spotts saw him follow us into the cemetery. If we showed up dead, she'd have known—"

"Doesn't matter. All he'd have had to do is say he tried to make an arrest and the two of you attacked him. The police knew you had a grudge against Montrose and they knew Lydia had a black belt in karate. He'd have said he was fighting for his life. Which was true."

"You think it's okay that we covered it up and lied to the authorities?" I ask in a taut voice.

"Absolutely! I'd rather talk to you as a free man than one serving life in prison. It was a justifiable homicide."

"Justifiable homicide," I whispered to myself. "I can live with that."

Dr. Grove meets my eyes. "The man committed a vile crime and was about to commit murder. He pulled in a swift punishment. You did society a favor."

"That's what Lydia said the night it happened."

He makes a gesture with his head. "You ready to open the Detective's letter?"

I nod anxiously and pick up the letter from Gerritsen. It's leaning against the saltshaker in the center of the kitchen table. I don't recall how it got there but after baring my soul I don't really care. "We know the truth, but what matters is what Gerritsen thinks. If he figured out what really happened . . . "

Dr. Grove swallows a big gulp of air. "Why don't you read it to me?"

"Okay." I'd half torn open the envelope when it arrived. Now I finish the job, a spidery chill running the length of my spine.

August 10, 1974
Dear Mr. Matthews,

Had a dream about you last night. You were posing for a mug shot and your eyes told me you were guilty as sin. I've never paid much attention to dreams but this one got me to thinking about Jack Montrose.

Back up a few months. When I arrested Vicky Spotts for drug trafficking, she asked if I could shorten her sentence in return for information that would close the Montrose investigation. Turns out Montrose busted her with a kilo of marijuana a month before his death. She claims she became hysterical when Montrose handcuffed her and told him she'd do anything if he'd cut her some slack. In return for a sexual act and the promise of future sexual favors, Montrose let her walk. Problem was, he got sadistic. Couple of weeks later he tied her legs spread-eagled and raped her with a beer bottle. My gut says she's telling the truth. As much as she hated Montrose, she wasn't very cooperative the first time around. Now she's providing new information about what happened on the night he died. Funny how your memory improves when you're facing ten years in lockup.

You're going down, Matthews. You're a brilliant guy, and maybe even a good guy, but you murdered a cop and you're going to pay. I don't care that Montrose was a lowlife, you killed a man. I'm going to close this case. Give me a call. Believe me, better for you to come to me than to make me come after you.

Gerritsen

P.S. I've sent a copy of this letter to the address Miss Redstone gave on the Pine Ridge Indian Reservation in South Dakota.

I leave the commune thinking about what Montrose did to Vicky Spotts and offer up a prayer for her to be healed emotionally. As always, Tuna prances ten feet in front of me, looking back every few steps to make sure I'm keeping up. "You're a dog of *routine*," I say playfully, pronouncing *routine* with a grossly exaggerated French accent like the witless Inspector Clouseau. She wags her tail, picks up a eucalyptus pod and tosses it into the bushes.

It has turned into a fine afternoon with a faultless blue sky. A cooling ocean breeze filters up from the floor of the canyon. I feel strangely unaffected by Gerritsen's letter, however threatening. I know why. Something shook loose in telling my story and Stubblefield has lost its power. At least that's the way it feels. I smile as I recall something Dr. Zaleski taught me in one of his Zen moments: *before you can fill the cup, you must first empty the cup.*

I'm contemplating the prospect of filling the cup as Tuna and I reach the dirt road that winds its way back to my cabin. The road is crudely engineered with a high, sandstone cliff on one side and a steep embankment that slopes down to Topanga Creek on the other – the part charred by the recent wildfire. We haven't had a decent rain in half a year and the road is bone dry.

Tuna kicks up little puffs of dust as she leads me along, step by step. Watching her grounds me, fills me with a strange contentment. I feel oddly light on my feet as I round a gentle curve. I slow my pace and focus on the sensations of each footfall, not so much for the purpose of being aware as to enjoy the experience of walking. Just ambling along, taking each step as it comes and feeling fully present in my body. Never before have I experienced such a deep affection for Mother Earth.

Stopping in my tracks I turn and face the sun. Bright light filters through the oak and eucalyptus trees rising grandly from the lower side of the hill. Enveloped in warmth, my breathing becomes lighter, more even. I'm taking deep down-through-my-body breaths. Soft, loving breaths. How good I feel just to breathe. Breath is life. *How have I not noticed this before?* Rooted to the earth, I stretch out my arms and stand like a tree, savoring a rush of energy that streams through my body. I feel a sense of kinship with the old oaks that surround me.

Tuna meanders off the road. She sniffs the ground where the hill begins to slope down to the creek. Watching her inspires in me an awe of the natural world and a reverence for her great spirit. Nose to earth, she begins to dig with great determination, like her life depends on it. She moves a considerable pile of earth using her enormous forepaws.

Something unusual catches my eye, just below the mound produced by Tuna's digging. It lies in a heap of ash left by the fire and looks like a smooth, colorful rock. A foot closer and it would've been buried. I step carefully down the steep embankment and pick it up. Red and berry-like, it's a piece of stone fruit that's fallen from a nearby manzanita. Scorched and defenseless, the manzanita had dropped the fruit to the ground. Two thousand-degrees of heat broke open the fruit's stony shell and exposed a fleshy seed to the ash-enriched soil. A little rainfall is all it needs to sprout and grow.

I recall something Annie told me the morning after the fire. We were out with shovels looking for hot spots in the dried up and brittle chaparral. The sky was the color of gunmetal and a veil of ugly, black smoke still shrouded the rugged hills. Gesturing to a badly singed shrub, Annie said, "You know, the fire isn't *all* bad. It takes an inferno of heat to crack open those stony shells on the manzanita." I asked her what purpose it served and she explained, "That way its seeds can germinate. Without fire, the manzanita would never sprout, grow to maturity and restart the life cycle. It's nature's way."

Looking now at the living fruit in the palm of my hand, I realize how alike we are. I, too, needed the fire of life to open me up—an act of God—and so by necessity my life had been an inferno. My early inability to speak, my mother's suicide, even Stubblefield and the loss of Lydia had something to teach me.

I gently squeeze the seed and consent to God's presence. God has always been present for me, but now I am present to God. My heart cracks open, wide open. At first this openness feels more physical than spiritual, as if I'm weightless and airborne in one of my flying dreams. Detective Frank Gerritsen can no longer touch me, no matter what he knows. Everything is okay.

Tears flood my eyes as I climb the embankment back to the road. Folding my arms around my chest, I hold myself in a warm embrace and release a lifetime of accumulated pain. My senseless fears and guilty conscience, the grievances I've nursed, the horrific memories, all vanish as I connect with something divine at the very center of my being. I close my eyes and forgive myself for how weak and dependent I've been. I forgive my mother for leaving me. I forgive Montrose for the harm he inflicted. The wounded perception of Bryan Matthews has been obliterated and an old story is ending, a new one mine to live. The moment seems timeless, though I want it to last forever. Standing in place, I haven't the slightest conception of what to do next. *It's okay,* I remind myself. *Everything is okay!*

I hear a door open and close a short distance away. Kaalaea hollers an enthusiastic hello from her front porch and I intuitively know it's time to return to ordinary consciousness. I turn and wave without speaking. Annie is with her. She offers a quick smile, then goes to one knee and double-knots Kaalaea's sneakers. A small rattler camped out in the bamboo last week and her daughter's barefoot days are over. I smile because I am pleased with the new policy, reorient myself and continue up the road.

"C'mon Tuna, there's work to do," I say. Again, my steps are mindful. I *know* I am walking and the bare awareness of placing one foot in front of the other makes me deliriously happy.

Popcorn eyes me from the low side of the corral and whinnies, long and loud. The high-pitched sound is so pure it feels like his soft mouth is pressed against my ear. Strangely, the old horse's golden coat and cream-colored mane have never appeared more vivid.

Tuna arrives at the cabin a few steps ahead of me and wags her tail impatiently. I hear Buffy Sainte-Marie on the stereo. *Little Wheel Spin and Spin* from her first album. I open the door and the big girl and I go in to-gether.

Lydia is standing at the sink. She tosses aside a towel and sets a blue and gray ceramic pie plate on the counter. The one we bought at a roadside fruit market on the drive down from Walla Walla. "You look like you're glowing," she says with a smile.

I smile back, mischievously. "I've been released by fire."

She lowers the volume on the stereo, walks over and wraps her arms around my neck. Her hands and arms are warm from the dishwater. "You better not be doing those magic mushrooms with Dr. Grove."

"Hardly," I say, with an air of mock indignation.

She takes a step back and meets my eyes. "What were you two talking about when I called?"

I hesitate. "I told him about Stubblefield."

Her body stiffens. "I wondered what was taking you so long."

"Actually I told him my entire life story."

"What brought that about?"

"A letter came from Gerritsen. In today's mail."

Her eyes go bright with fear. "What's it say?"

I shrug my shoulders. "He claims Vicky Spotts gave him some new in-formation. That he's going to get us. You can read it later."

She takes a moment to process the information, gives me a puzzled look. "You're not scared?"

I shake my head. "No. He's bluffing. If he really had something, he'd come after us with arrest warrants."

"What could she have told him?"

"Doesn't matter. She doesn't know anything and it's been five years. If he hasn't figured it out by now, he isn't going to."

"Are you sure?"

I nod, reassuringly. "I'm sure."

"We just live our lives?"

I nod again, certain Lydia can sense a change in me. "Everything's okay."

She gives me a smile that's like the sun emerging from a layer of thick clouds. "Do you have something in your hand?"

I show her, beaming with satisfaction. "It's a *red stone*. Tuna found it by the road, halfway to the mailbox."

"Hmmn. But what is it, really?" She reaches out and touches it with the tip of her finger, as if it were fragile.

"A manzanita seed. You want to plant it with me?"

She glances at the clock and I remember her meeting with the admissions director at Pepperdine. I promised to go with her, just before my run. "Sure," she answers. "If we do it right away."

Lydia follows me out to the tack shed, where I keep my garden tools. Tuna bumps her playfully, knocking her off the path and into a pomegranate bush, buzzing with fat, forgiving bumblebees. Lydia responds by threatening to send Tuna to bed without dinner.

Laughing at their antics, I jerk open the sticky door of the shed. The hot, stuffy air reeks of horse liniment. Assorted bridles hang from nails on the wall. An old and worn leather saddle perches precariously on a flimsy white sawhorse. Spider webs and dark shadows give the space an atmosphere of danger, but today I'm in no hurry. I rummage around, set aside a pair of cloth garden gloves and a rusted sprinkler. I find the trowel I'm looking for beneath a tangle of rope.

We hike about a hundred yards to a little bluff that's directly above the place in the road where I had the epiphany. There's an almost flat spot here where I maintain the first of two water overflow tanks that fill from an underground spring a half-mile up the canyon. This one's an old claw-footed bathtub Annie got for twenty bucks at the swap meet. The coyotes, deer and foxes that come for relief from the parched Southern California climate use it almost daily.

The ground at the low end of the tub is wet year-round from spillage. I get down on my knees, dig a shallow hole with the trowel and drop in the manzanita seed. It shines like a jewel in the afternoon sun.

Lydia smiles lovingly and says, "It looks like you're praying."

"I am."

Tuna snuffles the ground and moves in closer to see what I'm up to. I feel the caress of her thick coat as she settles in at my side. With great reverence, I scoop in handfuls of cool, damp soil and watch the seed disappear. The earth smells raw and rich and fertile, full of possibility. I tamp it down tenderly, thinking all the while of patting the belly of a pregnant woman. I say aloud, "God bless the soil, the water, the sunlight and the seed. God bless Lydia and Tuna, whom I love with all my heart." And then, as an afterthought, I silently bless myself.

CPSIA information can be obtained
at www.ICGtesting.com
Printed in the USA
FFOW04n1306081113
2287FF